THE STOLEN HARP

THE STOLEN HARP

PATH OF THE MANY WINGED GODS
BOOK ONE

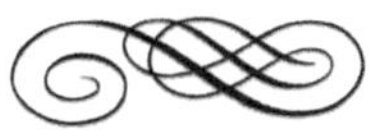

ASHER RICBRAHT

Dream Machine
Books

PATH
of the Many Winged Gods

To the spirit of Renaissance

*"A song of sorrows neverending is with them from the faraway lands.
Tremble and fear at the voice of the Seven O'rahs in their hands!"*

— *Book of Principal Covenants*

Contents

Chapter 1

The Sobbing in the Grove

The tragic and heroic deeds of the many winged Vheilyel are numerous beyond measure; their chambers filled with lengthy histories of triumph and those of utter dread, of creatures most excellent and others insufferably foul. And amongst these prized treasuries of wondrous works, there lives upon the records of the Order of Dathmahjen, that grand, matchless tale of the Seven O'rahs. This is a record most worthy of recounting before the vigilant eyes of the Council of Daylight. And as such, let us revisit the matter with the tale of the Shaifetnu, Saxfen, and his pursuit of the stolen harp.

Underneath those pallid, roseate skies of distant Eofendurk, there walked a silver-haired man along a snowy trail accompanied by a child. This was the land of the man's longing, the thirst of his heart. He had traversed across the starry gulfs above in search of old friends. His heart pounded with elation as he finally gazed yet again upon that wondrous arc above their heads, the astonishing Sky'erligg of Eofendurk. And this striking arc resembled an ever-present, uncolored bow spanning the pallid, roseate heavens, encompassing the lands of Eofendurk like a ring.

"Isn't it beautiful, Enos?" said the silver-haired man.

"Wow, it's incredible, Papa," Enos responded.

Saxfen smiled at his son and led the way across the snowy avenue so named, Sovereign's Pass, a royal pathway decked with lofty posts on each side, each bearing the royal crest of the Kingdom of Nith upon their banners.

"We should be arriving soon."

This was the tale of Saxfen of the Sevrinjiv, that noble champion of the many winged Vheilyel. He had traversed a vast ocean of stars to again tread upon Sovereign's Pass and behold again the place he once called home. He had longed to embrace anew his beloved gethwi friend and converse with the cheerful Neufs of his boyhood, to know of their safety and their health.

He glanced to his right, revealing a warm smile underneath his light, silver beard, and youthful, hooded face. Enos followed close by, filled with all the glee and wonder of a lad his age.

"Do you think Eukeris will remember you, Papa?" Enos asked.

"Yes, I think he'll remember me. It's hard to forget the things we experienced together."

Saxfen chuckled as he recalled the days he ventured with his old friend, Eukeris, the snow gethwi. He recalled how together they had challenged terrifying beasts amid perilous prospects, beheld the heavens fling open, witnessed the fierce battalions of the Council of Daylight come to their side, and traversed strange realms and lands full of woe.

The brisk wind upon Sovereign's Pass discretely hummed with the voice of serene solace, and the proud, snow-raided trees stood like vigilant sentinels, forbidden to leave their post. With the weight of the heavy snow stooping their arms, these fixed sentinels observed through the morning's haze as the victorious Shaifetnu cautiously passed by with his son. This was he who had recovered himself from the very bowels of terrors most frightful, and now he walked underneath the lovely Sky'erligg yet again.

The snow-shrouded trees beheld as he made his way to the abode of the snow gethwis, that grand palace that pierced the roseate heavens, that royal spire so named, Oclyd Tower. This enchanted edifice was the center of a once boastful kingdom that stretched across all the lands of Eofendurk. But the grave chastisement that came upon it had stripped it of its former masters, and instead, Oclyd Tower had been awarded to the lowly but majestic clans of the snow gethwis of Mount Tanlish.

"These lands are very special to me, Enos. You see, this is where Eukeris and I confronted the terrible creature that lived in the Sea of Nith, the Drukijaken of Eofendurk."

Enos looked on in suspense, desiring to ask his father about the Drukijaken. He took a breath in an attempt to conceal his troubled thoughts from his father. He finally dared to pry.

"A monster? Why did you have to fight a monster, Papa?"

"Well, I didn't actually want to fight a monster. Just the thought of it made my stomach turn. But it was truly my destiny to retrieve the precious thing that belonged to us. The Drukijaken had been guarding our family heirloom against our will, and the time had come to retrieve it. We *needed* it back."

"Well, what was it?"

"It was a very special and ancient relic, a stringed instrument entrusted to our people by the Vheilyel. It was a special harp, the O'rah Harp of the Shiggionoth."

For the first time in his life, Saxfen recounted to his son the journey to recover the ancient harp from the beast of the rubied sea and how the Drukijaken came to possess the O'rah Harp deep within its bowels. The kingdom that reigned over the lands of Eofendurk, the Kingdom of Nith, worshipped and feared the Drukijaken as their omnipotent god.

A terrifying and ancient deity dwelling in the depths of the Sea of Nith, the Drukijaken had the power to transform things. Amongst these, it could alter the beauty of Eofendurk's roseate skies into a calamitous tempest of furious clouds, blaring with punishing arrows of unwhole-some light. It could demolish whole mountains with its very thoughts. It had the power to peer into the hearts and plunge into madness the weak and timid. It shattered the heart with terror at the sight of its gargantuan form, and for these reasons, the Kingdom of Nith worshipped and served the Drukijaken of Eofendurk.

Twain sojourners treaded upon Sovereign's Pass as the misty haze that hindered the sun's luminance began to disperse. They had reached the crown of a sturdy hill and then came to an eerie, yet mesmerizing vista: the sight of a grand, abandoned city, overcome by the buffeting of a punishing blizzard, a formidable fortress threatening the heavens with the structural marvels of its defiant spires.

But most striking of them all was Oclyd Tower at its heart, rising high above all the lofty pinnacles. This was that once proud and imperial city, so named, Ujorg Stone City.

"Well, we're here, Enos. Welcome to Ujorg Stone," Saxfen announced. "Oclyd Tower is the big one, and that's where we're headed. That's where Eukeris lives."

The watchful snow-sentinel trees quietly observed at a distance as the faint mist finally parted. Saxfen and his son looked on at the potent hedges surrounding Ujorg Stone. The city walls had but one entrance by way of a great bridge, but the sojourners gazed upon it in disappoint-ment.

"Look, Papa!" Enos pointed at the ruins of the collapsed bridge in the distance. "How are we going to get inside?"

The city walls went on for leagues, as far as the eye could see, and the stone bridge leading to the principal gate had fallen.

"Let's settle here for a moment to rest and figure out our next steps," Saxfen said.

They cleared some rocks and used them for seats. Saxfen kindled a fire as he mused on how to assist his son across the shattered pathway.

He could, of course, find his way across by himself. He could efficiently make use of his ability to light-drift and safely reach the other side. However, Enos did not possess this ability. This would leave him behind, defenseless against the predators that might lurk in this desolate terrain. He glanced at Enos, but the boy had escaped his sight.

"Enos, where did you go?!" Saxfen shouted.

There was a brief, uneasy silence, and then the boy's voice finally shouted back from a faint distance.

"Over here, Papa! I'm gathering firewood!"

Enos had wandered into the snowy hills that encompassed their camp. Without hesitation, Saxfen light-drifted in the direction of the child's voice. His form instantly vanished out of sight, leaving in place but a faint, spectral contour only to reemerge atop an elevated hill. He re-emerged, accompanied by an equally faint silhouette of light. He looked on in hopes of determining Enos' whereabouts. And there he was, waving at his father in plain sight near a snowed thicket of isolated shrubs.

Saxfen gazed as if compelled by a trance at the elegance of the scene, a sea of snowed-covered trees reaching unto the farthest horizon. They appeared to prostrate themselves before the graceful arc of the Sky'erligg above. Its striking beauty spanned the roseate heavens by day in the form of a faint, spectral bow. And by night, it lit the way like the splendor of many moons. For there was no moon in Eofendurk, only the graceful band of the Sky'erligg in the heavens that could be admired from all terrains.

This imposing wonder ruling the roseate skies commanded instant awe at the sight of its striking beauty. Its excellent streak of phantasmal bows resembled some divine pathway reserved for the feet of holy beings not of this realm. Its likeness was that of a costly ring upon a betrothed, almost as if gifted unto Eofendurk by some celestial lover. And no matter how oft Saxfen gazed upon the dazzling beauty of the Sky'erligg, it never failed to thrill him and move him with a sense of wonder that refused to leave his side to this day, the day of his return.

Consumed by the amorous vista on that elevated outpost, he failed to notice the prowling peril that loomed ever closer upon his dear son. It was the stalking pose of a ferocious snow gethwi which had appraised Enos!

"Papaaaa!!" Enos screamed as he discovered the massive, four-legged beast and fled from its devouring maw.

With its twain, striped tails high in the air, the gethwi bounded toward the youth, ready to tear with its fearsome paws. Upon the beast's face were jeweled, azure eyes, fourfold in number, one menacing pair within each socket. And these were now wholly fastened on its prey.

Saxfen had recovered from his trance but remained unfazed. He light-drifted unto the gethwi's path, and the beast suddenly became reluctant to tear the Shaifetnu travelers in pieces. It was the scent. With the scent of the boy's father upon its nose, the ferocious snow gethwi bashfully retreated.

"Hello, Tonby, my old friend," Saxfen greeted.

It appeared that the Shaifetnu champion had recognized the wild beast at a distance by its distinguished stripes upon its hind legs. And the comforting sound and gentle tone in Saxfen's voice revived the creature's humbled spirit. Tonby leaped upon Saxfen, knocking him to the snowy ground. The gethwi head-butted the silver-haired Shaifetnu, and the loving gesture was returned. The sweet, caressing sound of Tonby's purr relieved the bewildered Enos as he exhaled deeply, struggling to recover from his passing fright.

"Oh, how I missed you, beautiful gethwis!" Saxfen said as he embraced the posh, white fur of his old friend. The moment stole a tear from the hero's eye, and it dropped and kissed the warm, black stripes upon the gethwi's coat.

"Papa! *This* is a gethwi?!" Enos exclaimed as he brushed the snow off his bright, golden hair. "Why didn't you say he was a big, furry cat?!"

Saxfen reached for Enos and embraced him while holding Tonby with his other arm.

"Well, of course, he's a big furry cat. What else would he be?" responded Saxfen, laughing in relief and joy at the sight of Tonby.

"As much as I'd love to bring him with us, this big, amazing furball has to stay here. You see, he needs to kill to stay alive, and this is not acceptable back home."

"Kill? What if we asked nicely? I'm sure they wouldn't mind."

"No, I'm afraid that will not do. Eating other animals is how he stays alive. He would've long eaten you if he wasn't my friend."

"Well, that doesn't sound like a nice cat," Enos said, frowning.

"Oh, he's a good boy. I've come all the way out here to see them. They're an ocean of stars away from us, yet they're always near my heart."

The three arose from the powdered snow, and Tonby led the way. The gethwi's twain set of jeweled eyes fixated on his visitors, and his right paw lightly patted the ground. This was the gethwi gesture that he wanted to be followed.

"Look, Papa, I think he wants to lead us somewhere."

They mounted the great beast and followed his lead. Saxfen gazed ahead at the structural marvel that was Oclyd Tower, which was also the place where Tonby was taking them.

"I've never quite told you how we met, huh, Enos?"

Saxfen looked at his dear son. It was like beholding the past and seeing his own face anew as a little boy. Save for the bright yellow hair, Enos was the mirror image of the triumphant hero when he was but a timid, young lad himself.

***

Long before the proud, vigilant trees outside Ujorg Stone City were consumed by the enduring, winteresque snow, the land was a lush, mystic place full of scenic romance. There was a time when the immersive beauty of the Sky'erligg crowned the heavens over the once lively, thriving streets of Ujorg Stone. It once graced the heavens above verdant fields and fragrant groves that stood in place of the snow-glazed desolation that now had engulfed the jewel of the Kingdom of Nith. 'Ujorg Stone, the Jewel of the Nithians,' as the place was once hailed.

And the Nithians were known for their love of those wild, deadly beasts of Nith, the ferocious, blue ujorgs, so named. With fierce snouts bearing deadly fangs, these four-legged prowlers possessed some opulent, blue coats highly desired throughout the realms. And so, the Nithians became skilled at handling the wild beasts and taught them to revere them by means of their various arts.

Long ago, within the city walls of Ujorg Stone, there could be seen one lavishly graced avenue decked with skilled, ivory sculptures of majestic ujorgs. Each of these bore a prized amber jewel upon their chest. The crafted beasts generously saluted all who would enter the royal halls of the formidable Oclyd Tower. In times past, this grand edifice was a glistering gem amongst gems in a vast treasury of cities conquered by the Nithians.

The king who reigned in Ujorg Stone at the time was an aged, old man, unable to depart from his bed. So, in his stead, the iron fist conducting the matters of the realms was that of a dark prince named Mafestus. And all was not well in the kingdom. He was cruel and brutal in his reign, as many also before him, and as such, the natives were known to plot and rebel in vain attempts to free their souls.

Amongst the enemies of the Nithians were the Bumbersing Neufs, who were known to be the most defiant of all neufs. They were whisker-faced, cat-folk with distinct, curled horns upon their heads. These kept to themselves within their concealed abodes in the woods but were compelled to wage violence against the Kingdom for the brutality against their kin.

On the eve of a final raid against the rebels amongst the Bumbersing Neufs, Prince Mafestus marched at the head of his armies. He strode atop the dark, cerulean coat of his ravenous ujorg, savoring the bloodlust in his heart like a hungry beast dreaming of helpless prey. His polished armor tightly fastened, the Dark Prince was quite eager for a taste of the battle ahead. He was youthful and face-shaven, with dark eyes mirroring his black hair.

The Bumbersing Neufs were exhausted with war, and the evil prince reveled in this, his finishing blow. The crimson and gold of his royal banners were proudly held high, announcing the impending doom to the rebels, and the ujorg crests upon them were like the menacing omen of certain disaster to come. Then suddenly, his gaze veered from its resolve by the curious sight of dim, flickering lights in the distant valley below. Something was amiss amongst the lush groves of Morwudell Forest.

"Lieutenant, do you see that?" asked Mafestus.

"Yes, sir."

"What do you make of it?"

"A distraction? A trap? Archers?"

"Take some men with you and find out!" the Dark Prince exclaimed.

"We will investigate and return with word, your Excellency."

His lieutenant strode onwards into the valley below with ten other riders. They left their ferocious, blue ujorgs behind to avoid being discovered, making their way through the trees and thistles of the mysterious grove from whence the flickering lights allured them. And finally, their quest ended at the source of the troubling lights.

"What do you suppose this is?" asked one soldier.

"Well, they're not neufs."

"Should we approach them?"

"No, let's return and tell His Majesty what we've uncovered."

The soldiers raced back to the camp and reported their findings.

"Well, what did you find?" asked the prince.

"They weren't neufs. They looked like us; only they had . . . white hair."

"White hair? As in aged men?"

"Well, yes, but no. They had white hair, but they were not old. They all resembled young men and women. There were some much smaller, also with white hair. I suppose those were their children."

"You mean a camp of young, white-haired intruders is carelessly prancing in my woods with lights . . . in my kingdom? And no one cared to inform me of this?"

"Yes, we suppose the lights were torches."

"The neufs will have to patiently wait for my sword to devour their fur and to smite down their horns," the prince assured. "We will rest here and ambush these silver-heads in the morning. In the meantime, take your best men and guard the place. Make sure they do not flee. If they escape, I will require your life for this. Understood?"

"Yes, my Prince."

The men of Nith rested while the pallid radiance of the Sky'erligg emanated upon the peaks and valleys of the Nithian night. The soldiers on watch were overly preoccupied in their post to admire the beauty of the Sky'erligg's mystical feast upon the eyes. The weary neufs of Bumbersing had been spared the mayhem of Prince Mafestus' bloodthirsty blade, at least for another night. The cruel monarch needed to know who these strangers were, or rather, *what* they were.

When the dawn finally arrived, Mafestus gave the orders, "Lieutenant, take two companies of your best men and march over the north and the east. We will take the west and the south. If any of them tries to escape, slay them on sight. Take no prisoners as we do not know what perils these might bring."

"Understood, my Prince," replied the lieutenant.

The lieutenant took his readiest troops and departed. The remaining warriors followed Mafestus into the mysterious grove. But the alluring lights that had intrigued the armies of Nith had vanished.

Could they have fled? The Dark Prince anxiously wondered. The warm embrace of the dawning light was dimmed by thick canopies of leaves above. The curious, faint cries of lingering wood creatures echoed nearby from all directions, but there was no sign of the mysterious intruders. And then came a startled voice whispering from the distance.

"My Prince, the strangers, they're up ahead," the soldier pointed westward.

"Where are the other two of you?"

"They remain at their post. The people, they appear to be harmless. They appear to be unarmed. They appear to be distressed and mournful, not happy at all. The mood is solemn and not festive. Somber and not at ease."

"Were you able to hear them? What is their tongue?"

"My Prince, I do not recognize it. I have not heard it anywhere in the kingdoms. We are awaiting your orders, sir."

"Well done, soldier. We will take care of this matter now."

The Dark Prince unmounted his blue ujorg and forged ahead. His troops unmounted as well and followed along. They carefully sliced through the lush greenery obstructing their path. Stealth was their ally; the element of surprise would not escape them. Finally, they began to hear them, the faint sound of weeping and lamenting.

The Dark Prince was perplexed. *Perhaps one of them had died? A funeral?* He thought to himself. *Perhaps it's a gimmick, an ambush.*

"Do not be deceived, men. Standby to engage the intruders," the Dark Prince ordered.

They arrived to meet the other two soldiers keeping watch.

"Well, what is this spectacle before us, soldier?"

"These people appear harmless. They are unarmed and only seem to quietly mourn. All of them together just keep . . . sobbing."

The Dark Prince peered through the heavy veil of widened leaves. There were thousands of them. It was a secret rendezvous of silver-haired people, and there were also children bearing the same age-colored hair. And yet, no aged or wrinkled person was found amongst them. Their clothes were clean and crisp, off-white in hue, some more adorned than others. They looked perplexed. The air was filled with the melancholic tone of a funeral ceremony. Some stood on their feet with their palms over their faces. Others laid prostrated while others sat or laid with their faces to the ground. They were lamenting something, and the Dark Prince was determined to uncover their reason.

"NOW!!" he exclaimed.

The order went forth, and the troops sounded their war horns. The warriors shouted as they charged at the silver-haired trespassers. They gathered them like cattle before slaughter. They were unarmed and surrounded by hardened warriors, clad in full battle armor and weapons drawn, ready to slay. Yet, not one of them ran away in fear or screamed. Instead, they remained mournful and serene.

"What is this unholy gathering in my lands?!" shouted Mafestus. "I demand to speak with your leader in the name of Ruminthumgath!"

But there was only silence. No response. Only a faint weeping continued into the ambush. The Dark Prince became irate. He violently grabbed one of them by the hair and aimed his sword at her neck. It was the lovely, rose-colored face of a youth. Startled that no one came to her aid, he looked about at the crowd with one vigilant eye on his captive.

"Lieutenant, do you notice something strange about their faces?"

"Yes, my Prince. They're all young. There are no wrinkles on them. There are no elders amongst them. Even the bearded ones appear youthful."

"Why are all these kids wearing white wigs!?" shouted Mafestus.

The lieutenant nodded at the troops, and they began to inspect the strangers. Some pulled at the white locks, hoping to uncover something else underneath. Others, cut away at their hair with the blade of their sword.

"It appears to be their real hair, my Prince," reported the lieutenant.

"Very well, then. Search them!" ordered Mafestus.

The soldiers searched the silver-haired people and found no weapons amongst them, just as previously noted. They appeared to be wandering in the woods without any belongings; no extra clothes, money, food supplies, or chariots to transport them. This further frustrated the Dark Prince.

"No chariots amongst them?" he pressed. "How, then, did they get here? And where did they come from?"

"My Prince! We found something!" shouted one soldier.

And then, the evil eyes of Prince Mafestus beheld it. He gazed upon the O'rah Harp for the first time. This was the O'rah Harp of the Shiggionoth and his eyes were instantly enamored by the graceful workmanship of skill unknown. He marveled at its golden form beautifully adorned with the likeness of twin, celestial ekeru beasts on each side, each spreading their wings towards the other. It had a polished, rune-inscribed bow at its base bearing the ancient tongue of the holy Vheilyel. The harp was composed of glistering, melodic strings that pleasured the soul with refreshing notes that indeed felt from another world altogether. He curiously held it, and he caressed it. The sound was foreign, soothing, and sweet. He had never heard such sweetness and tone in all the skilled glory of Eofendurk.

"This is all we found amongst the strangers, my Prince," explained the soldier.

Mafestus appeared to have entered another domain at the sound of the harp. The words of the soldier were faint and far placed from his hearing.

"Have you . . . ever seen or heard anything like this, lieutenant?"

"No, my Prince. This sound is utterly intoxicating, and the harp must be worth a fortune."

"Yes, it's beautiful. The best craftsmen in all Eofendurk could not produce anything like this. The best musicians in all the kingdom of Nith have yet to produce such an incredible tone."

Perplexed by the harp's obscure inscriptions and elegant form, Prince Mafestus considered its possible origins. *Oh, the massive wealth this instrument must have come from!* He pondered. Its sound filled him with a warmth and yearning he was unable to express with words.

And then, as he reveled in intrigue at the sight of the puzzling treasure, the Dark Prince suddenly recalled a night terror he had experienced in the wake of his siege against the neufs of Bumbersing. He remembered seeing the terrifying face of a cryptid ujorg, but it was no ordinary ujorg. Instead, the beast resembled a man because it stood upright on its hind legs. *Wait, it's . . . the beast from my dream! These people are the beast from my nightmare,* the prince thought to himself. *They are here to lead the rebel uprising!* He mused. At that instance, Prince Mafestus was convinced the Drukijaken had forewarned him of these intruders in a dream. He then realized what he must do. He had to slay them all at once!

"My Prince, awaiting orders," said the lieutenant.

But the evil prince, ever so eager to spill the blood of his enemies, did relent that day. The intrigue of their appearance, their foreign tongue, and the allure of the harp, all these compelled him to deny his impulse. He pondered momentarily and then finally announced,

"O legions of Nith, hear my counsel in this matter. These are the enemies of Ruminthumgath, our god, and they are here to assist the enemies of the kingdom, the Smoyjan and the Zafren, the Neufs and the Cathra, all the remaining enemies of Nith. The kingdom will not be mocked!"

"Just say the word, my Prince," the lieutenant swiftly replied, his sword in hand, ready to smite the strangers and show no mercy. The legions mirrored their lieutenant.

The silver-haired strangers became visibly worried for their lives. Some amongst them urged the others with hand gestures to remain calm.

"Lieutenant, this is my counsel. We will *not* slay these creatures today, whatever they are, wherever they came from."

The lieutenant became confused but retained his composure.

"Yes, my Prince, as you wish," he replied, glaring at the crowd with burning spite.

"Lieutenant, we will make these people our slaves. Furthermore, I hereby decree that no one in the kingdom may take any of them to marry or forcefully take any of them in any way. If anyone defies my decree, issued this day, in the name of Ruminthumgath, our god, that soul shall be certainly executed. We must not interbreed with these people because Ruminthumgath has warned me they are our enemies and they will attempt to overthrow the kingdom. I repeat, if anyone should interbreed with any of them, they have defiled the kingdom, and I, Prince Mafestus, will surely avenge the decree of the kingdom without mercy."

The soldiers were stunned. It was not what they were expecting to hear. Murmuring erupted amongst them.

"What a waste . . ." they said amongst themselves.

"My Prince, you are merciful to spare the enemies of Nith, but wouldn't this provoke the wrath of Ruminthumgath? They are, after all, enemies of the kingdom, as our god has shown you in a dream."

And truly, these were a grave peril to the Nithians, as the Dark Prince had perceived, but the greed of Prince Mafestus prevailed against him that day.

"Lieutenant, we will intercept the treasures of these, our enemies, and we will offer them unto Ruminthumgath, and then we will slay them once this purpose has been accomplished," Mafestus announced. "We will spare these strange people and make them serve us. They will learn to speak with us, and then they will lead us to the place of their treasures, and we will thereby increase the glory of Nith. For Nith!"

"For Nith!" the legions shouted back.

And so, the Dark Prince neglected the omen of the night terror given him in the hopes of uncovering the origins of the harp. Its beauty and ethereal sound had stolen at his heart, against his instincts. He no longer felt the gnawing impulse to slay the menacing trespassers. In place, he coveted with an unquenchable desire this rarest of treasures, one without rival in all of Eofendurk.

And yet, unbeknownst to the dark prince, the silver-haired Shaifetnu carried with them, that day, a second heirloom. But the perverse eyes of the Nithians were forbidden from gazing upon it, as it had been carefully hidden until the time determined. This was that sacred emblem of power also gifted to the silver-haired people by the many winged gods, and it was Saxfen's fate to one day wield its might against the fiendish adversaries of the Daylight.

The soldiers callously herded their Shaifetnu prisoners back to Ujorg Stone City, where they would seek to uncover the whereabouts of these treasures without equaling in all their lands.

But wrapped in lowly strands of soiled linen and firmly griped against a frightened boy's chest, the second heirloom had escaped the legions of Nith. The boy ran with all the vigor that remained in him despite the mind-numbing trauma he had experienced in the events leading to the capturing of his people by the Nithians. For the relic upon his chest gave him great hope. He had heard of its might; if he could only learn to wield its power! If he could only win favor in the sight of the ancient gods, if he could just be courageous enough! The Nithians had taken the costly harp, but what need had his captive kin of some elaborate, musical instrument? This the boy reasoned, for the purpose of the harp had long been concealed from the Shaifetnu within the mysterious runes inscribed upon its polished surface.

The boy desperately sought to hide the heirloom. He dreaded the thought of these vulgar brutes handling this precious relic. He ran without ceasing, never looking back, without regard to the possibility he may never see his family again. He collapsed in exhaustion.

Sobbing at the weight of the tragedy upon tragedy his innocent eyes had witnessed, the boy drifted into the merciful arms of slumber. He firmly gripped the heirloom against his chest and would rather die than release his clenched fists. But his peaceful slumber was violently disrupted by the cold talons of a monstrous sky predator. It was a fierce, crimson sky gylth! Upon its head was a crown of vertical, red feathers, and its neck was massive and elongated like a serpent. Its sharp, onyx beak could snap a tree trunk in half with little effort.

The boy knew he was doomed. He screamed in terror as the gylth soared across the verdant valleys and sparkling, roseate waters of the pristine lakes below. It raced skyward toward the lofty, snow-covered mountains on the horizon. But the looming haze of the mountains obstructed the hungry gylth's sight. Its wing dashed against the rocks, releasing the frightful screech so familiar to the terrorized natives of the land. The boy fell to his doom, and the sacred heirloom left his grip.

But the Daylight favored the boy that day, and he survived the plunge to his death. The boy laid unconscious, far from the comforting arms of his family or anyone else who could console him.

Then, a lone, hooded figure appeared in the distance. It approached him and raised him unto its merciful arms. The figure lifted its head toward heaven and exposed beautiful, white-feathered wings from its back, sixfold in number. This was a celestial keeper of the silver-haired Shaifetnu, a Holy Vheilyel of the Council of Daylight.

The Vheilyel had come to succor the lost lad from the frigid cruelty of the mountain. It soared into the air with the power of its six wings and parted unto Ujorg Stone City, where the boy's family mourned. And so, it seemed, the boy's appointment with death would tarry and return at another time. The many winged gods had determined to award this courageous, unsung hero many more days, and thus, they returned him to his grieving family.

But not merely the single lad's family grieved a painful loss that night. All the Shaifetnu captives within the towering walls of Ujorg Stone could be heard quietly lamenting their misfortune, the Great Vexation, and the loss of their home. Their faint cries of despair rose like incense, and they rose far above unto the very courts of Highest Ofandynth itself. Their sorrow pierced the nocturnal zenith like a sharpened dagger, piercing through the immense, starry gulfs of the black expanse so named, Ru'alameth. Their cries had moved the heart of heaven, the very hearts of the many winged gods.

***

Elsewhere, upon a land far placed from the grieving Shaifetnu of Eofendurk, there sat a beautiful damsel underneath the vibrant, uncolored leaves of a wiusk tree. She leaned against its widened trunk as she looked on at a group of children playing in the distance. A light cluster of whitened leaves came faintly coursing before her from the aged tree. A lone tear rolled down her face.

"What's wrong, Orilheart?" called out a voice.

"It's them. I think they're in trouble again," she replied. "I missed them so much. It's been a hundred years since I last saw them, and now their pain has reached my heart again."

Orilheart felt the piercing anguish of the Shaifetnu outcasts she had become endeared with. Their story had captured her heart. Her last visit with them was brief one hundred years ago, the saving of the lone boy on the snowy mountain. But the tales of their tragedy, the Great Vexation, as it was known, had stayed with her all these years upon the hallowed lands of Luwenkith. She fought back the tears by looking instead at the innocent children playing ahead and turning her thoughts into those of happiness. The children celebrated in a lush, verdant meadow underneath the crisp light of twain suns above. Her hooded, yellow hair partly veiled her face in an attempt to hide her tears.

The voice conversing with her continued, "Nuliette looks most pleased, does she not? If I may, her hundredth-year birthday today marks something special."

The voice referred to the happy little girl laughing and playing with her friends. They ran and danced and chased one another in celebration of her birthday.

"Well, what's that, Jrukell? Do you intend on telling me what that something is?"

"Yes, today concludes the measure of your days here in Luwenkith."

"What?" Orilheart asked in disbelief. "I've been having so much fun with Nuliette."

"Yes, but now it is time to proceed unto your next Mah'seyiud," Jrukell said.

"Oh, you're serious."

"Yes, and do you reckon where your path must now take you?"

"Well, hopefully not to Szobeknam. You know how much I hate that place."

"Well, not quite," smiled Jrukell. "You will need to return . . . to Eofendurk."

She swiftly turned to behold the face conversing with her. Those earnest whiskers refused to flinch. It was the face of a tiny osmu, but Jrukell was speaking through the tiny beast, as was their custom to conceal themselves from the prying eyes of their foes, from the enemies of the Council of Daylight.

"What? Wow, really? Please don't taunt me like that, Jrukell!"

"I taunt not; this is indeed the place of your new Mah'seyiud."

"Oh, what a high honor to return to the Shaifetnu! And we were just talking about them too! I will forever treasure this in my heart."

She removed the elegant hood from her head revealing a spirited smile. Her sorrow had turned to joy. Orilheart leaped upon her feet and sprinted toward the children playing in the meadow. She joined their childish glee at the thought of her new assignment from the Eth Master awaiting her; her new Mah'seyiud. She held the children's hands and began to rotate in circles with them and to sing their song. After concluding, she bid her farewells. Orilheart then revealed her majestic set of sixfold wings. She thrusted herself upward, toward the dual suns above, and the sky rippled like the crisp, clean waters of a lake. She vanished in a streak of light as the children of Luwenkith waved goodbye.

Though one hundred years had transpired upon sacred Luwenkith, Orilheart was nonetheless regarded a youth amongst the hierarchies of the Daylight. She came from a newer generation of Vheilyel, yet her skill was quite formidable, for she ardently applied herself in the celestial disciplines. And now, she had finally closed this chapter of her path in pursuit of a new, praiseworthy journey to be proudly inscribed upon the venerated records of the Order of Dathmahjen.

After a hundred years of being away from the world of her home, Orilheart had returned to those vibrant, living skies of that hallowed dwelling, so named, Eylundis. She sought to report to the honorable Otenhryen, chief amongst the ranks of the Order of Eth. This was that noble Ministry of Guides, those celestial shepherds sent forth to aid and console, and it was this divine Order that Orilheart had come to call her own.

These Eth Vheilyel were responsible for guiding, protecting, and counseling all beings entrusted to their care. And now, Orilheart must receive her new instructions at the hand of the mighty Otenhryen. *This must be the reason I felt the Shaifetnu's distress; I was meant to be sent to them*, Orilheart considered within herself. *I remember so clearly how the awful news of the Great Vexation reached me and the look on their faces as I looked upon them for the first time. Great Mebbukah! What tragedy! So many ages have passed since the Great Vexation, and now I have the honor to come to their aid again.*

There was a special place in Orilheart's tender heart for the distressed Shaifetnu. She had seen them newly vanished from the world of their abode and exiled unto Eofendurk. She beheld them in bewilderment and confoundment like stray birds without a nest. And she had been entrusted with the consoling and the caring of them, though only for a brief moment.

The thought of them was that of treasured, fond memories buried deep within and somehow resurfacing from the depths of an enduring age. Her loving memories had revived in that moment, and they consoled her with the same warmth she had felt in those bygone days.

She had reached that sacred haven of the Holy Vheilyel, the celestial dwelling of Eylundis. And that dazzling, azure sphere that was Eylundis radiated before her alongside a costly treasury of glistering stars stretching across the void like some wondrous river upon the black strata of Ru'alameth.

Upon piercing the cumulus layer hued in a faint, orange tint, Orilheart could now see the oceans below. The entire world appeared to be crafted from the sparkling surface of a single, turquoise gem. And from the depths of these delightful, vivid waters, numerous clusters of towering pillars decked with ivory structures arose unto the heavens. And the structures themselves were the startling, dignified palaces of the many winged gods of Lei'thrundall. This was that delightful city of the

Vheilyel upon Eylundis, that stunning dwelling Orilheart had come to embrace as her home.

The noble Vheilyel who lived there could be seen dispersed about in the skies amongst radiant schools of graceful clouds, soaring upon all four corners of the wind.

Her feet touched the polished floors of her beloved home for the first time in one hundred years. She leaned against a balcony and exhaled, immersed in the beauty of the scene: The turquoise waters far below, the towering pillars sustaining the Vheilyel castles, the river of stars faintly visible in the brightness of daylight—and even more striking at night. *I feel so loved*, she thought; *what an honor to serve the Shaifetnu again. This is so exciting. I wonder what's become of them? I hope all is well.* She then remembered the piercing pain that had haunted her upon Luwenkith, where she had received the news of her new assignment. *They must be in trouble*, she sensed.

Orilheart paced to her quarters, where she noted everything remained as she had left it, or at least as she remembered she had left it. She leaped upon her bed momentarily and embraced the soft, plush pillow at its head. But the brief moment overcame her, and her gentle, sapphire eyes slowly dosed into the pleasant slumber the many winged gods did enjoy.

While the Vheilyel did not require sleep to survive as mortal creatures require it, sleep was merely a pleasant activity they indulged in, not a necessary one. Unlike mortal creatures that need to eat and drink to sustain their life, the many winged gods enjoyed these activities for sheer pleasure. They loved to savor delicious delicacies from across the stars, sip exotic beverages, and feel refreshed after a long, soothing slumber. They dipped their bodies in warm and cool water alike, not to wash themselves as mortal creatures do but to undergo the delight of being submerged.

Deep within the strange, mystic lands of slumber, Orilheart ventured into the Path of the Sithrah, that boundless place between realms where amazing and terrifying creatures dwell. There, she beheld the faces of the happy children she had left behind in Luwenkith, that sacred land of peace and sanctuary. And her time there felt like a gift she would treasure evermore. Would she see them again? She wondered in her dream.

A curiously crafted window was upon Orilheart's ceiling, permitting the warm rays to pour in and caress her face as she laid in bed. But her eyes suddenly flung wide as she remembered in that blissful moment why she had returned home.

"Oh no! I have to report to Otenhryen!"

She arose abruptly and pounced off the gratifying comfort of her bed. She then light-drifted unto the nearby balcony which admitted the dazzling view outside.

"Farewell, my sweet home . . ." she whispered.

And with that, she playfully leaped off its edge, plunging herself unto the turquoise waters below.

Her shouts of joy could have reached the loftiest pinnacle encompassing her. One rectangular flap on her upper back exposed a tiny set of contracted, sixfold wings. On command, the feathered wings expanded forcefully and reversed her plunge, propelling her skyward instantly.

Soaring and playfully spiraling toward the swirling heavens, she raced unto the lofty crown of the ivory monolith. But she felt anew that piercing hurt she had felt in the lush meadows of Luwenkith. *This is destiny,* she thought as her left hand grasped her aching chest.

There could be seen various fellow Vheilyel rushing about matters of their own, but she could not be swayed to converse and visit. The brief repose had already delayed her against her will, and the sense that something was amiss would not leave her. She finally reached the summit and shouted for the chief Eth delegated to her well-being, "Master Otenhryen! Where are you!?"

The echo in her youthful, delicate voice resonated across the ivory halls of the pinnacle's palace. And then a handsome, dark-haired man mirroring her youthfulness made his way toward her. He was vested in the regal, white and gold hues customary to their order. This was Otenhryen, Song of the Ekeru, and Arch Vheilyel of the Order of Eth. He raised his right hand and saluted, "Peace of the Daylight."

"Peace of the Daylight," Orilheart responded, raising her hand.

"It is good to see you again, Orilheart. I see you have returned safely."

"Yes, thank you. Everything went well. I hope to see those children again someday. I love them so dearly. Sadly, they may no longer be children of Luwenkith if we ever cross paths again."

Chapter 2

A Shout Across the Royal Court

Notwithstanding that Orilheart of the Eth had been away for one hundred years, there had transpired upon far-placed Eofendurk a mare three years since the silver-haired Shaifetnu had been captured by the Dark Prince of Nith. This contorted passing of time was known as the work of the Decree of Unequal Seasons, where one world experienced time unequal to other worlds. And thus did the sacred decree ordain that after the passing of one hundred years upon Luwenkith, only three years had transpired upon Eofendurk.

And so, the cruel monarch of Nith was determined to extract from the exiled Shaifetnu the place of their kingdom in the hopes of looting their vaults of exquisite and unknown treasures, such as that he held in his hand. He patiently fed and housed the silver-haired strangers with a flattery found on the lips of serpents. His fascination with the stolen harp obsessed his every waking moment. It was mesmerizing to behold, and he craved the gentle sound of its sweet voice always. That marvelous, golden finish, those mysterious runes, and those fascinating, sculpted wings upon the twin beasts on opposing ends! These were sheer pleasure to the eyes and to the senses. The heartwarming notes of its finely tuned strings did cast enchantments of bliss upon the Dark Prince beyond description.

"It's like my soul leaves my body and treads upon unknown lands when I hear this sound," he declared to his court.

No doubt the ancient harp had stolen his wicked heart. And had it not, the Shaifetnu would have certainly been slain for their trespass upon the imperial lands of Nith.

Musing upon and savoring those rich, resonating notes, the Dark Prince could not help but quietly wonder to himself, *Where did you come from? In which of all the heavenly realms were you forged? Tell me . . .* he reasoned, fully engrossed in its beauty.

He had directed his wisemen to teach these strange people the language of Nith. And when wooing and hospitality failed, the brave ones that refused him were chastised severely. Therefore, the silver-haired Shaifetnu lived in fear, and some did compel themselves to speak the tongue of the Nithians.

And then, there was the other matter which most deeply disturbed and haunted Mafestus. And that was the matter of all his guest's uncanny appearance of youthfulness. At first, he had guessed that these were all stray children and youth, but upon closer examination of loose translations, the men of Nith were perplexed to find that they simply did not age like the natural creatures they had known in all their lands. Fathers, mothers, and grandfathers all did cease the natural aging that the Nithians were accustomed to.

"But we've labored feverishly these three long years, My Prince," said one. "And they still cannot explain to us this matter. The strangers seem to be just as puzzled as we are. From what our best trainers can discern, it's like we are strange to them."

The Dark Prince thus coveted the youthfulness the Shaifetnu appeared to be endowed with, rivaling his intense desire for their gold. He had ordered his wisemen to study their bodies and experiment upon them so as to find some clue that could be profitable in their quest to plunder these hidden riches.

"Bardceru!" Mafestus summoned.

The chief wiseman was swiftly summoned so as to answer an irate and increasingly impatient Prince Mafestus.

"My Prince," he pleaded. "We have all of the kingdom's best magicians relentlessly toiling day and night to uncover the secrets you seek. And still, we need more time. Three years is simply not enough time to uncover all this strangeness."

But Bardceru, the chief magician in Ujorg Stone, had boasted foolishly in the matter he had been commissioned. And now, Prince Mafestus demanded the boast of his mouth. All the wisemen of Nith had been ordered to attend to Bardceru in discovering the reason for this strange youthfulness. And now, after the three years had been accomplished, his boast had fallen to the ground, and the chief magician remained with hands empty and full of dread.

"So, what is this you are saying?" Mafestus interrupted his chief Wiseman.

Bardceru held his peace, afraid to his core of the prince's infamous wrath.

"Well, speak up!"

"My Prince, we . . . we have determined they are of a race foreign to all the kingdoms in Eofendurk. There are no references to silver-haired people who do not age anywhere in all our records. And, as you know, our records are the most reliable in all the lands underneath the Sky'erligg."

Mafestus suddenly became indignant. He glanced at his armored guard and nodded. The guard approached Bardceru, ready to escort him to the execution dungeons. To his horror, Bardceru knew what would proceed with this embarrassing failure.

He screamed and pleaded for his life, "Wait my Prince! We managed to train one of them a little better than the rest!" exclaimed the desperate Wiseman.

Prince Mafestus paused and gestured for the armored guard to release Bardceru.

"But there's a problem," he continued as he stumbled over his words, confounded by the strain of his own freight.

"Well, go on . . . why have you kept this from me? Do you wish to live or not?"

"My Prince, I've been reluctant to report this development. You see, the lad who learned our language best speaks dark things about you. I was afraid you would execute the lad for making threats against the Crown."

The Dark Prince grew impatient and took the guard's sword.

"If you do not start talking right now, I will execute you myself right here in front of all your wisemen!"

Bardceru took a deep breath.

"Very well," he began, "This is what the lad said. He said that you stole their costly harp and that the consequence of doing this, is that you will be punished unless you return it to his people. He said . . . the *many winged gods* will come for you."

The entire court listened intently, and the royal chamber was astonished into unsettling silence. Then, quiet murmurs slowly emerged. Prince Mafestus finally erupted in jeering laughter, "The many-what!?"

He stepped aside from Bardceru and handed the sword back to his guard, attempting to regain his composure from his laughter.

"Well, this clearly concludes the matter," he announced to his court. "Our dear, silver-haired friends are not from any of our known terrains. We can rest assured they are not from anywhere in all of Eofendurk. Had they been from any of our lands, they would not so much as dared to utter a single threat against the Crown of Nith! Nay, a threat against the

Crown of Nith is a threat against the god of Nith, the god of Eofendurk, the terror of the seas, Ruminthumgath, our god!"

The royal court erupted in consent, jeering and scoffing at the ominous words supposedly uttered by the Shaifetnu child. However, not wavering from his fury against the revolting things spoken upon his court, Mafestus proceeded in a taunt.

"How uncivilized of us to forego acquainting our guests with our master. Let us introduce them to the great Ruminthumgath. This way, there will be no question on who ought to be feared while sojourning in our lands."

And so, Prince Mafestus had determined to summon the monstrous horror deep within the rubied sea.

The day that followed, the evil prince called for a rendezvous upon the Temple of Ruminthumgath. He had gathered the youth who had learned the language of Nith, along with a few other Shaifetnu. He summoned these as well so they may witness the penalty for transgressing against the Nithians. They were ceremonially escorted to the mouth of the temple, and they were greeted by the striking height of its dual-arched doors inscribed with elegant words throughout.

This principal entrance towered far above the company like the gates of some sacred corridor for some giant thing to traverse. The lofty temple doors required the labor of five mighty chains on each side to open and close them. Within the sanctuary, the artistry was masterfully crafted, and the entire edifice sat upon the rim of a gaping cliff overlooking the sparkling, rubied waters of the Sea of Nith. Its walls were smooth to the touch, reaching high unto domed ceilings. The place was enormous, a monument of a structure built in honor of their monstrous deity.

Marvelous posts lent their soft light from curious, luminous gems. Warm sunlight also accompanied the visitors from the various, lavishly crafted windows. There was also a most generous source of light, but not from the crafted windows or yellow-hued gems. This light proceeded from deep within one central passageway, alluring the eyes with intrigue. At this corridor's end, there freely entered the crisp sunlight from the roseate skies above, and it smote upon the polished floors of a widened and spacious arena resembling the festive halls of some grand, ceremonial plane. The company found themselves outside again.

This was their destination. They had arrived at the venerated shrine of Ruminthumgath, the Drukijaken. This was the ceremonial threshold at the rim of the steep cliff overlooking the rubied sea. There was an altar and statues of Nithians with swords drawn. A grim, copper instrument reached unto the waters far below, and the priests of Nith stood beside it, as if awaiting to attend to some religious ordinance. Herein, the men of Nith would summon the Drukijaken, and if it pleased the terrifying beast to appear before them, it would surely heed their call.

The captive Shaifetnu became visibly anxious at the striking sight of the shrine. Were the Nithians going to cast them into the rubied waters below? And what was this Ruminthumgath? Frightened and perplexed, they whispered these things amongst themselves.

And then, Prince Mafestus finally nodded to his servant. They brought unto him twain children and placed them in front of the chief magician standing at his right hand.

The Dark Prince announced, "You will translate to your people what I am about to say, or I will throw these children one by one into the Sea of Nith. There, far below upon the crimson waters, they will be devoured by Ruminthumgath, our god."

Prince Mafestus nodded to his servants a second time. The grand arena was then filled with the clamorous clang of what appeared to be a giant bell. It was the eerie sound of the immense copper pipe reaching to the upmost depths of the scarlet waters. There came multiple, sonorous blasts in sequential tones like some cryptic message unknown. And then, finally, there was silence.

What came next seemed impossible. The splendid, roseate skies were suddenly assaulted by an intruding host of damning, menacing clouds, like the summoning of a thunderstorm at the whim of mere mortals. There came blinding flashes of light. It was the sight of terrible, red lightning, but not from the heavens above, as is the natural order. Nay, these fiendish bolts appeared to have surged from the depths of the crimson chasm itself! Ghastly, unknown howls also thundered from the watery abyss.

It appeared the prayers of the Nithians had been accepted in the depths below. The Drukijaken had harkened to their call.

***

"Papaaaa! Don't stop now! What did the Drukijaken look like? Did the children die?" Enos anxiously shouted.

The warrior of legend had been abruptly distracted. A subtle noise proceeded from a group of bashful shrubs, wholly blanketed in sparkling snow.

"Enos," Saxfen whispered. "Don't make a sound."

They unmounted the snow gethwi and listened intently. Tonby's twofold set of jeweled eyes were fastened, ready to pounce and tear into pieces whatever intruder lurked nearby. But the thing moving in the shrubs revealed itself without warning when it pounced upon the group. The ferocious, striped beast targeted Enos first, but Tonby's watchful gaze withstood the intruder. Tonby roared and pinned the assailant gethwi to the powdered ground. They fought one another like the wild creatures they were. But then, a familiar scent intercepted their savage combat. That scent . . . it was the gethwi, Kirrius, one of Tonby's own friends, who also lived atop the lofty Oclyd Tower.

Twain majestic beasts reversed their feuding and exchanged playful headbutts and purrs instead. Kirrius was slightly bigger than Tonby, with his right fang chipped. The shag on his upper back was also thicker and unkept.

"Whoa, Papa! Another one!" Enos exclaimed after recovering from the initial shock.

"Yes, I do remember this one as well. I know him from that mark on his head and the chip on his right fang. He is called Kirrius."

"Kirrius? I see . . . do you think he'd mind if I rode him?"

Saxfen glanced at Kirrius and stretched out his arm to the beast. He gently petted the heavy, unkept coat, and the gethwi replied with a friendly purr. Saxfen glanced at Tonby for his approval.

Tonby approved.

"It doesn't look like he'll mind, Son. Just hang tight so you don't fall off."

Enos approached the imposing, striped creature, but just as he was readying to mount, Kirrius unexpectedly growled.

"Ahhh, help!" shouted Enos as he raced to hide behind his father.

Kirrius was highly amused and proceeded to roll on the snow, exposing his belly. Saxfen burst out into laughter.

"Oh, yes! He sure fooled you quite good!"

"It's not funny! What if he was serious?" Enos retorted, trembling in fright.

"Nonsense. If that gethwi wanted you dead, he would have torn through Tonby and me already. Or at least die trying. Now, go on, let's try again."

Enos finally mounted Kirrius and tightly gripped the gethwi's coat. They then proceeded on their journey unto that sky-piercing colossus, Oclyd Tower.

"So where were we?" continued Saxfen, remembering where he had left off. "Ah, yes, the Drukijaken had awoken . . ."

***

With those chilling howls echoing from the depths of the Sea of Nith, the boy who had learned the tongue of the Nithians was compelled to accomplish the deed the Dark Prince had required. And those furious bolts of terror did surge unto the surface of the scarlet, restless sea.

"Now, I will tolerate your insubordination no longer, boy. I know you can understand me. Tell your people that if anyone refuses to learn Imperial Plierdurgeesh, we are compelled, as the defenders of Nith, to feed them to the great god of Eofendurk, Ruminthumgath, in whose temple your feet currently stand and whose divine voice you have witnessed this day."

The boy held his peace as he looked upon his frightened kin before him; such a good and wholesome race, a people of destiny. But now their lot was such that they had been abased and humiliated in a far-placed land with a beast for a god. He calmed himself and reiterated what Prince Mafestus demanded of him.

All Shaifetnu present that day nodded as they received the burden placed upon them. All agreed from the least to the greatest of them. It was not necessary to sacrifice their lives over a foreign tongue. Thus, they assured Prince Mafestus that day. They would strive to learn Imperial Plierdurgeesh and obey the prince's voice to the best of them.

And so, the monstrous howls of the Drukijaken erupting from the abyss; the fiendish, inverted lightning; and that sudden siege of menacing storm clouds concealing the lovely Sky'erligg—and altogether the roseate heavens—these had sufficed to persuade the Shaifetnu of the grave peril that had befallen them upon this foreign land.

But hidden from their weary and frightened eyes was that deathly Order of Vheilyel warriors defending the decrees of the Council of Daylight without ceasing. This was the Order of Sabbayoth looking down with burning eyes full of contempt against the terrible god of the Nithians and against their Dark Prince. Yet, the time appointed had not come for their legions to descend retribution upon Nith, and therefore, could not yet intervene.

One year did transpire since that frightful day when they almost became blood offerings to the terrible Drukijaken. At last, the best Shaifetnu students were summoned before Mafestus. They were to bring a good report on their promise in that shrine of evil before the chilling howls of Ruminthumgath. There came five students who were selected to converse with the Dark Prince, and they had better not disappoint. For all Shaifetnu now understood how Mafestus intended to heartlessly feed them, from the least to the greatest of them, to his god whom they had witnessed.

Bardceru, chief Wiseman of Ujorg Stone, eagerly marched to the quarters where the five elected students awaited. He opened the crafted doors of their royal chamber, and the sweet scent of freshly cut flowers filled the air. Despite the Dark Prince's impatience and contempt, the silver-haired Shaifetnu were nonetheless greatly admired throughout the kingdom. Thus, the locals were permitted to bring them gifts and colorful, fragrant flowers. After all, the goal was to befriend and seduce them in the hopes they might reveal to them the whereabouts of their treasures and the place of their kingdom.

"Look at you," Bardceru complemented, "So beautifully dressed and ready to impress His Grace with your newfound speaking abilities."

"Thank you, Chief Bardceru," they replied in one voice.

The five students were vested in royal attire fit for the finest of royal ceremonies. They made their way to the merry throne room, where Prince Mafestus awaited. The prince himself was also eager. He awaited them upon the throne while he reveled in the soothing, sweet melody of the O'rah Harp. What grand things will he finally learn today from the silver-haired strangers? The entirety of Ujorg Stone City was jubilant and overcome with suspense.

The royal announcer came forth and introduced the students with one resonant, commanding voice,

"Your Highness, Prince Mafestus, the five Silver Students!"

The royal court stood and welcomed them, and their eyes were fixed as they passed by. They looked on with a sense of awe, for a shroud of wonder and mystery had been their cloak these past four years. Joyous thrill, dense expectancy, and wild murmurings filled the royal chamber.

"Oh, look, they're adorable . . ."

"How delightful . . ."

"I wonder what they're going to say . . ."

"And that hair . . ."

Prince Mafestus arose from his throne. He spread his arms and greeted his guests, "Welcome, my Silver friends. This is an extraordinary day, and coming into these courts is a high honor!"

The five students bowed gracefully as they accepted the prince's affectionate welcome. The heralding trumpets blasted, and the royal court applauded.

"Thank you, Your Highness!" the Shaifetnu students replied as one.

"My Lord, I present to you, Liin," Bardceru proudly announced.

Liin was a small girl with a timid smile on her face. She paused momentarily and then began with an accent in her voice,

"Your Grace, we are called Shaifetnu by our friends. This is the name given to us by our friends, the many winged gods. What is our master, the royal prince's inquiry of this, his humble servant?"

The piercing silence gripped everyone present as they awaited a question from Mafestus.

"Well, let us see how well your speaking abilities have come along. Tell me, Liin, where is your home?"

The small girl smiled and gazed up with her silver hair faintly covering her timid eyes.

"My home . . . it is all. And all is my home, my master."

Unimpressed, Prince Mafestus glanced at Bardceru. Bardceru had a blank stare on his face and would not return the glance, but his eyes were solemnly fixed on the floor.

"I do not believe you understood me, little girl. Where is your home?" Prince Mafestus asked once again.

"As I said, my Lord. My home is all. My home is everything. My home is everywhere."

The court murmured and laughed.

Prince Mafestus was perplexed. He wondered at the small girl's answer and her new ability to speak the tongue of Nith. He pulled Bardceru aside and cautioned him, "This is no time for jokes, Bardceru. You are making a mockery of your prince. I told you beforehand what I was going to ask them. For your sake, they best furnish information on where they came from and how to reach that place, or you will die this day."

"My Prince, this is what they tell me when I pose the questions you presented. I told them this will confuse everyone in the kingdom, and that it will enrage you. Should I make them lie to my lord?"

The nervous Bardceru was at a loss on what to do with the student's bizarre answers. Prince Mafestus carefully considered what to do next.

"Very well, let us hear their speech," he concluded.

Bardceru dismissed Liin to return to her previous post and signaled the next student to come forth. It was young Svei, the boy who first learned Imperial Plierdurgeesh and conceded to the prince upon the evil altars of Ruminthumgath.

"My Lord, I present to you, Svei."

"Hello, Svei. How are you feeling today?"

"I am quite nervous, my Lord," the boy replied, also with an accent.

"There is no need to be nervous before me," Mafestus responded, offering a friendly laugh.

Svei glanced briefly at Mafestus with a look of disbelief. This was the man who had threatened to feed all his family to their monster god in the crimson sea! The boy was notably perplexed.

"Oh, come on, my dear boy. Are you still shaken by our last encounter? It was so long ago. And besides, I never truly intended to feed you to Ruminthumgath. We only wanted your cooperation. Now, be a good lad and talk with me."

And of truth, Mafestus did not intend to cast the Shaifetnu to the Drukijaken that fateful day; thus, the battalions of the Daylight relented their retribution. But the prince's patience had reached its measure, and now, he was prepared to fulfill his vow against them.

Bardceru nervously swallowed in the background. The life of this renown magician of Nith was now in the hands of these bizarre children.

"Your Highness, you truly frightened us that day, and it feels like only yesterday that you almost fed us to Ruminthumgath," Svei explained.

"My dear, Svei, I apologize for your trouble. I would not have resorted to that if your people had simply fulfilled what we asked. Truly, you need only to fulfill what we ask and we shall be best of friends. And perhaps, you also will one day find favor in the eyes of Ruminthumgath, and you will come to worship him as we do."

"Well, respectfully, that's not going to happen, my Lord."

"What's not going to happen?"

"Worship your god, Ruminthumgath."

"And why is that?"

"Because we already have a god."

"I thought your people worshipped many gods. Is this not true? You said you worshipped the many winged gods."

"Your Grace, we do not worship the many winged gods. We worship the king of the many winged gods."

"And who would that be?"

"My Lord, he is called . . . the Living One."

The murmurs of the anxious court could be heard again. Prince Mafestus paused to reflect on the boy's words briefly. He glanced at Bardceru, who in turn nodded back, signaling that he had previously heard the boy's answer. *What manner of taunt is this?* he reflected. *There is no rival to Ruminthumgath in all Eofendurk. All the gods of Eofendurk have fallen to Ruminthumgath. Would this foreign god not of this world challenge the great Master? A god that is called the Living One? What blasphemous speech is this?*

Mafestus continued, "So where is your home?"

"Our home is all, my Lord."

"Yes, we've heard that, but what does that mean?"

"Your Grace, it means . . ." The boy paused when he perceived that his answer would be ridiculed but proceeded nonetheless, "It means everything is ours."

The prince paused as he pondered what appeared to be some dark riddles provoking his ear. He then burst in laughter as his base instinct suddenly came upon him.

"This isn't a time for jesting, my dear boy!" he scoffed and warned as he reached for the guard's sword.

But the prince's scorn abruptly ceased as there came a series of violent shouts from across the crowded quarters,

"HALT! I command you!! In the name of the Prince of Nith!!"

It was the royal guard. They hasted and commanded one cloaked intruder, casually approaching the throne room. All swords of the watchmen were drawn, ready to punish without prejudice. It was a slender figure shrouded in a dark, hooded cloak. The trespasser stood at the mouth of the throne room, grimly staring at the prince from afar. The previously merry tone of the royal court became alarmed with gasps ringing in the air.

Then, as the stranger's right arm was raised against Prince Mafestus, there came the forceful demands of a calm, feminine voice.

"Prince Mafestus!" the voice scolded. "Be it known that the measure of blood spilled by your hand is now accomplished. Because your thirst for blood has rivaled that of the savage ujorg, thus will you now join their ranks. Because you have refused to return that ancient, holy harp, we will now therefore refuse you that which differs you from beasts."

Prince Mafestus was furious at the damning words pronounced against him in the presence of his royal court. But, unbeknownst to him, divine justice had come to his doorstep.

"KILL HER!!" he exclaimed.

The guards approached the stranger, their swords raised high and ready to spill her blood. But their deadly blows would not come, as their gazes were forcefully turned away toward the torturous screams proceeding from the throne.

"WhaaaaAAhhhh! AhHHHhhh!"

It was the screams of Prince Mafestus. He had fallen to the floor in gut-wrenching agony.

"My Lord!" rushed the guards to his aid.

The royal court panicked at the sight of this unseen display of power. They desperately fled the throne room by any means.

"HeeeeEEELP!!!" screamed Prince Mafestus.

His voice had somehow warped into deep, bellowing tones of a monstrous nature. The guards stood their ground, but their visages were appalled, and did not know how to respond. They were frozen with ice upon their feet as if bewitched into very stone by the utter dread of the sight. Their prince, he was *changing* before their very eyes! In place of men's hearty teeth, there had grown one menacing set of gruesome fangs. They were sharp and deadly unto all mortal flesh, and they were haughtily fastened upon a beastly snout most terrible.

His frame itself had grown, tearing the royal vestures from his back. He was covered in a thick, indigo fleece from head to toe—*Mafestus had become the very image of the vicious ujorgs the Nithians had come to domineer!*

The prince finally stood on his hind legs. He had grown notably taller than every fellow in the chamber. It was the image of the royal, blue ujorg, yet it obscenely stood upon its hind legs!

The hooded intruder defiantly raised her voice a second time, demanding Prince Mafestus surrender the sacred harp he had taken from the silver-haired Shaifetnu.

"Return the harp to its people at once!" she exclaimed.

The beast furiously growled and charged at the mysterious, hooded arbiter of his curse. She leaped and gracefully evaded, which only fueled the creature's rage.

"Return it, you fool!" she insisted.

Vexed and consumed with frenzied fury, Prince Mafestus seized the harp from the guards entrusted with its care. He fled the throne room with the prized heirloom in hand.

The hooded trespasser uncovered her head, revealing her long, golden hair and lovely, youthful face. It was the commissioned servant of the Council of Daylight, Orilheart of the Order of Eth.

She pursued the half-bred ujorg as he leaped and dashed through the royal corridors of Oclyd Tower. The creature was swift, but Orilheart light-drifted and would intercept the Dark Prince at every turn in that spectral silhouette of her vanishing ability.

In that instance, there came to her memory the words of that venerated Eth Master, Otenhryen. She recalled their talk upon that ivory abode atop the crisp, turquoise waters of celestial Eylundis, "And what . . . if he refuses, then what?"

She glanced at Otenhryen anew and saw the saddened look on his face.

"Then," the Eth Master replied. "I'm afraid we will strike at what his heart loves most . . . his beloved kingdom. Say unto him if he refuses, 'Because you have robbed that costly treasure of the Shaifetnu people, so now we will rob you of your prized treasure, that cherished city that is called, the Jewel of Nith.'"

In livid desperation, Prince Mafestus cast himself through a window and plunged unto the avenues of Ujorg Stone below. He dashed his heavy claws against the stone tower, and it appeared that his calculations had been correct. His massive, muscular body had survived the fall, and he had instinctively landed on both feet. The nearby Nithians screamed in horror and fled the awful sight of him.

Orilheart meanwhile appeared upon faint ripples of her silhouette from her light-drift. The Dark Prince would not be yielding that day. He seized a nearby torch and a curious flask from a market stand and proceeded to set a roof ablaze. The fire spread rapidly and compelled Orilheart to attend to the screaming Nithians within the dwelling place.

And then came one cryptid utterance that beckoned Mafestus, coming from deep within his heart,

"Come . . . to me . . . my child," the voice within him said.

It was the chilling voice of the Drukijaken, summoning the Dark Prince. Mafestus fled to the creature's shrine, hoping to be succored from his celestial adversary and be cleansed from the foul curse placed upon him.

Orilheart finally light-drifted unto the shrine, and Mafestus was fiendishly awaiting her at the threshold overlooking the Sea of Nith. Bleak, unnatural clouds hovered above, and raindrops suddenly descended. Violent spurs of red lightning surged from underneath the waters, defying the heavens. The chilling howls of the Drukijaken rumbled underneath both their feet.

"Don't do it, Mafestus! Your whole kingdom will suffer!" she pleaded. "Don't make your people suffer! You will always regret it!"

And with that, the Dark Prince sealed the fate of his kingdom by recklessly casting the O'rah Harp into the gruesome mouth of his god, Ruminthumgath. Mafestus had won, it appeared, for this lone intruder would now be compelled to contend with that ancient power that had reigned over Eofendurk from elder times primordial.

"So be it," Orilheart whispered.

But the boast of the man-beast's triumph would not last, as the dew upon the polished deck warred against the prince that day and provoked his fall into the rubied sea far below.

CHAPTER 3

A Night to Remember

Saxfen recounted the tale of how the stolen harp had been fed to the frightful beast of the Sea of Nith, but his beloved son, Enos, remained incredulous.

"So . . . what's the big deal, Papa?" he wondered as he playfully pulled on Kirrius' mane. "Couldn't they just, oh, I don't know, get another one? Did the Vheilyel run out of harps? Was that the last one they had?"

"No, Son, it was not the last one they had. You see, this act of defiance against the Daylight served many purposes that the Vheilyel had determined to accomplish. The Council of Daylight had purposed to raise an adversary for me, one that would test my heart to see if it was worthy to proceed with the destiny set before me."

"Oh, yeah? Many purposes? What else?"

"This rebellious act also brought severe judgment upon the Nithians because they were a cruel people full of blood on their hands. Also, the time appointed to judge the Drukijaken was drawing close."

"I see, what else?"

"Well, it turned out, this mischief against the Daylight would also test the Vheilyel themselves. Because, sadly, their hearts were not all with us. Not all were fully committed to doing that which is good. All were not worthy to walk amongst us, but many harbored dark thoughts and doubts against the Daylight and against their office of service."

"You mean, some of them were bad?"

"Yes, that's right. And that which is hidden in the heart must be brought forth from the darkness and into the light for all to see. The true heart of the Vheilyel needed to be revealed, and the thoughts of the heart are revealed when they are tested like gold is refined with fire. Do you understand this, Enos?"

"Yes, I think so."

The riders journeyed upon their gethwi escorts, who led their way unto hidden passageways they had knowledge of throughout Ujorg Stone City. Saxfen labored to explain his tale without sounding too frightening. Truly, the quest of the stolen harp was not for the faint of heart, and Saxfen took heed not to provoke night terrors upon the young lad.

"You still haven't told me how the gethwis came to live in Ujorg Stone."

"We'll get to that, but the first matters must come first," Saxfen smiled.

***

And so, many years passed since the bellowing creature in the scarlet waters devoured that most enchanting harp of the silver-haired Shaifet-nu. It seemed tragedy upon tragedy had come upon these exiled ones. Nonetheless, to their own relief, the silver-haired people could flee the city of their captivity now that its ruler had been rebuked and denounced by the very powers of heaven. The reign of the Dark Prince had come to a tragic end, and his kingdom was plunged into chaos.

Upon that beautifully adorned path of Sovereign's Pass, Saxfen recalled his childhood as the eager, wide-eyed lad he once was, full of zest and wonder.

"And the Silver Claw Gethwi Battalion remains . . . UNSTOP-PABLE!!" exclaimed the boy Saxfen, firmly holding a wooden sword raised above his bristly, silver locks.

He had just led a group of friends in a fierce dispute over a flimsy-built fort atop a verdant hill.

"Victory is ours!" he shouted.

His face bore a mask resembling the striped mountain beasts, the snow gethwis of Mount Tanlish. All of his fellows bore the same mask, while the other assembly that opposed them bore the ferocious likeness of blue ujorgs upon their faces. The children clashed in playful skirmishes for possession of the flimsy fort.

And so, the silver-haired people returned to a semblance of peace after they had been delivered from the Dark Prince of Nith. Thus, they were scattered throughout Eofendurk when that terrible curse visited the Nithians in their cherished city of Ujorg Stone.

Saxfen and his family took refuge within the faraway lands of Tunjunsora, where the warmhearted, whiskered neufs of Oakendunty Village comforted the strangers from their burdensome trials. The neufs were a mostly peaceful, cat-folk people but were known for their raids against the Nithians in defiance of the Kingdom. They were also known for befriending the trees of the forest, and the trees would in turn hide their villages from the dangerous, wild creatures of the land.

But the Nithians were wily in their crafts and would ofttimes find their secret dwelling places. It was said that the Drukijaken hated the neufs and would help the Nithians break their villages into pieces. Yet not all furry neufs sought to grieve the Nithian Kingdom. Only the most daring would challenge them; these were the ones hunted down, and their villages ransacked.

The whiskered-faced neufs laughed and played with the Shaifetnu children without a care in the world as they trusted the trees of Cimbri Forest to conceal them. And, besides, Oclyd Tower was far too distant from their pointed ears and curled horns for the Nithians to trouble themselves. The fierce kingdom and their cerulean beasts were merely a thing of talebearers around campfires within that secret haven that was Oakendunty Village.

"Okay, it's our turn to be the gethwi hims now!" one neuf exclaimed.

He removed his ujorg mask and revealed an eager look on his whiskered face. It was now their turn to use the gethwi masks, and none there be who would deny them.

"Alright, Qugam, we can be the ujorgs now," Saxfen laughed.

The children played and dreamt of being like the ferocious creatures they had only heard about in tales, never actually having seen one in the flesh. The gethwi group would charge at the fort in an effort to overtake it while the ujorg team protected it. They thrust and subdued one another, the Shaifetnu children careful to evade the curled horns upon the heads of the playful cat-folk.

After one extended, competitive bout, the gethwi group finally subdued the flimsy fort, and excitement erupted in the air.

"Ahhhh!! Yes!! And that's how we do it!! Fear the awesome power of the Ice Lance Gethwi Brigade!!" one neuf announced as he leaped and kicked the flimsy fort with his pawed feet. It crashed to the ground, and they laughed and pushed one another whimsically. It was time to return to their own dwelling places.

"So, your family is going to the Remembrance Torch? That's tonight, right?" one neuf asked.

"Yeah, Jix, you guys missed it last year," Saxfen said. "This is the night we go to the Remembrance Torch and light it. It's very special to us. Wanna come?"

"I don't know. I have to help Papa later."

"I can go help you guys if you'd like. That way, you can come."

Jix paused to consider the offer, carefully stroking the fur on his chin.

"Okay, yeah, that sounds good. Right now, I'm starving after that epic match. Let me go eat, and we can meet by the well in a bit."

"Alright, see you in a bit, Jix!"

The children parted ways. After his meals, Saxfen strolled to the village well as agreed.

"Hey, where are you going?" asked a voice along the way.

"I'm meeting up with Jix to help with their catch," Saxfen responded.

He turned and saw it was his longtime friend, Orilheart. But, in place of her long, yellow hair, her hair resembled the silver locks of the exiled Shaifetnu. She had cloaked herself in this manner from all the villagers in Oakendunty. And to Saxfen, she was just Orilheart, whom he had known as far back as he could remember. She was wearing a pallid, blue dress and was holding one adorable lyrbix in her arms.

"And who's your little friend?" Saxfen asked.

"This is Laseuke. We actually just met today, so he's not very talkative."

"So, this one talks too, huh?"

"Meeek meek, meeek meek," the lyrbix said.

"Wait . . . what's that, Laseuke? You think he's a stupid boy? Come on, be nice now! Look at that. I think you perked him right up."

"You're so funny, Orilheart. Well, I've got to meet Jix. I'm helping him with his chores so he can come with us to the Remembrance Torch later tonight. Wanna come too?"

"I don't know. Maybe I'll see you there. For now, this little lyrbix has some explaining to do after that last, rude remark."

"Okay, talk to you later!"

They parted ways, and Saxfen walked along the busied village. At last, he reached the well, but no one was there. Saxfen leaned into the mouth of the well and shouted into the dark,

"Hello, Jix! Are you down there?"

The echo resonated in a rich fading sound, but there was no response.

"Hey, Snowhead, why are you shouting at the well? Did we hit you that hard?"

Saxfen turned to see the familiar voice. It was Jix the neuf.

"Oh, hi, Jix. There you are. No, not at all. I was going to ask if you're okay from my famous catapult assault attack."

"Are you kidding me? You call that an attack move?" Jix laughed. "You're actually lucky I decided to take it easy on you back there. Had I failed to practice restraint, you wouldn't be walking around right now. So, yeah, you're welcome."

Saxfen paused to summon a pointed response swiftly.

"But you do remember that move, don't you?"

"I have no idea what you're talking about, Snowhead."

They playfully taunted each other until a second neuf approached them.

"What are you hims laughing at?" he asked.

"Oh, you better stay out of this, Qugam," Jix warned. "This Snowhead dares to defy the Ice Lance Gethwi Brigade after our duel had been long settled."

"Whatever," Saxfen retorted. "You're just mad I pinned you like a helpless little girl without breaking a sweat!"

Jix became visibly agitated.

"Hey, I know," Qugam suggested, "Why don't we settle this . . . on our way to the him?"

They agreed and made their way unto Ulfnell Lake as they continued to contend and rudely shout over one another. Jix's father could be seen in the distance. He was a gentle, bearded neuf. He had a warm, welcoming presence that instantly made the children feel welcome. He was preoccupied with cleaning the day's bounty and loading his cart with rakulfish.

"Hello, Pa!" Jix greeted.

"Hey, boys. Come help me get cleaned up and loaded."

The sparkling, roseate lake had awarded a generous load of wild rakul-fish. The boys began to put away the fish traps and load their cart alongside the elder neuf.

"Pa, I'm going with Saxfen to the torch-lighting thing later tonight," Jix said.

"Oh, yes, that's tonight. This is very special to our dear friends," his father responded.

"Yeah, they've kind of been through a lot. I'd say it's special."

"Well, I don't know about all that. All I know is that it's really nice to look at," said the senior neuf.

"You're welcome to come, sir," Saxfen offered.

"Probably not going to happen, Saxfen. As you can see, I have plenty of work awaiting me tonight."

"Oh, alright."

They finished the chores and rode the loaded cart back to Oakendunty. Twain, mighty kirok birds chattered amongst themselves as they pulled the company upon the neuf cart underneath the beauty of the Sky'erligg. The dusk had arrived, and they had almost arrived at the neuf abode. The faint village lights could now be seen within the mossy forest. They unloaded their bounty outside Jix's dwelling, and the kirok birds were visibly drowsy.

"Okay, Pa, we're off to see the lights now," Jix said. "I'll see you later!"

"Alright, Jix. You boys have fun over there," his father replied.

The three boys then made their way to a lone, towering hill in the distance. The mesmerizing Sky'erligg above lighted their way, and the dim twilight glowed amorously. They laughed and jested the entire way, each upon their own kirok bird.

"You know, Snowhead, you may be a little too busy in your own world, dancing in the clouds, to notice this, but I think Orilheart fancies you," Jix teased.

Saxfen paused, puzzled by the comment, his snow-colored hair above his musing brow.

"Huh? Orilheart? Oh, she's like a big sister to me. I think it's all in your head. Probably from me hitting you so hard earlier today."

"I think Orilheart him is so cute," Qugam snickered.

"Orilheart . . . is a babe, Snowhead, and if you can't tell she likes you, well, you might as well pack your things and head back home."

"Well, first of all, you know I can't just pack up and stroll over to our home. It just doesn't work that way. I mean, there's nothing left of the place, I don't think. Or so we were told. I wouldn't even know how to get there. Is it up there in the sky with all the night stars? Is it all the way at the bottom of the sea? Well? Do *you* know where it is?"

"Uh . . . no, actually. I don't know. But your feathered friends do, obviously," Jix challenged. "You can ask them."

"Hey, don't call them my 'feathered friends.' They are not to be trifled with. You have all heard what they did to the Dark Prince of Nith and his kingdom," Saxfen scolded.

"Well, we don't actually know that. But okay, okay, let's try this again . . . sorry about that. Ahem . . . You can ask the high and mighty, many winged gods, how to reach your lost home, right? I'd go with you."

"I bet this Shaifetnu him is somewhere deep underground. We just have to dig a real big him to get there. But how to dig such a big him?" Qugam pondered.

"Qugam, that is just nonsensical. If Snowhead and his friends came from underground, then where's the hole? Did they fill it back up? Couldn't they just back their way into it again? I swear, Qugam, sometimes I think you're not all there."

"Him is all there!" Qugam quarreled.

"Hey, take it easy," Saxfen defended. "For all we know, maybe we did come to the surface from some underground tunnel. Maybe the Star Sharveth on the Torch symbolizes just that very thing, a symbol of a hole in the ground. So, what if it's just a hole in the ground, but we can't remember where it is? Or they don't want us to know where it is."

"Oh, I think I get it now," said Jix. "That would be the reason they call it the Remembrance Torch! You guys are trying to remember where's that hole on the ground you came from."

The pointy-eared neufs laughed at the thought of Saxfen proceeding out of the ground from some forgotten lair.

"Yeah, from the ground like a yummy him!" Qugam laughed.

"I don't know. So what if we did?" Saxfen conceded.

They paused to briefly consider this, only to burst into laughter again, with even Saxfen joining in.

At last, they had arrived at a lush, verdant hill. Hidden amongst the moss and giant stones was a secret entryway into Delvikurf Hollows, where the silver-haired Shaifetnu gathered every year to light the Remembrance Torch. The torch was a solemn memorial for the great kindness the Council of Daylight had showed them when they had escaped their ravished world on that wretched day when the Great Vexation came upon them.

Within the secret caverns were rows of vibrant torches lighting the spacious corridors. Ahead, the merry crowd could be seen, casually mingling with one another. It was a gathering mostly comprised of silver-haired Shaifetnu. Scattered amongst them, there could be seen other neufs, cathra, and a few issorok. Everyone was in good spirits. There was laughter and jesting and dancing to stringed instruments. The boys made their way to greet some familiar faces.

"Hey, Saxfen, good to see you made it," said a fellow Shaifetnu. His white hair was longer than Saxfen's, and he was taller.

"Hey, Teyn, thanks. So happy the torch gathering is here again. But it sure feels like we were just here yesterday."

"Yeah, it's a pretty good turnout too. I think there's about two thousand people here."

Teyn was accompanied by a couple of friendly issorok. Their bodies were covered with grey feathers, but they did not resemble the birds of the air since they did not have wings or beaks on their faces. In place, they bore feathered snoots that drooped from their neckless heads, and their arms and legs also drooped slightly. Their round heads were graced with a feathered crown, like the heads of the mighty gylths that terrorized the roseate skies. Their language was obscure and brash to the ears,

"Urr Urr garr merr duurr," said one of them.

The three boys looked on in suspense.

"Well, what did him say?" Qugam finally asked after a prolonged silence.

"Huh? Oh, I have no idea," responded Teyn. "These guys speak a language I haven't quite gotten the hang of. They sure are friendly, though. We mostly communicate through hand gestures."

The boys wondered in disappointment.

"Actually, he said this is his first time attending the torch gathering," answered a familiar voice.

"Oh, hi, Orilheart," Teyn greeted.

Everyone went on to greet Orilheart.

"Orilheart him is so smart," complemented Qugam.

"Oh, I just pay attention. But thanks," she smiled as she brushed her silver hair back. "The issorok are quite welcoming and wise."

"Hey, Orilheart, you look amazing tonight," said Jix. "What do you say we dance?"

"Um . . . thank you. Sure, why not?" she responded.

Jix's whiskered face lit up, and his furry arm reached for Orilheart's hand. He then whisked her away for a round of customary dancing, with all the joy of having won some grand prize.

"That Jix . . ." Teyn laughed. "He beat me to it."

"Well, you have to be quick on your hims," Qugam replied.

"Garr urrr harrr murr murr," said the second issorok.

Everyone paused, expecting someone to translate what the feathered issorok said. The uncomfortable silence then provoked a round of nervous laughter. Twain issorok also joined in and laughed. Then came the lively sound of the Shaifetnu's wind instruments. They blew into wooden boxes held to their lips as one amongst them rose to welcome all the guests.

"Friends and family, thank you for coming to this year's torch gathering! We commemorate the wonders performed on our behalf by lighting this torch every year. This is our memorial to the Living One, whose servants have defended us and rescued us, time and time again, whose loving arms have carried us in times of trouble and have spared us from complete destruction. Though we continue to wander in this unknown land, uncertain if we will ever return to our home, we will continue to offer our gratitude to the King of the Vheilyel. Please join me in offering this year's prayer as we light the Remembrance Torch."

And so, they began in one voice,

"Our Lord, the Living One, whose servants have guided us by the hand all these years,

We thank you!

Who fills our mouth with bread, who fills our hearts with hope. Who crushes our adversaries with great terrors and wonders,

We adore you!

Accept us, we pray, so we may return to the place from whence we were vanished.

We long to be with you as in the bygone days, and we live in hope of that day to come!"

The gathering then erupted in jubilant shouting and celebration. The wind instruments blasted as if heralding some grand occasion. The Shaifetnu host then turned his back on the audience and raised his arms above his head. One dimly concealed structure was set before him. It was the night's chief event, the silver-haired people's special torch, waiting to be set ablaze.

The form of the torch was an elongated pole adorned with three polished rings at its center, one within the other. It was a structure forged of sturdy, Tunjunsora steel, gifted to the neufs by their guardian forest. The largest outer ring was crowned with three torches on opposing sides, each side ascending in height until they met the center torch upon the elongated pole. These seven torches bound unto the outer ring were regarded as one, and thus, these combined were known as the Remembrance Torch of the exiled Shaifetnu.

Twain attendants then made their way unto the structure, each carrying with them a snuffed torch in hand. They each climbed on opposing sides of the torch with the help of an elevated cart that was furnished for the lighting ceremony. The joyful guests looked on in solemn reverence as twain attendants prepared the center torch. A blazing, azure flame suddenly erupted, and the crowd loudly cheered some mysterious names followed by a redundant phrase.

"K'ash-iragav, arise again!" they shouted.

One attendant stood beside the center torch while the other slowly lit a second one to his left. He took fire from the center flame and set the second torch ablaze.

"Effronkizeh, arise again!" they shouted again.

He lit the third and the fourth, each new blaze provoking the triumphant shout of a new mysterious name followed by the same decree.

"Shelahuv'orot, arise again!"

"Tahmyd Tu'kaad, arise again!" the crowd cheered.

The attendant then returned to the center and replaced the second attendant. The second attendant likewise lit the opposing side of the torch, and the crowd shouted as before, a new mysterious chant after beholding each towering blaze.

"Olamshil'lumath, arise again!"

"Megu'rym Chama'dath, arise again!"

"Pahlaggi Magym, arise again!" they exclaimed with one voice.

With all seven torches lit, the crowd resumed their jubilant feast. The merry dancing and stringed instruments, the joyful piping, these all resonated anew, deep within the bowels of Delvikurf Hollows. It was a wondrous memorial, rich in meaning to the silver-haired people.

And so, the festivities were finally concluded, and the boys mounted atop their kirok birds and made their way unto their own dwelling places.

"The him was incredible!" Qugam said.

"Yeah, it's always been fun every time I show up," Saxfen replied.

"Yeah, she sure looked incredible. I think I'm in love . . ." Jix said.

"Wait, what?" Qugam and Saxfen pried.

"Huh?"

"What you just said."

"What did I say?"

"I think you said," Saxfen began but was suddenly interrupted by desperate shrieks coming from the woods.

"FIRE!!"

Saxfen lifted his eyes. An enormous pillar of smoke was ascending to the heights of the starry zenith, and it was coming from Oakendunty Village!

"Whoa, what's going on?" Jix exclaimed.

"I don't know. Let's hurry!" Saxfen shouted.

The boys rushed like the mighty winds of Y'orddrem atop their kirok birds and saw a host of scattered villagers fleeing for their lives. They looked terrified, and none dared stop to converse.

"We have to find Pa!" Jix exclaimed as they followed his lead into the burning village, leaving their kirok birds outside. They sprinted and searched the village for their families.

"What are you doing?!" shouted one fleeing neuf. "Turn around! Save yourselves!"

Jix finally seized a fellow neuf and demanded to know the matter at hand.

"What happened here?!" he shouted at the manic, horned she-neuf.

Hysteric and frightened, the neuf forcefully compelled Jix to release her. As she fled, the frantic neuf shouted the ominous words, "They're real! They've found us. It's them. It's . . . *the Wiljorgs of Nith*!"

It seemed Jix did not quite understand the words from the fleeing she-neuf.

"What was that all about?" he said.

"The who? The hims? What him say?" queried one bewildered Qugam.

"Oh no, this can't be," Saxfen whispered.

"What can't be? You seem to be holding back! Tell us what is going on," Jix demanded.

The mere sound of the word the she-neuf had shouted brought chills down Saxfen's back. Unless he had misheard, the she-neuf had said . . . *wiljorgs*. But this was but a mere campfire story the Shaifetnu people had shared with the peaceful neufs of Oakendunty, or was it? No respectable neuf actually believed the tale. After all, Oclyd Tower was leagues and leagues and days away from the lands of Tunjunsora. They stood in disbelief at the frightful word that had entered their ears and silently glanced at one another.

"Alright, snap out of it! We need to get out of here!" Jix finally ordered.

The boys returned to their senses and joined the panicked villagers in fleeing the sinister pillars of smoke. They fled with all their strength and would not look back. They had hoped to find their families, but if the stories were true, the wiljorg creatures were terrible indeed, and they would not spare anyone.

"Wait up!" shouted Qugam, struggling to breathe. "I have to catch my him!"

He halted to gasp for air, compelling Saxfen and Jix likewise to halt. They tarried for Qugam, as any dear friend would tarry.

"Let's go!" shouted Jix. "If those things are really here, they're going to tear us to pieces!"

Qugam continued to stall as he struggled to endure their pace. Jix's patience finally reached its boundary.

"I can't do this!" he shouted. "I'm sorry!"

He then proceeded to flee, leaving Qugam and Saxfen behind.

"Go on, Saxfen, I can take care of my him . . ." urged Qugam.

"What? You can't be serious. Let's go!"

A warm smile came over Qugam's whiskered face. The care of his friend filled his furred chest with a rush of fresh strength.

"For all his big him, that Jix is such a tunfoon, right?" he jokingly said, fighting back tears.

"Come on," Saxfen responded as he reached for the straining neuf.

But the tender moment was disrupted by the alarming sound of a sudden crash as one grizzly, blue ujorg leaped through a window unto the empty, ashen streets. But this was no common ujorg. This was an upright, muscular brute with piercing, onyx eyes. Indeed, this was no majestic, blue ujorg at all. This was a cursed Nithian from the royal courts of Nith, but now wholly consumed by that terrible curse upon them. These were the ferocious beasts the neufs of Oakendunty had only heard of in passing tales. These were the vicious and deadly Wiljorgs of Oclyd Tower, the Wiljorgs of Nith!

The ghastly creature attacked the timid Qugam, revealing a foul snout full of sharp, frightful fangs like the piercing blades of battle daggers.

"Look out!" shouted Saxfen, thrusting himself at his friend.

The greedy, azure beast was denied its meal, but not before slashing at Qugam's arm with its massive claws. The boys laid on the ground, screaming and desperate to escape the nightmare thing before them. It crept toward its helpless prey, savoring the fear that drifted in the air, mingled with burning embers and toxic fumes.

But, to their relief, the boys were spared by the burning blaze of a hurling torch. A strange bottle shattered upon the brute's bristled back, and the flames spread speedily. The howling wiljorg wrestled to extinguish the flames eating away at its blue coat. It rolled on the ground in uncontrollable rage.

The boys had escaped certain death but were unable to view who had thrown the blazing torch that had saved their lives. And, at that moment, they did not care.

Oakendunty Village was in chaos. Few amongst the courageous villagers fought back, denying the odds. They hurled fire bottles and wielded what melee weapons they possessed. Exhausted and terrified, Saxfen and Qugam found a place they could hide.

"It's over, Saxfen," whispered Qugam. "Our him is forever ruined."

"Yeah, we'll never be able to live in peace here again now that they've found us. Those of us who survive will need to find a new place and start over."

"You think Jix is okay, him?"

"Yeah, he can take care of himself. I'm so worried about Orilheart, though. Hope she's okay."

"We can't even look for them. Those hims are probably everywhere. It's not fair," Qugam said as tears rolled down his whiskers.

"And Mama and Papa, hims," he continued. "And my him! I'm going to bleed to death!"

"I know, this is terrible. But we have to keep our spirits up, Qugam."

Saxfen had wrapped a cloth around Qugam's injured arm, and the bleeding had stopped, but the trauma was unbearable to the startled neuf. The boys hid within the shadows of an empty attic, as the mayhem continued outside. Random screams and horrid growls could be heard. They felt helpless.

"I know. Why don't you ask your powerful hims to come kill them all?" Qugam finally suggested.

"Oh, believe me. I've been silently praying this whole time."

"The entire him?"

"Well, you know what I mean."

There was a brief, passing silence, and Qugam finally continued, "Well, can I him too, then?"

"Uh, what?"

"You know, pray to your hims. We don't have any hims of our own. Us neufs refuse to worship the Druki-him like others. Him sounds evil."

"Yeah, I don't see why not."

Qugam inhaled a deep breath and proceeded to offer a prayer.

"Okay . . . here goes my him. Ahem . . . dear many winged hims of my friend, Saxfen. It's me Qugam. I know you don't know me, but . . ."

"Ahem . . ." Saxfen interrupted.

"What?"

"Uh . . . you're doing it wrong."

"Oh?"

"Yeah, they get offended when you pray to them directly."

"Oh? Hims do?"

Saxfen explained but appeared preoccupied with discerning an escape from the doomed village.

"Well?" continued Qugam.

"Well, what?"

"How do I him correctly?"

"Oh . . . well, you have to talk to their leader because that's who they listen to. He's like their king, and they are his servants."

"Oh . . . I get it, him. Let me try again."

Qugam paused to gather his words.

"Dear, Living One, him. It's me, Qugam. I know you don't know me, but I wanted to ask you something. We are in big trouble, as Saxfen him has already told you. Please help us. Please make these evil hims go away."

He paused, expecting Saxfen to chime in.

"Well, do you think he heard my him?"

"Yeah. It's actually those guys out there who are in big trouble. We're in trouble, but not as much as those guys are."

The scared boys tarried within the safety they had found, but their hiding place in that isolated attic began to fill with smoke.

Cough *Cough* "Where's the him coming from?"

"I think it's coming from the floor, Qugam."

They looked at one another in alarm.

"The house is on fire!" they gasped.

The boys hasted unto a tiny window, and Saxfen cautiously peeked outside. It seemed safe to step out, but he was not certain. And time was against them before the flames ascended and trapped them inside. Desperate to flee, the boys climbed through the tiny window unto a nearby balcony. The bloodthirsty wiljorgs could be seen anew.

"Oh no, they're still here," Saxfen whispered. "Don't make a sound."

The smoke grew thicker as it streamed out of the windows.

"Qugam, it's going to be okay," Saxfen assured. "We can quietly make our way to the other roof and then find our way down."

"Yeah, let's do it," Qugam responded.

The neighboring roof was within reach, but the peril of reaching it without being found was apparent to both.

"Okay, I'll go first since I'm taller, and I can reach for you from above and pull you up," Saxfen suggested.

Qugam staggered to respond but finally replied, "Saxfen, him . . . if I die tonight, would you tell my papa and mama I love them if you see them?"

"What? You're *not* going to die! We will make it out of this and then hunt down those things that did this to us."

Qugam teared up,

"Okay . . . let's do this, him."

The boys calmed themselves and then proceeded with the plan. Saxfen carefully approached the edge of the roof. He kept his sight on the roof's edge all the while regarding the chaos below. The merciless wiljorgs could be seen fighting amongst themselves for prey, some searching out fresh victims while others merely lingered as the village burned to the ground.

Saxfen's heart broke at the awful sight. But this was no time for mourning. After all, Qugam depended on him to reach the top and pull him up to safety. His dear friend's stature prevented him from escalating to the rooftop alone. And all that coursed through his mind at that moment was his furry, whiskered face and saving it from a gruesome fate.

Saxfen stealthily reached the rooftop with a sigh of relief. He peeked at Qugam and gestured for him to proceed. The horned neuf nodded. After inhaling deeply, Qugam carefully climbed the balcony's rusty balustrade. His furry arm reached out for Saxfen's extended hand, and then, the unthinkable happened. Qugam slipped.

"*No . . .*" Saxfen gasped as he toiled to contain himself.

Oh, the agony that pierced his bowels in that moment! It was like someone took a freshly whetted blade and slowly drove it through his heart, compelling forth a scream against his will, "Qugam . . . NOOO!" he yelled.

He quivered as he realized he had shouted and immediately hid and covered his mouth. The hopeless look of despair on his friend's eyes would forever be etched in his mind. Qugam had fallen to his doom. And, what's worse, the ravenous wiljorgs had reckoned his fall! They greedily salivated as they raced towards Qugam's body on the earthen ground. Saxfen silently sobbed, wrestling to contain his pain.

"Dear God, what do I do?" he whispered through his sobs. "Save us, our Living One. Save your Shaifetnu once again . . ."

Saxfen finally mustered the strength to traverse the shabby roof of the burning lodge. He feared gazing at his friend one last time. The mere thought of gazing at his mangled body or being discovered by the wiljorgs dizzied him to the core. The fire had now reached the rooftop, but Saxfen safely enjoined to the neighboring roof.

It was serene atop the new rooftop, unlike the chaos of the burning abode that was behind him and the monstrous howls below. Yet he understood it was not safe to linger. One of those things could be lurking anywhere, hunting for his scent. He had to endure and press onward.

Saxfen leaped from one rooftop unto the other until the place of Qugam's fall was now far behind. Glowing, speckled embers wandered upon the warm, tranquil air underneath the pallid light of the Sky'erligg. His clothes reeked with smoke. He found a wide, sturdy chimney to lean against. The plan was now to patiently tarry in the hope the loathsome wiljorgs had finally had their fill. It was far too dangerous to come down.

Exhausted with dread and disbelief, Saxfen slowly began to doze into merciful slumber. But the sound of incoming footsteps suddenly roused him. He glanced up and saw the form of an incoming shadow, the source of the stealthy steps. To his dread, he realized it was one of them, one of those blue-furred brutes that had ruined his village. He gasped at the frightful revelation. And almost it seemed as though the scavengers had regarded him long ago, and now they had come to claim their meal.

Saxfen cautiously made his way unto the opposing end of the chimney. He peeked at the beast. It was massive and bulky, and its entire physique was covered in matted, dark-cerulean fur. And those fangs! It sniffed and traced the tranquil air, honing, hunting for Saxfen's scent.

Helpless and dismayed, Saxfen considered relinquishing. *I can't kill this thing. It's too big for me. If I run, it will catch me. Should I just lay here and die?* He thought in despair.

But then he remembered Qugam's frightened face as he plunged to his death. *Somehow, I must live and tell Qugam's papa and mama that he loved them,* Saxfen surged. His strength renewed, and he sought to loosen one of the chimney's bricks. He prevailed. He tossed the brick in the opposing direction he intended to flee. The wiljorg was deceived and pursued the lure.

Saxfen swiftly dashed to the edge of the roof, hoping to find a balcony or some other path to escape, but he could not find a cautious route. It appeared the only course was to dart himself off the roof and risk dashing his bones. Horrified, Saxfen searched for the gruesome hunter again, looking to know its whereabouts. But its foul gaze was now fixated upon the boy. The beast charged at the drained Shaifetnu and pounced for its prey. But Saxfen was able to evade its death path swiftly. The weight of the brute then collapsed the shabby roof underneath their feet. And both Saxfen and the cursed Nithian together plunged through the breach unto the wreckage below.

Chapter 4

Never the Same

When Saxfen finally recovered from his fall, he found himself alone on the second floor of a ravished home. Dazed and bewildered that he was yet alive, he gazed about and beheld a jagged opening on the floor. The manic wiljorg had crashed through unto the neuf chamber below. Without a sign of life in the room beneath him, Saxfen roused himself and dared to peep through the scraggy, wooden mouth. He exhaled a sigh of relief upon seeing the wiljorg, slain by the sharpened edge of a garden shovel. Its vile head had struck the common hand tool, and its blood had spilled unto sundry headings.

"Whoa, that was really close," Saxfen said, exhaling.

He rested on the abandoned dwelling place, staring at the ceiling, toiling to understand this tragedy that befell him.

He compelled his weary eyes to stare at the ceiling against his body's inclination, fearing one of those things would find him out if he fell asleep. Eyes exhausted, the lad could no longer bear, and he dozed into the distant lands of deep slumber. The faint cries and growls outside faded until they at last became a soothing mute.

Morning had arrived, and the warm, gentle rays of the early sun caressed his silver locks and nudged him awake. Stillness prevailed. The howls and screams had vanished like a bad dream. And like the passing of a bad dream, he suddenly remembered the horrid details, and tears began streaming down his cheeks. He fought them back, and also he strove against the urge to remain in the abandoned house and quietly sob. *I must find survivors*, he thought, urging himself forward.

The boy quietly made his way downstairs. He stared at the foul puddle of vermillion on the floor. Slight gratification came over him when he looked upon the slain wiljorg. Nonetheless, this was no time to celebrate. He seized the heroic garden shovel and reluctantly stepped outside the home.

Saxfen wandered throughout the abandoned ruins of his dear Oakendunty. Everyone had fled, it seemed. The birds mourned and sang a requiem for those who had perished. The pitiful sight was too much to bear. Saxfen embraced his nauseous tummy and fell upon his knees until finally collapsing with his face to the earthen ground. *I can't . . . do this. I will die here of heartbreak,* he thought.

The peaceful village of the horned neufs was mercilessly ravaged. The gentle peoples of Oakendunty had welcomed the wandering Shaifetnu for many years and had come to embrace them as their very kin. Kindness had been recompensed with cruelty. But in the midst of this cruelty, there came a gentle, comforting voice.

"Saxfen, get up," it said.

Striving to recollect himself, Saxfen finally looked up and gazed at the person talking to him. The sun startled his weary eyes, but he thought he could faintly discern who it was.

"Orilheart . . . is that you?"

"Yes," Orilheart responded. "Come, let's find the others."

She reached for his hand, and Saxfen embraced her. He was relieved to see his dear friend, but there was something different about her.

"Hey, what's with your hair?" he asked. "It's yellow."

"I'll explain later. You must be exhausted. Right now is not the time."

They walked together, hoping to find survivors.

"Are you sure the wiljorgs are gone?" Saxfen said.

"Yeah, I'm pretty sure they're all gone now."

"Are you okay? Did any of them hurt you?"

"I'm okay," she comforted. "I'm really saddened, though, that this happened. Those smelly wiljorgs; they sure have it coming."

Saxfen laughed in relief to see her in good health. Orilheart smiled at the sight of her friend beginning to feel better.

"This is so unfair, Orilheart. They killed Qugam. They just ate him. They ate him like he was just a piece of meat. Why did the Living One let this happen?" Saxfen asked, holding back his tears.

"Um, well. That's a good question. You see . . ." But before she could finish, Orilheart was interrupted by a shout.

"Hey, guys! Wait up!" said a voice from behind them.

"Jix!" shouted Saxfen. "Is that you?"

They embraced and felt a renewed appreciation for being together again.

"Oh, wow, am I glad to see you guys again! How are you feeling, Snowhead? Orilheart! What's with your hair? Hey, where's Qugam? I actually miss that little guy."

Saxfen's smile suddenly vanished from his face.

"Qugam didn't make it," he responded.

"Oh . . . I'm so sorry," Jix sorrowfully replied.

They stood in silence as the birds proceeded with their lamentation, and a gentle breeze sought to console them. Jix's eyes began to tear up, but he concealed it and resisted the urge, "We've got to go. Maybe we'll find others," he insisted.

The three friends courageously searched the village, but their endeavors proved fruitless. Not a soul was in sight.

"So now what?" Saxfen asked. "Looks like everyone ran for their lives. Or, worse, they've all been eaten."

"That's nonsense," Jix objected. "They couldn't have eaten *everyone* in the village. It's just not possible, Snowhead. Besides, they'd be so bloated we would still see them lying on the ground."

"What? It's totally possible! You just don't know," Saxfen suddenly snarked.

"Hmm . . . they must've fled instead of fighting back. I don't blame them. They never had a chance against wiljorgs," Orilheart said.

"Well, we can't stay here. They all know where our village is now. They'll be back. I just know it," Saxfen assured. "If a disaster like this happened to you guys, and you had to leave the village quickly, where would you go? Where should we look for the others?"

"Snowball, we need to start at Ulfnell Lake. We all need food and fresh water to live. I doubt they had time to pack a full-course meal for the road," Jix suggested.

"Yes, Jix is right. Plus, there's plenty of places to hide around Ulfnell Lake," Orilheart agreed. "Let's go find them."

With the noonday sun high above them, the three youths headed on foot to the sparkling, roseate waters of Ulfnell Lake.

"So, what's with the hair, O? Are you trying to disguise yourself from the wiljorgs? If so, that's the worst disguise ever," Jix taunted.

"Um . . . I'm not able to speak of it right now. The past couple of days have been really long for all of us," she replied.

"Oh? What's the big deal? I think it's a good look for you. Right, Snowhead? We should call you, Orilheart the Golden."

"Uh . . . no, don't call me that," she said.

"You look . . . dipped in gold. Like your head was doused in it, and you now bear the glittering, silky long strands of shiny, yellow gold."

"Wow, Jix. That was . . . poetic," Saxfen noted.

"Okay, you're being weird now," Orilheart sighed.

"I think we could've taken those guys had we been prepared back there," Saxfen mused. "Now we have to start over and build a new village from scratch in the middle of who knows where."

The three friends groaned in frustration.

"We'll get them, Saxfen, I'm confident of this," said Orilheart. "We just need a little time to get back on our feet."

"Thanks, Orilheart. I know you're just trying to be helpful and nice," Saxfen responded.

"No, really. You'll see. I just need to find . . . *him* . . ." she said, her eyes wandering and surveying the landscape.

"Huh? What was that?" Saxfen pried.

"What?" she responded, playing ignorant.

"You just said . . ." Saxfen began as a voice shouted his name in the distance.

"Saxfen, him!" said the voice.

It was Qugam.

"It's really you!" he joyfully shouted.

The four raced toward one another and fell into each other's arms.

"I've been waiting by this him all day for you!" said Qugam in relief.

"But how? I saw you die," Saxfen replied, wrestling with the tears in his eyes. "It's like you cheated death."

"Well," Qugam began, "I fell from the him to my certain doom. And then I hit the him really hard. It hurt very much. I couldn't run from the hims, and I knew I was done for."

He paused to reflect on the sadness of the moment, how he would never see Saxfen or Orilheart or any of his family ever again.

"Well??" Jix pressed. "Then what happened?"

"So, I closed my hims real tight. And then I realized I was still . . . alive?! I opened them and peeked. The hims were still standing in front of me. Huge, grisly hims and giant sharp teeth! They were looking for me, seriously, him! And I was still in front of them! I gasped in amazement."

Qugam then forcefully grabbed Saxfen and shook him, "*They couldn't see me, him*!!" he shouted.

"So, what did you do?!" one startled Saxfen pried.

"I got up, dusted my him . . . and snuck away," he concluded.

Saxfen and Jix were utterly amazed, their mouths gaping with astonishment. Orilheart, not so much. She knew it was the work of the Daylight that had spared the fortunate neuf, although she was not fully certain of his final fate until now.

"I'm so happy you're okay, Qugam," she said, embracing him again. "We had all feared you were dead."

"Yeah, glad you made it, Qugam," Jix said, smiling as he placed his paw on his shoulder. "You had us worried for a moment."

***

"Wow, Papa!" Enos exclaimed. "Those evil wiljorgs were going to make Qugam into neuf pottage!"

With fuzzy, yellow hair above his startled brow, the young lad was consumed with amazement at the strange creatures his father described.

"Yes, Son. It felt like my heart was carved from my chest when I saw my friend plunge to his death. I didn't think I'd ever see him again."

"So where is he now?" Enos asked.

"We'll get to that as well, Enos. The four of us made our way to the Treewinth Woodlands to find shelter and safety. But we had no idea that what we were about to hear in those woods would forever change our lives. There, we were destined to hear incredible things, and we were never the same again."

***

The four youths journeyed unto Treewinth Woodlands, where the frightened Oakendunty villagers had found refuge underneath some comforting shadows and vibrant leaves. The boys were greatly consoled to find their parents in good health there. That is, except for Jix. It appeared no one had seen his family since their escape from the carnage of the wiljorgs.

"Cheer up, Jix. We'll find them," Saxfen comforted his grieving friend.

The disaster that had visited Oakendunty Village left its people desolate and hungry for a new abode. But providence was with them, as Ulfnell Lake was a hearty source of food and clean, roseate water. They ignited small campfires and comforted one another to the best they were able.

"Snowball, stop hogging all the ejiberries! We're gonna have to eat tomorrow too, you know," Jix chided.

"Hey, this is all I've eaten all day. And it's not even that much I'm taking," Saxfen defended. "If you had helped us pick these ejiberries, maybe you'd have a say."

"Hey, someone needed to find the firewood you're using to warm you up right now. It wasn't gonna fetch itself, you know. Geez . . . sometimes I wonder about you, Snowhead."

"I helped gather hims, too," Qugam chimed, nibbling on a generous round of tasty ejiberries.

"I got your Snowhead right here," taunted an irate Saxfen.

"What's that, Snowball? I know, you want to fight, don't you? Wanna get a little rage off your chest? Well, let's go!" Jix challenged.

Tensions were high that night.

"Let's go, you pointy-eared furball!" Saxfen accepted the challenge.

Qugam reached for the swollen wound on his left arm, groaning to himself. He marveled at how he had survived the traumatic encounter with the wiljorg. Jix frantically rose and charged at Saxfen. Saxfen swiftly dodged and then proceeded to eat his ejiberries, seemingly unfazed by the assault.

"Him missed," Qugam laughed.

Jix angrily rose to his feet for a second assault.

"Oh, that's it, Snowhead, you're going down hard!"

"Oh, somebody, please help! Please don't injure me, you mean, pointy-eared neuf..." Saxfen continued to taunt, all the while engrossed in his ejiberry feast.

Furious, Jix charged at Saxfen yet again. And he missed a second time. Qugam fell to the ground, overcome with uncontrollable laughter.

"When I finally get you, Snowball, you're going to beg for mercy," Jix warned.

"Oh, look, he predicts the future!" Saxfen laughed.

"Him is seer!" Qugam joined.

"Ahhhhhh!!" shouted Jix as he charged.

"Hey!" shouted Orilheart from a distance. "Knock it off, you two!"

The three boys looked on and held their peace.

"Hi, Orilheart, him," Qugam greeted.

"Orilheart, where've you been? Want some ejiberries?" offered Saxfen. "They're so plump and juicy."

"Sure, I'll take some," Orilheart said.

"Hey," Jix greeted, calmly sitting beside her.

She took the ejiberries and gracefully nibbled. Her eyes blew wide open.

"Oh my God! These are amazing!" she exclaimed. She proceeded to obsessively consume the fruit. "Where? Where did you get these?!"

"Those, my dear, Orilheart, are the upmost rarest ejiberries of Treewinth Woodlands!" Jix explained. "How is it that you've never tasted them before? But I guess they only grow around this time for some reason. You will never find finer berries in all Tunjunsora."

"Um . . . I don't know about that," said Orilheart. "But they sure are delicious, though. Mmmm, that flavor!"

"We were starting to worry about you, O," Saxfen said.

"Well, I needed to be alone. A lot has happened recently, and I needed time to think."

"Yeah, these are scary times," Saxfen replied. "I can't believe we won't have Oakendunty Village to call our home anymore."

"We will build a bigger and better Oakendunty him," Qugam proclaimed.

Orilheart held her peace as if something heavy weighed on her mind.

"What's wrong, O? You seem troubled. Are you okay?" Saxfen asked.

She was reluctant to respond, but the burden on her heart needed relief.

"Hey, I have something important to tell you guys," she finally said. "I wanted to wait until things were a little better, but I have something very heavy on my mind I need to talk to you about. Come with me. We need to go somewhere a little more private."

They nodded, rose to their feet, and followed Orilheart to a solitary part of the woods away from the refugees. She carried with her a small torch, and the pallid light of the wondrous arc above also lit their way. The woods themselves were alive with the curious hums and chirps of unknown creatures concealed within every corner of the night's vesture. They had arrived at a modest pond where coursing light-bugs fancied themselves upon the mirror of the still waters.

The boys sat and listened intently as Orilheart proceeded to vent.

"Okay, let me begin. Do you remember how I said I would tell you later why my hair is different now? Um . . . well . . . you see, I needed to blend in amongst the Shaifetnu when they arrived at Oakendunty all those years ago. But this is actually my real hair color. And the truth is, I'm not really a Shaifetnu," she nervously laughed.

"Then . . . what are you, him?" a wide-eyed Qugam asked.

"Well, it all started about sixteen years ago, when the silver-haired Shaifetnu first arrived here in Eofendurk," she continued, "They quickly became the prisoners of an evil prince who wanted to trick them into leading his armies to their treasures."

"Oh, yes, we've heard this before. How the Vheilyel cursed the Dark Prince of Nith to look like one of their ujorgs; hence, they are called wiljorgs," Jix explained. "But it was just a story, right? We had no idea this truly happened."

"Yes, you see, the Shaifetnu's tears reached our home in the stars, way up there," she motioned at the starry, black zenith. "And, well . . . I was sent here to help them."

Without warning, Jix suddenly ejected a gulp of fresh water from his pouch in a violent burst. The spectating, roaming light-bugs were instantly drenched away by the outburst.

"Yuk! Watch it, Jix!" Orilheart exclaimed.

"Wait, what?!" Jix laughed in disbelief. "What do you mean you came from the *stars* way up there? Orilheart, don't taunt us like this. Just because you changed your hair color to hide from the wiljorgs doesn't mean you can tease us like that. We've been through a lot these past few days already, and it's not funny."

"Shh shh . . . wait, just let her talk," Saxfen hushed.

"Okay, I know this is shocking and hard to believe, so that's why I asked you to come here so we don't attract unnecessary attention. But I'm not making this up. I can prove it to you."

She turned around and showed them her upper back. There were slits on her clothes, fastened by a few buttons.

"You see that? That's so I can do this . . ."

She unbuttoned the slits on her back, and to their utter astonishment, six powerful, feathered wings flung out before their eyes! The silky, ivory feathers baffled the boys. Then suddenly, everyone realized what their most excitable friend would do next.

"Uh, oh! Grab him!"

"AHH**!!" Qugam began to exclaim, but the boys hurriedly muffled his whiskered face before his clamor reached the camp.

"Mmm . . . mm . . . mmm!!" the muffled Qugam struggled.

"Qugam, calm down. I'm going to remove my hand from your mouth, but you must be quiet, okay?" Saxfen instructed.

Qugam nodded in agreement, and then Saxfen slowly removed his hand. It seemed the young neuf had returned to himself as he deeply inhaled long, calm breaths.

". . . HIM IS A MANY WINGED GOD!!" he pointed and shouted.

Saxfen quickly muffled his mouth again.

"Um . . . technically, we are called Vheilyel, servants of the Council of Daylight. But yes, the Shaifetnu sometimes refer to us as the 'many winged gods.'"

"All right, give him a minute," Saxfen said.

Qugam finally calmed himself. The neufs had only but heard the legends and power of the many winged gods from the wandering Shaifetnu, but they had never actually seen them. Their little ones listened in awe as the strange, silver-haired people often talked about them as if they were always nearby. Saxfen had been born in Eofendurk, so he shared in the neuf's intrigue of the olden tales. And now, one of these celestial beings *. . . was their friend this whole time?!*

"Wow, wow . . . wow . . ." Saxfen whispered, pacing, struggling to contain himself. "You're one of them, and you never told us? What gives?!"

"Well, it's not exactly something I'm at liberty to just announce everywhere I go, you know. Oh, hi, everyone. Servant of the Daylight here, coming through. Make way! Excuse me, pardon, sorry . . . many winged god coming through," she playfully said as she made her way through an imaginary crowd. "That's not how this works."

"Okay, then, so why are you telling us? Why are you telling us *now*?" Saxfen asked.

"Wait, I've been in love with a mythical many winged god this whole time . . ." Jix muttered to himself, engulfed in a romantic daze.

They abruptly paused and looked at him blankly.

"But how do your hims fit back there?" Qugam examined.

"Anyways, go on, O. Tell us why, then," Saxfen insisted. "Does it have something to do with the attack on Oakendunty Village? Are you here to lead a counterattack against the wiljorgs and avenge us all? A rebellion to topple all the remaining kingdoms of Nith?"

"Um . . . well, I was getting to that before you so rudely interrupted me," she responded.

"Him is many winged god!" Qugam said anew with twinkling awe sparkling in his eyes.

"Yes, Qugam. We've been informed," said Jix, returning to his senses.

"Okay, would you just let me tell my story!" Orilheart exclaimed in frustration.

"Alright, alright. We'll shut up now. Tell us why you're here. Go!" Saxfen ordered.

"Okay, ahem . . . so a long time ago, about sixteen years ago, the evil prince of Nith had finally had enough and was ready to kill the Shaifetnu he had captured because they were not cooperating to his liking. That's when I stepped in to stop that crude fellow from doing this. 'Stop right there!' I shouted from across his royal court. Everyone looked back at my hooded face, and they were like, 'Who is this twerp? And who does she think she is, ordering our prince like that?' And, predictably, the evil prince did not heed my words and my warnings, and he was determined to slay the innocent Shaifetnu. He would've done it too! We had learned

that the measure of his patience was up. He failed, however, because . . .
uh . . . well, I turned him into a wiljorg."

GASP the boys exclaimed. "YOU WHAT?!" they said in unison.

"Well, guys . . . I warned him there would be consequences if he didn't
listen," Orilheart defended, nervously fidgeting with a lock of her hair.

"Oh, my God, Orilheart, my love! You turned *EVERYONE* into a
wiljorg!?" Jix exclaimed.

"Whoa . . . overkill much, him?" said Qugam.

"Wait, we had a good reason, okay!" she nervously defended. "And
honestly, it wasn't my idea. And, no, not *everyone*. Just the royal court.
I know how this looks, but please hear me out. There's something you
need to know about the Shaifetnu.

"You see, the Shaifetnu elders ordered everyone who witnessed something they called the Great Vexation to hold their peace for the sake
of all whose eyes were spared the horror of what happened. The Great
Vexation was truly nightmarish, and I will only relate what is necessary
for the purpose of this discussion.

"The elders feared that the heavy burden of the Great Vexation could
come upon the hearts of everyone whose eyes were spared. So they decided not to lay this burden on anyone if it was not needed. And so, all
the witnesses agreed to hold their peace. What monstrous things they
saw were best left unspoken, they reasoned."

"Okay, so if the elders don't want us to know, why are you telling us
now?" Saxfen asked.

"Because, Saxfen," Orilheart continued, "After taking a walk in the
woods tonight, it has come to my attention that it has become necessary
for me to share what I'm about to tell you. Don't worry, you'll understand. But first, about the Harp of the Shiggionoth."

"The Shiggio-what?" they asked.

"The O'rah Harp of the Shaifetnu Shiggionoth, the legendary harp
of the first Lords of the Shaifetnu," she continued. "As you are all well

aware, the silver-haired Shaifetnu are not from around here. They're not from anywhere in all of Eofendurk, really. Not from the sea or under the ground but from the sky. They're from a place far beyond the Sky'erligg above, a place far amongst those pretty stars you see at night.

"Now, the elders say the Shaifetnu home was stolen from them. And they're right. And they commemorate their loss and hope by lighting the Remembrance Torch, year after year. However, their home was not merely stolen from them. It was destroyed. An entire world was destroyed. Seven worlds, actually. The seven torches upon the Remembrance Torch are the memorial of them."

The lads listened on and could not believe their ears, but they trusted Orilheart, whom they had known all their lives growing up in Oakendunty Village. She continued, "To help the Shaifetnu escape their doomed worlds, the Council of Daylight led them through vast corridors we call Star Sharveth."

"Oh, yes! I've heard of those," Saxfen chimed. "The circles at the center of the Remembrance Torch are just that, they represent the Star Sharveth that brought us here to Eofendurk."

"Yes, correct. Think of the Star Sharveth as a bridge connecting the worlds that live up there amongst the stars. Hence, a *'Star'* Sharveth."

"I don't know. I always thought they were more like tunnels," Saxfen chimed.

"Or gates to somewhere else, but you had no idea where," Jix added.

"Um, no. A tunnel travels underground. A gate is merely an opening. Star Sharveth are bridges that connect the worlds above us."

"Shhh shhhh shhh, don't listen to them, him, continue," Qugam urged.

"So, the Shaifetnu who live here in Eofendurk, before leaving their home world, they were entrusted with a very special relic forged by us, the Council of Daylight. This relic is known in our writings as the lost

O'rah Harp of the Shiggionoth. You probably haven't heard of it because this is a burden only the elders wish to carry.

"The Dark Prince Mafestus, however, stole the Harp from them, and it is still there in Nith, to this day. So, this is my point, that the whereabouts of the harp needed to remain concealed, according to the elders. Can you imagine if some brave Shaifetnu wandered into the land of the wiljorgs and tried to retrieve it? It's a terrifying thought. So the elders agreed to also hold their peace regarding the fate of the Harp."

"So, the him is still there? What happened to it? We haven't heard of this him, only of the fury of the many winged hims upon the Nithians," said Qugam.

"Yes, and here's what happened. So, upon gazing at the beautiful, golden harp, the Dark Prince thought, 'There must be other treasures like this, wherever these people came from.' But there was one problem: he couldn't talk with them. He toiled for three long years to teach them their language so he could trick them into taking his armies to the vaults of their treasures. In the meantime, he kept the harp all to himself. The sacred harp being in the blood-marred hands of this vile prince was not acceptable to the Council of Daylight. And, of course, his heart's deceitful intent was fully bare before us.

"When the Shaifetnu's heartache in this new world became insuffer-able, and knowing full well what the Dark Prince would do, I was sent to stop him from spilling Shaifetnu blood. He would've done it too! He would've done it as the savage beast he was, had I not intervened.

"I confronted the Dark Prince to return the harp at once—in front of his royal court. But he refused to listen, so I obeyed my orders and changed him into the first wiljorg of Eofendurk. His entire royal court fled in horror at the sight of their prince. Furious at what had been done to him, the Dark Prince attacked me but could not harm me. He fled. He cowered in the sanctuary of his god, the Drukijaken, with the O'rah Harp firmly gripped by his ugly claws. He rang a huge bell to rouse the

Drukijaken from the depths of the Sea of Nith. He defiantly stood at the rim of the sea where his god dwelt. I pleaded with him. 'Don't do it!' I shouted. 'If you do this, your kingdom will suffer greatly!'

"Unfazed by my dire warnings, he went ahead and cast the harp into the mouth of the Drukijaken. The monster in the deep swallowed it. It swallowed the Harp of the Shiggionoth. And so, I had no choice but to obey and turn his royal court into the wiljorgs that burned down Oakendunty Village."

"Wait a minute," Jix interrupted. "So you're telling me these guys are just getting even for what you did to them? A little chip on the shoulder, have we?"

"Well, the trees of Cimbri Forrest did a good job of hiding us from outsiders," Saxfen suggested. "But I would think they would've found us a long time ago if that was the case. Getting turned into a wiljorg is not something you get over easily, especially if your closest friends were turned too."

"Hmm . . . him wiljorgs are still angry," said Qugam. "But how did they know him lived in Oakendunty with us?"

"Well, about that," Orilheart replied. "There's so much more to this than what I've just shared. I don't want to overwhelm you. I think it's enough for one day. Let's talk about it some more tomorrow after you're rested. Believe me, you're going to need some rest."

****

The exhausted youth could not help but remain in their beds the ensuing day. The attack on the village, Qugam's brush with death, Orilheart's incredible revelations, it was all much to take in. The leaf-knit blankets and pillows they had made felt amazing as they considered how fortunate they had been amongst those who had escaped death in the siege of Oakendunty. The warm afternoon sun comforted them while the extinguished campfire incense lingered in their nostrils. They finally roused themselves to be about the new day before them.

"So now what?" Jix wondered. "It's only a matter of time before they find us here. It's not like the most obvious place we could've gone to or anything, just saying."

"Yeah, we could've just headed to Delvikurf him and hid there," Qugam said.

"No, then what would we eat? Where would we find water in there? They could just as easily find us there since they can probably trace our scent. And besides, I don't think you can talk to rocks like you do to the trees, can you?" Saxfen responded.

The neufs shook their heads.

"Yeah, I'm surprised they haven't already thrashed this place, too," said Orilheart. "But take courage. The Daylight is looking out for us. They are not permitting them to come near us. At least not yet. Either way, I'm ready for them."

"Wait a minute, why couldn't you fight them off back there and prevent all this, O?" Saxfen said.

"Yeah, where were you, him?"

"Um . . . for your information, I did fight them. But . . . there were also nasty Urth with them. So, excuse me, I was a little preoccupied ensuring everyone and everything around was not utterly annihilated."

"Uh . . . thanks?" Jix suspiciously replied. "Thanks for fighting off 'nasty Urth' things for us, whatever that is . . ."

"What is nasty Urth hims?" Qugam pried.

Twain whiskered neufs, unfamiliar with the Shaifetnu lore regarding the Urth, looked on at Orilheart with blank stares as though she spoke in a foreign tongue.

"Sorry, guys, I don't know much about that either," Saxfen offered.

"Yeah, so what is that? That doesn't sound good at all . . . 'nasty Urth,'" said Jix.

"Well, simply put, Urth Vheilyel are many winged gods that became . . . evil," she explained.

"Ooh . . . him was fighting evil gods!" Qugam replied in amazement.

"Evil gods . . ." Jix nervously laughed. "Give me a break."

"Yup, fortunately, they decided to retreat," Orilheart said. "I was a little outnumbered here in Eofendurk, but help arrived."

"Well, what did they want?" Saxfen insisted.

Orilheart nervously laughed, "I was getting to that," she replied, fidgeting with her yellow hair. "Aren't you a bunch of eager poolfs! I'll tell you all about it soon enough. But for now, let's go fetch our meal."

The three boys agreed and strolled unto the sparkling waters of Ulfnell Lake, where they would catch some savory rakulfish.

It was a day filled with awe and mystery. They marveled at the sight of Orilheart, their long-time friend. Was this truly a fabled, many winged god in their midst . . . *fishing with them?* What would Orilheart reveal to them next? And evil Urth Vheilyel? What strange matter was this? There was so much to inquire about and to speak of, but they patiently waited on their newly discovered, old friend.

Although scared and deprived of a proper dwelling of their own, the boys were, nonetheless, filled with a profound sense of excitement and hope. The feeling was that of some grand herald alluding to enchanted mysteries unfolding in some unseen realm far beyond what their tender minds could perceive. They could not quite explain it with words, but it could be felt. After all, someone from the very stars was casually mingling with them, protecting them . . . and being a friend!

"Do you think she's just pranking us, Qugam?" Jix chatted. "It's just Orilheart, right?"

"Well, how do you explain him wings?" Qugam responded. "Can *you* make six hims pop out of your back?"

Qugam playfully glanced at Jix's back, skeptical to see if wings would indeed emerge. He was sorely disappointed. "No? No hims? I didn't think so."

"Hey, Jix, hurry up! Give me a hand!" Saxfen interrupted. "It's a big one!"

Jix hurried to Saxfen's side.

"Give me that, Snowball! Geez, do I have to do everything around here?!" he exclaimed.

He forcefully took the fishing rod from Saxfen's hand and toiled with the massive catch. The string snapped, and the rakulfish fled underneath the roseate waters mirroring the Sky'erligg above.

"Nice going, Jix," Saxfen said. "I could've done that myself."

"Stupid rakulfish. You live to fight another day," Jix taunted. "Hey, O, can't you just make rakulfish catch themselves for us?"

"Um . . . no, I don't do tricks, sorry," Orilheart said.

"Oh, come on! We're starving here," Jix insisted.

"Yeah, still, No. It doesn't work that way," she affirmed as she playfully swayed her fishing rod.

"So . . . I guess you've probably been expecting this," Saxfen curiously pried. "You've probably been like, 'When are they gonna start asking me all these stupid questions, *sigh*.'"

"Um . . . go on . . ." Orilheart said.

"Do you get hungry?"

"Nope."

"But you eat. I see you eat all the time."

"I like to eat."

"But you don't have to?"

"Nope."

"You just eat . . . for the fun of it?"

"Yup."

"I see. Do you sleep for the fun of it too?"

"Yup, it feels great."

Seemingly unfazed by her answers, Saxfen prepared his bait for another attempt at a rakulfish.

"O?" he continued.

"Yeah, Saxfen."

"I'm so glad you're our friend."

Orilheart playfully laughed.

"Actually, I think you'd be surprised that the pleasure is all mine."

"What? You're just being nice. We're just regular people. You're a celestial person we've only heard tales about, a slayer of giants, an avenger of Shaifetnu everywhere. You're one of those mythical winged people we've only heard about around camp fires and could only dream of meeting someday."

"Aw, you're only saying that because you don't know what you are yet."

"Huh?"

"What?"

"What you just said, that I don't know what I am."

"Oh, that. Why do you want to know that? What's the big hurry? It's not yet time to talk about that. But the time is coming upon us real soon."

"You're being weird."

"No, I'm not."

"Yeah, you are. You keep teasing us with all these secrets. Just out with it already."

"If only it were that easy, Saxfen."

"Him is many winged god," Qugam giddily interrupted as he made his way through.

"Okay, how about Jix's parents? Do you know where they are? Are they okay?"

"Yes, they're okay. I just recently learned this. But I don't know where they are. This is probably to keep him safe. That's why they haven't told me where they are."

"Okay, at least we know they made it. Do you hear that, guys? Jix's parents are okay!"

The neufs smiled back but did not quite hear what Saxfen had said. Orilheart smiled with them. She kept her gaze on her fishing line upon the crisp, roseate lake. The creamy, migrating clouds mirrored upon the glistering waters as they sailed across the faint, spectral bows of the Sky'erligg. Orilheart had much to share with Saxfen, but the thought of burdening her friend with her concealed revelations left her overwhelmed. *Wow, is this really him?* She pondered. *Sleep soundly just a bit longer, my dear Saxfen. The time is approaching when you must awake to destiny's beckoning.*

Chapter 5

The Decree of the Lightnings

The following day, the thrilled Orilheart made haste to deliver the wonderful tidings that the Council of Daylight had announced to her that very morning.

"Wake up, guys!" she shouted. "Come on, we need to go for a walk!"

"What's the big deal?" Saxfen resisted. "Why are you up so early?"

"Yeah, I wanna sleep in, him!" Qugam seconded.

"What gives, O? What are you gushing about?" Jix yawned.

"I have some big news! Come on, come on, come on! Let's get going," Orilheart urged.

It was another crisp, sunny morning upon the rustic lands of Tunjunsora, although life would never be the same. For the grim shadow of fallen Oakendunty would forever haunt its survivors.

The dazzling Sky'erligg greeted the dawning rays like a loving mother watching over her children. The fresh breeze was soothing, like a warm salutation from Eofendurk itself upon the early rise. Feathered haubians sweetly chirped as if hailing the rising sun for its generous rays upon their cozy nests.

The four friends journeyed anew onto Treewinth Woodlands, eager to talk with one another about the grand tidings Orilheart seemed so zealous about. They laughed and conversed in their usual manner as they coursed into the depths of the woods.

"Yes, but how do you know what a crocogrey tastes like?" Saxfen teased Jix, struggling to contain his laughter.

"Well, Pa and I were hiking along Gimizhy one day. And there was one, just slithering along, going about its way. So, if you must know, it was a long day. I had to do it. It was either me or him, Snowhead. Do or die."

"Well, did you at least cook it?"

"Nope."

A brief silence passed by.

"Well . . .?" Saxfen nudged.

"Well, what?" Jix responded.

"What did it taste like?"

"It tasted like . . . sweaty neuf's feet."

Orilheart and the two boys squirmed at Jix's response.

"Um . . . but how do you know what sweaty neuf's feet taste like?!" Orilheart exclaimed.

"Uh . . . well . . . hey, look at that!" Jix suddenly pointed, hoping to divert attention from his awkward words.

His three friends swiftly fixed their gaze ahead at the clean, lucid waters of the enchanted pond from the night before. The moss-vested trees and lush greenery were just as stunning to admire in the daytime when the warm, sunny rays pierced through the leafy canopy during the day. The lovely pond was serene and resembled some sacred sanctuary furnished by the spirits of Treewinth.

"This place is amazing, even during the day. I can't believe we've never been here before," Saxfen said.

"Yeah, pretty neat, right?" Orilheart smiled.

"Beautiful, this him," said Qugam.

"Very nice," Jix agreed.

They lounged in the pristine site as timid creatures peeped from the distance, from the still waters and verdant heights. Playful heewisps glided indifferently, oblivious to their foreign guests.

"Hey, so about that harp, what's the deal?" Saxfen wondered. "I mean, what does that have to do with us? You said we were not supposed to know about it, right?"

"Well, yes, under normal circumstances, I would never share anything about the harp with any of you and neither would your parents. First of all, the neufs were never told about the harp, so they, in turn, would not tell anyone else about it. But the Shaifetnu elders know it's still out there, in the belly of the Drukijaken. As for everyone else, all they know is that they had to evacuate their ravished world because of the Great Vexation, and now, they live in the hope of returning to those enchanted lands once again, somehow.

"And the Shaifetnu elders just refuse to talk about the harp with anyone outside their circle for their own good and safety. As mentioned before, they feared someone would try to retrieve it and get themselves hurt or even killed. The Drukijaken is real and truly a terrible monster. He could terrorize anyone he wanted without lifting a finger or leaving the Sea of Nith. Not that he has fingers, of course."

The boys attentively nodded.

"His wrath can destroy the very mountains, and the sight of him can make the weak-hearted die of sheer fright. Or, so the stories go, by the locals. And so, to be safe, the elders never spoke about the harp outside of their circle."

"Him Drukijaken is stronger than ten thousand Bumbersing Neufs!" Qugam exclaimed, recalling the tales he had heard.

"Right, who'd be dumb enough to go after that thing anyway?" Jix laughed. "I've heard the wiljorgs still serve him as their god to this day. So even if anyone wanted to get it from that Druki-thing, they would need to get past all those guards."

"I know, right? Complete lunacy," Orilheart agreed. "So, you can clearly see why the elders have been leery of talking about it with anyone. It really is for their own good."

"Okay, they're all scared, got it," Saxfen said. "But you still haven't told us why you're bringing it up now and talking about it . . . to us, to a bunch of stupid kids."

"Well, my dear Saxfen. These are very special, distinguished times we are living in," Orilheart explained.

"Distinguished?"

"Yup, you see, a long time ago, before any of you were born, Saxfen's ancestors found themselves mourning the loss of their home. With a heavy heart, they were sadly informed their home would be destroyed because gross creatures despised them, and they had come to destroy them. Now, please bear with me and try not to be scared, okay? I promise you there is a happy ending to all this, okay?"

The boys looked at one another with a hint of dread but nodded cautiously.

"Alright, so the ancient Vheilyel called those things that were coming to destroy the Shaifetnu, 'Light Eaters.' Those things terrorized and destroyed everyone who came across them. The peaceful Shaifetnu wondered with great awe that such cruel creatures could even exist! They devoured light, the light of nearby stars, and of their own bright, yellow sun. And they did so very swiftly.

"The terror of them spread like wildfire, and so the Decree of the Daylight came forth to contain these monsters within the worlds they had coveted. Seven Shaifetnu worlds were destroyed; within them, seven Light Eaters were imprisoned here in our realm, in what we call, Ru'alameth. When the Shaifetnu heard that their world would be destroyed, they were heartbroken and pleaded, but it was too late. They had to evacuate. This horrible destruction became known amongst all of us as, the Great Vexation."

"Wow, that's awful. Those things killed every snow-head on sight? Sorry to hear that, Snowhead," Jix said in a faint attempt to console his friend.

"Yeah, him is the saddest story I've ever heard," said Qugam.

Saxfen was visibly shaken by the tragic story of their desecrated worlds. He now understood this was truly an awful burden the elders wished to contain amongst themselves. He had never heard in detail what horrible things they had fled from. And not merely his own ancestors, but other Shaifetnu from six other worlds as well! He fought back the tears and motioned for Orilheart to continue, "Okay, don't mind me. I'll be fine. Go on, O."

"The Shaifetnu's profound sorrow moved the Living One's heart. He consoled them with the love of a gentle father and carried them far away from the Light Eaters. A place so far, they could never find them, even if they somehow escaped their prisons and even if they persuaded the very Vheilyel of heaven to join them and expose to them their secret hiding place.

"Indeed, this awful deed of wickedness, they heartlessly committed. They poisoned and deceived many of us, what you call the many winged gods, who were charged with the care of the Shaifetnu. The Urth Vheilyel searched and relentlessly scavenged the great chasms of Ru'alameth in the name of their Light Eater masters. But the Shaifetnu were nowhere to be found.

"They endlessly searched, but it was all in vain. And in their search, they considered some ominous words etched deep in their minds that haunted their hearts. The haunting words were a solemn Decree of the Council of Daylight, a prophecy against them, against the evil Vheilyel. These words became known as the ancient Legend of the Seven Lightnings.

It goes a little something like this,

He readies his Lightnings and grieves them.
He shoots his Lightnings, and unto perdition, they descend.
They span from across the heavens, and they strike at the foes.
Seven they are in number, seven they are their woe.
And none there was, able to unbind from the words of this Decree,
The Lightnings proceed, and they judge the Great Vexation of thee.

"You see, Saxfen, the Council of Daylight did not leave the Shaifetnu without hope. The Living One promised to avenge them and that he would use seven of their own, one for each Light Eater still imprisoned and awaiting judgment. And so, he will bring them home someday and renew their worlds. We call this hope and prophecy, the Decree of the Lightnings!"

Orilheart struggled to contain her excitement and giddily laughed to herself.

"O-kay . . ." Saxfen skeptically responded.

He briefly paused to consider all the things that were said. The silence became unbearable, so he glanced at his best friends, only to find they were all staring back, awaiting some response.

"What . . .?" he finally asked.

"Well, at least we know it's not because he's the brightest of the bunch, right?" Jix snickered.

"Him is . . . Lightning, him?!" Qugam gasped.

"YES!" Orilheart threw her arms in the air and finally shouted, unable to contain herself any longer.

***

"Wait, what?? You were one of the Lightnings they talk about, Papa?" Enos interrupted.

The grown Saxfen and his son, Enos, were yet sojourning unto that mystic haven that was Oclyd Tower. Mounted atop their regal, frosted gethwis, the sight of them was like that of conquering victors, returning from some epic quest.

"Yes, Son," Saxfen responded. "This is what the Vheilyel called me. And as you can imagine, it was surreal at first. Never in my wildest imaginings could I have thought this would someday be my destined path."

***

The boy Saxfen could not believe his ears. It was truly a frightful thought. Had he heard correctly? Did this mean he would one day have to confront . . . those Light Eater things? *Destroyers of worlds?!!*

"Wait . . . No! Don't tease me like that!" he objected. "How do you even know it's me? Does it have to be me?"

"Um . . . well, I guess it doesn't *have* to be you, but the honor has merely approached you. The Living One can raise a Lightning Bolt of whomever he chooses. He can even do it with that lowly heewisp over there if he is so inclined. Unfortunately for that tiny bug, though, he promised it would be one of your own kin. But I think you understand what I'm saying."

The wandering heewisp glided along, hopelessly oblivious to the marvels discussed before it.

"Well, Okay, O . . . I guess," Saxfen finally conceded. "But only because you have six wings you never told us about and because you are our best friend."

"Don't get me wrong," she explained. "I wasn't sure myself. These things don't just appear in front of us with a flashing sign. It takes a great deal of patience on our part to await further instructions. But then . . . this happened."

She flung her arms open, motioning everything surrounding them,

"That awful night of the assault on Oakendunty Village changed everything."

The three boys listened intently to their longtime friend. *What an exhausting past few nights!* They thought to themselves. What would she reveal to them next?

"You see, that night," she continued. "I was summoned for my routine briefing."

"You have routine briefings? Like this whole time?" said Jix.

"Yup, we must keep in touch with our superiors, you know."

Orilheart explained how she was strolling within Cimbri Forrest before the village was assaulted and destroyed. She would proceed to relate the happenings upon her path moments prior to the tragedy that befell the hidden, neuf abode.

She sought to meet with her fellow Vheilyel in the woods. This was to be a mere, customary gathering concerning the status of her duties in Eofendurk. A fresh, gentle breeze brushed through her long, silver hair. No one was in sight, none but the lonesome eyes of a single miziru staring at her intently. *Alright,* she thought to herself, *here we are. And now, where are you hiding, Jrukell?*

Then came a faint, ruffling sound from within an unruly shrub at the foot of an aiskol tree. It was a curious lyrbix, toiling inside the rumpled shrub. It sprung unto a trunk to hide as it sensed the peering eyes of Orilheart of the Eth.

"Well, hello there, Jrukell, there you are!" she greeted the curious creature. "Peace of the Daylight."

There was no response.

"What's with you, Jrukell? Is everything okay?" she continued.

"Ahem . . ." a voice finally responded, but it was not from the lyrbix peering back from within the trunk.

She turned around, but there was no one in sight.

"Down here, Orilheart," responded the voice a second time.

She looked down and saw another lyrbix innocently staring at her underneath the nocturnal lamp of the Sky'erligg.

"Oh . . ." Orilheart nervously laughed. "Uh . . . of course this little fella over here was not you . . ."

"Disregard that; we do not have much time," the lyrbix anxiously replied.

It hasted upon her left shoulder. Jrukell began to relate his message through the tiny beast, though its mouth did not move once when speaking with Orilheart.

"Orilheart, tonight is a night most pressing!" he said. "I have received confirmation . . ."

Jrukell paused for dramatic suspense.

"Well?" Orilheart urged.

"It's . . . Saxfen of the Sevrinjiv!" the lyrbix shouted in excitement.

Orilheart's eyes flung wide in astonishment. *Her* Saxfen? she thought.

"What? No way!" she abruptly replied.

Suddenly, she seized the adorable lyrbix and forcefully pulled it before her face, "Are you sure?! Are you sure it's Saxfen . . . of the Sevrinjiv?!"

"Calm yourself, Orilheart!" Jrukell replied. "These tiny beasts are truly fragile."

"Yeah, and so is Saxfen! I mean, he's just a boy."

"Well, I suspect that is the very reason the Living One has decided to send a fragile, defenseless boy to humiliate the Council of Night and their hordes in all their might."

"Yeah, it makes sense now that you mention it. It's consistent, I guess. Oh, that's wonderful news, Jrukell! The time to judge the Seven Thrones is finally here!"

Orilheart embraced the lyrbix in her arms as she whirled and danced with it to the sweet melody of her own voice. But then, she suddenly halted, for dreadful thoughts began to creep into her mind.

"Oh no, Jrukell," she said. "If I know Saxfen is the Lightning Bolt, then the Council of Night knows too!"

She then quickly placed Jrukell on the ground.

"Jrukell, do they know he's here in Eofendurk? Have they revealed his location in the judgment halls?"

"Yes, I'm afraid so."

Orilheart gasped.

And without saying farewell or uttering another word, she flung her six ivory wings and hasted unto Oakendunty Village. She thrust herself underneath the starry night sky with all the strength within her. She dashed and light-drifted to Saxfen's side as a prayer ascended in her heart. *Oh, dear Living One, please don't let it be too late!* She feared for Oakendunty's safety and, most importantly, her dear friends. And for the bearer of that ancient decree, spoken of in times before the rubied oceans of Eofendurk had ever been formed.

She was certain the Council of Night was on the prowl now that one of the Seven Lightnings had been revealed to dwell upon Eofendurk. *Is it too late? No, not if I can help it,* she assured herself as she conceived to veer from her course and intercept the hordes of the Night.

And the infernal hordes she had feared would surely follow. They would come with vengeful fury to persecute the one who bears the ancient name. The utter dread of impending doom pronounced against the Urth in bygone epochs would compel their villainous legions to search out and destroy the words of the Decree. The great retribution pronounced against the Council of Night had arrived at long last, or so it seemed, and the fiends would do all that was in their power to postpone the wrath, including the unlawful slaying of the servants of the Daylight. And they would not hesitate to deploy those corrupted amongst the noble hierarchies.

And so, after much distress and a lethal clash with the hordes of the Order of Zayd, Orilheart returned to the hidden neuf village. She was utterly heartbroken at the sight of the devastation. Her fears had come upon her, and she was torn within after gazing in disbelief at the bleak pillars of smoke, dismally ascending underneath the Sky'erligg. Her faint, spectral silhouette had emerged from her light-drift upon the plundered village, and all she could think was, *Oh no, I'm too late!* This was her beloved Oakendunty, so close to her heart, ravished and trampled to the ground.

A strange figure whizzed past her from the corner of her eye. *Alright, here we go,* she prepared.

She sensed the malignant gaze of baleful, bitter eyes stalking her at every move. She paused and gathered a deep breath. And without hesitance, she summoned the luminous fury of her essence blade, her deadly weapon emanating from her right arm. She thrust the piercing blade into the coarse, wooly coat of one savage beast charging at her. The slain wiljorg howled in agony and flopped its final breath on the ground as its blood departed from its blue coat.

Then followed twain growling brutes, swearing revenge for their slain brother. They clawed and snarled with snouts full of loathsome fangs. They charged at Orilheart. The first violently flung its huge clutches at her head, but she evaded and severed its trespassing arm in a single, clean stroke. She wielded a second stroke, and the head of the second raiding creature smacked to the earthen ground.

She then swiftly returned to the first combatant and drove her burning blade through its impaled body, exposing it on the opposing end of its azure, woolen coat.

She stood unfazed with her prey at her feet and noted the form of an animated shadow resembling a swollen worm escaping her slain adversary.

"Oh no, you don't," she said.

The slithering thing sought to flee the slain beast, but she skillfully pierced it through before it could escape.

"Gotcha!"

A second shadow likewise sought to save itself but was met with the same fate. And then came the sound of a faint, familiar voice into her ears from the burning village behind her.

"Qugam . . . NOOOO!"

It was Saxfen calling out for his dear friend as he watched him plunge to his death unto the pack of snarling wiljorgs below. Orilheart light-drifted to the scene.

"Move it, freak!" she shouted as she forcefully hastened, slashing all wiljorgs obstructing her. "Out of my way!"

And then she saw him, Qugam lying on the floor, ready to be devoured by the ravenous, blue wiljorgs. She then raised her right arm to the zenith and quietly demanded the blinding of the beasts.

"You will *not* lay your eyes upon him any longer this day!"

The brutes searched for their prey in vain. The savory morsel before them had instantly vanished from before their eyes!

"Come on, Qugam!" Orilheart whispered. "Now's your chance!"

The bewildered, injured neuf could not explain what had occurred, and he did not care to do so at the time. He rose to his feet and fled before the wiljorgs could return to their senses.

Orilheart squandered not her time and pounced upon the blinded brutes with the fury of a ferocious gethwi, ripping and tearing them apart, her eyes burning like the sun. No mercy would be extended that day. This was her beloved Oakendunty Village.

She gave a glance over her shoulder. It appeared to be safe. Not a soul was in sight to witness her carnage.

"Guys . . . I could use a little help down here," she muttered.

Where are they? This is huge. They must still be held up. Okay, I got this.

She was able to evacuate many, all the while closing all innocent eyes about her, so they may not witness the slaying of the beasts that dared confront her.

And then came the sneering taunts of a chilling voice she had never heard before, "What's the matter? Do you not fancy my new pets?"

Orilheart turned to face her adversary, but no one was in sight. The voice called out from within the Path of the Sithrah, that restless plane betwixt realms spanning across all domains within Ru'alameth. She light-drifted out of sight, escaping the Path of the Waking and instantly reemerging in the void.

Now, there is no day nor night upon the Sithrah, only a form of ever-present dusk. The sun, the stars, and the Sky'erligg alike are all diminished in their glory, and the heavens themselves contort. The verdant trees of Eofendurk and the proud mountains therein, all these appear as dimness in place of their common form. For it is a land where streaks of shadow stream to the heavens like a perpetual, inverted rain, and the ground resembles the dripping dew.

A restless plane—the Restless Lands, as also it is known. For the sound thereof is like the howls of the wind, ever toiling to find rest. And in every place upon the heavens, there could be seen the black suns of Hoviel'iggalot, those enormous dark spheres encompassed by a living halo of ethereal light each one. And all living creatures dwelling upon the Path of the Waking appear in the form of pulsating orbs of light, like phantom orbs they appear, faintly hovering upon the Path of the Sithrah.

Orilhart's eyes were met by the chilling stare of a hooded, sinister being cloaked in the doleful vestments of the Order of Zayd. Its face was shrouded, but its glare was malignant and could be felt. She was in the presence of the accursed, those persuaded by thoughts of darkness. These were the ancient Evil Ones, so named, the Council of Night—the Urth Vheilyel of Ru'alameth.

"Orilheart, is it?" the eerie voice continued. "It is said you are charged with the care of the fabled Shaifetnu in this place. So, it appears some have survived after all. Such base creatures, all of them. Why would you sacrifice yourself for them? Why, after ages of silence have gone by without a word in their name?"

"Um . . . what was that? Sorry, I was a bit distracted remembering what I wanted for supper later tonight. I think something about you returning to the filth that spewed you out?"

The lofty assassin became irate. How dare this novice taunt him so recklessly!

"Foolish Day Zarrar, I will not be mocked by an Eth! You know not who stands before you. Your overconfidence shall cost you your life."

"It's up to you . . ." she threatened with her gaze.

And without wavering, the loathsome being accepted Orilheart's summons. In a flash, the creature vanished, only to emerge at arm's length, hurling a lethal stroke at her exposed head. But Orilheart was prepared, and the fiend's weapon crashed against the radiant light of her essence blade. The fiend wielded an essence blade of his own, likewise emanating from his arm. But the glory thereof was ghoulish, like the bleak, extinguished soul within him. And a faint smoke followed it, like the toxic fumes of ghastly fire cinders.

"Today, I will drive you back into the womb that conceived you, O silly Day Zarrar. And I will savor the boast of slaying one of Eofendurk's champions."

"This is your last chance, creep. Leave now or be vanished to the darkness you came from!" Orilheart exclaimed.

Her haughty words reviled him, and his fury became a surging storm of rage. The creature lashed out at Orilheart from every side, but she cunningly deflected all of his blows with the skill of her searing blade and essence shield. The boastful adversary then understood this was no novice after all. This was an opponent most dreadful in combat, mirroring his aged might. It then stopped abruptly to consider again its ambition. Six leathery, nightmare wings then flung open from his back, and they surged him into the frightful, contorted zenith of the Sithrah.

"What's this? Leaving so soon?" she shouted.

The relentless Eth was unwilling to permit the wretched thing to escape. Nay, this was a matter most personal. The abhorrent thing had dared to threaten her friends! She flung herself after the fleeing Urth, halting his escape. They engaged anew underneath the contorted light of the Sky'erligg, high above the hazy pillars of smoke that could be faintly seen from the standpoint of this hidden domain.

"It's either us or them, you fool. Stand down!" the Urth ordered.

He beheld the skillful Eth, that she was but a youth and rued how he had underestimated her. She could not possibly have been around to witness the terrors of old or the things conjured from forbidden realms that emboldened the Night all the ages since. That might! How could he have known that the High Tribunals of S'hyeru Kadash had prevailed on her behalf? How could he had known that the Order of Aedyr had decreed in her favor, and thus, the decree would stand and none would be able to withstand her that day? It appeared that the Urth's allies had busied themselves and had failed to dissuade him from this, his futile ambition.

"Prepare yourself for what's coming!" the Urth warned. "They're coming! The Sign of the Eighth is upon us . . . the Gods of the Naloz'oth shall rise, and there will be no mercy for the kingdoms of the Daylight when they shall reign!"

The vile creature was crafty and evaded the wrathful strikes of Orilheart's essence blade.

"No . . . *you* better prepare yourself!" she shouted back.

She stunned the adversary with a sudden counter-slash across his chest and quickly transported herself behind him. She severed three of his horrid leather wings, and the fiend plunged into freefall. The injured Urth swirled from the heights of the battle but light-drifted safely to the inverted drips proceeding from the ground. Orilheart light-drifted to the dying foe. Ebon, runny ooze escaped from the wounds of its severed wings and chest.

She waved her hand, and his head vesture flung, only to reveal a set of hateful, sulfur eyes and that repulsive, scaled flesh underneath. It was the loathsome mark of the curse, the Curse of the Morning upon the Urth Vheilyel. This scaled form was the judgment against the wicked Vheilyel of old, an ancient curse from the dawning age of Ru'alameth.

Its face was garnished with pointy horns, curiously assorted through-out. Its head was void of hair of any sort. One slit, sharpened tongue could be seen within its fanged jaws as it wheezed its final breaths. It trembled in dread as one realizing some unseen horror lurking in the shadows, stalking to consume its prey. A faint sense of restrained sobbing could be felt in the air.

"You'll be lucky if they spare you from the Vaults of the Naloz'oth for what you've done," Orilheart glared.

She raised her right arm to the night sky, and the creature knew what would follow.

"Orilheart . . . Nooo . . .!! *caught* I am the Zayd chief, Lakkemhok-mu, and I wield great power. Join us and be spared the wrath of the Seven Thrones. Join us, and I will give you a throne of your own . . ." he tempted.

SWOOSH!

She drove her essence blade through its pleading, fanged mouth.

This Order of Zayd, so named, was the Order of those fiendish hunters and assassins sent forth to search out much-coveted prey in the name of the Council of Night, which also is named, the Sevens Thrones of Ebelsaddon.

There came a brief silence as Orilheart stood the victor over the slain captain at her feet.

"And now . . . the fun part," she muttered.

The surroundings became dense and oppressive, as if struggling to contain some burdensome mass. The unnatural, contorted heavens rumbled with a cry above the howling of that restless plane. The rumbling appeared to proceed from some concealed source.

And there it was. It was the faint, enormous image of a Daylight Reaper sent forth to gather the bodies of deceased Vheilyel from all four corners of Ru'alameth. This was the frightful sight of the Order of Kozeroth, discreetly concealed from mortal eyes within the secret expanse of the Sithrah. It had emerged from impossible leagues to lay claim to the remains of the perished Lakkemhokmu. Sixfold, gigantic wings covered its body, and upon its head, there stood twain massive horns. Its face was fourfold and resembled that of the majestic War Ekeru, with the beak of a terrible sky gylth and the eyes and mouth of a man.

The Kozeroth Vheilyel extended its plated arm, and the remains of the fallen Lakkemhokmu dissolved into a streak of light. The fate of this haughty adversary was such that it would now be forcefully transported in disgrace unto that awful darkness Orilheart had warned of.

***

"And that's what I was up to when Oakendunty Village was attacked," Orilheart concluded.

The three boys stared at Orilheart in utter disbelief, wide-eyed and bewildered at her incredible story.

***

The grown-up Saxfen glanced at the boy Enos and beheld that he was notably startled. "You alright over there, Enos?" he pried.

"Yes, Papa . . . keep going," the boy responded as he tightly gripped Kirrius' shaggy coat.

***

Orilheart discreetly motioned with her hand on her lips to the astonished Jix.

"Um . . . Jix," she said.

There was a hint of dribble running down the left side of his whiskered face. "Oh . . . oops. Sorry, O."

"How embarrassing, him," Qugam chided.

"You've got to be kidding me, Orilheart," Saxfen erupted. "This really happened while we were hiding for our lives?!"

"Well, yeah. It's not like I'm making it up for attention, you know."

"Yeah, I know, but it's just too much! It's just so much—so many questions. I don't even know where to start. Should I even start?" Saxfen complained.

The silver-haired boy then suddenly realized the painful truth. "Oh no, that means . . . those creatures destroyed Oakendunty Village because of me. It's all my fault. I put everyone in danger."

Tears began to roll down Saxfen's cheeks at the revelation. His heart ached at the thought of those who perished.

"And you knew Qugam was alive! Why didn't you tell us he was still alive back there?" he sobbed.

"Yes, I saved Qugam when he fell off the roof, but I wasn't sure if anything happened to him after that. Believe me, this has been an extremely emotional experience for all of us," Orilheart explained.

"Why did it have to be my fault, O? I didn't do anything to anyone," Saxfen continued. "How can I even think of being this Lightning thing when I'm sitting here crying like a baby?"

Orilheart embraced him.

"It's okay, Saxfen. Don't doubt, only believe. You'll see. You'll see great and astonishing things if you are able to believe," she comforted.

"Maybe I don't want to see great and astonishing things, O," he sobbed. "Maybe I just want things to be the way they were before this nightmare we can't wake up from. Maybe I just want to bring back the innocent people who died because of me and play with my friends in the Kedfrin Green."

"Maybe you will. But, for now, many good people are counting on you, Saxfen. A lot of Shaifetnu, a lot of beautiful neufs . . . a lot of my own kind, a lot of us."

Saxfen paused to consider Orilheart's words.

"The Living One believes in you!" she assured him.

He wrestled to regain his thoughts, wiping the tears from his eyes and toiling to take heart. And finally, the lad regained his composure.

"Okay, O. This seems really important," he responded. "And you will be with us the whole time, right?"

"Yup, that's right," Orilheart muttered, slightly preoccupied with a generous helping of delicious ejiberries. "I'm here to help the Lightning Bolt retrieve the O'rah Harp, don't you know. And I'm also here to assist in judging our Light Eater prisoners."

Her fondness for ejiberries would not be doubted for one second.

"Wow, these things are incredible!"

The boys looked on in awe. Was this really the same Orilheart they had known all their lives?

"What?" she asked, as the boys gazed blankly.

Slightly startled, they quickly removed their fastened eyes.

"Uh . . . nothing," Saxfen replied. "Well, it's just that . . . you're a fabled many winged god, you know, hero of my people, slayer of fallen Vheilyel and other monsters, and yet, here you are . . . chatting away with us with a mouth full of ejiberries."

Orilheart appeared to ignore his remarks. She seemed wholly immersed in savoring that fine ejiberry flavor she had become enamored with.

"Seriously, these are incredible! And believe me, I've traveled to a lot of places. But these right here!"

She finally acknowledged their anxious, prying eyes.

"Ahem . . . sorry, we just don't have these in the places I've been. They're just so tasty!" she said.

"Yeah, they're pretty fantastic," Jix interrupted. "Anyway, so where do we go from here?"

"Yeah, what is Saxfen him supposed to do now?" Qugam said.

"Right, this brings us to the big news I was telling you about when I dragged you out of bed. Now that we have established that our dear Saxfen here is one of the promised Lightning Bolts of God, destined to judge the imprisoned Light Eaters, I think the time has come for us to meet with . . . the Fire Seer."

"The Fire-who?" the boys wondered.

"The Shaifetnu Fire Seer. I learned this morning that he's here in Tunjunsora already. This is the seer appointed by the Daylight to announce the Lightning Bolt's appearance here upon the Path of the Waking. You see, Saxfen has already been announced as such within the Daylight Tribunals of Highest Ofandynth, but he is yet to be announced upon the Path of the Waking, which is . . . all this is!"

She motioned her arms about her and gently swirled herself as if dancing to an unheard tune.

"Okay, I think I get it. I think you're saying Saxfen now has to be announced here in Eofendurk, right?" Jix guessed.

"Almost, but not quite. It's a little more than that. The Path of the Waking is where all mortal creatures have their being, not just Eofendurk. And the Path of the Vheilyel is where we have our being. It's our life course that is set before us and that we journey in, hence we call it a

Path. And it is where Saxfen has already been announced as the promised Lightning.

"Anyways, it's crucial for us to formally announce Saxfen here on the Path of the Waking because, in so doing, we are adhering to our sacred code, enshrined forever in something we call, the *Book of Principal Covenants.*

"And this brings us to the Fire Seer. The Fire Seer has been sent to Eofendurk to perform the Annunciation Ceremony. He's traveled a very long way to do this, and it's going to be a little tricky finding him because he must remain hidden for his own safety. If the Council of Night gets word, they will surely kill him, or at least try."

"Alright, so how are you supposed to find this guy?" Jix asked.

"Yes, about that. You see, the key is to never mention his name. The Council of Night does not know who's been appointed to announce the Lightning Bolt upon the Path of the Waking, so they can't know his location. But we know who he is!" Orilheart explained, giddy with excitement. "We know who the Fire Seer is, and we will find him!"

She noted the puzzled look on their faces at her sudden burst of burning zest.

"Sorry, this is all so very exciting for us Vheilyel. These are truly exciting times. We've been waiting a very, very long time. To be honest, we're talking about well before even the very foundations of Eofendurk were formed. And well before even I was born. Yes, it took a very long time for all this to unfold . . . and *finally,* here we are! So, as you can imagine, I can hardly contain myself right now just merely talking about it!"

The boys were stupefied with astonishment. What could she possibly mean by 'before Eofendurk was formed?' And how old was Orilheart exactly? The questions poured in without ceasing, but the boys were simply too timid to pry and just plain exhausted with the shocking unveiling of Orilheart's secret world.

She veered off into song again while the boys mused, humming joyous, sacred notes to herself while whirling in celestial dance. The three boys scratched their heads and congregated to debate their course.

"So, Jix, you're coming too, right?" Saxfen asked.

"What?! Snowhead, are you out of your mind?" Jix chided. "You want me to wander into who knows where and look for who knows what? And then, you want me to march into Ujorg Stone City, yes, *that* Ujorg Stone City! Which, by the way, is riddled with wiljorgs? And THEN . . . you want to pick a fight with . . . *the Drukijaken?!* Well, what do you think I'm going to say?"

"So, I guess that's a, 'No.'"

"Yeah, it's a hard no, for me, Snowball."

"Qugam? What say you?" Saxfen asked.

"Him is right. Him is far too dangerous for us," Qugam responded.

"Wow, really, guys? Alright, you do have a point, though," Saxfen conceded. "I wouldn't expect you to come along, anyway. It really does sound way too dangerous. You could die, and it would be my fault. Even I could die out there. But if it's really me that the many winged gods have chosen for this, and there's no doubt Orilheart really is one of them, I have to see what comes of this."

He glanced at his friends, and his heart broke anew at the thought of their beloved village destroyed. It wasn't fair. Their kindness had been rewarded with destruction. Their compassion had been repaid with death. His eyes drew down in sudden anger. This wrongdoing must be rectified, he reasoned.

"I really hope you guys rebuild a bigger and better Oakendunty Village," he continued as he fought the tears in his eyes. "I will avenge all our friends and family they killed. Somehow, with Orilheart's help, I will avenge us all. Just don't forget me."

The silver-haired boy paced as he anxiously wrestled with the daunting labor placed upon his young shoulders. But his eyes turned to Orilheart, who gently smiled back.

"I *will* see you guys again. Unless I die, of course. And we'll talk and laugh together again, and I'll tell you stories of how we avenged Oakendunty Village on all those dirty wiljorgs and slew their monstrous sea god, Ruminthumgath."

And so, with a fresh sense of resolve, the Shaifetnu boy raised his fist in the air in defiance of the fear that had come upon him and his breath became heavy.

"Yes, Saxfen, Lightning Bolt of God!" he exclaimed. "Slayer of Evil Gods and Grand Avenger of Shaifetnu and Neufs everywhere!! You'll see, guys . . . I promise you!"

Jix and Qugam looked on in admiration. That raw valor, that burning vendetta! The blood of slain wiljorgs at his feet! The slayer of the dreaded Drukijaken itself? It all sounded . . . *amazing!!*

"Those cowards must pay for what they've done to us," said Jix. "It's just not fair!"

"All those evil hims cannot get away with this," Qugam agreed.

The more the boys spoke about the tragedy that came upon their home, the more they felt compelled to pursue justice.

"This is why the Living One has given me life!" Saxfen exclaimed. "This is my purpose for being alive. This is my reason, to avenge Oakendunty Village, to avenge the Shaifetnu, to avenge the neufs . . . to avenge the very Vheilyel of heaven!"

"You know what? Curse those dirty wiljorgs! They took everything from us!" Jix exclaimed. "This is our chance to make things right. We have a many winged god on our side, in person!"

"Him is powerful many winged god!" Qugam cheered.

"YEAH!" they shouted.

Orilheart finally joined in, her mouth tinged with the golden tint of the irresistible berries, "Great, guys! So, we go . . . together!"

Chapter 6

Into the Forbidden Streaks

Elsewhere, amongst far-placed stars and frightful seas of luminous, ethereal mists, the foul spirit of the slain Urth captain, Lakkemhokmu, had returned to the place of his own origins, unto the desecrated world of Ga'nost. And thus was the fate of failed Urth who were forcefully evicted from the worlds in which they indulged in their mischief.

Now, depending on the gravity of their offenses against the treaties with the Daylight, some of the Urth would be returned to the worlds from whence they were commissioned. And yet, there were others whose crimes would reach far beyond the tolerable measure. These most threatening foes were sentenced to the soul-shattering despair of the Naloz'oth Vaults, those dreaded dungeons where the ancient enemies of the Daylight were imprisoned for tormenting spans of undefined epochs.

And the failed Zayd captain had truly committed cardinal trespasses warranting the maddening Vaults of the Naloz'oth, for he had controlled the damnable raid against Oakendunty Village. He had directed the unlawful destruction against the Shaifetnu boy who was said to be heir of the fabled prophecy of the Lightnings.

Nonetheless, the Night had secretive allies within the noble hierarchies. Therefore, the defeated Urth captain had evaded the stern sentence of the Naloz'oth Vaults, though his legions could not be so fortunate.

And so, to his own terror and devoid of his potent Vheilyel frame, Lakkemhokmu roamed the savage wastelands of the nightmare world, Ga'nost. He wandered the desecrated terrain in the hazy hope of obtaining relief from his masters. A captured world of the Urth, this was the place which had commissioned the Zayd chief, the place of his origins and the darkness from whence he came.

He now existed in the form of a fatted shadow worm, and within the capitol of this nightmare world, he would be compelled to answer for the grievous loss of the sizeable host entrusted to him. And, as chief amongst the infernal ranks of the loathsome Order of Zayd, the Lords of Ga'nost demanded answers for his failure to obtain the head of the Shaifetnu boy dwelling upon Eofendurk. For it was said this boy bears that ancient name of their dread, the *Lightning Bolt of God*.

And the Council of Night, which also is named, the Seven Thrones of Ebelsaddon, did not look favorably upon failure, but instead, they chastised and made examples out of such, for all others to heed. Their punishment was appointed according to the measure of their loss to their Daylight rivals.

This, Lakkemhokmu, had squandered much. He had squandered costly legions of Zayd hunters under his care, and now the gruesome beasts of Ga'nost came forth, prowling for his wandering soul. These came searching for the creeping shadow worm so as to retrieve it for the Urth masters dwelling within the ancient chambers of one, Castle Burning Skull.

The disgraced Lakkemhokmu slithered upon the lurid, unholy lands desecrated by the Dark Kingdom. The heavens were cloaked in swirling, dismal brumes, furiously objecting unnamable miseries with violent thunderings and crashing bolts. The flashing, clamorous bolts revealed the grim terrain as the whole nightmare vista was engulfed in perpetual twilight. Glittering, poisonous streams issued upon ghastly rivers of death. Foul rivers these were, mirroring the fury above. And there could also be seen other, even more terrifying flows of molten rock in the distant, towering monoliths shrouded in somber haze.

There were curious growths resembling withered botany scattered throughout. These leafless, tree-like growths featured alarming images of what appeared to be faces, and they were petrified in a state of torment and horror. Lakkemhokmu slithered along these shocking fixtures, only to discover a greater terror looming nearby. The faint, eerie howls of the one-eyed cerumogs had come for him.

The Lords of Ga'nost had knowledge of Lakkemhokmu's arrival, and their vile, four-legged cerumogs had found him. These were abysmal beasts whose grotesque bodies harbored living things, shifting underneath their skin. Their jagged teeth salivated like starving wiljorgs. Their single, hateful eye burned with contempt. They howled and snarled at the shadow worm that was Lakkemhokmu, absorbing him into their foul bodies.

The nightmare beasts then returned to their masters, who awaited them upon the elevated heights of that hellish, ancient citadel, Castle Burning Skull. There could be seen gigantic, four-armed beings restlessly roaming at the base of a severed head more enormous than they and its flesh had long perished from its bizarre, skeletal form. It was a gargantuan, three-eyed skull that dwelt amongst the vast, burning rivers and wrathful mountains which spewed brimstone and blazing cinders. Overlooking this maddening sight was Castle Burning Skull of Ga'nost, where the gruesome cerumogs had arrived with their prey.

Within the malignant corridors of Burning Skull, those villainous servants of the Night instantly appeared and vanished in spectral silhouettes. Serpentine hissings and jeers and fits of manic anger could be heard throughout the devilish fortress.

There were hunters of Zayd who pondered and contended the co-ordinates of highly coveted souls. There also labored the Order of Yith'doni, who busied themselves with bizarre machinery and profane tomes amassed from forbidden corners of Ru'alameth.

All carried out their malignant craft without disruption within those unhallowed walls. But most fiendish of them all was the much-feared Order of Mefflezet. This was that infamous order that presided over the ghoulish hierarchies of the Night.

The Mefflezet Lord overseeing the works underneath the nightmare skies of Ga'nost was known as, the Great Kel'torh of Castle Burning Skull. This was that fierce Urth Lord who had summoned Lakkemhok-mu and now demanded answers for his slain hunters.

The menacing, hooded face of the Great Kel'torh brooded upon his grim throne as there came one formidable Urth General, one Beosigeus of the Order of Kaabaldur. And this Beosigeus could be seen interrogating the failed Zaid captain on behalf of the feared Urth Lord.

"And what is this tiresome speech that you bring before us?" Beosigeus interrupted. "Was not the might of Ga'nost sufficient? Twelve legions of Zayd, were they not sufficient to accomplish our deed against one harmless Shaifetnu boy? And our astounding labors to enlist our covert brethren for this deed, was this not sufficient? Furthermore, we gave you power over the blue vermin to utilize while the Day Zarrar busied themselves. And your tiresome speech says all these were not sufficient?"

No response was returned. It was an utter humiliation of a defeat. Whispers and piercing scoldings from an onlooking Urth court filled the insufferable air.

"ANSWER ME!" Beosigeus shouted.

The vicious cerumog beast being interrogated was reduced to a frightened, whimpering. Its one-eyed gaze turned to the masoned floor in shame, not daring so much as to look upon his inquisitor.

"Our retribution will be increased tenfold if you do not begin to speak," the Urth General continued.

The response finally came.

"It was not sufficient, my lord," replied the cerumog in a deep, unwholesome voice.

"You boasted unto us, the head of the supposed Lightning Bolt. But you return to us . . . with no Lightning Bolt. And now, for reason of your failure, the words of the Day Zarrar gain credence, and their detestable Decree looms closer to the Seven Masters!"

"The Lightning Bolt was well guarded, my lord," the possessed cerumog defended.

"You *knew* he would be well guarded. You *knew* the wagers. And so, you deceived us and squandered twelve legions of Zayd. You squandered our hidden resources amongst the Aedyr, amongst the Miyshmaoth, amongst the Eth!"

The gruesome cerumog eerily howled in despair.

"Perhaps we should have given you over to the dungeons of the Day Zarrar for this failure. Take him away!" Beosigeus ordered.

The ghoulish spectator audience of wicked beings clamored in mockery and scoffing. They spat and shrieked at the terrified cerumog, escorted in heavy chains about its neck. Their horned, scaly faces abhorred the sight of the failed Lakkemhokmu.

Imprisoned within the foul cerumog, the failed captain was then subjected to numerous tortures prescribed by the indignant Lords of Ga'nost.

"This cannot be!" Beosigeus exclaimed. "After ages of silence and without testimony, after ages of vain research, the supposed Lightnings emerge without omen!"

The serpentine multitude became tumultuous, and they contended and shouted amongst themselves.

"Silence!" Beosigeus demanded. "We shall unleash all the wrath of the Night if need be. The full fury of the Seven Thrones from every corner of the stars must rain down upon this . . . Eofendurk. We shall destroy their world in its entirety! I, Beosigeus, will accomplish this myself, and I, Beosigeus, will ensure the endurance of all our Urth brethren upon Ru'alameth."

The ghastly crowd shouted in accord with the words of their dark champion. He was prepared to unleash full annihilation upon Eofendurk that very moment, and they loved him for this.

But one earnest dissenter lifted his voice and disrupted the reveling.

"Cease this fallacy at once!" one vulgar, commanding voice ordered.

The chamber held its peace.

"My brethren, why so hasty?" the dissenter continued.

This was that infamous and revered fiend, Morskelis, Arch Counselor to the Great Kel'torh.

"Heed my words, O Servants of the Night. To send all our might and to send Beosigeus at its head is to secure the extinction of Ga'nost. Why, I say unto thee, shall we gather ourselves for the Living One in this manner, to our own destruction? Is this not his own counsel? One clean strike unto all our elite ranks? But, is this truly our own desire?"

There spurred murmurings anew and contentious whispers at the counsel of the ancient fiend. And then, the sinister voice of the Great Kel'torh finally spoke.

"We shall not gather ourselves in this manner for the Living One. We will prevail against the Day Zarrar by sending steadfast waves upon their Panni. We shall stalk them, and we shall weary them. We shall persecute them relentlessly and slay this supposed bearer of the Name. Ga'nost will accomplish this with their legions, and the glory shall be ours.

"We will prevail in shattering the words of the Decree, for these are the days of reckoning against the Day Zarrar!"

The Urth king uncoiled himself from his gruesome, serpentine frame.

"The *Sign of the Eighth* is upon us!" he loudly professed. "The Seven Masters shall be released upon the Council of Daylight to devour them all, once and for all!"

This, the Urth king confessed, for the Urth had oracles and prophecies of their own, insisting that the words of the Daylight may be refuted and denied passage.

The fiends shouted and celebrated their ghoulish king.

"Excellent words, my lord," said Morskelis.

"You are wise, O Great Kel'torh," said Beosigeus.

The Great Kel'torh raised one arm to the air and pledged, "We shall begin by immediately sending the might of . . . Dolaam, your prince."

The fiends were incited the more feverishly at the mention of the execrable name. For this was Dolaam the Perjurer, that ancient Ulkazak Knight infamous for slaying that most loathed adversary, Hielandar the Endbringer, who had tormented and vexed Ga'nost for many ages.

But Hielandar was most abhorred above all for the slaying of their three-eyed master, Hauggousanth, Desecrator of Covenants, whose gargantuan skull resided outside the citadel walls as a perpetual shrine of wickedness. Truly, the Urth court lauded this Dolaam; Dolaam who had deceived, Dolaam who had prevailed against the loathed Hielandar.

"He shall take his legions," the Great Kel'torh continued. "And he shall test the bearer of the Name and shall find him a liar! He shall deny the supposed Lightning Bolt passage, and the Decree shall not stand with this Shaifetnu boy. And the Seven Masters will prevail against the Daylight, when they shall return and lay claim to Ru'alameth and deliver us from the covenants of the Day Zarrar! *There will be Perpetual Night!*"

Upon hearing the Urth creed invoked, the hordes shouted and they hailed their king and their prince. They chanted the Urth creed in one direful accord.

"There will be Perpetual Night! There will be Perpetual Night!"

And then, the brute, menacing figure of the mythic Dolaam stepped from the veil of shadows to accept this new provocation against the Daylight. The serpentine hordes became inebriated with bloodlust as they praised the wisdom of the Great Kel'torh and of Morskelis, his counselor.

As for the failed Zayd captain, it seemed as though an eternity had transpired within the torture chambers underneath Castle Burning Skull. His scourings finally concluded, and Lakkemhokmu found himself within the body of a different cerumog. The first cerumog had perished in the stern penalties imposed.

The new, grotesque creature wandered unto the haunting wastelands outside the evil fortress. With the heavens engulfed in furious lightning and faint, cryptic monoliths peering at its every move, the hellish beast had reached its destination. It was the strange fields of twisted growths past the flowing, metallic rivers mirroring the mayhem in the heavens. The vile cerumog convulsed and spewed an abominable stream of black ooze in that place. The odious ground then drank the ebon filth, and it slowly formed into a new, enigmatic growth. The tormented, petrified face that was now etched upon this new growth was that of the condemned Lakkemhokmu.

And thus, most of the failed Urth were castigated within their own worlds. For this was the ordinance prescribed by the ancient Covenant of Spirit Vials in place of the vexing anguish of the Naloz'oth Vaults, where only the most grievous enemies of the Daylight dwelt in torments without a known end.

***

The grown Shaifetnu champion, Saxfen of the Sevrinjiv, wrestled within himself, struggling to dampen the frightful things pertaining to the Urth kingdom as best as he was able. But no matter how he posed his words, the utter horror of that realm could yet be felt. The tender Enos could no longer contain himself and finally shouted, "Ahhhhh! Ga'nost sounds terrifying, Papa!"

"Yes, Son, it truly is a bitter, scary place. It was really one of many nightmare worlds ruled by the Council of Night. For ages, the Urth had been sending their armies throughout all the stars you see at night from these very worlds. You see, the Urth think they alone should be above all others because they helped defeat the great enemies of long ago. And so, they feel the worlds are in their debt. They feel that Ru'almeth is theirs.

"Long ago, in their senseless anger, they waged war against the Living One and against all the creatures he made. This war took place after the rebellion that came to be known as, the Apostasy of Power, when those great spirit-beasts we call the Soggseraf, believed themselves to be superior to the Vheilyel.

"Wow, you mean there were evil Soggseraf Ekeru?" said Enos.

"Yes, and after the defeat of these evil Soggseraf, there came the rebellion known as the Apostasy of Vanity, and this is when the victorious Vheilyel demanded not to merely rule the worlds in Ru'alameth, but to be worshipped as the Living One is worshipped.

"And also, there was the Apostasy of Envy and the Apostasy of Despair, to name a few.

"But all the rebellions were crushed because there is no living being capable of defeating the power and wisdom of the Living One. Yet, for some reason, our enemies do not see this truth, so they insist that they are wiser and could somehow overcome the very power that formed Ru'alameth."

"So, does this mean there will be more rebellions in the future?"

Saxfen hesitated to respond, not willing to trouble the young Enos with matters to come, but he proceeded nonetheless. The boy needed to know the truth and to guard his heart from errors; past errors, and even more so, the great errors to come.

"Yes, Son, there will be another rebellion," he finally said.

"Whoa! Really? Can I join the fight? Maybe I can take down one of those dumb Urth creatures with my very own essence blade like yours, huh, Papa?"

Saxfen was amused with his son's zeal as he watched him motion with his arm atop the regal fur of the striped gethwi.

"You'd make a fine warrior, Enos. Your courage takes you halfway there already."

Escorted by their gethwi friends, the two journeyed into the mouth of a concealed entrance amongst the formidable walls of the desolate, frozen city of Ujorg Stone.

The bygone days of his youth, when Saxfen and his three best friends ventured underneath the wondrous arc of the Sky'erligg, were long behind the coronated hero. But their memory did course within him as if only a few days had transpired all these years away from this dearest place of his affection.

***

After having accepted to undertake the quest for the O'rah Harp, Orilheart, the boy Saxfen, and twain furry neufs prepared themselves to journey into the wild, untamed lands of Tunjunsora. The boys discretely embraced their parents on their final night, and even Jix had been reunited with his own, only to be unable to say a proper farewell. They inscribed letters explaining that they needed not disquiet themselves for their care. But they omitted their reasons out of the seer absurdity of them. There was simply no reasonable way to explain that Orilheart was a fabled Vheilyel and that they needed to contend with the Drukijaken of Nith.

Having placed their letters each, they set out in search of the concealed Fire Seer. But, in order to find him, they first needed to meet with a fellow

Vheilyel messenger to learn about his location. This stealthy method of contact is how the Council of Daylight intended to conceal the Fire Seer's whereabouts as he awaited them somewhere within the wondrous lands of Eofendurk. For if the Fire Seer was openly made known, the Night would most certainly discover him and devour him in their wrath.

"Here you go, O, I caught this one just for you," Jix said as he presented Orilheart with a confounded kirok bird.

"What? What's this? Hello, I have wings, remember?" she responded.

"I understand you have wings. But this is so we can keep up with you, so you're always by our side," Jix said.

"Alright. I guess that makes sense . . . I think."

Orilheart mounted her kirok bird, and the three boys did likewise.

"Alright, guys, where to?" Saxfen said.

"Well, according to my last talk with Jrukell, we need to meet him at the Yiedsso Hills for further instructions," Orilheart said.

"What? The Forbidden Streaks? This is stupid," Jix began. "Why can't this Jrukell just meet us here? Is he not aware of what lives in Yiedsso? Why should we risk our lives going to the Forbidden Streaks and be devoured by gegnazugs? Tell him to relocate."

"Gegnazug hims are disgusting! They'll eat us all!" Qugam exclaimed.

"Oh, come on, guys! If Orilheart can take down Urth and wiljorgs, don't you think she can eat gegnazugs for supper?" Saxfen said.

They cringed in disgust at the thought of eating the slimy mass of the foul gegnazugs. Prompted by the piercing glares of the company, Saxfen suddenly realized what he had just suggested. The repulsive creatures evoked one unanimous chord.

"Ewww!" they exclaimed.

"Okay, sorry about that. But you know what I meant, right?" Saxfen continued.

"Yeah, I guess, but eating those things?" Orilheart mocked.

"So unnecessary, him," said Qugam.

"Snowhead, remind me to prepare supper for you later tonight," Jix mocked.

The three friends laughed and teased Saxfen for suggesting anyone should eat a slimy gegnazug. They reluctantly journeyed unto the Forbidden Streaks but were comforted that Orilheart was on their side.

"Anyways," Orilheart started, "As I said before, it's quite necessary to go to Yiedsso because we can't just openly announce what we're doing. The Urth are watching closely, up there, far past the Sky'erligg. They may see us and wait for the perfect moment to make their move, like a pack of ujorgs stalking their prey. They need us to stumble so they can attack. I'm sure they're trying to confront us even as we speak. Sorry for the trouble, everyone. But it's completely necessary to work covertly like this."

And so, they traveled eastbound intently as the warm rays faded into evening twilight and the clean, roseate skies exchanged vestures with those of the enchanted, starry nights of Eofendurk.

The following day, the four friends enkindled a campfire and prepared their meals. But then came suddenly, the abrupt screechings of a soaring sky gylth echoing from above.

"Gylth!" Jix exclaimed. "Quick! Take cover!"

The verdant, open meadow did not offer many hiding places except for some scant, puny trees and scattered boulders. The frightened boys ran for cover, each to a hiding place of their own choosing. The scarlet-feathered beast was lord of the skies. It cast its enormous shadow upon their camp. Its bright, lengthy tail adorned the heavens with a deceitful beauty, lethal to all living things that would dare gaze upon it in plain sight.

The gylth taunted its prey with the resonant echo of its piercing shrieks. It was the kirok birds that had caught its eye! In their gripping fright, the boys had forgotten them. The massive sky predator readied its sharpened talons and it savored the thought of feasting on its meal below. The kirok birds fought desperately and wrestled to escape the sturdy vines that bound them to a lonely stone. They snapped with their frightened beaks, but it was futile.

"Oh no! We forgot our kirok hims!" Qugam shouted.

The soaring gylth plunged its scarlet, feathered body upon the panicked kirok birds—it had captured two—and thrust itself back unto the great heights of the flush, roseate sky.

"Nooo!" exclaimed Qugam, fighting back tears.

Orilheart was furious.

"Oh no, you don't!" she exclaimed.

Her eyes flashed with a wild, threatening glare previously unseen by the boys all their lives.

"Give us back our kirok birds!" she shouted, immediately surging to intercept the fleeing gylth.

"Whoa!!" the boys marveled at her sudden pursuit.

With one watchful eye on the boys at all times, Orilheart had reached the massive, winged bandit, but instead of slaying it, she pleaded.

"Give them back!" she demanded of the soaring beast.

The hungry gylth shrieked and maneuvered out of reach from the irate Eth. She gained upon the scarlet, sky terror and again made her demands.

"Don't make me do it!" she announced.

Orilheart then drew her essence blade. The radiant weapon reflected wondrously on the polished, onyx eyes of the now startled gylth. It shrieked and snapped at Orilheart with its massive beak and elongated neck. She swung at the giant fowl's elegant, feathered crown and severed it on the first attempt. The gylth was sorely grieved when it saw its proud, red feathers drift underneath its sharp talons.

"See! Don't make me do it!" Orilheart warned yet again.

But the stubborn gylth would not yield. Orilheart became distressed, unwilling to slay the monstrous, crimson fowl.

"AHHHHH!!" she screamed as she finally attacked.

But instead of driving her essence blade into the stubborn gylth, Orilheart launched a single, forceful kick using all the strength within her. The enormous winged creature shrieked anew, but this time, in piercing anguish. It finally conceded and released the terrorized kirok birds from the injury inflicted. The kirok birds plunged to the ground from the dizzying heights of the bleached, soaring clouds. Orilheart instantly dove to their aid. She caught them, but the terrified kirok birds refused to be comforted and squawked uncontrollably.

At last, they arrived safely to the ground. Whirling and reeling from the fall, the kirok birds collapsed in relief and felt profound gratitude for being safely back on solid ground.

"Now, now. It's okay, guys," Orilheart comforted as she gently petted their heads.

"Wow, Orilheart, that was amazing! Did you get that stupid gylth good?" Saxfen said.

"Yeah, I got 'em," she responded. "These poor kirok birds were almost done for."

"Amazing, him," Qugam said. "I was so worried about you . . . and the kirok hims, too!"

"Yeah, you were up there for a while, O. What took you so long?" Jix jested.

"I tried to hurry, honestly. And I couldn't just leave them. We need the kirok birds to get you to Yiedsso."

"Well, we could've just found new ones," Saxfen bashfully said.

"I know, Saxfen. But these were so scared and helpless," she insisted. "I mean, did you see the look in their eyes as that hungry gylth flew away with them? Seriously, I had to get them back."

"Alright, I'm just glad you're okay, and the kirok birds are okay too," Saxfen responded. "And at least that gylth will not be bothering us anymore."

"Well, about that," said Orilheart. "I may have made her a little mad. You see, gylths are very proud birds. They love the feathered crowns on their heads. I may have angered it a bit by snipping it off . . . a tad."

"You mean you didn't kill it?!" Jix exclaimed.

Orilheart shook her head.

"What? What if it comes back to get its revenge, O?"

"Well, at least it knows what it's getting itself into," she responded, motioning with her hand above her golden hair.

"Yeah, we'll be waiting for that baldy him!" Qugam threatened.

The four friends laughed and ridiculed the gylth together. They imagined the lofty sky predator, humiliated by its embarrassingly clipped feathers.

After the startled kirok birds finally recovered from their shock, they again turned to their curious, friendly selves. Orilheart reached with her arm to comfort them as if conversing with them, "Well, yeah," she chatted. "You guys were the main course for her babies. I told her not to take it personally. But she sure is upset about her trimmed feathers."

Orilheart chuckled and mused as she conversed with the alleviated kirok birds. They seemed to enjoy chirping with her as if talking with one of their own.

"Some nerve, that pesky gylth, taking our kirok birds," Jix chimed.

"Well, I guess she needed to eat, and so did her babies, right, Orilheart?" Saxfen said.

"Yes, they need to eat. You all do."

"Great, now I feel sorry for her and her babies. Is she going to be alright?" Saxfen said.

"Oh, she'll be fine. She can take care of herself," Orilheart assured.

The striking beauty of the cloudless night had closed in again on the four friends, and they arranged camp underneath the soft glow of the lucid arc above. Serene, sparkling trails of stars looked on in suspense like the captivated eyes of a spectating audience. Indeed, the heavens looked on in merry bliss as the concealed Fire Seer was being sought after upon the Path of the Waking. After all, this was the long-awaited unveiling of the mysterious, ancient words concerning the Decree of the Lightnings.

"So, this Fire Seer guy we're trying to find, do you know him?" Saxfen asked.

"I don't know him personally, but he is quite popular in Vheilyel circles. Hence, the giddiness, as you can imagine. He is a man of great honor and courage. He actually comes from a place that imprisoned one of the Light Eaters I've been telling you about. He is a slayer of evil, a weapon forged by the Living One . . . a fellow Shaifetnu like you, actually."

"Wow, really? One of us?" Saxfen responded.

"Yup, and you'll meet him soon enough."

"Great, all this trouble to meet another snowhead," Jix sneered.

"He's not just another Shaifetnu. He's the *Fire Seer*! This is a huge deal. I'm really excited to finally meet him," Orilheart responded.

"Yeah, Jix. Haven't you been paying attention?" Saxfen defended. "This guy's pretty important, you know, for us to get that harp back."

"Well, excuse me, mister high and mighty Snowhead people. Us little people down here are just trying to go about our lives without your grand importance blocking the sun from all Eofendurk."

"Well, we don't mean to be important or block anything. We just want to return to the place where we belong," Saxfen said.

"Him ejiberries is smothered," Qugam frowned as he reluctantly nibbled his meal.

"Ooh, I sure love ejiberries!" Orilheart said, nibbling on her portion. "You know, I've only tasted these here, in all my travels. Why, after our journey has long ended, I'd come by to visit just to savor these sweet, savory ejiberries one more time."

"Yeah, we get it. You love ejiberries," said Jix.

"Ejiberries are alright," said Saxfen.

Orilheart abruptly paused and stared at Saxfen with keen bewilderment upon her face. She could not grasp how the intoxicating flavor of her esteemed ejiberries did not enamor her silver-haired friend as they did her.

"Hmm . . . I suppose it's because Vheilyel bodies are made differently," she assured herself, savoring another delicious bite. "Yes, that must be it."

The boys snickered at Orilheart's fascination with ejiberries. They couldn't believe a fabled many winged god preferred Tunjunsora's ejiberries above all others.

"No, really, guys! They're that great!" she insisted.

Their laughs continued into the night as the crackling flames danced along in their comforting warmth to the cadence of their youthful mirth. It was almost as though they lounged upon their beloved Oakendunty Village again, like the violent whirlwind of the wiljorg assault never occurred. Their friendship had carried them through the cruel ravaging of their abode, and there was now within them a newfound hope that did comfort them like the warmth of the campfire before them.

"Hey, and then . . ." Orilheart explained as Jix interrupted mid-sentence.

"Wait, did you guys hear that?" he said.

The four friends held their peace. Only the serene, cool draft of the night and crackling fire could be heard. Orilheart's hair glided as a gentle blast of soothing gust coasted through. The stilled company was then startled when Qugam gazed across Orilheart's hair and marked the hateful eyes of a four-legged creature charging from the shadows.

"Look out, Orilheart!" he shouted as he pounced to her defense.

The brave neufs intercepted the beast's assault on their friend and wrestled with it on the ground.

"Ujorgs!" Saxfen exclaimed.

"Help me, him!" Qugam shouted.

Orilheart instantly grabbed a nearby vine they used to fasten their kirok birds and quickly bound the ravening beast.

"Oh no. Wait here," she ordered as she dashed into the shadows.

But the deadly jaws of the blue menace prevailed against the vine, and it snarled and raged. Jix then pounced on the beast and gripped its huge fangs from behind.

Saxfen grabbed a nearby branch and lit it with the dancing flames.

"Orilheart, where'd you go?!" he said.

He waved the flaming stick at the hungry ujorg and managed to stab it in the face. The ujorg yelped in pain and violently howled.

"Oh, great, Snowhead, you made it mad!" Jix shouted as he wrestled with the injured beast.

Saxfen then firmly clinched the burning branch and jammed it into the ujorg's throat. It howled miserably as it convulsed in pain and spewed its blood unto the ground. The wounded ujorg then broke free and retreated into the shadows for comfort.

Orilheart could be faintly heard contending in the distance. The three boys rushed to her side and beheld a slain ujorg at her feet, perished from the fury of her essence blade. Four others growled and threatened with their cunning, piercing eyes.

"Stay back, guys!" Orilheart ordered.

She then proceeded to reason with the majestic, yet savage creatures,

"What?! No, I'm not going to give you at least the little one! Keep that up, and your friends here will be eating you instead!"

But the hungry ujorgs would not relent. They were determined to seize their meal.

"Don't be foolish!" Orilheart pleaded. "Why do you want to end up like your dead friend here?"

One ujorg suddenly pounced before she could finish another word. Orilheart then forcefully shoved its fanged snout with one arm and thrust her bare fist into its left eye with the other arm. The ujorg slumped to the ground with the cry of an unsettling yelp.

"Just kill them already, O!" Jix demanded. "What are you waiting for?"

"That's not how we do things, Jix. Just stay back!"

The three boys stared in admiration at their guardian Vheilyel and then stared at one another in disbelief. A real many winged god was truly protecting them right before their eyes! The evidence was overwhelming, but they could not help but wonder whether this was truly the same Orilheart they had known all their lives.

"There! Is that what you wanted?" she shouted at the ujorg on the ground. "Have you had enough? You cannot have these!"

The remaining pack howled and gnashed in vexation. They studied their celestial foe and their deceased brother on the ground.

"Choose . . . *to live*," Orilheart answered.

And so, with Orilheart's unwavering gaze burning at their core, the pack finally conceded, ceased their greed, and retreated in pitiful whimpers of defeat. They cowered into the night in failure. They had chosen wisely to live.

"Whew! What a relief," Orilheart exhaled. "I do not enjoy killing the Living One's creatures, although it is sometimes necessary."

"Oh yeah? They're just stupid ujorgs. What's the big deal?" Saxfen asked.

"Well, they may be just stupid ujorgs to you, Saxfen, but they speak and have families, friends, and memories," she explained. "And they feel happiness and sadness, like you and me."

Saxfen paused to reflect as her words resonated with their recent, painful loss.

"I guess if you put it that way," Saxfen responded.

"They wanted . . . to eat us, O!" Jix erupted.

"Yeah, that ugly him almost devoured me in one bite! I thought I was done for . . . again," Qugam reflected.

"Would you just listen to me!" said an irate Orilheart. "All I'm saying is that we must be very careful about killing any creature because we can sense them on a different level than you, that's it. And we also empathize with their need to survive. Most creatures, you know, are not malignant at heart. In most cases, they kill merely to stay alive."

The boys paused and briefly considered what it would be like to be a hungry ujorg struggling to survive.

"Just kill them next time, sheesh . . ." Jix finally blurted out.

They then erupted in sudden laughter at how Jix so casually dismissed Orilheart's passionate rant.

And so, the friends returned upon their pursuit of the mysterious Fire Seer, who was said to be dwelling amongst the fair slopes of the Yiedsso Hills.

The curious hills finally came into view in the distant range. It was a massive, hued landscape, astonishing to the eye and exciting to the heart. Grand, dainty bands of scarlet and rose, of titian, copper, and hazel, graced the lovely vista.

"So pretty, all these hims," said the awe-struck Qugam.

Few an adventurous neuf had ever wandered into these lovely hills. Only wild tales of their treacherous beauty were heard amongst the Oakendunty Neufs. For therein, there lived those evil masses of living hate upon these enchanted hills, and scant they were who had lived to recount the tale.

These were the feared gegnazugs of the Forbidden Streaks, and they resembled breathing, vile pits of blackened pitch. Their food consisted mostly of the rich nutrients from the streaked hills, but if ever a stray wanderer or pitiful adventurer dared to cross their path, these crawling nightmares of ebon ooze were known to pounce and fling themselves upon their victims and would dissolve their bones like the devouring acids within the hungry bowels. Such was the terrible fate of those who ventured into these delightful hills so rightly named, the Forbidden Streaks.

"Don't get too comfortable, Qugam," said one vigilant Jix. "Everyone, stay alert. Remember, neuf-eating gegnazugs are lurking in these hills. We cannot be too careful, even with Orilheart by our side."

The boys nodded in agreement. These lovely, streaked hills were truly a perilous place to sojourn. The sluggish gegnazugs were not to be trifled with, as every responsible neuf was well aware. This was their kingdom, and terrible was the fate upon all unfortunate souls who dared to intrude in their reign.

"Just stay close to me and don't wander off, okay?" Orilheart instructed as she led the way. "We're almost there."

***

The striking beauty of the hued bands resembled the likeness of rings, and these summoned a warm reflection hidden deep within the shepherd Eth. Instantly, Orilheart was swept away into a tender time when she was escorted herself in like manner by a hero of her ranks.

"Do not wander off, little ones. We are nigh to the place," said the familiar voice of her reflection. "Behold, it is ahead."

The voice was that of the high and venerated Vheilyel, Jiosu'dahlar of the Eth. He was an Arch Vheilyel, entrusted with teaching a band of young Learners who followed closely. Orilheart eagerly and attentively awaited instructions as the mighty Jiosu'dahlar directed their attention to the curious marvel before them. It was a cluster of revolving rings in the sky, composed of orderly rows of stones, duteously gliding upon some unseen orbit.

"The Dancendi are at hand. Follow me," Jiosu'dahlar urged.

The celestial Learners of the Daylight followed in sheer delight and admiration of their guide. This was, after all, Jiosu'dahlar, Oath of Anguish, and the righteous slayer of that unholy fiend, Domierrynth the Spirit Collapser. Just and resolute and wholly devoted to the Daylight, Jiosu'dahlar was heroic and beyond reproach.

His companions were young, inexperienced Learners of the Eth. One studious, fascinated company they were, and rather eager to grow and to obtain the aged wisdom of the renowned Eth Master.

"Therefore, in response to your query, Orilheart, yes, the Dancendi also are light-drifters, as we are. They were graced with this ability but in a rather lesser form."

"Okay, but how can the Dancendi also light-drift when their bodies are mortal and fragile? Wouldn't they just dissolve?" Orilheart replied.

"You are correct that their bodies are fragile and made of dust, but the knowledge of light-drifting was awarded them nonetheless. And, because of their mortal condition, the Dancendi have also been gifted the wisdom of moderation, so they may know not to light-drift in excess. Furthermore, they have learned how to heal and to recover from the practice of light-drifting."

"I see. They have learned to light-drift cautiously, then," Orilheart pondered.

"Yes, when the Living One gives in generosity, he does not add a single measure of sorrow."

The group conversed and queried their heart's content regarding the curious stones in the sky that gracefully encircled their unseen orbit.

"Look!" one observant Learner pointed.

The company gazed from their concealed place amongst the verdant hilltops.

Below was the ancient city of the Dancendi, the stone citadel, Ophauvis.

The great bridge thereof was lowered, and there came from the midst of the fortress, one formidable host riding strong upon the backs of their armored steeds. The warriors gathered in battle formations and strode to confront some imminent threat from within the surrounding woods. The comforting breeze accompanying the waning sun was all that could be heard as all creatures of land and sky held their peace.

And then came the chilling growls. The adversary had arrived. It was the foul bellowings of strange brutes with elongated arms and short hind legs. They appeared to be armored for battle, and they heeded the voice of some unseen master. Their small heads and faces were loathsome to behold, and these charged at the forces of the Dancendi like some ghoulish, infernal horde. They swung with their arms at the valiant defenders of the coveted citadel, whereas others used sharpened weapons of deadly steel. The battle raged, but the valiant Dancendi made use of their light-drifting abilities to evade and effectively restrain the monstrous intruders.

They gracefully slew the abysmal foot soldiers in the eyes of their cheering dames and noble masters, watching atop the fortress walls. And almost they began to celebrate their victory over their hideous persecutors until, suddenly, there came one thunderous blast unlike they had ever heard.

"Master Jiosu'dahlar, what was that?" said one.

"That, my dear Learners," he announced. "Is the voice of glory's call! The voice of Triumph over Peril. It is the voice of Orilheart's first *Mah'seyiud.*"

The young company of Learners looked on at Orilheart with great admiration in their eyes. They silently cheered her on. At last, the moment had arrived for her to prove herself worthy before the Order of Eth.

"Go, Orilheart!" one cheered.

"You're gonna be great!" assured another.

"This is your moment!" whispered another.

The thundering boom was frightening even to the obscene brutes who clashed with the light-drifting Dancendi. And then came the face of the clamorous blasts terrorizing the feud below. It was the brazen, haunting voice of the Sagurk, or rather, the voice of their menacing sky chariots! There came an entire fleet of them, like some soaring war navy upon inverted, azure waters! Fifty in number at minimum had appeared, and they were now in full view.

This was the source of the bizarre thunderings heralding the Sagurk. And the audial of them struck terror in the hearts of the Dancendi, *but the sight of them!* Their woeful semblance most closely resembled that of lifeless ghost cities of the damned, like soaring cities that had come from some unnamed abyss, ready to usher in inescapable doom wheresoever their shadow neared. And so, these looming cities in the sky sparked a raging panic within the walls of Ophauvis, for how could these vessels live and soar? How could they clamor like the voice of vexed thunder clouds?

So grave was the dismay upon the dwellers of Ophauvis. But the Dancendi pleased the Council of Daylight, and they had prepared Orilheart the Learner for this dismal hour of their need.

She opened her sixfold, ivory wings and took to the heavens. She raced to the side of the Dancendi with all her fervor, she light-drifted and she summoned her royal vestures of white and gold upon her body.

The soaring terror was posed to inflict great death from the heavens until the valiant Learner suddenly emerged in the midst of the mayhem. The startled Dancendi began to point and shout. They could not believe their eyes! What was that? Was that . . . *a damsel with wings in the sky?*

This was the young Learner, Orilheart, fully engulfed in her luminous splendor, and her eyes burned with the blazing fury of the noonday sun. This, who had intervened and succored the bewildered Dancendi, was Orilheart of the Learners, soon to be known as, Orilheart of the Eth.

CHAPTER 7

THE ANNUNCIATION CEREMONY

"**O**rilheart! LOOK OUT!"

The three boys shouted at their guardian Vheilyel in the hopes she would return to her senses. She had been musing over her adventures as a Learner of the Eth and had momentarily failed to heed her surroundings. But she swiftly regained her guard as there flung one hazardous mass of ebon ooze upon her. Her heightened senses and battle training saved her from a torturous and embarrassing devastation. Her head skillfully evaded the darting stream of living ooze but not without taking its toll upon the bystander Qugam. The ebon mass altogether was denied the full meal of the fortunate neuf, but instead, it had clipped the tip of his curled horn.

"Whoa, that was close, Qugam!" Jix shouted.

"Orilheart, get that him!" Qugam demanded.

The matter occurred quite suddenly, but then came the retribution. Without warning or her usual sympathy, Orilheart severed the slimy arm as if severing the limbs of some unholy adversary. The awful thing's severed limb splattered and twitched on the ground. The injured gegnazug shrieked in a hideous pitch as Orilheart stood firmly in her battle stance.

The slimy beast appeared perplexed that injury had befallen it. This was a trespass against the startled gegnazug most unheard of, and the anguish provoked it to engage these curious intruders.

There came another limb from within its ebon mass, and at its apex, the creature toiled to form what it imagined resembled the likeness of a face. And it did speak, but not as common words are uttered. The ebon slime grumbled and sputtered gibberish, thinking it could be understood. The boys gazed at one another in confoundment.

"Is it . . . *talking* to us?" said the wide-eyed Jix.

"What?! No, we are not sent here by Ruminthumgath to destroy your kingdom. Cease these lying accusations at once!" Orilheart vehemently rebuked the querying gegnazug.

"Bruuulm . . . baaaarm . . . braaaahl," it continued.

"Okay, I understand you must destroy us for defiling your lands. But you've seen what I've done to your arm over there . . ."

The gegnazug bemoaned its severed limb as it admitted to Orilheart that it could not be reattached again. The foul mass went on to grumble about its duty to destroy them. And how the humiliation of this day would haunt it for the rest of its life, if it did not devour them all at once.

"Uh, is it done yet?" Saxfen sighed.

"Shhhhh! Quiet, guys! Do you want to anger it again?"

"Did she just 'shush' us?" Jix retorted.

"Him totally did," Qugam chimed.

But Orilheart prevailed as she contended and explained how she could slice its slimy body into pieces without hesitation if she so desired. And so, the disgraced gegnazug retreated, valuing its remaining life and the rich nutrients it was permitted to feast on while dwelling upon those vibrant, streaked hills. This deadly, ebon mass was amongst the rarest of sights in all Tunjunsora, and had it not been for Orilheart, twain neufs and the lone Shaifetnu boy would have certainly perished.

The devastated gegnazug finally parted ways. The company proceeded in their search for the Fire Seer as they carefully treaded the forbidden hills, so as to not provoke a second feud.

"So . . . what else did the gegnazug say, O?" Jix playfully queried.

"Oh, nothing. Don't worry about it."

"What? Nothing? The smelly him would not shut up!" Qugam pressed.

"Yeah, Orilheart. That thing back there sure was chattery. What was that all about?" said Saxfen.

"No, it's far too scary. Just leave it alone."

"Oh, well, now it's impossible," Jix said. "You can't just tease at something like that and then expect us to forget all about it. If you don't tell us what it said, I will ensure Qugam here relentlessly sings that awful song you hate until we save the world from the Drukijaken."

"What? You wouldn't . . ." Orilheart squirmed.

"And a one, two, three . . ."

"Wait! Alright. But you asked for it."

The boys gleefully glanced at each other in excitement.

Orilheart sighed, "Alright, the gegnazug was telling me they were not always that way and didn't always look like blobs of black goo. A very long time ago, they were actually once a noble people from the lands of Otov. They had cities and chariots and lived at peace with their neighbors. But the greed of the Nithians had reached their cities, and then they learned of the Drukijaken. And so, they foolishly purposed in their heart to find this Ruminthumgath of the Sea of Nith and kill it. Needless to say, it didn't go well for them. The Drukijaken ridiculed them and smote them with an awful curse. And thus, they became the living masses of goo we see today."

"Whoa!" Qugam panicked. "You mean that Druki-him can turn us all into gooey hims?!"

"Well, I did warn you, didn't I?"

"Okay, O, you win. Maybe we'll take a hint next time," Jix conceded.

"Told you."

"Wow, I don't want to be turned into a blob!" Saxfen protested.

"Yup, pretty scary," Orilheart assured. "But you must overcome your fear. This is part of becoming the promised Lightning, you know? Anyway, I didn't want to alarm you all, but I did find interesting what the Drukijaken said. He was so amused with their ridicule and their feeble war against him that he declared that if any son of Eofendurk should touch a living gegnazug and live, death itself would flee twice. But if death should come yet thrice, then death must have its prize."

The boys stared in amazement; no words came, not even the usual snarky retort.

". . . or something like that," Orilheart mused.

"Whoa! So does that mean Qugam here has three lives now?!" Saxfen finally exclaimed.

"I don't know. You guys really believe that thing?"

"Well, why would it lie?" Jix pondered.

"Yeah, that him back there sounded pretty serious."

"It's just a story. I wouldn't make much of it."

The group encamped under the vigilant eyes of their celestial escort. They were nigh. She could feel it. There remained but some short distance further.

The morning came, and the company was allured by the faint sound of what appeared to be melodic singing.

"What is that?" Saxfen said.

"Yeah, I hear the him, too."

"Should we see where it's coming from?" said Jix.

"Yeah, that sound. It sounds like faint singing, but I cannot tell where it's coming from. I wonder . . ."

Orilheart staggered not and sought the source of the faint, pleasant sound.

"This way!" she led.

They followed their guardian Vheilyel across the beauty of the deadly, streaked hills, and fortunately, there wasn't a single gegnazug in sight to challenge them. At last, they reached the fount of the faint singing. It was a lone man in the distance, sitting cross-legged with his back toward them, his arms resting with his palms opened toward the sky.

"The Fire him?" said Qugam.

They approached the sitting man as he sang, oblivious of the adventurers looking on in suspense. His hair was dark, bristled, and unkept. His beard was peppered with debris. There rolled tears down his cheeks, and he appeared completely absorbed in a sort of trance. He finally ceased and noticed the shadow of his audience behind him. He rose to his feet and appeared to address the company with a series of questions.

"O, what's he saying?" Jix said.

"Hang on, give me a minute."

Orilheart grabbed a woody shoot from a nearby shrub and instructed the man to take the shoot in her hand, break it into fourfold pieces, and eat it. The Fire Seer did not tarry. He consumed the woody twig and proceeded to query anew.

"I was saying, how long have you been standing there?" asked the Fire Seer.

"Are you, Greizeiros Esh?" Orilheart asked.

"Yes, I am come to these lands to search out the one who is called, the Fifth Lightning."

And suddenly, Orilheart could no longer refrain from her zest.

"WOW!" she erupted. "FIRE SEER! It's such a pleasure to finally meet you! You are so well admired where I'm from. That might! That valor! That triumph over foul evildoers!"

"Geesh, O, give the guy some space!" Jix chided.

"Oh, my God! Oh, my God! Oh, my God! It really is him, right here with us!" she continued to gush.

The boys were visibly stunned. They seemed uneasy and unsure how to respond. The Fire Seer himself became quite bashful that Orilheart would gush about him to such extent. Although greatly admired by the many winged Vheilyel, the famed Greizeiros Esh never quite became accustomed to the lavish praise poured upon him by the Celestial Ones.

"Greizeiros is highly favored by the Council of Daylight," Orilheart finally calmed. "And now he's been given the distinct honor of performing the sacred ceremony that will announce Saxfen as the promised Lightning! All the hiding, all the secrecy and patience, it's all finally paying off, and it all comes down to these incredible moments. We get to see the Decree of the Lightnings unfold before our very eyes! So, you can probably imagine why I get so giddy."

"I see," one studious Jix noted. "So why isn't your hair white like our friend, Snowhead, here?"

"Huh?" Greizeiros puzzled.

"Jix, that's silly," Orilheart responded. "Why would he have white hair like Saxfen? Greizeiros is from a completely different generation than his."

"Right, of course. And that would also explain why he looks so much older than Snowhead, too," Jix snarked, rolling his eyes.

"Yeah, we were expecting you to look like me, Fire Seer, but it's nice to finally meet you," Saxfen welcomed.

"Thank you, and you must be Saxfen of the Sevrinjiv, correct?"

"Yes."

He held the Shaifetnu boy's hands upon his own and humbly said, "The honor is all mine to stand before the very fulfillment of the ancient words of the Holy Vheilyel."

"So, have you been here in Tunjunsora this whole time?" Saxfen asked.

"Well," Greizeiros began. "I was first summoned to the lands most sacred, where they talked with me about the Legend of the Seven Lightnings. It's an ancient legend of some importance, so much so that the holy gods thought it necessary to transport me to their realm to discuss this matter with me in person."

***

Greizeiros proceeded to recount the first time he had set eyes upon that grand, celestial city, Yeilundor Athi. He thought upon the striking, colossal towers, whiter than the soaring clouds and whiter than the whitest, snowed summit he had ever seen. He recalled the radiant, swirling skies of splendid cerulean hue that appeared to throb with life as though the heavens were alive themselves. He recounted to his new friends how his feet were counted worthy to tread upon the polished, hollowed avenues of Holy Yeilundor Athi. There were intoxicating waves of melodic, stringed notes and pleasant scents from all directions as he journeyed through this sensory feast. The citizens, the Holy Vheilyel, adorned themselves in fine, costly garments, cleaner than the mountain frost.

All who passed by appeared to recognize the cherished seer, and they would smile and greet him like the greeting of an old friend. He intently observed the holy gods as they coursed about their matters, some carrying mysterious volumes, others carrying curious orbs, whereas others fancied the lustrous jewels in their hands.

There were voices slightly chattering throughout, which complemented the serene ambiance with a sense of restrained excitement. Some cordially conversed while others randomly broke into lovely songs in rich notes that had never reached Greizeiros' ears. Some would pause their curious business to wave at him in the friendly manner he became accustomed to.

"Is everyone this friendly all the time?" Greizeiros asked his escort.

The Fire Seer was amiably escorted by the somber and beautiful, Cinnia of the Eth.

"Yes, Greizeiros," Cinnia responded. "However, they are especially friendly today because we have a very distinguished guest in our midst. You see, you are rather well known amongst us, the Council of Daylight. It is an honor to have you join us this day."

Greizeiros openly marveled at the striking beauty and warmth he felt while pacing the hallowed avenues of Yeilundor Athi.

Ahead, children could be seen playing with a massive, winged beast. Its fearsome fangs playfully gnawed at the children as it subdued them to the ground.

"Cinnia, what is that beast playing with the children over there?"

"That is a celestial ekeru," she responded. "A spirit-beast with high intellect."

"Oh, I see. They look like lions. But our lions don't have wings, and their fur isn't white. It's more of a golden color."

"Oh, yes. We know lions, such amazing beasts. However, ekeru resemble many other beasts. The one before us is a War Ekeru, and they look like lions, whereas others are graced with great horns upon their heads. We call those Crown Ekeru. Others resemble your gallant falcon, and those are Scribe Ekeru. And also, there are the Sage Ekeru, these mostly busy themselves in the temples. And there are the Builder Ekeru, which are the eldest of all. And none are without the glory of their beautiful wings. And, unlike the beasts in your world, ekeru in our world speak many tongues."

Greizeiros gasped.

"This beast . . . speaks?"

Cinnia smiled, her dark, silky hair glimmering in the sunlight. She was pleased to share the wonders of Yeilundor Athi with Greizeiros.

"Perhaps you would be pleased to ride one of our ekeru later?" she replied.

"That would be incredible," Greizeiros agreed.

"Yes, they are quite enjoyable to ride and converse with. We do love our ekeru very much."

Greizeiros and Cinnia arrived at the stunning entrance of one of those breathtaking towers. Brisk, rejuvenating melodies, much sweeter than previously enjoyed, could be faintly heard inside.

"What delightful music, Cinnia. It's refreshing and dizzying to my heart, like the taste of sweet wine to my lips!" Greizeiros exclaimed.

"Yes, we do love music. Some of us travel far and wide in search of new sounds and strain ourselves diligently to create the lovely tones gracing your ears. We are very pleased with the gift of music from the hand of the Living One."

Within the ivory edifice, the halls were lit with vibrant lamps and elaborate, open windows, enabling the vivid, crisp rays to furnish the royal chambers with lucid lighting. There were other Vheilyel lounging upon nearby furnishings, and they conversed and enjoyed curious morsels while sipping unknown potions.

"Now, Greizeiros, don't be frightened, but I think you will be delighted to find that most of these people are here to get a glance of you. Sure, they have other matters to attend to, some very busy indeed, but they have heard the good tidings, how yet another Lightning is about to be unveiled. And what a relief to all of us that this is so!"

The somber Cinnia was moved at the thought of the wondrous things her own mouth had spoken. The many winged gods had longed to see with their own eyes the Decree of the Lightnings accomplished upon the Path of the Waking, a thing of legend for some, but to others, the reward of much-guarded patience.

The Fire Seer and his celestial escort finally reached an extravagant chamber where the Arch Vheilyel, Naerym-dul the Valor Sword, awaited upon his royal throne. He sipped from an elegant chalice but then rose to his feet upon seeing the lovely Cinnia and Greizeiros entering the room. The accompanying Vheilyel in the lavish chamber also rose to their feet.

The ancient hero welcomed his guest with a warm smile and cheerful laughter, "Greizeiros!" he shouted. "Welcome to Yeilundor Athi!"

This was Naerym-dul of the Order of Aedyr, those celestial kings and judges in matters pertaining to all the realms within the starry chasms of Ru'alameth. This was the highest and most venerated of the Daylight hierarchies. Thus, this highest of orders amongst the Vheilyel was also known as, the Ministry of Fates.

"Thank you, O great Naerym-dul. It is an honor to stand here in this incredible place and to walk amongst you," Greizeiros responded, respectfully bowing his head.

"We are greatly honored by your visit," Naerym-dul said. "You see, these are truly prestigious times that we have been brought into. Greizeiros, *the Greizeiros*, it appears you have heeded the call to coronate the Fifth Lightning!"

***

"Wait, what? To cora-what, the Fifth Lightning?" the boy Saxfen interrupted Greizeiros.

"Yes, that's why I'm here. I have been sent to announce before all the Vheilyel of heaven that you are indeed the Fifth Lightning. And the ceremony I am to accomplish is done to coronate you before them, with this very name. When you are coronated the Fifth Lightning, we will announce to the Council of Daylight and the Council of Night that the Decree of the Lightnings is truly and finally upon us."

"Wow, Snowhead, it turns out you're more and more important as the days go by!" Jix taunted.

"Coronation, like . . . a crown, him?" Qugam pried.

"Uh, I'm not sure what a 'crown him' is, but yes, I am here to place a crown upon Saxfen's head. This crown is that sacred name bestowed upon him, the Fifth Lightning," Greizeiros explained.

"A crown like . . . a king, him?" the curious Qugam continued.

"Yes, like a king. As a king has the power to command legions, so will the Fifth Lightning command the legions of the Daylight. Hence, a coronation."

"Oooh . . ." the boys marveled with intrigue.

"Well, yes," Orilheart chuckled. "What else would the Annunciation Ceremony be?"

"Wait, but why does it have to be you, Greizeiros?" said Saxfen. "Why couldn't Orilheart just coronate me and save us all this trouble?"

"Well, it didn't have to be me. But the honor is reserved for us, Shaifet-nu. And the ancient words must be fulfilled, that they of their own kin must bring the knowledge of the Lightnings to light, as the words of the holy gods say . . ."

One grand power to rectify the wrongs is bestowed.
Their brethren arise, they of their own kin shall herald their woe.

"And, so," Orilheart gleefully chimed. "The Lightnings must be announced upon the Path of the Waking as they have been announced upon the judgment halls of the Daylight."

The boys mused in fascination at the marvels explained before them. So much had been revealed and so soon. *What marvels awaited them next?*

"So, where was I . . ." Greizeiros continued with the account of his sojournings upon the celestial Yeilundor Athi.

The Fire Seer proceeded to recount of that dreamy, heavenly dwelling merely guessed at by the wild burnings deep within the hearts of mortals.

***

Elevated upon his ivory throne, the mighty Aedyr Vheilyel, who also is named, the Valor Sword, rose to his feet and welcomed his highly esteemed guest.

"Come, Greizeiros, share in our joy and our zeal for the wondrous things unfolding before us! After countless ages ensnared within their prisons, the time is upon us when the accursed Fathers of the Urth will finally be judged, and the thrones of their children will know a proper end. Woe, indeed, unto the Council of Night. The *Mystery of the Seven O'rahs* shall soon be unveiled!"

Naerym-dul then raised his opulent vessel into the air, "Let us celebrate our guest!"

The majestic court rose from their seats and raised their bleached, feathered wings in a sort of salute. They pointed their wings in the direction of Greizeiros and of Cinnia, who stood at the center of the chamber. They honored and saluted their guest in this manner and with clenched fists pressed against their chests.

"Cinnia, what are they doing?" the stunned Greizeiros whispered. "Am I supposed to say something?"

"They honor you, Greizeiros. We honor you."

Cinnia joined in the homage, and finally, Naerym-dul joined in as well.

Greizeiros knelt and lifted his palms toward heaven. He gently whispered to himself, "O Great and Dreadful Living One, truly you show your servant wonders without measure."

And so, after the warm welcome from the enthroned masters of Yeilundor Athi, the Fire Seer was escorted to another chamber, much larger than the throne room they occupied. It was a large place full of feasting and celebration.

There were curious dancings, and the fragrant air was accompanied by soothing, melodic cadences. There were sweet, enchanting melodies oscillated from the voices of stringed instruments and merry creatures not of Vheilyel origins.

Delicious scents emanated from hearty, steamy plates of unknown nourishments. And yet, there were no manservants or maids to furnish the guests with food and drink. The delicious beverages and delicacies the Vheilyel consumed simply replenished themselves, all of their own accord.

Greizeiros looked on in astonishment as his savory drink was replenished on its own after having sipped the final drop. He merely desired more of the delightful content, and it was as though someone or something had heard his thoughts. The honorable Naerym-dul noted the seer's audible gasps and playfully mused, "Do you marvel so greatly at the cup filling itself when your desire beckons?"

Greizeiros was seated beside the Aedyr Lord; therefore, his astonishment was not concealed. He respectfully answered, "Yes, my lord. We do not have such wonders in the lands where I am from. We require servants to come by and assist us. Or we may also get up from our seat and replenish our drink ourselves."

Naerym-dul continued, "Yes, you are correct. It is quite different here. I've never been to your world, but I know of its constellation and of its tragedies and people. Please eat and drink as much as you like. You are our most honored guest."

The surrounding court smiled and nodded as he timidly glanced across the table. They talked amongst themselves discretely, but Greizeiros understood they were conversing about him. He noted the hint of fascination in their eyes when he peeped at their faces.

Naerym-dul sensed his uneasiness, "Greizeiros, in due time, you will understand why you are so special to us and how we would wage great wars if it meant keeping you safe. So, please, feel at ease. You are amongst friends, my dear friend."

The kind words of the celestial king assured him. The startled seer felt well-favored and beloved. And after sharing many laughs and pleasant talks, they concluded their meal. Cinnia then rose from her seat.

"Now, how about those ekeru? How about we ride into the sunset?" she said.

Greizeiros' face lit with surprise, but he wrestled within himself to conceal his zest. After all, these were the Divine Ones from heaven, and the utmost reserve should be observed, he reasoned. He took one last sip of the delightful drink and rose to his feet. He timidly glanced at Naerym-dul, and a warm nod met his eyes. The accompanying Vheilyel masters lightly smiled and nodded in approval as well.

Greizeiros and Cinnia made their way down the towering, ivory fortress, and the seer was unable to restrain his prying, "Cinnia, do you know what the honorable Naerym-dul meant when he said 'in due time, you will understand why you are so special to us?'"

"Well, Naerym-dul could be referring to a number of things, actually. But I believe he was referring to your calling at hand, how you will traverse the ocean of sparkling stars to a faraway place. And from there, you will announce that the Fifth Lightning is indeed amongst us. This is truly a special honor, Greizeiros. You see, there are many amongst us who would relish the opportunity to avenge the honor of the Daylight in the manner you are sent to accomplish. This royal calling bestowed upon you will become clearer as you progress in your journey. But, for now, it must remain concealed from your heart, and this is for your own sake and safety."

Greizeiros shivered at the mysterious things his celestial companion spoke of. Cinnia noted his troubled thoughts, "Have peace in your heart and wage war to retain it, Greizeiros. You are our champion, elected and commissioned for these very things. We observe in envy the crown of honor that is yours, and yours alone!"

The astonished seer and his lovely escort approached the royal quarters of a slumbering War Ekeru. Cinnia gently petted the beast, and it arose from its sleep, "Cinnia, why all the commotion to disturb my slumber?" the ekeru asked.

"Kallata-ruthol, I'd like to introduce you to our special guest. This is Greizeiros Esh, the Fire Seer. He's come to receive a Decree at our hand. It is our great delight to deliver the Holy Decree, and so we honor him this day. And we would like you to join us in our celebration."

The great beast arose and respectfully bowed its bleached mane and feathered wings upon gazing at the seer.

"A seer of the Living One amongst us in this place and the gleaming rays of an unfolding decree, this is very good," the War Ekeru said.

Cinnia then motioned the Fire Seer to mount the majestic ekeru, and so he carefully mounted Kallata-ruthol and wondered whether Cinnia would come along.

"Cinnia, will you be coming with us?" he asked.

"Why, yes. I shall return momentarily."

The thrilled seer's beautiful escort dashed toward the rim of the sky palace and flung herself into the depths below. Kallata-ruthol and Greizeiros could hear the faint roars of a new ekeru nearby. And then, without warning, Cinnia swooshed above them, mounted upon the colorless coat of another fierce War Ekeru of her own.

"Come, Greizeiros!" she shouted. "Let us soar upon the heavens!"

Greizeiros and Kallata-ruthol then plunged likewise into the lovely, open skies of vibrant, cerulean hue. The regal beast pounced and flung its massive wings. The deep, resonant sound of its roar echoed in the heavens like the mighty thunders of Zumkelles.

Twain, majestic ekeru soared above luscious, verdant fields and amongst lofty, green summits and striking monoliths. Ahead, there were nine other silver ekeru watching over a group of children as they laughed and played in an open field. The reposing War Ekeru playfully roared as if to greet their brethren soaring above them upon those lucid skies. The children laughed and pointed, and they waved as they hurriedly mounted each a beast of their own.

The company of ekeru made haste to rendezvous in the pristine sky, and they swayed and jestingly drifted into each other's way.

"Hey, look out! You almost knocked me over!" Greizeiros exclaimed.

The playful child laughed and taunted, but to Greizeiros' dismay, the towering water spouts of the Thrundanah Sea suddenly came into view! Great, swirling pillars of crisp seawater ascended unto mighty clouds as the ferocious ekeru fearlessly scrambled to meet them. Greizeiros took heart in the company of his new friends, and he reached with his hand to feel the cool, ascending waters of the curious fountains upon his fingertips. The company freely soared amongst the spiraling water towers which cleaved unto the heavens. And the whole vista seemed to Greizeiros Esh, like the bizarre wanderings of a vivid dream from which one does not wish to awake from.

***

The boys carefully listened as they reflected over Greizeiros' unbelievable story, savoring what it would be like to mount a snow-colored, winged ekeru. And those water fountains! How does swirling water soar to the very heavens in such manner? They quietly wondered to themselves in astonishment.

"Yes, it was incredible; it was like a dream, but I was wide awake the entirety of the time, and I was truly seeing these things!" Greizeiros explained to his friends as they pondered his tale intently.

The three boys were visibly stunned at the grand, celestial place Greizeiros described.

". . . and that's how I came to visit these lands, my friends. The Holy Vheilyel summoned me, and they charged me to search out the Fifth Lightning and to do the honor of coronating him," he explained.

"Amazing, him," said Qugam.

"Wow, yeah, they sure seem to like you up there, huh?" Saxfen chimed.

"So . . . couldn't they, oh, I don't know, lend you one of those ekeru creatures? You know, for safe travels?" Jix chimed.

"I'm afraid not, but truly, they are wonderful companions," Greizeiros responded.

"Yes," Orilheart agreed. "I'm quite certain those ekeru were already committed to the care of the children entrusted to them, so sneaking off with one of them would not be a good idea. And, besides, they wouldn't come with you anyway, even if you asked them nicely. They'd probably just snarl and laugh at you."

The company strolled along the elevated heights of the Forbidden Streaks, where the winged sorrelum soared high upon the pale, roseate skies and where the castaway gegnazugs prowled below. They laughed and conversed as the day dwindled into faint twilight, and the lambent rays of vermilion from the setting sun pleasingly complemented the luminous arc above.

They had settled camp, and there came an accompanying sea of sparkling stars, silently looking on as the Annunciation of the Fifth Lightning took place over the crackling voice of their campfire embers.

Greizeiros, the famed Fire Seer, commenced the Annunciation Ceremony by uttering the solemn words he had prepared.

"Saxfen of the Sevrinjiv, I present you before that Dreadful and Worthy One and before all the Holy Vheilyel that serve him night and day. I present you, O beloved Shaifetnu, a weapon forged before the worlds came forth, a vessel crafted to execute judgment upon that which you were born to rule. Therefore, O Saxfen of the Sevrinjiv, elect of God, take upon you now that sacred crown of oil ordained for your head this blessed day."

Greizeiros raised his arm above Saxfen's silver, bristled locks. And upon his hand, there was a worn, leather pouch that the seer carried with him, reserved for this very hour. He poured an oily content upon the Shaifetnu boy's head, and it slowly dripped down his cheeks. The Fire Seer continued.

"Take upon you now, the name feared greatly by the servants of darkness, the name that strikes terror upon the hearts of the sons of wickedness, for I announce before the heavens this day that the Decree of the Lightnings is upon us! Go forth now in this might of heaven's power bestowed, O Lightning Bolt of God."

There was a brief moment of silence. Only the crackling voice of the fire embers could be heard. No splendid, mighty sign accompanied the words of the Fire Seer. Only solemn quietness came forth in that moment.

Saxfen finally said, "Well, I don't know what just happened or what any of that means, but I feel really good."

He turned his sight to his friends, and to his own surprise, there were tears in their eyes. He hurried to their aid, "Qugam, are you okay? What's wrong?"

He didn't respond, and neither would Jix answer him a word. No usual, taunting jests were offered or bursts of laughter; they simply sobbed to themselves quietly.

"Oh, come on, Qugam, stop that!" He then looked to Orilheart, "Orilheart? You too?"

Orilheart quietly sobbed as she discreetly covered her face from Saxfen's prying eyes.

"Greizeiros, what's wrong with them? What did you do?"

"Saxfen, give them some space. They cannot help themselves. Their minds may not know why they are sobbing, but their spirit knows. Their spirit knows of the great joy and of the great wonder that just took place. You see, this coronation is a sign of the long-awaited age when the Seven Lightnings should finally be revealed. One by one, they must be announced, thereby fulfilling the words of the ancient Decree. Now, is the fifth one unveiled. Now, they arise and will satisfy a thirst found deep within every living creature. This thirst, is a thirst for justice, and the unveiling of the Lightnings speaks and resonates to the innermost parts of our being."

"I . . . I don't know what happened, him," Qugam finally replied. "I was just standing here, and all these hims just started pouring down my face."

"Okay, I'm alright," Orilheart chimed. "I just needed a moment. The crowning of the Lightnings is a very special moment for us."

"Yeah, I don't know what that was all about, but I feel so refreshed," Jix said.

"Fire Seer, when you said 'coronation,' I was expecting something different. I can't say I'm disappointed, though. I feel so good right now," said Saxfen.

"Good, the crown you received today may not be a crown of gold like you may have imagined, but rest assured, it is very much a crown. Soon, the ancient enemies of the Daylight will bow their power to yours, and they will plead with you for their lives. Now, let us rest, Saxfen. Tomorrow begins your first day as the coronated Fifth Lightning."

The weary neufs enjoyed the deepest, most peaceful slumber in their lives that night. Saxfen had never slept so well, to his remembrance, either. They slept in the bliss and serenity of a comforted babe in the arms of a loving mother.

And so, Saxfen's first day as the coronated Lightning Bolt of God had arrived. With the warmth of the crisp morning rays upon his face, the young Shaifetnu awoke to the playful smile of his dear friend, Orilheart.

"Geez, O. How long have you been sitting there spying on me?" Saxfen asked as he rubbed his sleepy eyes.

"Oh, long enough," she responded. "Hey, I have some friends I'd like you to meet. We are so excited to be selected to accompany the Fifth Lightning on his journey! You are going to love them."

"Friends? What kind of friends are we talking about here?" Jix yawned.

"Oh, they're the best. They're just like me. Only, we live really far from each other, so we don't see each other often. Actually, now that you mention it, it's been a while."

"Wow! More many winged hims like you! That's incredible, him!" an astonished Qugam exclaimed.

"Yup, they're on their way. Now that Greizeiros has performed the ceremony, they are released to meet us here. You'll have to excuse the red one, though. He's still somewhat of a novice. Actually, I think this may be his very first Mah'seyiud."

"His Ma-what?" Saxfen questioned.

"His very first Mah'seyiud. Last I remember, Wolsage was still a Learner."

"Yes, but what exactly is a him?" Qugam pried.

"Oh, right. A Mah'seyiud is like an assignment that we must carry out. Like me being right here with you. This journey is my Mah'seyiud, and Saxfen is what we call, my Panni."

"Oh, okay, that makes sense now. So, I guess a Learner is a student then, right?"

"Correct, Saxfen."

"Whoa, a student, like in a school of many winged hims?"

"Uh, what else would that be?" Orilheart pondered.

"Wait a minute. Really, O? They're sending a newbie to come along?" Jix scoffed. "For a minute there, I thought we were up against terrible monsters from other worlds and such. Oh, and not to mention that terrifying Drukijaken from our own. I guess I can sigh in relief now, knowing it's not as bad as I thought it was."

"Yes, well, as ill-advised as it may seem," Greizeiros responded. "The Living One, in his wisdom, proudly pits the weak against the strong, the low against the high, and the feeble against the terrible. He does this in a sort of taunt and mockery of those who think it wise to oppose Him."

"Like he . . . toys with his enemies?" Jix asked.

"Yes, that's exactly what he does," Orilheart replied. "The Living One laughs at his adversaries and humiliates them to make examples of them. He tramples the wrathful and haughty, and he thrills us with his mighty acts, and we applaud him for it. So, you can probably get a sense of why I get so excited to be a part this Mah'seyiud!"

Orilheart playfully broke out in graceful dance to melodies no one else could hear. She swayed and twirled and hummed to herself to unknown song, seemingly unfazed by the puzzled looks over her random spur.

"There she goes. She's doing her him again," Qugam said.

They wondered and stared at Orilheart's bliss.

"Ahem . . . we're still here, O," Jix waved.

"Yes, I'm doing my . . . him . . . again," Orilheart smiled.

"Wolsage, Starrelos, Eluryn," she gently chanted in song. "Water, tender tree, and snow. Wolsage, Starrelos, Eluryn . . . water, tender tree, and snow!"

She continued in her blissful whirling while Greizeiros cautiously smothered the dying campfire.

"Right this way, everyone!" Orilheart giddily led the way. "I saw them. I saw all three of my friends. One by the lake waters, one by a tender tree, and one in the snow."

"You saw them?" Jix challenged. "Where did they go? Did they forget something? Are they coming back?"

"No, silly, not in person. I saw them in a vision. I saw them in my mind. These are the places we will meet them," she explained.

"I see," Saxfen responded. "Can't we just wait for them here? The nearest snow is on Mount Tanlish, where the deadly gethwis live."

"No, actually, we can't just linger here and wait. It's far too dangerous for that now. We have to keep moving."

"Uh, hello, Saxfen, we have Orilheart him with us," Qugam said.

"Yeah, I guess you're right. And you have escaped death twice now in the past few days already. What could go wrong?" the young Shaifetnu reasoned.

"Saxfen, my dear, when I say it's not safe here anymore, I don't mean we are in danger from wild creatures or anything of the sort," Orilheart continued. "Although true, there are dangerous creatures around us. What I actually mean is that, now that you have been announced here on the Path of the Waking as the official Fifth Lightning, set out to bring doom upon the Seven Thrones of Ebelsaddon, I think you can imagine the Urth are not too happy with you right now, or me for that matter. So, what that means, as happy as you may have noticed me these past few days, is that there are powerful creatures, not of this world, sent forth to oppose us and to kill us all if they have the opportunity."

The boys stared at Orilheart in utter astonishment,

"They're . . . hunting us down, O?" Jix finally responded.

"Yup, this appears to be the situation we are in."

***

The young Enos abruptly exclaimed and disrupted his father's story,

"Wow, Papa, I'm so glad we are friends with the many winged hims, and we know so many of them!"

"Yes, Son. We are very fortunate to be amongst the few entrusted with this honor of walking alongside the Holy Vheilyel and to freely converse with them. And the stories were true. It was always said we would once again walk amongst them, as in the days before the Great Vexation. And here we are, Son. However, this honor should not be taken lightly, no matter how good of friends we are with them. Do you understand, Enos?"

"Yes, Papa."

"What did I mean by what I said?"

Enos paused to respond.

"Um . . . I think you mean that their friendship is a gift, and we should take care of it."

"Correct. These are wonderful times that we are living in; full of peace between the Shaifetnu and Vheilyel and full of happiness other people can only dream of. But understand this, Enos, it will not always remain this way. There will yet come a new rebellion, a new Apostasy, as they are called, where a new generation must be tried like a furnace tries the most precious gold. So, take very good care of this gift that's been given to you, okay?"

"Yes, Papa."

Saxfen laughed in his friendly manner and continued his story as they made their way into the stunning chambers of the snow-ridden structure, Oclyd Tower.

***

The following day after the Annunciation Ceremony, the group had risen early and now their hearts were set on searching out Orilheart's three celestial friends. The Fire Seer was filled with joy after having fulfilled his charge, but the time had come for him to part ways.

"Well, everyone," he said. "It has been a great joy of my life to be gifted the opportunity to meet you. It has been an honor to coronate Saxfen and to be a part of ushering in the due justice that the works of our God have been eagerly yearning for."

"Greizeiros, the great Greizeiros, the pleasure has been mine to finally meet you," Orilheart blushed. "We shall meet again, and hopefully not under perilous circumstances as these."

"Yes, thank you for meeting with us, Fire him," Qugam said.

"Thank you, Greizeiros," said Saxfen. "What amazing things you have shared with us. And to think, someday, I too, could ride on the back of a winged ekeru!"

"So where are you headed now?" Jix wondered.

"As for me, I must travel back to my home, where there awaits for me a foul beast that must be confronted. You see, I too, must face a Drukijaken of my own."

The boys marveled in admiration, greatly desiring to know more of the bizarre creatures and peoples he had met throughout the zenith above, far upon foreign stars and distant planes. The beloved Fire Seer blessed them and said farewell. He then gracefully strolled away into the forthcoming pages of the volumes written of him.

CHAPTER 8

In Matters of the Realm of Decrees

At last, the Shaifetnu boy of the Sevrinjiv family had been coronated with that forgotten, ancient name, the Fifth Lightning, and he had been properly announced in the sight of the many winged gods. This wholesome deed by the revered, Greizeiros Esh, was a bold witness against the damnable Seven Thrones of Ebelsaddon. For therein had the seer proclaimed that the Decree of the Lightnings was indeed upon them after bygone ages had transpired in a veil of secrecy and silence.

And now, Saxfen and his three closest friends would gather three additional Servants of the Daylight, appointed to herald the words of the sacred Decree unto completion. Nonetheless, be it Saxfen or another more worthy than he, the Council of Daylight had vowed to never rest until the Decree of the Lightnings was fully accomplished upon Ru'alameth.

"Well, there it is! The lake I saw in my vision," Orilheart said, waving toward the roseate waters ahead. "Let's set up camp here."

The group enkindled a fire on the shores of the nearby Ruddlelet Lake, and they nibbled on what food remained. They laughed and conversed, but their musings were interrupted by the sudden gust of a violent wind. Their campfire was snuffed out, and in stillness they sat, all of them.

"What was that?!" Jix whispered.

"Oh no! Is it the sky him?! Has it come back for revenge?" Qugam feared.

"Steady, guys. Let's not panic," said Orilheart.

The company carefully gazed about for any sign of life, but nothing was out of place. No vengeful, red gylth in the sky, no ravening ujorgs, and not even the kirok birds seemed startled by the unannounced gust. But then, the urgent plea of an unknown voice shouted from afar, "Orilheart! Is that you!?"

The voice came from a stranger in the distance, swatting his clothes and hastily approaching the camp.

"Wow, it is you! I got here as fast as I could! Is everyone okay?" the stranger asked.

"Wolsage!" Orilheart shouted as she leaped off her seat and greeted her friend with a warm embrace.

Orilheart studied Wolsage, whom she had not seen in many years. She had missed that wavy, orange hair, and those gentle, emerald eyes.

"Everyone, I'd like you to meet my friend whom I've been telling you about. This is Wolsage of the Eth! As mentioned, please be kind. This is his first assignment, and it's a big one."

"Thank you, Orilheart, but it's Wolsage of the Learners . . . still," he corrected. "I've yet to earn the title of Eth alongside my name."

"Oh, I see. Very well, then. Everyone, please welcome my friend, Wolsage, Learner of the Eth!"

The group exchanged greetings and welcomed their new comrade in their quest for the stolen Shaifetnu harp.

"So, it's an Eth class, huh? Like Orilheart, perhaps?" queried the whiskered Jix.

"Well, not quite. I have yet to accomplish a great deed to be awarded that worthy name of the 'Eth' Vheilyel. Hence, it is merely 'Learner of the Eth' for the time being."

"Oh, I get it. So, if we fail in retrieving the lost harp, you will fail to receive your name as well?"

"Yeah, that sounds about right. And, besides, Orilheart has much more experience than I do, and she could definitely show me a few tricks. I wouldn't dare compare myself to the noble Eth; and I stand far less than such a one as Orilheart."

"I still can't believe you were selected for this assignment, Wolsage," Orilheart chimed. "This is a very important mission, and the peril is horrendous."

"Yes, I can hardly believe it myself, but this is what was determined," Wolsage explained. "When the contentious Bogedoth heard Eluryn was selected to protect the Fifth Lightning, they were deeply distressed, and they objected without relenting. It was embarrassing. Eluryn is a titan of a warrior, and she was responsible for the healing of the broken Akaz'ath, which saved countless Learners from certain doom. But that was so long ago, right? And this is, after all, one of the seven Lightnings we are supposed to protect. So, it's completely fair and appropriate to select Eluryn.

"But the Bogedoth insisted that there must be balance, and their contention prevailed. They cited a long list of reasons and provisions from the *D'ath Pithgam*. And finally, they agreed to appoint a Learner, so that there may be balance. And guess who they went with?"

This he spoke referring to the heated contentions upon the judgment halls of the Vheilyel, where the adversaries of the Daylight are permitted to present their grievances. There, they present their disputations, fiercely contending the sacred ordinances governing the Dark Kingdom. Thus they are given power upon the judgment halls to invoke the ancient treaties inscribed within the *D'ath Pithgam*. And Aedyr Judges are compelled to be impartial to their voice.

"Well, that's just fantastic. I guess that's supposed to balance the scales a bit?" Jix scoffed.

"Okay, whatever the reason, I'm so glad you can join us," Orilheart said.

"Yes, thank you for being here," said Saxfen.

"The honor is truly mine, Shaifetnu Saxfen, Lightning Bolt of God."

The group dismantled their camp and agreed to head east, where their next rendezvous was said to take place.

"Sorry, Wolsage him, we're out of kirok hims for you to ride," Qugam said.

"Oh, don't mind me. I'll have one come to us," he replied.

The newest member of the company raised his hands to the air and sang a line in an unknown tongue. The resonating tone in his voice reached the ears of nearby kirok birds, and three of them hurried to the source of this lovely sound. The kirok birds assessed the company and cautiously approached the beckoning melody. They felt the warm, cordial presence of Orilheart and Wolsage, and casually lingered amongst them as they randomly pecked at the ground.

"Well, I guess, that solves that," Jix said.

"Oh, great! You know how to call them already," Orilheart exclaimed. "It took me forever to do that!"

"Yes, I've been pushing myself in my studies and training, and it looks like all the hard work has been in preparation for this very hour. Yet, I have much, much to learn in the Way of the Soulshift," Wolsage replied, as he mounted the studious kirok bird that had come to his side. "Alright, Orilheart, lead the way."

***

The young, orange-haired Learner was flattered to have been selected for this mightiest of deeds. Oh, the glory to be attained! Though a mere Learner of the Daylight, he would be hailed and remembered for generations to come if found triumphant. Nonetheless, he could not help but feel angst over his inexperience; how it could make him a disappointment in the end, or worse, put somebody in danger. Or even worse, put Orilheart in danger! These are the things that troubled the mind of the young Learner. But the Decree of the Daylight had gone forth, and this journey had now become his own path, and his own solemn duty. This was now his sacred lot upon the path of the many winged gods.

His troubled mind wandered unto the instruction most ardent he had labored in so devoutly. He recalled those punishing consultations in the fleeting moments preceding his commissioning to the side of the Fifth Lightning.

There came the stern, earnest voice of his counselor echoing in his head.

"It is not about strength," the voice challenged. "It is not about power. It is not about size or even numbers. Wolsage of the Learners, in all your perils and in all your strivings, it will always come down to this one word . . . *valor*.

"When the adversary is before you, when the obscene forms they present themselves in, are before you, you must *know* to retain your resolve. And yet, it is not enough to know. Also, in that moment, you *must* retain your resolve. You must retain . . . your valor. For when you forfeit your valor, my dear Learner, you shall enter grave woe, the peril of becoming seduced and consumed by the *Shadow Terror* itself. Now . . . strike at me, I command you!"

At once, the novice Wolsage drew his essence blade, but to his dismay, it flickered and strained to remain drawn like the flickering of a lamp void of oil. He charged, nonetheless, and attacked the demanding presence before him. But his staggering weapon was not sufficient in his pursuit. The fierce combatant he faced skillfully quelled all his attempts with a blade of his own.

Unlike the common creature of mortal flesh and blood, the Vheilyel did not make use of weapons forged of ore. Instead, they commanded Ru'alameth and the elements heeded their thoughts and their voice. Also, they commanded their own essence, and it became the searing blades and shields that burned upon their arms.

Wolsage took to the sky with his six powerful wings and flung a raining host of piercing, wind blades upon his opponent. But the clever gambit of deadly blades did not land a single scratch upon the challenger master he faced.

"Casting them at me will not help your cause, Wolsage," his opponent taunted.

In a desperate, irate burst, Wolsage light-drifted from above and smote with all his remaining strength. But to his disappointment, his ambitious attack was effortlessly deterred. His chest was then repelled by the sudden strike of a counterkick. The flickering blade finally gave away and dissolved. Wolsage's opponent light-drifted to his side and comforted the injured youth. He extended his right arm in a warm gesture to assist.

"Come, you are improving every time we meet," said the victor Vheilyel.

"Oooouch!! Iobrenn'yon, take it easy on me. Are you trying to kill me?!" Wolsage exclaimed. "That kick to the chest was a little uncalled for, don't you think?"

He reached for the extended hand of his counselor, Iobrenn'yon of the Order of Dathmahjen, those celestial keepers of divine wisdom who serve the Daylight as counselors, advocates, and scribes. This was the Order that faithfully upheld the exalted office of the Ministry of Knowledge throughout the stars, which Order was known for the golden etchings upon their flesh.

To Wolsage's surprise, there came lone applause and a familiar voice that appeared to taunt the aching Learner.

"Well done, Wolsage. At this rate, we know exactly who to count on if the Urth decided to revolt tomorrow."

"Ruvaen! Peace of the Daylight," Wolsage greeted. "What are you doing here? And yes, of course, you can always count on me to defend our beloved city of Neuvundiel."

Their guest was clad in the onyx battle plates and ebon cloaks of the Daylight war legions.

"Peace of the Daylight, I come from Highest Ofandynth," Ruvaen said, raising his hooded head.

Wolsage and the Dathmahjen Master suddenly gazed at their guest in constrained amazement at the mere mention of this, most sacred of worlds in all Ru'alameth. They closely heeded his words.

"Wow, really? Well, what is this about? Am I in trouble?" Wolsage asked.

"You have been summoned to appear before the High Tribunals of S'hyeru Kadash, your first Mah'seyiud awaits you," Ruvaen solemnly announced.

The Learner became visibly perplexed that his first Mah'seyiud from the Council of Daylight should be awarded . . . so soon? Did they really think he was ready? Was he worthy to proceed? He glanced at Iobrenn'yon for approval.

The ancient master nodded, "You have worked hard. I have full confidence in you."

"It has been an honor to train under the great Dathmahjen Master, Iobrenn'yon, himself. I won't let you down, master," Wolsage assured.

The youth said his farewell and parted ways from his counselor. He was beaming with zeal, yet anxious to have been selected for his first assignment. *But why send Ruvaen? And why so soon?* He thought to himself, *There's still so much to learn.*

He walked alongside Ruvaen, pondering to himself and also out loud at what his first Mah'seyiud could be.

As the longtime friends conversed and journeyed unto the lands of Highest Ofandynth, there opened before them those celestial passageways, so named, the Star Sharveths of the Halls of Ru'alameth. These resembled the circular face of rippling water upon entry. And they served as immense corridors conjoining the impossibly distant worlds as one, unified plane. These are they which Orilheart had spoken of with the Fifth Lightning and her beloved, whiskered neufs.

The Vheilyel made regular use of these passageways effectively to reemerge unto far-placed, mystic landscapes. They knew the paths well, which paths to favor and which to shun. To mere mortals, the grand Halls of Ru'alameth seemed in their eyes impossible gulfs never to be fully breached or explored. But to the many winged gods, all worlds were unified, like the lavish entryways of a single, cosmic house, and the far-placed worlds were like mere chambers within this house.

Bizarre, yet approachable beasts of all sorts could be seen in these voyages. There were upright beings that stared but remained unfazed by the sudden emergence of the many winged Vheilyel upon their lands. Dazzling, brilliant suns ruled the day in some worlds, whereas in others, there ruled over them the faint, comforting twilight of fading elder stars. Luminous streams of starry constellations shifted from one zenith to another as they sojourned, and thus, no heaven was alike. Wondrous architecture and ruins concealing vast histories from bygone peoples, came into view upon forgotten lands.

On certain occasions, the nearby beings would wave and smile at twain wanderers. Some there were of these strange creatures and simple peoples along the way who had become accustomed to the comforting presence of the Holy Vheilyel. Their dwellings, it appeared, had become a regular course for some of these. Others, indeed, knew them well and had befriended the Vheilyel on some accounts.

And twain sojourners had agreed to deny themselves the comfort of traversing upon Vheilyel chariots. For if they so desired, there could come to their aid, Water Seffinahs, as they are so named, which could transport them across the chasms with much ease. These transport vessels of the Vheilyel resembled sizeable orbs of shifting water, but with them came the risk of exposing their location to the Urth kingdom. And this could not be risked, for this was a journey of utmost significance and they would conceal their distinct signature to the best of their ability.

At some point, the strain of the prolonged journey through the rippling passageways wearied the celestial drifters, and so they were compelled to rest and recover themselves.

"Okay, I'm beat. Let's rest here for a moment," Wolsage suggested.

The friends rested underneath the fragrant leaves of an oxabbey tree that crowned the dome of a verdant hill. They overlooked the busied arms of one Balaalt giant, wholly engrossed in the craft of its massive hands. It appeared to be crafting nets of braided fabrics or skins.

"It's too bad you can't come along. It sure would be nice to go on my first Mah'seyiud with the Omen Breaker himself," Wolsage said.

"I yet remain, Ruvaen, your humble servant. We must not permit our vanity to consume us."

"So, you really don't know what this Mah'seyiud is about, huh?"

"No, the details have also been kept from me. It must be truly important for them to keep this concealed to this degree."

"Maybe," Wolsage pondered. "They're afraid of what would happen if I knew what it's about. Or maybe they're afraid of what could happen to you if you knew the purpose at hand."

"Well, they're certainly being cautious. I can discern that much," Ruvaen replied as he nibbled on a tasty morsel he had brought along.

"You don't think it's . . . dangerous, do you?"

"My guess is probably not, why would they send a novice to an overly perilous Mah'seyiud?

"I don't know. To test my worth?"

"Probably not."

"To be . . . the strategic bait!?"

"I suppose we will find out soon enough."

"Well, you have to agree something is not right, Ruvaen. Why are they sending a Sabbayoth and not an Eth to summon me before the judgment halls? And we may not even board a Sky Seffinah?"

This he said referring to Water Seffinahs, which also are named Sky Seffinahs.

"They would not say a reason," Ruvaen insisted.

The friends shared a few laughs and continued their journey for some time yet, until finally they had arrived. Appearing into full view, there came those splendid vistas and glorious avenues gracing the sacred lands of Highest Ofandynth. They beheld clusters of hovering spheres made of crisp, sparkling water that gleamed with the lucid radiance of a turquoise sky. In the distant haze, there walked winged giants bearing striking, golden crowns upon their heads. There could be seen orderly companies of ferocious War Ekeru.

Also, there soared the dignified snouts of the feathered Soggseraf, bearing magnificent horns upon their heads. Their massive, elongated frames soared underneath the gentle rays of threefold suns. And the suns radiated a soft, blue hue most pleasing to the eyes.

Before them, there finally stood that cardinal city of the Daylight kingdoms, that majestic city of the High Tribunals—that most worthy city—S'hyeru Kadash.

Throughout the city's venues and upon the vibrant, turquoise skies, there hurried the busied Servants of the Daylight, vanishing and emerging by the skill of their light-driftings. There could be seen the studious Scribe Ekeru and other articulate, celestial beings, also avian in semblance. And there were colossal towers, pristine monuments, and living fixtures.

There were elaborate memorials constructed in honor of ancient sages and valiant warriors. There were lovely, living fountains that appeared to sing in rich, consoling notes. Sweet melodies and pleasant, floral aromas reigned in all directions. Warm, clean rays ceaselessly descended from the cloudless, turquoise skies, gracing the grand capitol city of the High Tribunals.

"So, how long do we have?" Wolsage asked.

"It appears we are one arch revolving of Iddan and three lesser revolvings early," Ruvaen replied.

By this, they referred to the Stellar Revolvings of the Prime Iddan, which the Holy Vheilyel observed to measure time as a sort of Master Clock from which all other time was inferred throughout the Daylight kingdoms.

"Alright, let's find a place to lodge."

They made their way to the cozy quarters of a nearby banquet hall. They joined in as fellow Vheilyel from all corners of the heavens conversed and shared their heroic deeds with one another.

There were empty seats at a table in the depths of the splendid hall, and they settled in. The two listened in fascination of the grand exploits and wild ventures their fellow pilgrims boasted and of their pressing matters upon the hollowed grounds of the High Tribunal City.

"It's a great honor and a gift from the High One," one stranger exclaimed. "To be sent unto the mountains of Gloinurvesh. Indeed, we are prepared. The cunning fiends therein shall not survive our inquisition. Numerous rebukes have been made, and now . . . for the retribution!"

The stranger raised his cup in the air to the roars of his companions.

"Well, our party is sent to the oceans of Voodor Nygol," said another. "Where the great beast Hok'dolddrun awaits us! The citizens of Zorjen have suffered long enough in its reign of terror, and now the Daylight must intervene!"

His fellows likewise roared at the raising of his cup.

The table looked on at Wolsage, who remained timidly silent in the midst of the jubilant feastings and celestial merriment. The fierce battalions awaited as they gazed at Wolsage and Ruvaen.

"Ahem, I think they expect us to share our commission," Ruvaen whispered.

Wolsage indulged the guests, "Uh, we do not yet know our Mah'seyiud."

The table then turned away from the bashful Wolsage and returned to their boasts and festivities.

Slightly embarrassed that they could not rival the grand feats of them all, the two maintained their upmost reserve, hoping not to be queried a second time.

"So where are you two from?" one at length pried.

"Us? We are from Hyirius-nu, the place of the legendary city, Neuvundiel T'hem," Wolsage responded.

The inquiring stranger was the beautiful Arryndel. Her wavy, golden hair complemented the golden cup in the Lerner's hand, and her warm smile made them feel welcomed and at ease. She briefly paused as she sipped from her cup, "Oh yes, I have heard of Neuvundiel. That's where Vhalyun, the Slayer of Ashes, held off the detestable armies of the Muuwol and defeated the foul Ghrakarhegg," she replied.

"Yes! Correct, that's the place," said Ruvaen. "The noble lands of Hyirius-nu will miss our beloved Wolsage as he duteously journeys on his first Mah'seyiud."

"Oh, is that right? Congratulations. Wolsage, is it?"

"Thank you, and yes, Wolsage of the Learners. And this is my longtime friend, Ruvaen, of the Sabbayoth."

Upon the head of their lovely guest, there rested that distinct adornment of the Oracles of the Daylight. *That beautiful crown of wreathed gold and those blue colors on her clothes. Could that be?* The youths wondered to themselves.

"It is nice to meet you. I am Arryndel of the Sodd."

Yes, they were right! This was indeed that distinguished, golden crown of the Order of Sodd. The youth paused and looked on in admiration. They had never met a Sodd in person, as the Ministry of Oracles was known to be quite reserved. They mostly attended to the matters of the temples and were sworn to secrecy, thereby guarding the Daylight Decrees entrusted to them.

"What an honor, a Sodd Vheilyel amongst us," Ruvaen said.

"Yes, what mysterious and profound things must be concealed in your heart! It truly is a pleasure to converse with you today. We've never met a Sodd Vheilyel in all our voyages," Wolsage said.

"Well, thank you. And yes, the mysteries concealed within me are just that, concealed, until the time appointed for their unveiling comes," Arryndel responded.

The Sodd were not oft seen mingling with others, for they were primarily absorbed in their service. These were fervidly given to the study and contemplation of profound revelations, old and new—the Decrees of the Daylight past, present, and Decrees yet to come. And when the appointed time should arrive, this Ministry of Oracles would sing upon the temples their revelations, infused with divine ordinances and epiphanies. These alone were entrusted to minister the wisdom of that hidden realm so named, the Realm of Decrees, where all knowledge of the past and future dwelt.

According to the Dathmahjen Masters, all knowledge of the past and the future resided within the Realm of Decrees, and the Order of Sodd was the sole, priestly authority appointed to distribute its secrets when they would arise to present their much anticipated, Hymnals of Decrees.

"So, what is your advice for my Learner friend, Arryndel, as he ventures forth on his first Mah'seyiud?" Ruvaen politely asked.

"Well, you say this is your first Mah'seyiud, correct?" she considered. "I would preface with this, that, in the end, it matters little what I suggest or what advice you suppose to heed because your path is already ordained before you of long ago . . . before the realms were made . . . before the very first war ever took place, or even before the Age of the Morning."

The youths were startled, unsure of how to respond, afraid and unwilling to contend with a holy Sodd. But she then proceeded to playfully laugh in light of their astonished faces.

"But take heart, my friends!" she continued. "Do not let my words confound you or remove from you your resolve. We have been ordained to cross each other's paths, and therefore my words will guide you unto the purposed end. Hence, my advice is this . . . learn to rest. Appreciate and enjoy the moment, feel the thrill, learn from your errors, and always, always rise again when you fail."

They shared a laugh and a sigh of relief when she unexpectedly returned from the lofty heights of her initial, disquieting remarks.

"I like it!" Ruvaen responded. "You hear that Wolsage? Do not fret. Try to enjoy yourself."

"Yeah, that's easy for you to say, you are much farther along on your path than I am."

"Remember, it's not me saying it. It's Arryndel of the Sodd!"

Wolsage considered her words, and then, there arose upon his heart many pressing questions he had long considered.

"So, Arryndel, up till now, we've only heard secondhand from the Dathmahjen masters of how the Sodd draw the waters of mystery from the Realm of Decrees. But have you ever been there yourself?" Wolsage asked. "I do not quite understand the explanations I have heard."

"Let's see, in matters of the Realm of Decrees. What can be said? Well, to answer your question, yes, I have been there, and so have you. The Realm is all of us and everything. And yet, the Realm is nothing. It is all things and nothingness. I say nothingness because the Realm of Decrees is not an actual place you can visit but rather a place you glimpse into. So, it is everywhere, and it is nowhere all at once.

"It is all spans of time and all events together coexisting upon Ru'alameth and all other realms beyond. It is all things together frozen for all ages like a fine portrait spanning across the eons without end. A brilliant, beautiful paradox, more real than the passings of the Prime Iddan you and I observe."

The youth contemplated the mysterious Realm that Arryndel described, and Wolsage could not help to interject, "But . . . *that* doesn't make sense. If all our actions are fixed in the Realm, why are we subject to rebukes and to scorn for our errors? It doesn't seem fair, don't you think?"

"Or so, the Urth would argue," Arryndel responded. "And that is the error of our fallen brethren. You need not convince me of your novice status, my young Learner. You see, the Urth cannot accept the fairness that proceeds from the Living One like a clean, invigorating river that satiates the thirst of all.

"Instead, they have said in their heart, '*We shall decide what is fair and what is just.*' Therefore, theirs is an existence of denial, believing against hope that the Realm of Decrees is not real. It simply does not exist, but rather, it is a clever device of the Daylight to suppress them from obtaining preeminence above all thrones. To them, it is a mere invention crafted against them to suppress their brand of justice upon Ru'alameth.

"And then, there are those who will say, 'Surely it exists, but it can be altered.'

And lastly, there are those who say, 'Surely it exists, and it cannot be altered, but we despise the High One for creating it.' But make no mistake, the Realm exists, and the Realm is good. The Realm of Decrees is us, and it is everything, and it is nothing because it is nowhere. We are merely carrying out our lives like the Learner carrying out the words inscribed upon a book. All must walk their path like the stars. And just like the worlds they govern, all must walk the path appointed to them by their orbit."

The novice Wolsage was conflicted, "Respectfully, you still haven't answer my question, why are we, in the end, ultimately responsible for actions that have always been inevitable?"

"This is a matter quite simple, I suppose, to us Sodd. You see, when your spirit makes a decision in the present, you have come into agreement with the Realm in that decision you made, so in a sense, that decision becomes . . . you, the present you.

"Although, the knowledge of the Realm teaches us that it was always you all along, the act of agreeing in the present actually validates the Realm. This act of agreeing is an act of accepting and validating that this, indeed, is you. Our future selves, exposed as such by agreeing in this, our present form.

"Ah yes, the future calls out to us and draws us from horizons far beyond the present epochs of our paths—fluid, it is, so we may freely swim like the fish in the waters. But truly, what is to come is also steadfast, because that which is ordained is that which comes to pass. A brilliant, beautiful paradox.

"To illustrate, this present decision of you sipping from your cup and conversing in this place, has emanated from the endless chasms of the future and announced to us all, that this is indeed, you. And hence, you are responsible for your choices, because you have agreed with the future . . . by the act of deciding."

"I see. So, if we are agreeing with what is already ordained, how is it that we are able to choose our own paths?"

"Because it is the only way for any living thing to experience perception. Without perception, there is no life. And without choice, there is no perception. Thus, choice and perception are life.

"But do not be fooled, we are all subject to *limited* choice. We may not be able to alter the destination, but we may decide how to voyage our journey along the way."

"So, what if I folded my arms and never made a decision again?" Wolsage chimed.

"Sorry, you still agreed because, if that is what you conclusively, fundamentally decided, then that is what the Realm portrayed you as deciding."

"So, who's at fault for my decision, then? Me or the Realm, for making me fold my arms and never doing anything again?"

"As stated before, young Learner, it is your decision because you agreed with the Realm, that this is indeed what you would have decided. But, as far as 'fault' is concerned, whether folding your arms and not doing anything ever again is good or evil, that would be a separate matter altogether because we do not know the circumstances for you folding your arms. I think you may have heard where these matters are resolved," she hinted.

"Yes, in our honorable Daylight Tribunals, of course," Wolsage replied.

"Arryndel, be gentle with our lowly Learner!" Ruvaen intervened. "My head is aching trying to conceive these things."

Arryndel appeared puzzled for a moment but then proceeded to playfully laugh.

"My apologies. I do not mean to trouble you. I'm merely answering a few questions," she explained. "I suppose, what appears simple and obvious to us may not be accepted the same way by others. Anyway, it sounds like you are visiting Ofandynth for the decree, and not for the Festival of the Lightnings, correct? What will you be doing for your first Mah'seyiud?"

"Uh, we don't know. We were summoned to appear before the High Tribunals tomorrow," said Wolsage.

"The High Tribunals? Fascinating. No Lesser Tribunals? And they have summoned . . . a novice? I see. No details, just summoned. Such secrecy! And where is your Eth?"

"No Eth, they sent Ruvaen to escort me."

"A Legion Prime? I must say, this is extraordinary! It feels like something truly grand is underway. And the *Mystery of the Seven O'rahs* is also tomorrow! I sense a monumental shift in the air."

"Oh? What do you mean?"

"Well, when a Mah'seyiud involves truly extravagant events, the decree is usually closely guarded until the last possible moment to shield the one bearing the charge from himself and from others that might intervene. This also prevents the Urth from intervening, or better yet, presume to intervene."

"Oh, right. Because the Urth cannot actually change a Decree, only make things difficult for everyone and everything along the way. It's like, why do they even bother, right? Why do they have to be that way? Why can't they just be good and stop with their foolishness?" the Learner guessed.

Wolsage lifted his gaze and noticed the blank stare in Arryndel and Ruvaen's faces. After all, Arryndel had just explained why the Urth elect to course upon their evil paths.

"What?" he asked.

"You speak that way," Arryndel reiterated. "Because you actually believe the Realm of Decrees is good, and you believe in the Council of Daylight, but the Urth . . . well, they feel quite strongly on the contrary."

"Ahem, clearly you fail to give your full attention to our special guest, Wolsage. Shame, Shame," Ruvaen jokingly chided.

"No need for reprimands. I do not expect everyone to fully grasp what I say. I am quite used to it and possess the upmost patience in Highest Ofandynth."

"So, I guess it makes sense now, then, that they sent you to escort me, Ruvaen, and not a typical Eth. If Arryndel is right, and this is a real important mission, that would explain the secrecy and why they sent the Sabbayoth Omen Breaker to escort me."

The friends shared and laughed till the time for parting arrived. Exhausted with excitement and suspense, Wolsage and Ruvaen finally made their way unto the cozy, sleeping quarters where comfortable beds were furnished for the sojourning visitants of exalted S'hyeru Kadash.

"Very well, let us rest, Wolsage."

Refreshed and woozy with suspense, a new day was upon the youth, and they coursed unto the appointed chamber within the ivory halls of the High Tribunals. They beheld as the revered Ministry of Fates contended with the Urth emissaries appointed to their judgment halls. And these lawfully clashed without end over the undetermined outcome of occurrences throughout the worlds. Faction upon Urth faction was thus permitted to approach the Ministry of Fates, for so had the olden accords ordained.

"Enough!" one infuriated Aedyr Vheilyel exclaimed. "Truly, there was reason for alarm, but thine host needed not burn down the village!"

The Aedyr Judge was fully clad in the dreadful garments of their office, those ethereal vestures resembling shifting lighting currents about their frame and about their visage.

"O Excellent Aedyr, we ordered them to cease the folly of their ambition," another contended, searching for a refuge of an excuse, "But this . . . this is no ordinary circumstance! Our distress is grave beyond measure. This advent, this revelation, it is a sign of a certain doom against us. We are filled with dread. And thou, what knowest thou of the terror hanging over our heads? These were, therefore, correct in exacting their penalty in a time of our greatest calamity."

"Ye do well to fear," the Aedyr ominously responded. "Yet, it is no reason for vindication."

He further reflected on the appeal presented. They contended over the fate of the slain Urth who had raided Oakendunty Village.

"The judgment shall stand," he sternly replied. "The slain Zayd shall remain in our custody and they shall be confined within the Vaults of the Naloz'oth. And, as for the fugitives, Howarmog and Azbele, we demand they be surrendered immediately for this obscene and unlawful deed they have accomplished."

The audience seated on half of the chamber discretely snarled, and they gnashed in objection while the other half quietly murmured.

Upon hearing this final verdict, the contentious Urth violently pounded with his fist. The outburst of anger gave way to the horrid visage of cursed, scaly flesh and scattered horns of another figure concealed within him. The outburst provoked his flesh to eerily flicker in this state but then quickly reverted back to his previous, fair form, thereby concealing again the Curse of the Morning upon him.

Such was the work of the crimson arrayed, Order of Bogedoth, within the halls of the Just. These were scheming, diplomatic Urth sent forth from all corners of Ru'alameth unto the halls of Daylight Tribunals everywhere. These lawful Emissaries of Darkness fervently toiled within the celestial judgment halls so as to win for themselves kingdoms and peoples and judgments favoring the Seven Thrones of Ebelsaddon. For there lived within the sacred volumes of the Daylight, the olden Covenant of Spirit Vials. And this ancient treaty it was, which bestowed this power upon the crimson cloaks of the Bogedoth Vheilyel.

The honorable Aedyr judge proceeded with the matter of the young Learner summoned for his first Mah'seyiud.

"And now, unto the matter at hand. Wolsage of the Learners, come thou forward," he announced.

The timid Wolsage stepped unto the center of the judgment chamber.

"Welcome, young Learner. Peace of the Daylight," the Aedyr greeted.

"Peace of the Daylight, O Excellent Aedyr," Wolsage replied.

"Receive the Decree appointed unto thee this day."

Wolsage humbly lifted his palms toward heaven as his body became encompassed by tiny, white flames.

The judge continued, "Wolsage of the Learners, thou art hitherto advised by this High Tribunal that thou hast been elected to escort he who bears that sacred name, the Fifth Lightning. Thou art hereby commissioned to escort your Panni on his calling to execute that judgment prepared of ancient times. This is in accordance with that elder Decree inscribed upon our most hallowed, *D'ath Pithgam,* which decree is named upon our sacred volumes as, the Decree of the Lightnings."

The startled, emerald eyes of the young Learner flung wide at this most astonishing of announcements. He had vaguely heard the olden Legend of the Seven Lightnings and their promised retribution against those nether fiends confined within their sealed vaults throughout Ru'alameth. He marveled at how he had faintly heard of those ghastly things summoned from those cryptic, forbidden voids; the fiends whom the Vheilyel had known as, the T'ohuvohu, and who also were named, the Light Eaters. He had scantly heard of the mass devastation that befell the heavens in ages past because of these. Legions upon legions of fierce Vheilyel once failed long ago to subdue these nightmare creatures. And now, this lowly Learner of the Eth would be sent forth to confront them?

***

And so, it appeared the eon-worn, primordial phantom that was the Legend of the Seven Lightnings had come alive anew, and had gone forth upon a steed of doom to haunt and to torment the hearts of the crooked Vheilyel. For ages, these had deceived countless legions of the Daylight with a false faith of their perceived dominion over creatures fallen as they themselves were. Great epochs had transpired, with no further testimony of these supposed Lightnings, who were said to, one day, be the very demise of the haughty Urth kingdoms.

Therefore, many of the faithful Vheilyel had lost hope and were enticed to forfeit their allegiance in exchange for that of a seemingly endless dominion alongside the Urth. Truly, many there were who had been seduced into imagining that the Living One had abandoned his works to the thrones of the Night. For the Council of Night contended that the Living One had limited power to undo that great evil that had been recklessly released upon Ru'alameth so long ago.

Elsewhere, far beyond the High Tribunal City of S'hyeru Kadash, amongst the great chasms of blazing stars, there journeyed a lone servant of the Night. The Urth Bogedoth made haste unto that grand, ghoulish chamber within the ancient Urth palace that was Castle Burning Skull.

The Great Kel'torh of Ga'nost, that wicked ruler of the devastated Urth world, awaited.

"The Day Zarrar said, No, my lord," the Bogedoth reported. "There will be no forbearance granted for our slain, and as such, they will remain in their custody."

The crude voice of the shrouded Urth Lord thundered in vehement revulsion along with his encompassing, fiendish court.

"AHHHH! My hunters! My slayers of all that is good and wholesome!" he exclaimed in a manic rage.

The Urth emissary quivered and was reluctant to proceed.

"Well, what else, servant?" the Great Kel'torh inquired.

"And . . ." the servant cowered. "They want us to surrender the fugitives, Howarmog and Azbele."

The Urth Master cursed in an obscure tongue and denounced his informant.

"You have failed me! You have let the Day Zarrar trample all over you once again! You have disgraced your Lord for the last time by failing to secure Zaamkut for Ga'nost."

The servant fell to the ground and pleaded with the Urth Lord not to be carried away, "I beg you! Don't vanish me, Master!"

"Take this embarrassment out of my sight at once, he is hereby stripped of his crown as High Ambassador!" the Great Kel'torh ordered.

At the fiendish king's rebuke, there heeded his voice those foul, creeping shadows bound to the service of the Night. The frightful screeches of the loathsome Salmurvet came forth, and the shadow fiends eerily emanated from the chamber walls and ascended from the floor like a plague of toxic fumes. They seized the pleading, doomed Bogedoth, and cast him into torments unnamable.

"Sandathus!" the Great Kel'torh beckoned.

"Yes, Master!" another Urth servant answered.

"Ga'nost favors you this day. You are now appointed as the new High Ambassador of Ga'nost!"

"It is my privilege and duty, my lord," the bowing servant responded.

"In these, your opening matters, tell the foolish Day Zarrar that the two fugitives are on their way," the Great Kel'torh instructed. "And this is how you will earn a great name for yourself. You will earn for us a new assault on this Fifth Lightning, that we may slay all his friends. You will prevail, and you will win for us . . . Zaamkut for Ga'nost!"

"*Zaamkut for Ga'nost! Zaamkut for Ga'nost!*" erupted the devilish court.

For this Zaamkut, so named, was the lawful power to conduct a matter upon Ru'alameth.

"You will tell them that the Night demands the lives of his friends," the dark master continued. "And when they shall ask on what grounds, you will say, 'Ga'nost of the Throne of Lezuth finds fault . . . in the Fifth Lightning himself.' And then you will tell them, 'Herein is the trespass in dispute: the Shaifetnu boy is most guilty of . . . *Cowardice!* Because he had tempted his friends to accompany him in the great peril of this labor placed upon him!'"

"Excellent words, my lord, this will be done."

"And don't you dare fail me, O Sandathus," the Great Kel'torh warned. "And one last thing, tell them . . . that there will always be night, but the daylight must surely cease. There will be Perpetual Night!"

"There will be Perpetual Night! There will be Perpetual Night!" the fiendish court shouted their dark creed in manic zeal.

The frightful Urth master laughed at his own ominous words and dismissed the new High Ambassador of Ga'nost. The devout Sandathus of the Order of Bogedoth then returned to his quarters, where there awaited twain acolytes for his arrival. He gazed at them with those slitted, sulfured eyes.

"What is thine bidding, master?" said one.

"I am become the new High Ambassador of Ga'nost, and we have much work before us."

The threefold, crimson emissaries made their way across the dimly lit corridors of the ghoulish palace. They marched outside the lurid fortress unto the restless, whirling black clouds above, and they boarded their sky chariot resembling a crystal orb filled with shifting shadows. These were the Urth chariots, so named, Shadow Seffinahs, for the waters of Ru'alameth despised the Urth. But the shadows heeded them indeed, and thus, shadow Seffinahs were formed for their service. And the Star Sharveths, likewise, opened unto the Urth as they did for the Vheilyel, for Ru'alameth was also compelled to adhere to the solemn Covenant of Spirit Vials.

And so, because Ru'alameth was compelled to observe the treaties of old, the Urth likewise made use of the worlds like stepping stones upon a watery pond. And the creatures ill fortuned to gaze upon them as they passed by, these were oftentimes struck with maddening fear. Wild brutes and bizarre men alike fled at the presence of the Urth. And at certain times, the brave creatures that dared to infringe were met with fates more terrible than death.

The emissaries traversed many worlds of varied suns and eerie landscapes resembling the wild, lucid dreams of a lunatic. There were ruins and towering monuments veiled from mortal eyes for millennia. And, finally, there came the lawful bounds where the dominion of the Urth reached its limits, and the laws of the covenants changed.

They unboarded their Shadow Seffinah, which also are named, Sky Seffinahs, and proceeded upon their own leathery wings by the forbearance of those rippling passageways enjoining the heavens.

They traversed many more a world until, finally, they had reached the hollowed lands of Highest Ofandynth, where they would earnestly contend with the Ministry of Fates.

Unlike the noble Vheilyel, the Bogedoth's visit upon Highest Ofandynth was strictly limited to their designated quarters within the tribunal cities. They were not permitted to sojourn in the splendid land during their stay, and neither were they permitted to mingle with the other sojourners. However, this statute suited them well because they did not care to wander the land nor to engage its people.

For there lived a profound contempt within twain, feuding families of the Vheilyel, and this enmity was most irredeemable. The good despised the evil, and the evil despised the good without remedy. Only there were the watchful eyes of the Order of Miyshmaoth, who prevented violent quarrels from erupting between the opposing hierarchies. The feared Miyshmaoth were an elite class of war battalions, giants in stature and reserved for the guardianship of precious sites, and also they served as wardens of Daylight prisoners.

This regulated presence upon the judgment halls was the manner in which the defector Council of Night sustained a measure of power amongst the noble Vheilyel. Nonetheless, this measure of power was one of necessity, as prescribed by the Covenant of Spirit Vials, which required the emissaries to obtain certain approvals from Aedyr Judges before they could lawfully intrude upon the scattered worlds of Ru'alameth. And this lawful power was willfully bestowed upon them by the Daylight, for the Seven Thrones of Ebelsaddon had been charged with upholding the Ministry of Scales; which power comprised of the trying of hearts and words of the mouth.

And so, there lived great volumes of divine ordinances and guidelines, exceptions and divine criteria governing the Urth's interference throughout Ru'alameth, and those who resisted against these ordinances were castigated in what befitting manner was prescribed in these books.

The summation of these governing volumes was composed as one, singular compilation. Thus, the most highly regarded codex within their governing archives was the volume, so named, the *D'ath Pithgam,* also known as, the *Book of Principal Covenants.*

Amongst the enumerated grievances harbored within their wicked hearts against the Daylight, it was this celestial codex that was at the core of the Urth's unquenchable loathing. How they despised to be governed by the Daylight! Yet, a measure of power was preferred over the much-dreaded Naloz'oth Vaults, which was the agreeable exchange at the time the Covenant of Spirit Vials was first established.

The dark emissaries of Ga'nost had arrived upon their designated judgment chamber. That, most grievous, trespass that was the brutal assault upon Oakendunty Village was undergoing consideration. For this assault was no ordinary assault. This was the insufferable and unlawful attempt at the life of the one who was named, the Fifth Lightning.

"And now, unto the matter at hand," began the Aedyr Judge. "The matter of the fugitives, Howarmog and Azbele. Those who unlawfully destroyed the village of the Fifth Lightning upon his announcement within these honorable chambers and who afterward fled when subdued. The first query, when can the Daylight expect their extradition so we may render due justice? What saith the Bogedoth of Ga'nost?"

Sandathus, Chief Bogedoth of Ga'nost, then responded with the monotonous formality of the office left to his charge.

"In the matter of the fugitives, Ga'nost of the Throne of Lezuth is conducting stern reprimands upon the trespassers, Howarmog and Azbele. We assure the honorable Aedyr that Castle Burning Skull of Ga'nost shall see to it they are properly chastised. And they will require two, full Arch Revolvings before surrendering them so as to fully impose the reprimands warranted."

The Aedyr Judge glanced at his notes with those imposing, luminous eyes.

"The Bogedoth's appeal is Denied," he sternly replied. "They shall be surrendered immediately. The reprimands shall be conducted by the Ministry of Wardens, considering the gravity of the transgression."

Sandathus continued, "Ga'nost insists the fugitives acted in reasonable desperation as the unprecedented circumstance of the Legend of the Lightnings has come to our attention. And the ancient Decree against the Seven Thrones appears to be unfolding as we speak. The Lightnings were thought to be but a mare tale for the extracting of wisdom, and their recent sightings have disrupted our society to the point of mania. There is no precedent for a decree of this magnitude, an utterance of doom against our entire people! Therefore, the fugitives are justified in their fear, and so Ga'nost insists on extending two additional Arch Revolvings to account for the reasonable dread imposed upon them."

The judge briefly considered the appeal for the additional time.

"This chamber's Denial shall be sustained," he affirmed. "The mere appearance of the Lightnings shall not excuse their murderous raid against the innocent. The *D'ath Pithgam* is clear, and no forbearance shall be extended. Furthermore, these proceeded without regard to our previous denial for Zaamkut."

Sandathus then responded in a sudden outburst and insisted upon his plea.

"Most noble Aedyr, this 'Annunciation' of them upon the Path of the Waking, it is the sign and the token . . . of our extermination! That is, if the prevailing interpretations ought to be believed."

But the Aedyr judge would not yield.

"The Denial shall stand. There is no reason for observing the Principal Covenants if the Urth may violate its laws out of unrestrained passions. We perceive thine fear, and rightly so thou fearest. Nonetheless, this chamber shall not suffer the fugitives to remain at liberty for another revolving, Arch or Lesser or otherwise. They shall be delivered within the hour, without exception.

"In the event, that Ga'nost doth not yield, its kingdom shall incur additional losses at the hand of the Sabbayoth when they shall forcibly retrieve the fugitives."

There was nothing more the refused emissary could offer to spare his fellow Urth and win additional time for their schemes, but a much greater objective was now in sight.

"We shall now proceed unto the additional matter . . ." said the Aedyr.

"Very well, Castle Burning Skull of Ga'nost shall be informed," the Bogedoth conceded. "Be it cataloged that Ga'nost is prepared to satisfy the aforementioned demands. They shall surrender the fugitives immediately. However, Ga'nost shall now at this time petition to advise . . . Shul-kahn."

The judge paused, as the mention of Shul-kahn compelled his attention. This was that lawful exchange between the powers, useful for the advancing of much-needed relief upon the conflicting realms.

"Very well. Permission to advise Shul-kahn. What is the Ministry of Scales prepared to forfeit to the Daylight?"

"Ga'nost of the Throne of Lezuth is prepared to offer not one or two, but three . . . Ulkazak Knights of our revered Order of Ulkazak. Ga'nost shall forfeit three Ulkazak Knights alongside the two fugitives immediately, contingent upon the issuance of . . . Zaamkut for Ga'nost."

The highly coveted Zaamkut had been invoked, which was the lawful granting of power to perform a deed proposed.

"This judgment hall shall now hear the Bogedoth's terms for the proposed Zaamkut."

"Ga'nost shall surrender the aforementioned resources and this shall be contingent upon the issuance of Full Denunciation against twain, mortal friends accompanying he who bears the sacred name, the Fifth Lightning."

The chamber murmured at the daring proposal presented.

"And the grounds for Full Denunciation are as follows," Sandathus continued. "Ga'nost has found the Fifth Lightning to be guilty of the vice of . . . *Cowardice.* The Shaifetnu boy, in spite of beholding and obtaining a Holy Eth by his side, has desecrated the generous gift of the Daylight because he is now exposed before us to be a coward.

"For he could not endure the labor of keeping the charge with an Eth in the flesh by his side. But instead, he tempted his friends to join him on the perilous journey, endangering their precious lives. Therefore, Ga'nost of the Throne of Lezuth lays claim to the lives of his two companions for this indulgence most abhorrent to the Daylight, and now demands Full Denunciation upon them."

The room silently resumed their murmurings, quietly disputing the words of Sandathus, as Full Denunciation meant that the Bogedoth desired the opportunity to slay the beloved neufs. They had charged Saxfen with endangering them for the cowardice they perceived within him. And so, the question posed to the judgment hall was this, was the Ministry of Scales correct and Saxfen was indeed a coward?

For amongst the enumerated flaws of the heart that the Daylight despised, Cowardice was amongst the most shunned of them all. It was said that from the well of cowardice, there came the waters of deception and treachery. And if found guilty, the Fifth Lightning could not be trusted, as cowardice had long been the downfall of many of their own kind. Therefore, the Council of Night demanded to test Saxfen's heart with the death of his friends as he had now been formally presented as a Coward before the Ministry of Fates.

The Chief Emissary continued, "For this reason, Ga'nost requires Full Denunciation against the company of the Fifth Lightning in order to satisfy this grievous indulgence against this, most holy, *D'ath Pithgam*."

The Aedyr quietly considered, for what coward did not predictably disappoint, or worse, *betray*? He then inquired of the assembly to his right hand, "And what saith the Lesser Nelcailith in the matter of this query for formal Denunciation?"

The assembly continued their whispers until they had reached one accord. One amongst them finally spoke out on behalf of the rest, "O Excellent Aedyr, this Lesser Nelcailith shall deny the Bogedoth's petition for Full Denunciation, seeing that Utterances Twelve, Three and Two shall be observed."

The judge quietly considered the words of the Lesser Nelcailith. And having reached an outcome, he assumed the hazard presented by the Bogedoth and replied, "This chamber shall hereby deny Zaamkut for Full Denunciation as proposed. The Daylight shall bare the guilt and obligation"

Upon hearing the firm denial and how the familiar Utterances from the *D'ath Pithgam* had been invoked, Sandathus then knew further dispute would be in vain.

His fate had been sealed, it seemed. Nonetheless, the shrewd Bogedoth prolonged the session in a vain attempt to persuade the Nelcailith with every maneuver that was in his power. But would he be returning to the terrifying Urth Lord of Ga'nost empty-handed, knowing of the impending rebukes, utter humiliation, and unspeakable chastisements awaiting him? He had been given power over threefold, much coveted Ulkazak Knights and he would have nothing to prove his worth upon his return. There would be no forbearance for this failure. *There must be a way to free my soul from this snare,* he carefully searched.

***

The kingdom of Ga'nost would soon be violently sieged by the armies of the Daylight if they so persisted in harboring the fugitives, Howarmog and Azbele. The trespassing fiends had brought such cruelty upon Oakendunty Village and now the High Tribunals demanded their extradition at once.

As for Wolsage and Ruvaen, they had stepped outside of the celestial judgment hall, and together they pondered this impressive Mah'seyiud entrusted to the orange-haired Learner.

"So, they chose you precisely because you are weak, it appears." Ruvaen said as they stepped down the marble steps. "You must feel quite special right now."

"Yeah," Wolsage responded. "I guess they wanted to make it fair for the Urth, you know, how they're always whining about unfairness and balance? Someone in there made a good case to have me go along, that's for sure. But at least they sent the Omen Breaker to ensure I made it here safely. I should be fine now, heading back on my own."

Wolsage could not overcome the initial shock of the dizzying revelation. But then suddenly, he remembered his dear friend, Orilheart.

"Oh no! Orilheart! I must get to her, Ruvaen!"

The young Learner hastened away, leaving his friend behind.

"You sure you will be alright without me?" Ruvaen said laughing.

Wolsage laughed and waved in the distance. He hurried along, but as he turned his sight forward, he unexpectedly clashed with an incoming company.

"Take heed how you thread!" exclaimed one menacing voice.

"Yes, we are prepared to destroy you, should you dare oppose us," said another as he drew his mighty essence blade.

"Whoa, relax guys! I mean no harm!" Wolsage frightfully assured.

The group before him were fierce warriors, dreadful to look upon. They were clad in the onyx plates of the Sabbayoth, and their eyes burned to the depths of the soul. They appeared to be escorting a silver-haired Shaifetnu with his gaze to the ground.

Wolsage proceeded to apologize and hurried along without engaging small chatter, "I am so sorry for the trouble, but I'll be on my way now. I'm off to my very first Mah'seyiud!" he shouted as he sped away.

"Very well then!" one warrior shouted back, "Peace of the Daylight. The Seventh Lightning sends his regards!"

Wait, what? The seventh one is found already? I . . . I can't . . . Orilheart! He thought. This was all that coursed through his mind at that moment as he traversed the worlds to the aid of his friend.

Chapter 9

The Contention Against the Eth

The orange-haired Learner had safely arrived upon those pleasant lands underneath the silver arc adorning Eofendurk. There, he was greatly relieved to find that Orilheart, his longtime friend, was safe and well. The young Saxfen and twain, whiskered neufs trailed the orange-haired Learner, and they stared in awe at their newfound guardian. They couldn't believe they had now met not one, but two celestial, many winged gods!

"What? You defeated a *captain* of the Zayd? A captain of the ruthless Order of Hunters and Assassins?" Wolsage marveled at Orilheart.

"Yes, but in all fairness, I had no idea it was an Urth chief at the time of our clash. Also, the Eth Master informed me earlier that the High Tribunals had decreed in my favor, and that none would be able to overcome me that day."

Eager to learn more about their new, Vheilyel companion, the boys could not help to interrupt.

"So, Mr. Wolsage, sir . . ." Jix said.

"Oh, just plain Wolsage is fine. This is what I'm called in the Path of the Waking, but my real name, you may not know it."

"Oh, really? How strange is that?" Jix pondered.

"Yes, our ways may seem strange to you, but we must work covertly, considering the great bounty on the Fifth Lightning's head. And it's actually also for your own good that you don't know my name."

The Learner's tone then suddenly transitioned into one of a dark, ominous scourge, "For if any mortal creature dared utter my name without consent, a dire curse and most terrible fate would surely fall upon them."

The boys stared with eyes wide in incredulity, but this provoked an even more intense fascination.

"Oh, stop scaring them, Wolsage!" Orilheart chided. "That was way too much information."

"So does that mean Orilheart is not really called Orilheart up there where you're from?" Jix pried.

"That's right," Orilheart answered. "Our Cloak Names, as we like to refer to them, amongst other things, prevent our enemies from finding us and stirring up trouble. It would be so annoying to have to deal with Urth and Dreggut and Szaivoomi, and so on and so on, every time we decided to go for a stroll in a lovely garden nearby. Hiding our real names works out quite well. And it's actually a little fun. I happen to love orils, so I went with Orilheart. They're just the cutest!"

"So, what's an oril, him?" Qugam asked.

"Oh, that's right. You don't have those here. Well, if you were to visit Eylundis, where I'm from, you would see them playing and giggling, leaping and rolling on the green grass and drifting on their wings. They look like tiny people, and their four wings look like flower petals. They have long tails and they grow many horns on their heads that look like crowns upon their bristly hair. They're highly social, and you would see large groups of them, freely hovering through the fields underneath our bright, blue skies."

"Blue skies?" Jix chimed.

Orilheart playfully laughed, "Yup, blue skies. They are so beautiful to look at, but I suppose all you've ever known is the pink one here, so I can see why this is bizarre to you."

"So . . . you get to pick your own names?" Saxfen asked.

"Correct."

"And you can pick whatever you want?" Saxfen continued.

"Yup."

"Hey, I know. Let's pick a name for our him!" Qugam exclaimed.

"What? Qugam, that's ridiculous," Jix scolded. "Why in the world would we do that? This is a serious matter, can't you see?"

"Oh, come on, it'll be fun," said Saxfen.

"A group name, huh? Well, what did you have in mind?" asked Orilheart.

"Uh . . . I don't know. We are a group of friends . . . and we are on a quest to find a magical harp. How about . . ." Saxfen pondered. He paused momentarily as the soothing caress of the evening breeze enhanced the suspense. The young Shaifetnu gathered his thoughts and then finally made the contribution.

"How about . . . the Sages of the Harp!" Saxfen dramatically announced.

The group paused. They carefully considered the proposed name for their group.

"Nah!" they replied together.

"What?!" one perplexed Saxfen said.

"Snowhead, that has to be the lamest suggestion for a group's name in the history of selecting group names," Jix scolded. "I mean, how embarrassing was that!"

"I kind of liked it, him," Qugam comforted.

"Uh . . . come up with something else," Orilheart said.

"The Ferocious Five hims!"

"Nope . . ."

"The Wiljorg Slayers!"

"Really, how many wiljorgs have you slain?"

"The Masters of the Harp!"

"What? Unspeakably lame."

"The League of the Lightning!"

"Wait . . . no, probably not . . ."

"The Warriors of the him!"

"I don't think so . . ."

"Oakendunty's Revenge!"

"Nah . . ."

"Sword of Oakendunty!"

The group finally held their peace.

"Yeah, that sounds kind of him . . ."

"I kind of like it . . ."

"Nice ring to it, I suppose."

"It's nice."

And with that, it appeared the contentious company had settled on a name in the aged tradition of the many winged Vheilyel. *Sword of Oakendunty* had been born.

"So, Wolsage, you know we just have to ask," said Saxfen. "If you don't mind, can we . . . see your wings?"

"Sure," he responded.

Wolsage then proceeded to fling his sixfold, powerful wings from within the loose flap on the back of his coat. He stretched his frosted, feathered wings atop his kirok bird and almost knocked over the jeering Jix.

"Hey, watch where you fling those things!" he yelped.

"Yeah, I love them," Wolsage playfully laughed. "They sure come in handy when you're in a hurry like I was on my way here. I was in such a hurry, I didn't even stop to say hello to the Seventh Lightning. Pretty sure I'll regret that one later."

"Wait, what?!" Orilheart exclaimed. "You saw the Seventh Lightning?! What is his name? What did he look like? Was it a he?"

"Well," Wolsage recounted. "As I said, I was in a hurry and didn't realize who it was. I did glance but did not get a good look. I don't know. He may have been a girl, but he or she was looking down, and their silver hair was covering their face so I couldn't tell. It was silver, like Saxfen's here. I didn't catch a name because I didn't stay long enough to find out. I was in a hurry to get to you. I was so worried about you, Orilheart."

"Wow, this is all really happening. And look at us! We just happen to be right in the center of it all!" Orilheart said in her gleeful way.

The group laughed and conversed with Wolsage, their curious new ally, until Orilheart finally shouted, "Look, over there! It looks like somebody is sitting down!"

The company approached the scene with spirited zest mingled with caution. *Could that be the third Vheilyel they had been looking for?* The hazy figure turned out to be a person sitting down indeed—or rather crouching. But it was not what they had suspected. The being rose upon twain muscular legs and exposed a set of grisly, clawed arms and a bristly, blue coat. It howled and sneered at the sight of the group. And then five others like it suddenly appeared from within the woods. It was a ravening pack of those cursed Nithians, hungry wiljorgs ready to rip and devour flesh.

"Guys, stay back!" Orilheart warned.

"We'll handle this," Wolsage assured.

Twain Vheilyel unmounted their frightened kirok birds, and they drew their luminous essence blades, ready to confront the cursed men of Nith. But there came one punishing voice from an unknown place, demanding restraint and the wavering from unneeded bloodshed.

"Halt!" the stern voice ordered. "Why so hasty to perish, O cursed ones of Nith?"

The hungry wiljorgs quivered at the resolute voice and slowly fled until none remained. Then, from within the scattered woods that housed the wiljorgs, there stepped into view the source of the menacing voice. It was a slender young man with dark hair and thick, dark brows.

"The tender trees from my vision," Orilheart remembered. "This is where I saw them. This must be Starrelos."

The young man approached. It was the tried war hero of the Daylight battalions, General Starrelos of the Sabbayoth, who also is called, the Liar's Bane.

"Orilheart!" he exclaimed. "I have found you! Peace of the Daylight."

"Peace of the Daylight," she responded.

They greeted and embraced.

"These vulgar creatures . . . what annoyance they are," Starrelos said. "They wander the lands and do not cease to appear. I'm glad to see you are well, Orilheart. I was not sure what had happened to you after we deflected the Zayd we hindered. That's the last place I saw you."

"Yes, and as you are now well aware, that was no ordinary assault or act of mischief from the Urth. And that was no ordinary village they came for. They were after something big, or should I say, someone," Orilheart said as she glanced at Saxfen.

Starrelos stared in admiration.

"So, this is him, the dreaded Fifth Lightning, the long-awaited doom of the Urth, and the praise of the Council of Daylight."

"Yes, meet my longtime friend, Shaifetnu Saxfen of the Sevrinjiv," Orilheart introduced.

"Longtime friend?"

"Yes, I've known Saxfen almost all his life. I had no idea I was, in fact, friends with the Fifth Lightning this whole time! And this is Wolsage of the Learners, and Jix, and Qugam of the Neufs. They're from the assaulted village, Oakendunty Village. Everyone, meet General Starrelos of the Order of Sabbayoth."

The company greeted and welcomed their new guest. *Now there were three of them!* The boys secretly mused.

"Welcome, General, to Sword of Oakendunty," Saxfen said.

"Pardon, to what?"

"Sword of Oakendunty, him," Qugam responded. "This is what we are called."

"We took it upon ourselves to give our group a name in honor of the Vheilyel practice of naming themselves," said Jix.

"I see. Well, thank you, for your warm welcome. I am honored to join Sword of Oakendunty," Starrelos gracefully said.

"This is wonderful!" Orilheart exclaimed. "Only one more Vheilyel to complete our team!"

She raised her arm and playfully pointed to the snowy summit that crowned the majestic mountain in the distance.

"To the snow!"

The company was in high spirits and had much to talk about. The traumatic and profound loss the boys had lived through only a few days ago was mercifully eased by the excitement of their newfound friends. The matter of Oakendunty's ravaging was far from settled. These were set on avenging their beloved abode and slain loved ones as the assault on Oakendunty was a damnable, cruel one indeed.

***

The evil Vheilyel that had learned of the Fifth Lightning's Annunciation upon the Path of the Waking, these were sorely consumed with cursings and restless vexings. The long-decreed advent of the supposed Lightnings was to be but a mere tale of symbolism, or so, they were instructed. For there had transpired before them many an age of muteness and void of testimony. The Legend of the Lightnings was to be but a mere fable, not to be understood in a literal sense. This was the conviction of the faithless amongst the celestial hierarchies, amongst the schisms they were persuaded to believe.

But now that the Lightnings were being unveiled by the elect Seers, the Council of Night did not relent as they desperately searched for new methods to sway their fate. This in a frenzied attempt to delay the severe chastisement that was foretold would surely follow.

And thus was the conviction of the Urth, that they had power to sway what was ordained within the mysterious Realm of Decrees. The Urth therefore made use of their liberties prescribed under the *Book of Principal Covenants* to alter their fate, or so, they supposed they had the power to accomplish.

And none there were amongst the celestial hierarchies, good or evil, released from the *Principal Covenants*. But all were subject to the supreme ordinances and judgment halls of the Daylight.

All were subject to the exalted Ministry of Fates, and as such, there came an adversary upon the holy judgment halls against Orilheart of the Eth. And there came stern, railing charges against her in the hopes of altering the Fifth Lightning's path. Let us return to the days before the beloved neuf village was destroyed and the time when the Ministry of Scales devised grave charges against the courageous Eth.

Before the assault on Oakendunty Village, there arose stern contentions amongst the ranks of Ga'nost. And Castle Burning Skull greatly coveted the glory to be attained in postponing the Decree of the Lightnings against them. Therefore, they conspired to commit their unlawful destruction against the peaceful neuf village. It was a scheme of madness, but madness is that which desperation breeds, even amongst the tarnished, many winged gods.

Whether the Decree was truthful or invented, slaying the supposed Fifth Lightning would compel the Daylight to restructure their purpose for their elect champions. Thus, their desperate design against fate was perceived to be a worthy one.

"They call the place, Oakendunty Village, O Great Kel'torh," reported one hissing Urth.

The eerie voice of the Lord of Ga'nost became irate.

"We care not what it is called! All is now in place. Find this Shaifetnu boy and slay him at once! And do not dare fail!"

At once, the grim company of Zayd Hunters attending to the Great Kel'torh departed. They had received proper instruction to destroy the Fifth Lightning and thereby halting the damning pronouncement lingering over their fleeting power and their kingdom; over their entire race. Alas! This grave transgression against the *Book of Principal Covenants* they had set out to accomplish.

The dark host of hunters boarded the Shadow Seffinahs awaiting them and took to the restless, spiraling skies. Fury and chaos followed their path and they had but two more worlds to traverse until they had reached the bounds of roseate, Eofendurk. Then suddenly, their soaring sky chariots were halted by the sight of threefold, luminous orbs revolving upon the blacked, foreign sky. It was the sight of the Daylight's own sky chariot, and the Vheilyel within gazed with eyes full of retribution.

"The Sabbayoth have found us," one Urth announced.

The Urth captain gave the order and the hordes of darkness mounted their monstrous, spirit-beasts of war. These vile creatures also resembled winged serpents like the Urth, yet their frame was larger and useful for transport and warfare.

And the Vheilyel likewise mounted their spirit-beasts and set out to vanquish the unlawful raid; their beasts also readied in the skill of light-drifting for the purpose of warfare. And, amongst them, there rode upon one plated War Ekeru, Orilheart of the Eth, accompanied by the imperial, black cloaks of the Sabbayoth. This was that much-revered order of those battle-forged battalions, the Order of Sabbayoth, faithfully attending to the Ministry of War, night and day without ceasing.

And at the head of these dreadful adversaries of the Night, sent forth to quell the Urth uprising, there rode that mighty Vheilyel Prince, Starrelos, the Liar's Bane, General of the Sabbayoth. His burning essence blade was drawn, ready to unleash divine fury alongside Orilheart.

The Urth transgressors were incited at the sight of the holy Sabbayoth and would not relent. Starrelos extended his hand and confronted the foul legions of Zayd.

"Halt this madness, in the name of the Daylight!" he thundered.

"Flee, O foolish Day Zarrar, and be spared the oblivion that awaits you!" one fiend threatened.

"Treachery! The Covenants shall be avenged! Surrender now, the time of the Urth is coming to an end!" Starrelos demanded.

"End?" the hissing Urth scoffed. "This is only the beginning. We shall spare no one when the Sign of the Eighth is come. Join the Seven Thrones now and escape our vengeance. There will always be darkness . . . *there will be Perpetual Night!*"

"Blasphemies!" Orilheart shouted as they charged the invading army.

The clashing battalions roared. They battled above the perilous wastelands of Chaantulmit. The slain plunged unto radiant streams of magma below, violently flowing from the onyx bowels of the forsaken world.

"We do not have time for this!" one hissed. "The Fifth Lightning *must* be slain . . . NOW!"

The scaly, hissing thing gathered many warriors to its side and fled the battle.

"They must not escape!" shouted Starrelos. "We shall pursue them. Legion Prime, hold the rest here!"

Orilheart and Starrelos clashed and light-drifted with all their might in their pursuit, and other Sabbayoth likewise joined.

"We need to slow them down!" Orilheart shouted. "They're going to reach the village before us!"

One Sabbayoth then raised her right arm to the sky as she shouted with all the breath that was within her, "O Great Keundruintanth, I command you, come forth now from your dwelling within the Path of Sithrah!"

With that, there came a sudden surge of thick, baleful clouds, clamoring with the voice of violent thunderings and blinding flashes.

Whoa, could that be? Orilheart marveled, for she had yet to win the fidelity of the great spirit-beasts dwelling within the depths of the Sithrah.

The chilling howls of the Soggseraf Ekeru, were frightful, even to the infernal legions. The massive, horned shapes upon its head peered into view from the midst of the menacing vapors, and it did prevail in hindering the siege of the fleeing Urth. They were scattered and shaken by the ravenous beast that heeded the call from its dwelling within the unknowable depths of the Sithrah.

These hidden depths were the confines of the great chasms and the unseen domains of spirits, those boundless depths that enjoined all the scattered worlds. Indeed, these were the depths that made the Star Sharveths of Ru'alameth attainable to the many winged gods. For, without this unseen domain of the Sithrah, the Vheilyel would not be permitted to traverse the worlds in the manner to which they had been accustomed. Neither could they speak to one another across those confounding, impossible spans had their knowledge of the Sithrah been denied. Truly, the Vheilyel themselves would marvel with the marveling of mere mortals at the very thought of breaching the impossible gulfs, without the Path of the Sithrah.

The ivory, feathered Soggseraf devoured with its monstrous snout, and it hurled piercing lightning of azure terror. It greedily consumed those unfortunate to become its prey. Its potent feathers were like heavy armor, and they withstood many searing blows from the foul blades of the Zayd.

The Sabbayoth had prevailed, and they swayed the assaulting fiends, but it was no time to celebrate.

"We must get to Oakendunty!" Orilheart exclaimed.

The heroes traversed the final world and raced to the peaceful neuf village. But it was too late. There could be seen the smoke of Oakendunty Village in the distance. Terror had reached the neufs and the silver-haired Shaifetnu, before they could be evacuated.

"Oh no!" Orilheart exclaimed, fighting back tears. "We're too late!"

She stared in disbelief. She was cut to the core with the heart-piercing wound of her failure.

"Orilheart, behind you!" shouted Starrelos.

The foul essence blade of one charging Urth was flung at her head. She drew her own weapon and barely intercepted the incoming death blow. She guarded her face, but the blow prevailed to forcibly unmount her from her startled ekeru. The raiding fiend taunted and hissed as she plunged to the ground in a confounded daze.

"Feel the failure, feel the defeat. Feel . . . the *despair*!" it hissed from within its ghoulish, shrouded face.

"Silence! We will not be mocked!" Orilheart shouted.

Twain, dueling adversaries had reached the ground while wrestling to fend off one another's deadly weapons. Orilheart's face was dangerously close to the murky Urth blade. With her back firmly against the ground, she mustered the strength to thrust off the transgressor while she remained injured on the ground.

And then, a second and a third hunter light-drifted into view. She was all alone. General Starrelos and the other Sabbayoth were nowhere to be found.

***

And so, upon the emergence of the third hunter, there came the thunderous tumult of numerous Vheilyel, roaring from within the royal courts of the celestial city, S'hyeru Kadash. They sneered and vehemently dissented against the lawless assault upon the distressed Eth. They looked on intently at the carnage of Oakendunty from across the vast, starry spans of Ru'alameth, from within the very halls of the High Tribunals of Ofandynth.

Indeed, the many winged gods earnestly studied the chaos underway, for at the heart of these unfolding matters was the very fate of the conflicting, celestial kingdoms. They eagerly observed in angst and suspense as Orilheart was forcibly unmounted from her winged ekeru and was now injured on the ground, left to fend off not one, but three damning hunters of the Order of Zayd.

"Release her!" one spectator pleaded while others demanded swift vengeance upon the assailing Urth.

"Seize them! Seize the transgressors! They are in breach of the Principal Utterances!" shouted another.

The Principal Utterances were those divine entries inscribed upon that hallowed volume that is the *D'ath Pithgam*, which also is named, the *Book of Principal Covenants*. And now, the Council of Daylight demanded severe retribution for the breaching of its most revered codex.

The vast host of the Daylight railed and interjected with divine zeal. They anxiously looked on with an unbearable, burdensome sense of helplessness. Any one of them would gladly descend and rain down punishing judgments in the name of the Daylight. But the *Principal Covenants* would be observed. Nay, they *must* be observed. And without prejudice, they must be observed, with all the vigilance and vigor that dwelt within them. For any breach of these hallowed treaties would release curses upon curses and wrath most dreadful upon all offenders.

"Arise, Orilheart! Do not despair!" the shouting continued.

But the railing charges brought against Orilheart also persisted, and would not spare, for the Urth wielded the power of the Ministry of Scales.

"Most Excellent, Aedyr," one Urth ambassador contended. "The reckless Eth, Orilheart by Cloak Name, is most guilty of abandoning her sworn post! This dedicated Council of Adversaries has uncovered that she shamelessly forfeited her duties to the Fifth Lightning!"

And with these damning charges presented in the judgment hall, there came the voices of other Bogedoth, also railing in assent against Orilheart.

The vehement, principal adversary continued.

"The Throne of Lezuth therefore demands her fall for the careless breach of Utterances Eight, Twenty, and Three."

"This is correct," yet another concurred. "The sacred codes are breached, honorable, Aedyr! There must be a ransom for the satisfying of this breach."

The Aedyr judge paused to consider the charges against Orilheart in the transgressions presented. He glanced at the principal advocate rendered unto Orilheart for her defense. It was the beautiful and shrewd, Casdynbiel of the Order of Dathmahjen.

"Noble Advocate Prime, the Throne of Lezuth demands ransom for the charges set forth against this Eth. What saith the advocate in defense?" the Aedyr queried.

Casdynbiel carefully considered her response. She calmly brushed her dark, silky hair from her face, exposing the faint, golden etchings of her order upon her face. She turned her sparkling, azure eyes to the Aedyr before her and gracefully related her defense.

"Honorable, Aedyr, the defense of Orilheart of the Eth is as follows: The Bogedoth of Lezuth speaks in error. The slandered Eth did not abandon her post, but rather, she engaged the intruding menace in defense of her Panni. This Council of Advocates determined Utterances Eight, Twenty, and Three were not subject to breach, but rather, the *D'ath Pithgam* was indeed upheld. The trespassing legions, in fact, qualify as 'sizable and imminent' under the provisions of Utterances Three and Seven. Hence, she is in full subjection to the *D'ath Pithgam* for the entirety of the span in dispute.

"Furthermore, through the execution of said provision, she has thus demonstrated she is wholly given to her solemn oath, which binds her to her Panni. She demonstrated her commitment in the very courageous act of joining the counterassault in question, placing her own life in peril for the Shaifetnu's sake.

"Finally, Orilheart of the Eth received knowledge that her Panni was, in fact, one of the fabled Lightnings that very night, that very eve of the unlawful assault upon the neuf village. She is therefore also entitled to the provisions prescribed under Utterances Ninety and Four."

And at this calm and composed articulation of the heavenly ordinances, there followed the clamorous heckles and hostile outbursts from the Bogedoth court. They discreetly gnashed and scoffed at Casdynbiel's defense, and there stirred amongst these, great wrath for her words.

The Aedyr busied himself with the study of certain material, not in sight of the quarreling chamber. He then gazed again at the contending adversaries before him and quieted their ruckus.

"Silence!" he exclaimed, with burning eyes and shrouded in dreadful, lightning vestures. "Upon closer inspection of the occurrences in dispute, the contention of the advocate is correct. Petition for ransom is hereby declined."

The Servants of the Daylight roared in joyous triumph!

The Aedyr Judge continued.

"Furthermore, the charges set forth by Ga'nost of the Throne of Lezuth have brought grievous ill to the Eth and she must therefore be remedied. This noble chamber hereby decrees that Orilheart of the Eth will prevail against all her opponents for the remaining duration of her native revolving. This is hereby decreed, and it shall stand."

The thunderous shouts echoed in the vast judgment hall. The disconsolate Bogedoth burned with revulsion. And thus, the weary Eth lying on the ground upon distant Eofendurk facing certain death would escape a tragic end that day.

***

But Orilheart herself could neither hear nor feel the ecstatic tumult of festivity that roared on her behalf within the halls of S'hyeru Kadash. Only the pulsating anguish of her slim, celestial frame could be felt as she laid, unable to rise to her feet. Her foe also remained on the ground as there approached twain combatants with their weapons drawn.

The foul smoke from their essence blades was terrible to gaze upon. They resembled weapons forged in the abyss, weapons that accomplished more than to sever their victims. Rather, they appeared to scorch and torment with flames spawned far beyond the Path of the Waking. The approaching Zayd uttered profanities in an obscure tongue. Their faces were concealed within their dismal vestures, and their eyes glowed with a loathsome, sulfured hue, not at all natural or native to Eofendurk.

Orilheart glanced at her would-be executioners with her remaining breath, she raised her arm to the night sky, "Save your servant, I pray," she said in a pitiful, quivering voice.

She collapsed from exhaustion.

Mere moments the span of a single breath would pass, but time itself would lose all sense and reason. And then a warm, familiar voice called out to her.

"Why so saddened, Orilheart?" the voice said.

"What? Am I dead? Is this . . . what it's like to die?" she responded.

The figure talking with Orilheart was none other than the Eth Master, Otenhryen, Song of the Ekeru.

"No, not dead, only resting," he said.

"Resting? What happened? Is Saxfen okay? I can't rest now. He needs me."

Orilheart realized that she had returned underneath the enchanted skies of Eylundis. It was the world of her home, far from Eofendurk where Oakendunty laid in ruins several paces ahead only moments ago.

"Oh no! This . . . this is Eylundis. If I am not dead, why am I here? The Fifth Lightning has arrived. He's counting on me!"

"Orilheart, observe," Otenhryen calmly said.

He waved his arm, and the air gently rippled like the striking of still water on a pond. She gazed at the rippling before her, and she saw her own body lying on the ground. The looming Urth hunters stood above her with their weapons raised, ready to execute her helpless body.

"Is that me? Well, why aren't they moving?" she asked.

"They are moving, yet not as you are accustomed."

"I see, so this is all still going on in Eofendurk?"

"Correct."

"But if I'm not dead, and they are about to kill me, what does this mean?"

Otenhryen gently smiled, "Do not fret about them, Orilheart. They will be handled accordingly. All things in their time. For now, I have very important tidings to report."

"Oh, I see. This must be a vision."

Orilheart continued to gaze at her exhausted body as twain combatants remained suspended in time, their weapons ready to strike.

"Orilheart, your integrity was challenged at the High Tribunals of S'hyeru Kadash. But be greatly consoled, you have overcome! These incoming Urth standing over you were sent to execute you for the slander uttered against you. Nonetheless, the decree has gone forth in your favor and none shall be able to withstand you this day."

Orilheart was visibly relieved.

"Whoa, I guess that was a close one, then?" she nervously laughed.

"Indeed, but your adversaries were found liars. Now gaze into the Face Sharveth and tell me what you see."

She gazed at the rippling vista, "I see . . . a beautiful lake of sparkling, pink water."

"Great, what else?"

"Um . . . there's, some plants. No, wait, they're trees and young tender trees. It's like the entrance to some woods."

"Very good."

"Also, there is a mountain. It's a snowy summit."

"Yes, that would be three, then. Orilheart, you must travel to these sites in the world in which the Shaifetnu Saxfen dwells. There, you shall find three friends to assist you in escorting the Fifth Lightning. Find them, Orilheart. Wolsage, Starrelos, Eluryn."

At the mention of the three Vheilyel names, the voice of the Eth Master became faint until it finally vanished from Orilheart's mind. She found herself in the place where she last remembered, lying on the outskirts of ravished Oakendunty Village.

Her pain had been relieved, and she felt comforted and refreshed as if waking from a deep, restful slumber. Her eyes flung wide; they burned white with fury. At this gesture, there came a fearsome noise far above in the zenith. The sound thereof was like the frightful blast of a calamitous thunder roll.

The cryptic hunters were stricken with dread so maddening and so fearsome as though they had heard a stern utterance in place of thunder. They searched in vain for the source of this awful rebuke as they considered flight. And then came a ravaging, violent pillar of fire crashing down upon the injured fiend lying on the ground with Orilheart. The engulfed fiend screamed in agony and despair as the flames seared and scorched its scaly flesh.

"NOOO . . . not yet!! More time I . . . *beg you!*" the tormented assassin pleaded with hideous howls and laments as the heavenly vengeance consumed.

The fiend's body was utterly dissolved by the descending flames. And yet, within the fiery pillar, a faint figure could be seen plunging like a gylth upon its prey. It was the bewildering semblance of the many-faced Kozeroth, reapers of parting, celestial spirits; servants of the Ministry of Harvest.

The remaining Zayd fled in manic fear, leaving Orilheart at last to recover from her injuries. These that fled became the fugitives the Daylight would come to forcefully demand at the hand of Ga'nost, the fugitives, so named, Howarmog and Azbele.

Orilheart crashed her body unto the ground and threw her arms above her head.

"Whoa! That was close!" she exhaled.

But it was no time to rest. She suddenly gasped and remembered her Panni.

"Oh no! Saxfen!"

The early rays were now upon the ruins of plundered Oakendunty Village. Grim pillars of smoke ascended unto the morning sky, and dimly lit embers drifted across Orilheart's saddened, jeweled eyes. It was quiet, not a soul in sight. She paused and raised her palms towards heaven, "Where . . ." she whispered.

Her eyes flung open, and she soared and light-drifted to the northwest part of town. And there he was, helpless and collapsed upon his knees with his gaze to the ground. Orilheart approached and urged her beloved friend in her gentle, comforting voice.

"Saxfen, get up."

***

The shamed Zayd fugitives, who nearly slew Orilheart, received no comfort from their distress. The dread of seeing their brother consumed in holy flames was a difficult sight, even for the heartless creatures they were. For they knew that the fearsome Vaults of the Naloz'oth awaited the perished hunter. *And that could have been their own fate!* They could still hear the desperate cries within their scaly, serpentine heads.

They cursed and raged, "The Seven Thrones must not fail. There will be Perpetual Night!" hissed one.

"No mercy, no mercy, no mercy for the Daylight!" raged the other.

The manic pair traversed the worlds across barren lands, rivers of iron, and haunting monoliths. The horrid, restless skies mirrored their burning fury. Monstrous, winged beasts cowered as they passed by. They fled unto the far-placed, ever-shunned depths of the starry gulfs. They searched for relief and sanctuary within the ghoulish halls of that dark fortress, Castle Burning Skull.

The failed assassins knew they had little time. The profanity and grievous trespass of their scheme would not be dismissed, and they would soon be forcefully seized. That is, unless their Urth brethren would conceal them, but that could mean a confrontation with the Sons of Light.

Would they be worth sparing? Would their master surrender them? They consulted within themselves. Ga'nost was the world of their home. They could not utterly abandon the nightmare world. But if they remained therein, they could only expect the heavy hand of their lofty rivals upon them.

They hurried through towering, iron gates, and sought to report to the Great Kel'torh of Castle Burning Skull. They thrust and snarled at onlooking Urth. The onlookers stared at their desperate flight. Some heckled their failure, whereas others murmured and queried amongst themselves, "Fools! Did you think they wouldn't uncover your destruction?" chided one.

"Are they coming for them now? Must we go to war over this? A truly grave matter is upon us," another pondered.

"No, clearly you cannot hide here . . ." one rebuked.

"Whaw haw haw . . . it's a Mevu'yash!" yet another taunted. "For you, it shall be the Naloz'oth Vaults! There is no place to hide, not here, not anywhere!"

At the mere mention of the dreaded Vheilyel dungeons, the hateful fugitives glanced at one another in accord, and turned to the latter naysayer. They seized its scaly, elongated throat, and instantly it cowered before them.

Cold and unannounced, one proceeded to expose a set of massive, fanged jaws while the other held the cynic in place. They ripped and greedily devoured their prey down to its torso. None dared intervene. The vicious fugitives cursed and thundered and pointed their scaled fingers at the gazing horde.

"We are doomed, you hear! The *Mystery of the Seven O'rahs* is upon us. Prepare yourselves, all of you!" the hunter threatened.

The ominous words did not resonate well. The gazers had been provoked to wrath. They hissed and bellowed in the manner of their kind, in that deep, bone-chilling howl. Their eyes burned with that detestable sulfured hue, and their reprobate essence blades were drawn, ready to execute the fugitives, Howarmog and Azbele.

"BLASPHEMY!!" the serpentine crowd shouted.

"You dare confess the words of the Day Zarrar in this place!" others challenged.

"Oh no, no, no. It is you who are doomed . . ." hissed yet another in an eerie, menacing tone as it revealed from within its hooded head, one monstrous maw full of fangs.

And so, violence and rage filled the house of the Urth tyrant upon the appearance of the Zayd fugitives that day.

***

"Papa, that's enough!" Enos exclaimed.

The yellow-haired boy could no longer bear the horrors of the Urth and their cruelty. Kirrius, their ferocious gethwi companion, could no longer bear the strain of the child pulling his proud, unkept coat. He growled and protested his rider,

"Huawrr . . . grawrr," Kirrius announced.

"What, Papa? What's he saying?"

"He actually seems very upset. I think it's because you keep pulling on his coat."

"Oh, I'm sorry, Mr. Kirrius. I'll try to stop now. Please don't eat me." Saxfen playfully laughed.

"I know this part of the story is scary, but you must understand how the Urth behave and how they think. You will grow up to understand this one day," he assured.

The lone Shaifetnu and his son strode upon their majestic escorts, Tonby and Kirrius, who had led them past the bleached, ujorg monuments and unto the entryway of that massive edifice, Oclyd Tower.

"Are you sure we are welcome in this place, Papa?" Enos timidly wondered.

"Don't worry, Son. You are amongst friends. The gethwis that live here have been living here for many years now, but I'm sure they'll be happy to see me. It is said they even tell stories to one another in their own way about how the Vheilyel and their Silver-haired One saved them long ago."

Saxfen proudly led the way as they proceeded to enter the frozen tower. It was pleasantly lit inside from the windows adorning all walls.

There were curious shadows lurking in all directions, creeping, stalking, dashing. And then the assault finally came,

"Grrrl, hurrawl! Rawrrrl!!" the unseen gethwis shouted.

They crept on every side, ready to pounce and devour the intruders. But then Kirrius and Tonby responded with roars of their own,

"Grrawl! Grawl rawrl!!"

The silence that followed was stunning, only the shrill whisper of the eve's wind could be heard. And then, the snow gethwis revealed themselves. They encompassed Saxfen and his son. They made not a sound. Only their azure, twin set of eyes firmly fixed upon the sojourners.

Finally, there approached one amongst them who proceeded to bow to the ground, and then all gethwis in like manner followed. They bowed in the hundreds, from the onlooking floors above to the far corners of the corridors. Indeed, the beasts remembered the silver-haired Shaifetnu that stood before them. It was his scent, the scent they had told tales to one another about, all these years, amongst their fellow gethwis.

"Whoa, Papa. They're beautiful!"

Enos watched in awe at the majestic, four-eyed beasts. He gazed at their regal, striped fur and the proud, unkept manes upon their upper backs.

"Are . . . you sure they're not going to eat us? How do all these cats eat?"

Saxfen laughed. It filled his heart with joy to behold his son imbued with such curiosity.

"Yes, I'm sure they will not be eating us. You don't need to be afraid. They typically feed on the wild gemips that love the cold of the snow or the delicious fish of the red sea. The Vheilyel did not give them this sturdy tower only to starve them to death here."

"Wow, so how did they get here, then? There's so many of them," Enos wondered as he petted another nearby gethwi.

"We're getting to that. Patience, Son. For now, we need to rest until the sun comes up. We will look for Eukeris in the morning when the day breaks."

But the gethwi clans could not contain themselves, for they had all heard of the grand exploits of this, Saxfen of the Green Star. Therefore, they eagerly sought after their gethwi fellow, for Eukeris. And at last, they found him and announced that the Snow-haired One from his tales had come again to see them! And Eukeris was most delighted with the tidings. He hasted down the elaborate corridors of Oclyd Tower with twin tails in the air until finally reaching Saxfen. And upon seeing the silver-haired Shaifetnu, he pounced on his old friend and playfully swatted at him on the ground.

"Wow, it's so good to see you too, Eukeris!" Saxfen laughed.

He rose to his feet and introduced Enos. Eukeris greeted him with friendly purrs and a headbutt in the manner of their custom.

"This is incredible, Papa! I love them so much!" Enos exclaimed as he petted the wild beast.

The beautiful gethwis looked on in admiration. After all, this was he who had slain the dreaded Drukijaken of Nith! This was he who had come long ago with many winged gods by his side, which had warned them of the impending doom of Mount Tanlish.

Exhausted from their journey, Saxfen and his son found a place to rest. And the cordial assembly did not appear to mind that their guests reclined themselves against their posh, cozy fur.

"I wonder how many there are?" Enos guessed.

"I'm not sure of their number, but it looks like they're very happy here. Plenty of room, that's for sure. They have the fortress all to themselves."

"So, this is where the wiljorgs lived, huh?"

"Yes, and their terrible monster, the Drukijaken, lived in the red sea nearby. It was a scary sea monster, even scarier than the stories said. I honestly don't know why I even agreed to face it. But it seemed right at the time, I guess. Probably from my anger for what they did to our village. Those eyes, that mouth . . . and that awful red lightning . . ."

Saxfen glanced at his son. He was sound asleep.

"But I wasn't alone, my dear boy. I wasn't alone . . ." Saxfen murmured as he himself drifted into the lands of slumber.

The warm, morning rays swiftly arrived, and they gently provoked the waking from their fortifying rest.

"Good morning, Enos. Did you sleep okay?"

"Yes, these gethwis are so comfy."

They rose to their feet and found that Eukeris was patiently waiting for them. The ferocious beast patted the cold, masoned floor.

"Look, Papa. I think he wants us to follow."

"Alright, let's get moving."

Saxfen mounted his old friend and Enos rode Kirrius again and they made their way through the stately halls of Oclyd Tower. No one else had dwelt in these quarters for many years, nor any other place in Ujorg Stone, except the cursed wiljorgs.

But those creatures had long abandoned this jewel of a city. And now, the ravenous, yet gentle-hearted snow gethwis of Mount Tanlish had laid claim to it as their new abode.

Twain beast companions led their guests until they finally halted at the elegant entryway of some royal chamber.

"This must be it, Enos. They're urging us to go in there."

Eukeris led the way, and ahead, there laid a small group of slumbering, four-eyed beasts. They were roused by a gentle growl from Eukeris. And then, there suddenly came a group of adorable gethwi cubs from the midst of the slumbering group.

"Whoa! Baby gethwis!" Enos shouted.

The cubs pounced and purred. They swatted playfully at Enos as he struggled to pet their soft fur. They curiously studied the strangers with their duel set of azure eyes.

"Eukeris, you're a father?!" Saxfen exclaimed. "They're incredible."

Saxfen held the loving cubs in his arms and was unable to stop smiling from the joy he felt for his friend. *This is great!* he thought. *I can only hope that Jix and Qugam are also doing okay.*

Saxfen of the Sevrinjiv, the triumphant Fifth Lightning, had traversed from across far-placed stars to look upon his beloved gethwi friend. And now, his thoughts drifted unto the courageous neufs of Oakendunty Village who had comforted him, and had come to accept him as one of their own.

Chapter 10

Sign of the Eighth

S word of Oakendunty, as the company of sojourners had named themselves, proceeded in their march throughout Tunjunsora in search of the third Vheilyel sent forth to accompany them. They now treaded the frigid, desolate regions of Mount Tanlish, where the deadly snow gethwis were known to dwell.

"Are we there yet, him?" Qugam complained.

"Hey, take it easy, Qugam. You're free to go back if this is too much for you," Jix reprimanded.

"You take it easy, Jix," Saxfen defended. "Where is he gonna go? Throw himself into the mouth of a wiljorg?"

Tensions were high, as they had ceaselessly traveled unto the snowy terrain of the gethwi mountain.

"Now, now. There's no need to quarrel," said one diplomatic Starrelos.

"Remind me again why this Eluryn can't just come to us?" Jix impatiently wondered.

"Well, I know this may be hard to understand," Orilheart calmly explained. "But we are working covertly, in secret, that is. Eluryn herself is looking for us at this very moment, but we just can't announce, 'Hey, over here! Come and get us!' I mean, of course, we can, but we are being cautious not to emit energy surges so we may avoid clashes with the Council of Night. If we used celestial power to communicate or to travel, for example, the Urth may pick up on this and trace us to our location. Make sense?"

"I don't know. I guess? If you say so, O. This Council of Night sounds like a real pain in the nether-fur, that's for sure," Jix sighed.

"Hey look over there!" Saxfen shouted.

The company was met with the jagged entryway to a cavernous orifice in the solitary distance.

"Let's take refuge there for the day. We'll continue in the morning," said Orilheart.

The group established their camp in the snowy cavern. The sun shortly faded into one splendid, vermillion horizon. They had found shelter in good timing.

"Look at that, luck is on our side," said Jix.

"Yes, we are highly favored indeed. This is providence," said Orilheart.

"Providence? Don't mind me asking. I mean no offense, O, you know me," Jix said. "But why does your god make us go through all this trouble? Why can't he just 'providence' us with the harp so you can be about your way? I'm no expert, but wouldn't that make more sense instead of risking our lives?"

Orilheart briefly glanced at her fellow Vheilyel. She then glanced back at Jix with her customary, warm smile.

"I guess we take it for granted that most creatures don't see the world like we do. Well, Jix, if the Living One just magically handed us the harp, what would be the glory in that?"

"Ahem, the what?"

"You know . . . *the glory* . . ." Orilheart responded with eyes widening and with arms raised above her head as if heralding something grand and extravagant. "*The renown*! *The honor* from the Council of Daylight! *The praise* at the High Tribunals! This grand *legend* that is unfolding before your very eyes! You will talk about this with your children, and their children with their children.

"Tell me, my young neuf, how else would this great *glory* ever come to light? How would it ever be born upon the Path of the Waking, if there was no triumph over villains and trials? And no triumph over things larger than ourselves? I ask you, how else would these stories ever exist? How else would General Starrelos have become the *Liar's Bane?* How else would Eluryn have become the *Mender of the Broken Akaz'ath?* If you knew the tale ahead of time, and you were given the opportunity, wouldn't you want this everlasting glory yourself?"

Jix paused but could not retort in his usual snarky manner.

"Uh . . . I guess we're just lowly little neufs in this big world, and we don't think about stuff like that," he finally said.

"The glory, huh?" Saxfen chimed.

"Yes, Saxfen. If you truly are appointed to overcome the great adversity that awaits us, your name will live on throughout the ages like the stars live on in the night sky. Your name will echo to the depths of eternity like the wondrous echo within the depths of this cavern."

She raised her voice and proceeded to shout into the hallow cavern, "SAXFEN, LIGHTNING BOLT OF GOD!"

The cavern responded with the resonating, echoing sound of her delicate voice as she playfully laughed in her usual way. The boys quietly pondered over the crackling fire, this curious explanation she had offered. They had yet to truly pause and consider that their quest was becoming quite the extravagant tale, the kind they would recount to their friends over a campfire such as this; the kind that would be told for generations.

"Sounds like this glory thing is a big deal to you guys, O," Jix said.

"Well, yes. It is our wealth and high honor to be accepted and celebrated by the society of the Daylight."

"Whoa, this is way too much to take in, guys. I'm just a kid!" Saxfen exclaimed.

"You're doing very well, him," Qugam assured. "Most other kids would never stop crying like scared little hims!"

"Yes, young Shaifetnu prince, the road ahead is very long, but we are here at your side, every step of the way," Starrelos said in a comforting manner.

"If it makes you feel better, Saxfen, I'm actually new at this too," Wolsage explained. "So, I understand how overwhelming all this may feel to you right now. You're probably thinking, 'Why me? What if I fail?' Honestly, I think the same things too. I can't help but wonder, 'Why are they sending such a novice to something so important?' It doesn't make sense to me. Orilheart might as well be a Sabbayoth with her extensive fighting skills, Starrelos is a great general of the armies of Jiobb'rynarth, commanding great legions of the Sabbayoth. And Eluryn is a powerful Aedyr Queen."

Saxfen was exceedingly comforted by the Learner's warm words. He was refreshed to find that even the fabled Vheilyel shared his disquieted thoughts.

"So, General, you lead armies, like, to real wars?" Saxfen asked.

"Yes, I have been leading campaigns against vast armies for such a long time, it would give you night terrors," Starrelos shared as he briefly recalled the haunting creatures that had fallen at his feet.

"Starrelos, the triumphant war general, huh?" Jix chimed. "Yeah, I guess that makes me feel a little better."

"Yup, Starrelos has survived many wars," Orilheart explained. "We are all so proud of him, and we are honored to have one of such rank and caliber come along to secure the harp. We truly are lucky!"

"Hey, what about us, hims? We're in this too, you know," Qugam interrupted.

"Yeah, I know I said we're just lowly neufs back there, but we're still here, ready to pledge our lives for Snowball."

Orilheart playfully laughed.

"Jix, Qugam, I'm afraid after we secure the harp, you will not be able to join us," Orilheart replied.

"What?!" the whiskered neufs exclaimed. "You're kidding! You're taking Saxfen, him . . . from us?!"

"I'm afraid so."

"Well, we have better things to do than be slapped around by some Light-feeder, or whatever, anyway. Don't we, Qugam?" said Jix.

"What? No . . . I want to go with you, hims!" Qugam responded with slight tears in his eyes. "Please don't take our him from us!"

Saxfen placed his arm around the teary-eyed neuf and comforted him, "It's all right, Qugam. This is the right thing to do."

And, with that, the saddened neuf was compelled to make peace with Saxfen's eventual parting. He would only be permitted to share in the journey until the stolen harp was restored to the Shaifetnu boy. After that, they would part ways and may never see each other again. He laid down his curled horns and wiped the tears from his whiskered face as the thoughts of their fond memories consoled him through the night.

The warm, morning rays rapidly arrived, and Sword of Oakendunty was hailed by faint, merry chirps outside the cavern. The company arose and persisted in their search for their third, celestial companion.

"It's so calm and peaceful around here," said Saxfen.

"Don't be fooled, Snowhead," Jix responded. "It may be peaceful in these parts, but the deadly gethwis that roam nearby could devour us in an instant."

"Perhaps," Orilheart concurred. "But any troublemaker gethwis looking for a fight will have to go through us. I'll be sure to have a good talk with them and explain the nature of our business here so there will be no need for fighting. Gethwis are actually very sensitive creatures, you know. They love to snuggle and purr, but don't mess with their food or their territory because then they turn into completely different persons!"

"In all my expeditions, I have yet to encounter a snow gethwi," Starrelos said.

"Come to think of it, I've never seen one either," Wolsage seconded.

"Yup, me neither," Qugam chimed. "I've never seen the hims in person, only in stories."

The mere thought of beholding a real gethwi in the flesh thrilled the young lads, who had long heard of these majestic, wild beasts around their cozy campfires. They eagerly wondered what they would look like at a short distance. Would they see any, whatsoever, during their visit to Mount Tanlish?

And then, the gripping uncertainty finally culminated. In the faint distance, the group spotted one crouching, striped predator, stalking a careless fayen pecking away at the base of a tree trunk.

"Hush . . . don't let it see us," Orilheart whispered.

"Yeah, let's wait here until the him leaves," Qugam agreed.

They studied the regal, four-eyed beast as it calculated the opportune moment of its pounce upon the doomed, feathered fayen. The hungry gethwi patiently tarried until the sturdy fowl cleared its head from view. But the meal was foiled by the sudden, alarming shouts of one terrified neuf.

"AHHHH . . . get it off me!" Jix exclaimed from atop a snowed tree.

The terrified neuf firmly gripped his own tail. It seemed a second gethwi had discovered him and was now raging at the foot of the tree.

"Grrr Hawrrll Graww!" the gethwi announced.

But the fierce creature was suddenly diverted by quite the unexpected reproof.

"NO! We are NOT stealing his fayen!"

It was the chiding voice of Orilheart, and it had silenced the raging gethwi's mouth. The three boys glanced at one another in utter amazement. The gethwi itself was baffled that Orilheart understood his tongue and his thoughts.

"Uh . . . alright, you heard her. You can go away now," Jix gently nudged.

The gethwi then growled some more in response to Jix as it clawed at the snowed tree with its massive paws.

"Well, I'm glad you asked," Orilheart responded. "Let me introduce myself. My name is Orilheart. We are looking for a friend who's somewhere on this mountain. She's slightly taller than me, has long red hair; bright, green eyes; and at times she has a set of six wings on her back."

The gethwi growled yet again.

"Yes, wings . . . on her back. Six of them. Have you seen her?" Orilheart asked.

The gethwi was slightly amused, and the offended Orilheart was quick to defend, "What? No, that's *not* ridiculous. It's what we look like. Here, let me show you. Look, see this flap on my back? It opens so these can come out."

Orilheart thrust out her sixfold, beautifully feathered wings for the cynical gethwi to behold. The gethwi was visibly shaken at the sight of the curious wings and proceeded to sniff and inspect them. It growled and hissed.

"No, they are not made out of snow, I'm afraid," Orilheart responded.

And then there came a second growling voice that intervened in the ongoing quarrel.

"Why, thank you. And I'm terribly sorry your fayen got away. We were not planning on stealing it. I promise!" Orilheart sincerely insisted.

The striped gethwis were dazzled by the stranger's huge wings. Their jeweled, azure eyes were fixated on how fluffy and powerful they were. *Where did they come from? How do they fit back there? Could she do it again?* They thought to themselves. The curious beasts gently swatted and even nibbled at them playfully.

Having gained their trust, they then proceeded to formally exchange names.

"Oh, it's nice to meet you, Ridtiil and Eukeris," Orilheart responded. "Yes, that would be amazing! Would you so kindly take us to her? Look, to show you we mean no harm, we will replenish that which we caused you to lose."

Orilheart then stepped away from the crowding beasts and spontaneously sang a sweet melody. There was silence, and only the midday gust could be heard sailing across the pallid, roseate skies. The quaint, serene moment was then disrupted by the sudden ruffle of flapping wings. It was flock upon flock of eager fayen, racing to catch another hint of the magical melody proceeding from Orilheart's voice. She sang a while longer, and the speckled fayen were now everywhere.

"See, we are friends!" she exclaimed as she motioned her arms to view all the fayen she had called on their behalf.

Twain gethwis each effortlessly seized their meal and they insisted their guests follow them with mouths full of bounty.

"You mean she didn't care to feed you guys like this? How rude, Eluryn," Orilheart chatted.

"Wow, Orilheart talks to hims like it's nothing," Qugam whispered.

"Yeah, she's totally got this!" Saxfen laughed.

"I knew she was in charge all along," Jix said.

"Whatever, Jix, you cried like a baby neuf back there!" Saxfen teased.

They laughed and taunted the nearly-devoured Jix as he grumbled under his breath.

"I must say, these gethwis truly live up to the touting of them," Starrelos said.

"Oh, they're adorable!" Wolsage admired. "Those bright, blue eyes! Two in each eye! And those stripes! I kind of want to take one with me back to Hyirius-nu."

"Well, I'm quite certain they would die if you brought them to Hyir-ius-nu," Starrelos said.

"Oh, how so?"

"Well, if I may," Starrelos explained. "The air is different in Hyir-ius-nu. I know this because I have been there. Also, their bodies may not be able to withstand the food or water there because they are not accustomed to anything outside Eofendurk. And even if you somehow find suitable food and drink for them, they would be required to use a kobanuk the entirety of their stay."

"I see . . . and you're sure about this, then?"

Starrelos nodded as he looked across Wolsage's shoulder and inspected their surroundings for intruders, his vigilant eye always on the alert.

Their newfound gethwi friends finally led them to the mouth of the famed, Wintebrek Caverns, atop the stout mountain, so named, Mount Tanlish. The gethwi colony growled and threatened with deadly glares, but they seemed to calm as Ridtiil and Eukeris responded with ferocious growls of their own.

One hazed figure then approached from within the shadows.

"Eluryn, is that you?" Starrelos shouted.

The figure then came into full view. It was the slim semblance of a gor-geous, young woman with long, rubied hair and frosty, pallid skin. She approached the company from amongst the gethwi clans, her delicate frame clad in royal battle armor. This was indeed Eluryn of the Order of Aedyr—Eluryn, Mender of the Broken Akaz'ath.

"Queen Eluryn, Peace of the Daylight," Orilheart respectfully greeted.

"Peace of the Daylight," she responded.

There was a brief exchange of warm greetings. The onlooking gethwis curiously observed while maintaining their safe distance. That cozy cav-ern of their frigid rendezvous had several openings permitting the radiant sunrays to illuminate several of the furred families lounging therein.

Scant cubs were playfully racing as their mothers kept watch. There was a pool filled with fresh, pristine water where the striped beasts congregated and appeared to socialize. Glamorous, crystalline rocks graced the icy abode like the gleaming jewels of a royal crown. This was that icy sanctuary, so named, the Wintebrek Caverns, a natural, frozen wonder only a few had lived to recount.

"So, how long have you been here, Eluryn?" Orilheart asked.

"Well, by the sun's measure, I have only tarried since yesterday. I hope I'm not late."

"Oh no, you're just in time. All of us hims were just heading to Oclyd Tower," said Qugam.

"Hims?"

"Yes, we're so glad to have you. But don't you think this place is a bit dangerous?" Jix pried. "I mean, why the gethwi caves? These are actually ferocious animals, you know?"

"Oh, are they not adorable?" Eluryn smiled. "You have to meet the rest! They are quite charming and hospitable once you are acquainted with them, once you are accustomed to their growls."

"Yes, well they are pretty amazing, I must say," Jix replied.

"But, truly, I am glad you asked, Jix. There is reason for my sojourning to the gethwi abode. I am come to these caverns because I wanted to retrieve . . . this."

Eluryn then presented to the company a long, mysterious object enveloped in soiled cloth. She pulled the dirty rags aside to reveal the ancient rod within. And behold, it was the fabled Scepter of the Shiggionoth!

"Whoa . . ." said the boys at the sight of the golden scepter. "Uh, what is it?"

"This, my young Shaifetnu prince, is called the Dominion Scepter of the Shiggionoth. Your kin dropped it when they arrived in this world. It is your heirloom, your heritage, the legacy and destiny of your ancestors."

The boys studied the mysterious relic, and their innocent eyes glimmered with awe as they gazed upon the bizarre inscriptions, and their imagination exploded with questions. Truly, the scepter was amazing to gaze upon. It was forged of fine, radiant gold in the manner of the O'rah Harp, and as the Harp of the Shiggionoth, this too was beautifully inscribed with an upmost, elder tongue. At its apex, there adorned the crafted likeness of golden wings raised to the sky, sixfold in number, three on each side fastened upon the rim of a polished ring.

"Well, what does it do?" Saxfen eagerly queried. "Does it shoot fire? Does it call down lightning?"

"Uh, no, not quite. Why would it do that?" Eluryn replied, lightly amused.

"I don't know. I figured it has magical powers so we can defeat the Drukijaken and retrieve the harp, or something."

"My, you have quite the imagination," Eluryn responded. "But you're close . . . it's even better!"

She raised the fabled scepter above her head and proudly announced its significance.

"I do not believe you heard me the first time. This, my young Shaifetnu prince, is the envy of the gods, the legendary Scepter of the Shiggionoth! Long thought to have been forever lost since the elder days of creation's Morning, and now, here it is before us once again, just as beautiful as the olden legends had said."

***

Now, it is needful to return our care unto elder epochs, unto the bleak, final hours of what came to be known as the Great Vexation of the Shiggionoth.

These were indeed the days of the Apostasy of Vanity before the vast chasms of Ru'alameth had been polluted by the Shadow Terror of the loathsome Light Eaters; those detestable fiends that proceeded from the forbidden void known as, the Dark Xoloth.

Long ago, in the age of that tragic rebellion, so named, the Apostasy of Vanity, there came the honorable Shaifetnu king, King Ryffeon. He wielded that grand weapon much revered by the Holy Vheilyel, that rune-inscribed scepter spoken of so highly by Eluryn, Mender of the Akaz'ath. This was a weapon most mighty, for it was forged by the crafty skill and wisdom of those immense, elder spirit-beasts, the Soggseraf Ekeru. These, who later became known upon the Path of the Waking for their evil deeds by a host of names, as some called them—Hexadrakes, Drageleons and Dragons.

That beautiful, royal scepter! And, O so mighty a scepter was thus entrusted to the Shaifetnu kings, who also were named, the Shiggionoth Lords, for they were charged with overseeing the matters of the sil-ver-haired Shaifetnu.

And that grand weapon was no weapon as one would expect. The Dominion Scepter itself was not used to injure or smite the adversaries at hand, but rather, it was used to summon the might of heaven's bat-talions, *to gather and command the fierce warriors of the Daylight!*

And so, as fate would have it, the Shiggionoth Lords in the days of the Apostasy of Vanity, were but mere novices in the skill of war and battle. They had long enjoyed generous epochs of peace after the quelling of the Apostasy of Power. But there came once again those rogue, apostate Soggseraf against them. Fallen from the Covenants of the Daylight, they were, but they had attained new opportunity to usurp and reign over the works within Ru'alameth. And thus, a new woe had befallen the excellent, cardinal cities of the Shiggionoth Lords.

At the time of the Great Vexation, Shiggionoth Ryffeon reigned from the exalted heights of the Cardinal City of Vydendoth, and the new uprising reached his beloved kingdom as in the bygone days of the Apostasy of Power. But this was a much different peril than the former rebellions of the past. For the adversaries had obtained the strength of newly forged confederacies, unlike anything they had witnessed since.

Reprobate, fallen spirit-beasts had returned with black hearts, and these were set upon the domination of Vydendoth—nay, of all worlds where Shaifetnu had their being.

Alas, this was the dreaded Apostasy of Vanity, when vengeful Soggseraf prevailed in the persuasion of the once-celebrated heroes amongst the Vheilyel! Heroes who had tasted the glory of vanquishing the great opposers of old, the holy knights of ancient times, these had indeed betrayed their oaths. The elder Soggseraf deceived them and therefore they waged war against the Council of Daylight.

And so, the majestic, Cardinal City of Vydendoth was sieged. Its defenses were breached, and the time to wield the power of the golden scepter had arrived once again. It was a sudden, brutal assault that not only tempted the noble king but also tempted the resolve and loyalty of faithful Vheilyel everywhere. The true heart of the many winged gods would surely be exposed through the awful return of the covetous, Soggseraf Ekeru.

In the days prior to the violent siege of Vydendoth, the days before that lovely city was overthrown, there lived few within the city that remembered the old war of the Apostasy of Power. The citizens of Vydendoth were a novice people, one consecrated to the learning of wisdom so as to properly rule, at the appointed time, those pristine, scattered worlds furnished throughout the stars. And so, the Council of Daylight was also established to lead and oversee the young silver-haired people and instruct them in good and correct paths.

But throughout the four corners of Ru'alameth, there lived contempt against the King of the Vheilyel amongst the servants of the Daylight. And it was their own King, the creator of Ru'alameth, the God of Beauty and of Virtue, who deemed it imprudent to perpetually entrust the worlds to the proud race of the Vheilyel. But rather, their dominion was one of necessity. And it was said that it would one day cease, at the time appointed.

Thus, some there were amongst the Urth who feared that long concealed oracle of enmity so great, which oracle was named, the *Mystery of the Seven O'rahs*. For it was said that it revealed the appointed time when the Ministry of Scales shall be abolished.

The God of the Vheilyel was well aware of his servant's limitations and of their covert ambitions. And thus, he was also aware of their predictable, final fate, their downfall driven by their hidden contempt for their Maker. The true heart of the many winged gods would indeed be summoned to light by the tragic events that would transpire.

Imbued with ever-expanding knowledge, the Vheilyel were destined to someday learn of the forbidden realms, so named, the Shunned Beyonds. Amongst these realms was that dreaded place of deepest gloom, that evil plane, so whispered as, the Dark Xoloth. Therein did the evil dwellers lurk, the accursed things that devastated the Shaifetnu kingdoms, those loathsome things, so named, the Light Eaters and the T'ohuvohu.

The Holy Vheilyel would someday discover these hidden realms, these Shunned Beyonds, and that which was contained therein. But most frightening of all, they would someday league themselves with the apostate Soggseraf. And they would conspire to release those shunned dwellers from the maddening chasms of the Dark Xoloth, and unto Ru'alameth.

Consumed with tormenting spite and hate, the immense spirit-beasts conspired diligently. The unbearable insult of endowing a lesser race with power over the worlds was unforgivable in their eyes. It was the mischief of the Living One, they reasoned, for forging the excellency that was their own being, only to subdue them and compel them to grovel at the feet of these silver-haired ones.

To be compelled to exist with this awareness was grievous and unforgivable in their eyes. It was an injustice. After all, *they* were the exalted Soggseraf of the heavens, *they* were the Builder Ekeru of old, imbued with wisdom and beauty and might, rivaling the powerful Vheilyel themselves. *They* had preeminence, *they* possessed abilities no other creature could even conceive, freely traversing the worlds like the fish of the waters freely traverse the seas. It was *their* workmanship and it was *their* own power that had built the glorious, ancient cities of the Daylight!

And to further impose grievance, there was that golden scepter. That loathed scepter! How they hated that scepter! It was the symbol of their everlasting servanthood at the feet of the unlearned and naive Shaifetnu people.

And so, those massive beasts that were the apostate Soggseraf, nay, the *Naloz'oth Soggseraf*, so named, these had conceived a great revenge for the humiliation of them, ushering in the Apostasy of Vanity. Their fair, ivory feathers stripped from them, they toiled covertly and prevailed in persuading the multitudes of the Sons of Light. And also they prevailed in the releasing of the Seven Light Eaters, who would defile the works within Ru'alameth with the Shadow Terror that proceeded from their flesh.

The dreaded day had arrived, when the evil, Naloz'oth Soggseraf would reveal their wrath anew. And so, with the aid of the betrayer Vheilyel, the Naloz'oth unveiled those seven most terrifying things from the forbidden void for all to see. Light Eaters, so named, from the shunned realm of the Dark Xoloth they did unleash. Their profound hatred for the silver-haired Shaifetnu and for the Living One Himself would now be satiated. This, through the utter destruction of the seven cardinal worlds of the Shaifetnu. And neither one of their former rivals of the Daylight would be able to withstand them this time, as there came with them, those accursed abominations that were the seven T'ohuvohu.

"...and now you must all learn the true source of all power!" shouted one evil Vheilyel with blazing eyes.

The adversary withstood the armies of the Daylight in full splendor, for the Urth had not yet been cursed with the Curse of the Morning.

The Shiggionoth Lord raised his arm above his head and firmly gripped the gleaming scepter in hand. It pulsated with might and contorted the ambiance as though it had power puncture the frame of Ru'alameth.

And at his command, the vast legions of the Order of Sabbayoth were summoned by the Dominion Scepter and fiercely smote at the impending forces. The celestial clash was brutal and merciless. There would be no prisoners. Vheilyel dashed against Vheilyel, and majestic ekeru of all forms warred against their own, far above the desecrated ruins below. And then the monstrous call of the things from the Shunned Beyonds erupted.

"Oh no, it's here!" one exclaimed.

"How much longer?" Lord Ryffeon shouted.

"Almost. We must withstand them for just a small measure now," another replied.

Below, there hurried a vast, frightened crowd of Shaifetnu citizens, streaming out of sight in a frenzy. They desperately sought to escape the sieged city. And there came to the aid of the fleeting crowds, one merciful Star Sharveth that was their shimmering hope of escaping the horror that would soon come upon them. This was that stellar passageway that would transmit the silver-haired peoples unto worlds far beyond their own.

"You must flee at once!" the Shaifetnu king shouted. "They shall need you amongst them!"

"No, I will not leave your side, my Lord Ryffeon," replied his attendant.

"Look at this! We have lost the city! Leave at once!"

"I will not!" the loyal attendant insisted.

With one wave of the golden scepter above his head, the king summoned many more Sabbayoth warriors to succor the smitten palace. But the forces of the Daylight failed to defend Vydendoth that day, for this was a peril far more perplexing than all prior.

This menace was unlike any the holy gods had ever witnessed in all wars past. Something terrible was amiss. There had come with this regrettable calamity, a strange influence upon the Sons of Light. This unknown dread later came to be known as, the *Shadow Terror*. For there came madness and fear most unbecoming and perplexing upon the holy Vheilyel. There had entered Ru'alameth, some inexplicable dread compelling them against their will to succumb to an unseen horror, like some widespread plague of celestial delirium.

But at last, the intruders revealed themselves in the flesh. The newly uncovered horror of the encroaching Light Eaters overwhelmed the righteous Vheilyel. Never had they encountered such a menace, much less imagined such things could exist!

The apostate Vheilyel closed in on Lord Ryffeon. The valiant king handed the scepter to his attendant.

"You must take this. It must stay with our people. I cannot bear the thought of those things seizing it," said the king. "We have held them back as long as we could."

Cithrel, his loyal attendant, was faithful in all the will of the Shiggionoth Ryffeon. He reluctantly received the golden rod and said his farewell. He then fled with all his strength as his master had ordered. The trauma of the loss was devastating. He could hardly escape the chaos of the royal tower. He pressed and strained until he was no longer able. There were hordes of apostate Vheilyel everywhere.

Alas, the tragedy! Those beautiful wings and those fair faces, *they had regrettably turned into instruments of vileness!*

They jeered and raged at the fleeing Cithrel. They flung their essence blades and blasted deadly currents from their palms. But the noble ekeru and the valiant warriors of the Daylight shielded him, some sacrificing themselves along the way. He finally collapsed, and the scepter flew out of his hands.

"NOOOO!" he shouted. "This can't be!"

The scepter slid off the edge atop the towering structure and tumbled far below upon the fleeing crowd.

The evil legions fought to prevent the exiles from leaving the doomed city, but their struggles proved to be in vain, for they faced the searing essence blades of the Sabbayoth armies. The golden scepter plunged out of Cithrel's sight, but it was now safe amongst the fleeing refugees below—for the time being, at least.

And thus did the Great Vexation visit the exalted Shaifetnu city of Vydendoth when the T'ohuvohu freely roamed upon Ru'alameth.

***

"This scepter," Queen Eluryn continued with her arm raised above her head. "It commands the legions of the Daylight! And now it is in your hands where it belongs, my dear Shaifetnu prince."

She placed the Dominion Scepter upon Saxfen's hands.

And this very act, this presenting of the lost scepter, this was yet another great marker of that ancient Decree of the Lightnings, and the Holy Vheilyel looked on in awe as the thing unfolded before their eyes. They filled their hollowed cities and tribunals with loud cheers and with shouts like the reveling of some grand, gladiator arena.

The Daylight had now advanced one step closer to the final triumph over their cosmic adversaries and over the damnable things that had been shamelessly unleashed from the void unspeakable. The sweet melody of a new, resonating chorus commemorated the event,

The storm clouds thundered, and the waters did rage.
But the Daylight pierced through and could not be restrained.
The fabled scepter, at last it is found and the Lightnings waged war.
Seven they are in number, Seven they are that vanquish them all!

Wondrous joy immersed their temples and sanctuaries. They sang and freely soared as the caressing sound of string instruments and surreal, choral harmonies encompassed the hosts. The great commotion could be heard outside the celestial palaces like the blood-thirsty cries of an invading siege.

Yet, not all Holy Vheilyel were assured of the meaning of these events. For there dwelt amongst them, those who harbored doubts. And there arose controversy and schisms underneath the threefold suns of Highest Ofandynth.

"The Lightnings are real!" some shouted.

"But this can't be correct. Those were fables, nothing more than mere parables meant to teach the great wisdom of the Living One," others responded.

"It is blind zealotry of the Urth! They have infiltrated the Aedyr of the High Tribunals to compel reason for war!" yet others frantically admonished. "They must have their war. Do you not see!?"

"The doom of the T'ohuvohu is upon us!" another shouted.

Schism and tensions were on the rise, but also within the tribunal cities, the time had come for the matter of the rogue fugitives, Howarmog and Azbele, to establish swift resolution. One Chief Sabbayoth, Oexiusdor by name, had summoned his formidable warriors. They were to seize and retrieve the fugitives in the grave matter of their unlawful assault upon the Fifth Lightning's village.

"Therefore, we have no other remedy than to apprehend them forcefully," Oexiusdor admonished. "We shall use robust force, if necessary. The fugitives may not be permitted to remain unfettered. Any questions?"

"Sir, is it true the Seventh Lightning has arrived in Highest Ofandynth?" one asked.

"Yes, that is correct."

The Sabbayoth ranks discretely whispered amongst themselves.

"Silence, please," Oexiusdor continued. "I understand this may be rather bewildering to many of you since the era of the T'ohuvohu was ages ago. Our adversaries, the Urth, have ruled for time immemorial for most of you, so I understand the tales and legends surrounding the Lightnings might appear to you like mere parables.

"But regardless of what you have heard, rest assured, the Lightnings are real. And because they are real, we will risk an all-out war with Ga'nost for the invasion of the Fifth one's village. Ga'nost knew full well what it was doing when it waged war against the Daylight in this, most grievous breach against the Covenants."

"Sir, when did the Seventh Lightning arrive?"

"He arrived only moments ago. Of truth, he must be preparing for this eve's festivities."

"Sir, considering the gravity of the crimes and in light of the unparalleled events, are we at liberty to destroy the Urth stronghold, Castle Burning Skull?"

"Yes, you are at liberty to demolish Burning Skull. But, be forewarned, the Urth may have developed weapons previously unknown to us in anticipation of the Lightnings. This latest act of desperation was only the start, so be prepared for anything. Tensions are high, so you must guard yourselves with the upmost caution."

The Sabbayoth commander concluded his instructions, and the war battalions were dismissed.

***

Elsewhere, underneath the restless skies of Ga'nost, the residents of the ghoulish fortress feuded with the fugitives at hand.

"How dare you blaspheme this High Temple of Corruption you tread upon?!" shouted one rageful Urth.

The desperate fugitives, Howarmog and Azbele, prepared themselves as the castle hordes closed in on them, ready to devour them.

"We would rather endure tortures at your hands than succumb to the Naloz'oth dungeons," the fugitives defied.

"I'm sure you would . . ." retorted another.

The menacing hordes screeched and howled. Piercing horns and sharpened claws, elongated necks, and hunched backs, duplicated heads and limbs, and scaly tails; all these demanded the blood of Howarmog and Azbele. Bulging, sulfured eyes filled with hate and mouths full of fangs lusted to tear apart their flesh for the words they had uttered, giving credence to the oracles of their adversaries. How dare they utter those things upon the halls of this, their most revered, Castle Burning Skull!

That is, until the sinister voice of the Great Kel'torh halted the brooding carnage.

"ENOUGH! Cease your folly at once, O Children of Darkness," he ordered.

The evil lord uttered in his chilling tone and addressed the quarreling fiends from the edge of an onlooking deck above. He uncoiled his serpentine frame and extended his scaly arm over the fuming hordes.

"There will be no need to destroy these Zayd this day. The Day Zarrar shall come for them, but we are counting on them to come. They shall come, and they shall put forth their demands to retrieve your brethren. And they shall expect to cast them into their prison without incident.

But they do not yet know they shall come face to face with our latest . . . *guest.*"

The hordes clamored and reveled at the sacrilege that had been announced, leaving off from their prior ambition of tearing into pieces twain fugitives.

A second figure accompanying the Urth Lord stepped from the shadowy balcony.

"Our Great Kel'torh speaketh correctly!" the orator announced in an eerie tone. "Hearken to my words, O Devotees of the Night! The rumors do not lie. This is the much-awaited unveiling! We surmised additional time was needful, but we have favorably summoned more . . . *attendees* for our great banquet. They hail from afar, from a banished sphere. Ye may have heard of it, from the hidden realm, from the *Dark Xoloth*."

The hateful, burning eyes of the serpentine horde became wild with excitement and bloodlust. They celebrated with awkward strokes and manic motions, with howls and piercing screechings. It was the unveiling they had secretly conspired for, at long last!

"And now, all ye Brethren of Darkness present this day, ye shall witness with thine own eyes what the Elders only dreamed of but could not bring to pass. Let us make haste unto the Yathruhnan Crypts!"

The agitated hordes scrambled and celebrated as they hastened unto the subterranean quarters of the morbid citadel. They hurriedly arrived at that ancient, cryptid arena they revered as, the Yathruhnan Crypts.

The place was adorned with nightmarish sculptures of nameless creatures of blasphemous origins. Images of beasts unknown to most conscious beings, images of their imprisoned gods, the T'ohuvohu, images commemorating Urth warriors for their savagery, and the slaying of the Sons of Light. These were sacred memorials the wicked Urth venerated, far-placed from the wholesome eyes of the Daylight. These were crypts so offensive and repulsive, that the Daylight had abandoned them altogether; hidden quarters and domains shunned and left to their profane devices, or so it was said.

The spectator, serpentine race rendezvoused in maddening cackles and eerie sneers, expecting to behold the things rumored about in this supposed, unveiling. For this was indeed the unveiling of a new rival to the Daylight, a malignant creature foreign to Ru'alameth, a newly summoned abomination from the forbidden realms of the Shunned Beyonds.

Many an Urth had merely heard of the great infamy of their captive gods, those things imprisoned throughout Ru'alameth, whom the Naloz'oth spirit-beasts first worshipped. They had marveled at the tales of how these once polluted the venerated temples, how they once trampled the disheartened souls of Daylight battalions; how they had devastated the untouchable, sacred cities and brought to ruin the cherished worlds of the abhorred Shaifetnu.

These were all but mere tales, forgotten in lost tomes in the profound oceans of time. But now these reveling fiends had been gathered unto one, unholy table, where they would savor the ruthlessness and wrath of the fabled T'ohuvohu of long ago—the dreaded Light Eaters, the *Gods of the Naloz'oth*.

The covert dwelling was filled with eager monstrosities and adversaries of all that is good. They looked on as their malignant host presented one curious, mechanical device at the center of the arena. It was the sight of luminous halos, eightfold in number, shimmering like silver, each suspended in midair. There came wild flashes through the center of each of these, like the surges of railing thunderclouds. And the base of the device revolved and pulsated with countless eyes made of eerie lights.

"Brethren! The Day Zarrar . . . shall envy us!" the Urth presenter declared to the tumult of the horde. "The Shaifetnu vermin shall wish they had never survived the carnage of the Seven Masters!"

The maniacal shouts continued as the Urth Lord of Ga'nost gazed from his grim throne. The vile seat of the Great Kel'torh was surrounded by heinous figures spewing bursts of filthy ooze. The throne itself was crafted in the likeness of a three-eyed monstrosity, resembling the remains of the gargantuan skull outside the citadel walls. Swarms of serpentine fiends filled the air, searching for a place to rest and observe the spectacle.

"The Lightnings, so called . . . shall bow to us!" the presenter boasted. "And they shall plead with us to spare them. Brethren, behold! I present to you . . . the Sign of the Eighth . . . *Gha'shuulmog, Dissolver of Realms!*"

The fiendish presenter eagerly activated the bizarre device, and there erupted amethyst bolts of haunting light. The sudden, blaring tumult of an ominous gust filled the lair of Urth worship. The flashing bolts from the infernal machinery were followed by the emergence of an abysmal rift, like the emergence of some malignant, searing Star Sharveth, foreign to the Halls of Ru'alameth.

They beheld and witnessed the inversed passageway intruding upon the Vheilyel realms outside the hellish shrine. This lawless breach from the shunned realm engulfed itself and plunged into the condensed mouth of a newly formed whirlpool, enjoining Ru'alameth to the forbidden Dark Xoloth against the natural order.

And the Urth revelings were suddenly suppressed as they timidly awaited what would follow. They were not disappointed. For there came the seething howls heralding the vengeful monstrosity summoned for war, emerging from depths far beyond the path of the many winged gods. It was that loathsome dweller from the shunned abyss, the eighth T'ohuvohu upon Ru'alameth, Gha'shuulmog, Dissolver of Realms!

The joyous feasting of the Daylight would soon be violently halted by the conjured terror from the sinful void. The time of madness had come, when the Urth would risk all their dominion and all their wealth in one final, desperate assault. Their wrathful eyes were now set upon the most sacred lands of them all, the lands of Highest Ofandynth.

Now that the Lightnings had been revealed and the ancient lore revived, there was no return. Truly, this was a brazen declaration of war; an uncontestable act of war, indeed. And now it had been published in the sight of all.

The Apostasy of Despair had arrived.

CHAPTER 11

OUR LEIYENWURI ROAR

The eve's twilight had set in, and Sword of Oakendunty purposed to settle their camp amongst their newly found friends, the tender, yet ferocious gethwis of Mount Tanlish. The air was bitter and icy upon that frigid summit, and it chilled the boys to their core. But the amiable, four-eyed beasts were happy to snuggle beside them and keep them warm. They curiously stared in fascination at their guests, as they were not accustomed to visitors, especially such bizarre creatures as the many winged gods.

The gethwi colony conversed amongst themselves about the strangeness of the mighty wings hidden underneath the Vheilyel's garments and about how delicious and crunchy they supposed the neufs would taste. They debated and guessed at their texture and flavor. And yet others expressed a more civil tone, in their own manner of conversing, by bringing food to the group from their treasury of bounty.

"So, what do you suppose the hims are doing?" Qugam asked as he studied the gethwis' subtle commotion.

Orilheart snickered as she struggled to contain her amusement, "Uh . . . I think it's been a long day. Try to get some rest, Qugam. Tomorrow, the real quest for the harp begins now that all three of my friends are here."

"Yeah, Qugam. I think they're talking about eating you while you sleep. I wouldn't keep them waiting if I were you," Jix teased.

"I think they're talking about us," Saxfen said. "They keep looking over here like they're talking about us."

The four Vheilyel glanced at each other, hoping for clues on how to divert the subject.

"Nah," Jix objected. "They're probably talking about what they're going to do tomorrow with all their free time in this lonely place."

"Well, I'm glad we've found some new allies in our journey," Saxfen offered. "No, Sword of Oakendunty has gained new allies!"

He then briefly paused and dramatically announced, "The legendary Sword of Oakendunty and its fierce army of immortal gethwis!"

"This, our army of immortal hims!" Qugam joined.

"Hey, what about us? Are we invisible now?" Wolsage said.

"Oh, you guys are great too," Saxfen assured. "But these are *real* gethwis here!"

Starrelos proceeded to give Saxfen a challenger's gaze, beckoning for a skirmish.

"And . . ." Saxfen continued. ". . . there's absolutely no way we could've seen them up close like this, if it wasn't for you guys!"

"I don't know about you, Snowhead," Jix said. "But I would take Orilheart over a smelly gethwi any day of the week. No offense, Eluryn."

Eluryn playfully laughed as she brushed her vibrant, red hair from her face, "No offense taken."

The band of adventurers teased and laughed until they finally dosed unto the mystic, nocturnal lands of slumber. And it was there that the young Shaifetnu prince was imbued with a glimpse of the thing that lurked underneath the waters of the Sea of Nith.

There, in the far depths of the realm of dreams, the Fifth Lightning found himself racing with all his strength in an unknown field, fleeing for his life. He found himself sore afraid. He was tormented and distressed.

He was alone. It appeared the dreaded, monstrous god of the wiljorgs had awakened to confront this contested Shaifetnu, which had disrupted its slumber.

That terrible giant of the deep, so named, Ruminthumgath, thundered and vehemently denounced the boy, taking great offense at the puny frame of this Shaifetnu, who was said to seek out the harp hidden within its bowels. The Drukijaken taunted and boasted of its devouring of the stolen harp. It raged and ridiculed the youth. Its hoary, deep voice was terrible and sardonic.

The wise and ancient creature of the scarlet sea chillingly inquired, "But who shall save you from me? This is my world. I rule the land and the air. I rule it all from the depths of this watery, red abyss."

Saxfen fled and wrestled to think clearly as the horrible thing pursued him. He desperately searched for refuge and relief. There, above him. He lifted his eyes and could see the proud summit of the gethwis, the snowy peak of Mount Tanlish. The warm, cherished memories of his friends, the snow gethwis, these suddenly returned to him at that moment and filled his heart with joy. Tears began to roll down his cheeks.

But the moving, fleeting sight did not go unnoticed by the monstrous god of the deep. He used the touching sentiment of that moment to further punish the frightened Shaifetnu youth.

"And what is this? You miss . . . your friends? Are they going to help you? Will they dare rise against me? Have they not heard of my wrath in all Eofendurk?!"

Saxfen held his peace in a cluttered medley of fear and bewilderment. The cruel, monstrous beast was then impulsively inspired by diabolical whim.

"I know. How about we ensure your friends do not intervene in this . . . our little dispute? How about we teach them not to meddle in the matters . . . of the god of Eofendurk!"

The Drukijaken then raised its tormenting voice as the piercing words burned within Saxfen's very being.

Then, in benumbing horror, Saxfen understood the heartless intentions of the evil Drukijaken. He screamed uncontrollably and could not refrain any longer.

"NOOOO!" Saxfen pleaded.

The heartless beast had no regard for Saxfen's tears nor for his heart-wrenching pleas. The crisp, roseate skies suddenly turned dense with haunting, menacing clouds. And at once, there came one raging, perilous thunderstorm, summoned and sent forth to barricade those enchanting Wintebrek Caverns. Saxfen rubbed his eyes in disbelief. Where did such awful clouds come from?

And then, as if heeding some unseen hand, the wrathful, dismal vapors blasted and rampaged in a maddening frenzy. The beaming power of their fury was unleashed upon the peaceful summit of Mount Tanlish. Raging blasts of ruinous bolts ravaged the proud mountain, and the gethwi abode was no more. The food bounty treasuries, the crisp pool of fresh mountain water, the jeweled crevices of the Wintebrek Caverns . . . *all gone!*

Saxfen screamed in desperation as he roused himself from the clamorous doom that came charging down from the heavens.

"Whoa, are you okay? It's okay. You're safe with us now," Orilheart comforted as she held the startled lad in her arms.

The three other Vheilyel rushed to his side as well. They watched attentively, ready to avenge against all trespassers.

"NO!! THE GETHWIS! The gethwis! No! Save them! Please save them!" Saxfen uncontrollably shouted, tears streaming down his face.

He slowly returned to his senses as the comforting arms of Orilheart embraced him. His silver hair was soaked in cold sweat from the trauma of the night terror. He gazed about and was visibly relieved to see the gethwis were in good health. The startled gethwis themselves anxiously looked on in bewilderment.

"Grrwl HuawrrL Rawrrr," said one.

"I think he's going to be okay, thank you," Orilheart responded.

She turned again to the terrified Shaifetnu and proceeded to console.

"See, they're alright, Saxfen. Try to take deep breaths. We're here to protect you."

"Orilheart, it was so real. And you were not there when I needed you. Neither was Starrelos or Wolsage. Not even Eluryn! It was just me and . . . that thing. It talked with me. I couldn't see it, but I could feel it. It talked to me with that horrible voice. And . . . and . . ."

Saxfen could not continue with the retelling of his nightmare as he wrestled to recall what followed.

"And what, Saxfen? It's okay. It was just a dream. You're here safe with us now."

Saxfen could not hold back his tears and could not finish his story.

"You know what?" Orilheart smiled. "Let's forget all about it. Let's not worry about this right now. Actually, we never have to talk about this, if you don't want to."

Saxfen agreed and began to feel better. He exhaled a sigh of relief. The startled gethwis returned to their matters as their guests slowly returned to their pleasant, cheerful selves.

"Alright, everyone. Let's try to get some sleep now," Orilheart said.

"Saxfen, I assure you," Starrelos said. "I command many legions of the mighty Sabbayoth, ready to rain down fury upon all our adversaries. Be greatly consoled."

"Yes, you are in highly capable hands," Eluryn said. "Believe and do not doubt in your heart."

"I may be a novice, Saxfen, but you have my devotion. I will serve you with the fervor I serve the Living One, to my last breath," Wolsage offered.

Orilheart smiled, "And . . . of course, I'm always here for you. Anyone trying to hurt you will have to come through me first."

"Yeah, Snowball, relax. We're here for you," Jix assured.

"No dirty him can stop us," Qugam said.

Saxfen smiled at the warm, comforting words of his friends.

"Thanks, guys. I really needed to hear that. I feel so much better knowing you're here with me."

The company conversed a while longer until they finally dozed unto the peaceful realms of slumber once again.

The morning rays descended from the pristine, roseate skies, and the sweet chirpings of wild fayen lauded the sunrise. But Saxfen was sound asleep, and the gentle songs could not arouse him from his bliss.

"Saxfen, Saxfen," said a warm, friendly voice. "It's me, Orilheart."

"Orilheart? Hi, how are you?" Saxfen responded. "What is this place? Where are we?"

The friends found themselves surrounded by the grand, ethereal beauty of what appeared to be a celestial capitol of the Vheilyel. They sat upon the ivory rim of an elaborate fountain, flowing with mystic water that appeared to resonate divine melodies when touched.

"The water . . . it's singing?" Saxfen marveled.

"Uh, yes. The fountain speaks . . . in its own way at least," Orilheart smiled.

"What's it saying?"

"It's saying, 'Saxfen, beloved Lightning Bolt of God, welcome to Eylundis.' It's glad to meet you."

"Oh, I see. Well, thank you, beautiful singing fountain thing. It's a pleasure to meet you as well."

"Yes, well, this place, this is the city of Lei'thrundall . . . my home."

She gazed into the surreal, towering pillars and majestic spires, piercing the swirling azure heavens. There could also be seen, neatly paved avenues and curious flora, beaming with radiant, luminous life. There soared the citizens of Lei'thrundall, drifting upon their sixfold wings and smiling as they passed by. Playful orils also wisped by, hurriedly about their day upon their fluttering wings.

The friends found themselves conversing atop one elaborate, dazzling tower, rising high unto the vivid heavens, surrounded by other opulent structures. And all of these were encompassed by a sea of coursing clouds. Also, there were gentle, bizarre creatures that could be seen roaming in the distance.

"Orilheart, this is amazing! This is where you come from?"

"Yes, this is actually where I was born, and it's always been home to me."

There came one tiny oril, and it rested upon Saxfen's shoulder.

"Oh, hello, little guy," Saxfen greeted.

"Don't mind her," Orilheart said. "She's just curious about the new visitor and she'll be on her way soon."

"What is it? Is this one of those orils you told us about?"

"Yes, that's an oril," she responded. "This one's name is Ennix, actually."

"Oh, you know her?"

"Yup, I practically know every oril here," she said, laughing.

"Every one of them? They're so pretty. That tail! And are those horns?"

He reached to touch the crown of ivory horns gracing the oril's head but the tiny being objected and wisped away.

They briefly stared into the excellent surroundings in the bliss of comfortable silence. The view was of upmost delight to the young Shaifetnu as he sat there immersed in the vast, heavenly sea of plush clouds, which slowly drifted amongst the exalted monoliths.

"Saxfen," Orilheart finally interrupted. "I wanted to show you this. I wanted to show you my home. And I also wanted to show you that I'm with you, even when you're asleep, in your dreams. So, you don't have to be afraid when bad dreams come."

"So, this, this is just a dream, huh?"

"Yes, it's a dream. But this place really does exist, and we really are there . . . well, in a way."

"In a way?"

"Yes, you're looking at a memory of Eylundis. You're walking in one of my memories of my home world. I can't actually take you there because that would give away our location to the Urth. It's the same reason we have to communicate in secret instead of our Face Sharveths. But if I could bring you here, it would look just like this, full of these little guys flying around, the sparkling water that sings when you touch it, the sea of clouds, the gentle wooths you see over there . . . that's really what they're like, if you came here in person."

"Whoa . . ." Saxfen said with a gasp.

"And this is just the start," Orilheart smiled. "There is so much more to see and to learn and to explore! But also, to prepare for."

"Oh, what do you mean?"

"I mean, just like this place and its beauty is real, there is also another side to it. There are very scary places and beings out there that you will no doubt encounter in our journey. This is your calling, so long as you choose to accept it.

"You see, it's not that we want you to see those dark places and bad creatures. It's that, well, the bad creatures will no doubt come for us. And they will stand in our way, opposing us and guarding the way. You are a threat to their survival, the Fifth Lightning. And, as such, our paths are destined to clash."

"I think I understand, Orilheart. You are with me, even when I'm asleep, so I can have peace in my heart, right?"

"Yes, and that's what I wanted you to see. No matter how awful our adversaries present themselves, no matter how scared you feel, you

must remember this place I brought you to. You must remember . . .
our friendship. And you must remember our power is greater than the
monsters of the Council of Night. Because, Saxfen, it is in your doubts
and your fears that they wield the most power over you and, believe it or
not, over us Vheilyel as well."

Orilheart's comforting voice gently faded as she pleaded with the
young Shaifetnu to believe and to be strong in the face of peril. Tears
of joy rolled down Saxfen's slumbering eyes until he finally arose to the
sweet melody of the chirping fayen outside the gethwi cavern. He awoke
and glanced at Orilheart as her loving gaze was firmly fixed on him. He
embraced her and wept in gratitude.

"Thank you, Orilheart. Don't ever leave my side," he sobbed.

"Shhh . . . it's okay, we will always be together, in our hearts."

The group prepared some food to nourish themselves for the long
journey ahead.

"Oh, it's ejiberry time!" Orilheart exclaimed as she eagerly devoured
her delicious meal.

"Easy there, O, you're gonna choke on your ejiberries," Jix said.

"Orilheart, I would think you'd mind your manners around your
Panni," Starrelos questioned.

"Yeah, and are you forgetting that this isn't just any ordinary Panni?"
said Wolsage.

"Oh, leave me alone! Me and Saxfen go way back," Orilheart laughed.

"How fortunate are you, to be such close friends with the Fifth Lightning?" Eluryn chimed.

Orilheart seemingly ignored every word from her friends and proceeded to obsessively devour her delicious berries, "That flavor! That
flavor! How do you not marvel at these incredible ejiberries as I do?!"

The group playfully teased at Orilheart's intense fascination with
Tunjunsora's ejiberries.

"So, anyway, I think I'm ready to talk about my dream last night," Saxfen said.

"Go on, tell us about your him," Qugam hurried.

"Alright, so I was standing in a field. No, wait. I was running in a field from something. I didn't know at the time, but I think I was running from the Drukijaken."

"Oooh . . ." said the neufs. "Well, what did it look like?"

"That's the thing, I didn't get a good look at him. I just heard his deep, horrifying voice. He taunted me and ridiculed me. He seemed offended I would challenge him for the harp in his belly. And . . . I was alone. No mighty Vheilyel warriors. You guys weren't there. It was just me and that thing."

The group intently listened.

"So, I was running from it, and I saw this very place right here, the mountain of the gethwis. I looked up, and it was the snowy peak of Mount Tanlish. The Drukijaken knew I was looking at the mountain and then . . ." Saxfen fought back his tears as he recalled what followed, "And, and then . . . the Drukijaken decided to take out his anger on the mountain. No, on our friends. On the snow gethwis!"

"Oh, I see why your him was so scared and sad," said Qugam. "And then what happened?"

"Well, that's the real scary part. The Drukijaken somehow called these thick, black clouds and commanded them to shoot powerful lightnings at the mountain. Guys, he completely destroyed this place in my dream!"

The friends sat in silence, carefully considering the dream as they nibbled on their savory ejiberries.

Orilheart finally spoke up, "Saxfen, my feeling is that this is no ordinary dream. I think what you saw was . . . the Realm of Decrees."

"Yes, this quite feels like the unveiling of something that is to come, a Foretelling Vision," Eluryn suggested. "Considering the circumstances, the Order of Sodd must be alerting us to some grave peril. We must take this to heart. We must take our gethwi friends out of this place."

"The Realm of the who and the Order of what?" Jix puzzled.

"Wait, what? You mean that's really going to happen?"

"Yeah, I'm afraid so, Saxfen," said Orilheart.

"How do you know, him?" Qugam said.

"Well, because the Realm of Decrees may at times be peered into from the land of dreams," she explained. "There are Foretelling Visions as Eluryn said, where future events are revealed. And there are also Endurance Visions, where only a potential outcome is revealed and we could prepare for it, like a warning. It's hard to tell right now, in our current state of stealth. We could ask the Daylight, but this may jeopardize our location."

"Oh no! Then that means the gethwis are going to die?!" exclaimed a frantic Saxfen. "That means the gethwi home will be destroyed! Can't we do something about it? Why does it have to be this way?"

"Okay, calm down. One question at a time," Orilheart replied. "Yes, we can do something. We can prepare. But if this truly is a Foretelling Vision from the sacred realm, and not a forgery, then there isn't much we can do to stop it. We can only prepare in anticipation and try to save as many gethwis as we can."

"Oh no, the gethwi hims are going to die?!" Qugam panicked.

"Well, did you actually see them die?" Wolsage asked.

"Uh . . . well, no, not really. I just saw this very mountain blown to pieces," Saxfen responded.

"Okay, that's a relief, then," Wolsage pondered. "So, it may not be totally hopeless after all. Perhaps you were given this vision so we can save the snow gethwis from some impending calamity we are not yet aware of."

"Okay, hold on a minute," Jix challenged. "Why don't we find out for sure, before we go through the trouble of getting everyone out of here?"

"Yes, we could," Starrelos responded. "But as Orilheart said, we risk exposing our location, and so our problems will be multiplied by incoming hordes of Urth warriors. And we cannot risk a confrontation at the moment."

"Well, that's lame. So, what do we do, guess our way through this?" Jix continued.

"Not guessing, my dear neuf, but rather, having faith," Starrelos said.

"Oh? What does that supposed to mean?"

"It means faith does not require certainty, but we press onward in spite of not having certainty."

"Right, so we're guessing."

"No, guessing does not have the confidence of faith. We have confidence that this is a genuine vision from the Daylight, and we will take the warning to heart. We will prepare for the worst, in the full confidence of faith."

"Alright, fair enough," Jix conceded. "But how are you going to persuade our four-eyed fur balls to abandon their precious mountain?"

Starrelos glanced at his fellow Vheilyel, "Any suggestions?"

"We can lure them with vast treasures of food?" Wolsage answered.

"Um, no," Orilheart responded. "They love their home more. Besides, there are no shortages of food in these parts of the mountain."

"We can transport the hims through one of those watery doors you speak of," Qugam said.

"Nope, they may not survive."

"Okay, bad idea, him."

"We can frighten them out of this place with one of my servants from the hidden realm," Eluryn offered.

"What? No. They'll hate us forever. Besides, they'll probably fight to the death defending their home."

"Can't you, like, give them a sign or something, so they can take a hint?" Jix suggested.

"Um . . . that's it! Yes, I got it!" Orilheart announced. "We will explain to the gethwis the reason for our visit. We will tell them we are here to warn them of an impending doom that is about to strike this place. We will tell them they need to evacuate for a year, which should be plenty of time for us to get the harp and plenty of time to kill the Drukijaken, if that's what it takes. And we will confirm all this by furnishing them with a sign in the night sky, as well as a sign in the day sky."

The seven friends concluded their careful devisings and began to announce the prophecy amongst the gethwi clans. The gethwi, so named, Eukeris, he had grown deeply fond of their guests. And he was gravely alarmed to learn of the imminent doom that was said to destroy his family and his beloved abode.

"Grr Grawl Hawl," said Eukeris.

"Yes, I'm afraid this is the only way," Orilheart explained. "Very soon, anyone left on this mountain will be slain by the destruction that will come from the sky."

Eukeris was visibly grieved. The gethwis loved the mountain, but most of all, they loved the cold. The freezing, perilous gusts of the mountain felt amazingly fresh on their bristled, striped coats. The thought of living anywhere else made the four-eyed beast dizzy with anxiety.

"Rawr Rawrr Herwl," he continued.

"We understand you love your home. But we are here to save your lives. Thank you for believing us," Starrelos said.

Eukeris offered to accompany the Vheilyel in their labors to convince his fellow gethwis of the danger they were in. There came, Tonby, a close fellow of Eukeris, and offered to assist in communicating that an impending cataclysm would soon be upon Mount Tanlish. For the message would be most effective if the gethwi families heard it from one of their on kin.

"Alright, Starrelos, you take Tonby and head north," Orilheart direct-ed. "Eluryn, you take Ridtiil and head west. Wolsage will go with Kirrius to the gethwis of the south, and I will take Eukeris with me east."

"Hey, what about us? We want in on the fun too," said Jix.

"Why are you hims leaving us out?" Qugam protested.

"You guys are welcome to go along with whoever you like. I think we are safe in these parts, and you are in good hands."

The neufs did not hesitate to accompany Orilheart. She was, after all, their best friend. Eukeris asked a few of his friends if they could join them in carrying the three boys. The curious gethwis, enthralled by their bizarre guests and their ominous message, gladly went along and carried the boys. The kirok birds were safe in the enchanted cavern and enjoyed a brief rest along with the generous hospitality of the gethwi clans. The gethwis secretly dreamed of devouring them, but they would not dare commit this deed against their new friends.

The mountain gust roared, and Orilheart's company defiantly pressed against it. Onwards they marched unto the eastern region of the snowy summit. There were scattered groups of wild gethwis along the way, and Eukeris snarled at them. The onlooking, double-tailed beasts heeded Eukeris' beckoning without much hesitation and followed. This matter seemed most important, the gethwis reasoned, as they had heard for the first time in ages, their Leiyenwurl Roar, so named. They formed one orderly arrayed caravan and followed him unto the upmost rim of the eastern bounds.

"What's he saying to them, Orilheart?" Saxfen asked.

"Yeah, all the hims are following us? What's he saying?" Qugam chimed.

"I think it's some sort of trivial code. It roughly translates, 'Our Leiyenwurl Roar,' or something. They sure take it seriously, though, as you can clearly see."

"These furballs are pretty neat, I have to admit," Jix admired.

The stirring expedition unto the eastern bounds finally ended when the trailing caravan of wild gethwis had reached the outermost rim. Eukeris engaged a few of his nearby kin, invoking that curious, feral code to gather everyone for this most urgent matter at hand. The clan was gathered throughout. Some murmured while others threatened. Some scoffed at the rumors that had already spread, and yet others eagerly awaited to hear the matter plainly.

"Now, Eukeris," Orilheart instructed. "I'm going to address your fellow gethwis, and I need you to relate what I say very carefully. It will be best if they hear it from you. This is not a game or a joke. This is a life-or-death situation. They are all in grave danger, you see."

Eukeris agreed and exhaled a solemn roar that captivated everyone's attention. He had announced the event was about to commence. The wild colony of ferocious, four-eyed gethwis was not so savage after all, it seemed. They were attentive and appeared to adhere to basic etiquettes of civility. And, yet again, this apparent civility could also be explained by their burning curiosity concerning these 'winged ones,' and thus they observed the spectacle with obsessive wonder.

The assembly engaged in solemn observance at the mention of the Leiyenwurl Roar, and the cold, mountain gust only increased the tension felt. All eyes were fixated upon Orilheart, whom they had heard could expel glorious wings from her back. And she did not disappoint. She began by flinging her beautiful set of sixfold wings, and she soared high above all their heads like some awe-evoking, crimson gylth. The gethwis all but gasped at the sight of the winged damsel. They had never seen such a marvel, and so they looked on the more intently.

Orilheart then proceeded to summon her royal garb, those celestial gowns of the Daylight Eth. These emanated from tiny, faint threads of light, engulfing her body. The luminous threads then converted into fine attire of white cloth, elegantly garnished with vivid adornments of golden hue. The gethwi clan was much impressed, and if they could, they would have applauded. They conversed amongst themselves in their curious way, wondering, disputing, admiring the incredible sight before them.

And so, Orilheart began her admonition, "Friends, I call you friends because we are here with sincere concern for your lives . . ."

The solemn growls and heartfelt pleas of Eukeris could be heard as she continued.

"I am Orilheart of the Eth Vheilyel. I come from the stars above you to warn you of a great evil that is coming to your cherished home. A great evil has been summoned to destroy your beloved mountain. This mountain will be demolished by forces you cannot imagine.

"We plead with you, save yourselves! Save your families and loved ones. You must evacuate this mountain and flee the catastrophe that is coming! All of your gethwi kin are also being likewise warned. Again, I plead with you as my own friends, you must flee this place and escape the tragedy that will follow.

"Look to the emerald star in the sky! You don't have to take my word for it. The blazing, emerald star in the sky will visit us in three short days. It will be with you in the night sky and in the daytime for five days and five nights. It will come to comfort your doubts, that what we are saying to you this day is true. It will tell you of the impending doom that will come upon Mount Tanlish. Believe the emerald star, my dear friends!"

Orilheart concluded her plea and the gethwis were astonished. But only momentarily. For they shortly returned to themselves and scoffed and derided the prophecy. Gethwis do not laugh, not out loud at least, but internally.

"Well, what are they saying, O?" Jix inquired.

"Uh, well . . . they're laughing," Orilheart said.

Eukeris was not amused. He roared and growled in objection to their careless response.

"Grrwl Hawrl Grrl," retorted one.

"Hrrwl Grrwl Mawhrr," another exclaimed.

"Hawrl Grrawl Huawrrl," yet another said.

Saxfen looked at Orilheart in curious expectation.

"Hmm . . . they sure are cynical, these gethwis," Orilheart observed. "Once the initial shock was gone, they just brushed it all off. They say the beast of the sea, the Drukijaken, would not allow a mountain in his world to be removed."

"I see," Saxfen said.

"They say that nothing can destroy so mighty a mountain. And they say emerald stars don't exist."

"Oh, so they think we're crazy. Great," Jix chimed.

"Well, it's the best we can do. We can't force them to leave," Orilheart said.

"Maybe all the hims really do die," Qugam wondered.

"This is awful. Can't you use your power to just carry all of them out of here?" Saxfen pleaded.

"I'm afraid we cannot force them," Orilheart explained. "They have to decide for themselves because it is unclear what their ultimate fate is. If I knew their ultimate fate, I could tell you with certainty the outcome. But this is not yet revealed to me; the Daylight is silent in this matter. We are left to carry on by faith. And so, by faith, we must carry on."

"What do you mean by this 'ultimate fate?'" Saxfen asked.

"I mean, the final sequence of events encoded in the Realm of Decrees, as you have seen for yourself. But you have only seen a partial outcome, so the rest is still veiled in mystery and secrecy."

Saxfen's tears began to roll down his cheeks, "I don't want them to die, Orilheart. It was so real!"

"None of us do, Saxfen. But we cannot force them. Or rather, we must not force them."

Saxfen's friends comforted him as best as they were able and then proceeded to lodge for the night with the gethwis of the east.

And so, the gleaming, gentle rays of the morning swiftly arrived, and the party headed back to the Wintebrek Caverns. They were disheartened and afraid of what would become of their beloved gethwis. They had reached the wintery abode and found the others had already arrived.

"Well, how did it go?" Saxfen asked.

"We warned them as instructed and . . . they just laughed at us," Starrelos said.

"They sure love our wings, though. They were utterly infatuated with them," Wolsage recalled. "At least we made some good friends, right?"

"Well, you know the rules, we cannot compel them to listen to us," one anxious Orilheart reminded.

"Indeed. And there is no word from the Daylight in this matter with us either," said Starrelos.

"I didn't think so," Orilheart responded. "Well, let's get going. We have a stolen harp to retrieve."

The group mounted their kirok birds and were relieved to find their gethwi friends had made good on their vow not to devour them. Not a single feather on their head was harmed, as promised.

They said their farewells and parted ways. The saddened friends did not share their usual laughs. They felt the strain of defeat and failure as their labors to persuade the gethwis were met with ridicule. Saxfen could not help but look back.

"Guys, hang on!" he shouted. "What's that over there?"

He pointed at the faint figure in the distance. It was the semblance of a striped gethwi sprinting with all its strength. The parting company halted and awaited.

"Who is that, him?" Qugam said.

"Could that be . . . Eukeris?" Saxfen wondered as he unmounted his kirok bird and ran to meet the sprinting beast. Indeed, it was the snow gethwi, Eukeris, who had endeared the distinguished visitors. Saxfen embraced the twin-tailed gethwi and mounted immediately.

He growled at Orilheart.

"Yes, Eukeris, you are welcome to come along."

And so, the company was slightly relieved to find at least one gethwi would be spared, and that their labors were not entirely in vain.

Chapter 12

Mystery of the Seven O'rahs

Deep within that ancient, shunned fortress, Castle Burning Skull, the temperament was quite unlike than that of Sword of Oakendunty, who had failed to persuade the gethwi colonies that great destruction would soon be upon them. There, within the lurid corridors of Burning Skull, the fiendish rivals of the Daylight maniacally hailed the forbidden summoning of an eighth Light Eater upon Ru'alameth. The forbidden conjuring of a new T'ohuvohu from the bowels of the Dark Xoloth had now been accomplished.

They shamelessly lauded their high crime against the Daylight covenants, a trespass so lewd and brimming with such wrath that they would not dare commit under any other occasion. But these were no common times for serpentine Urth. Nay, this was a damnable epoch for their kind, the foretold hour of their condemnation. Thus, there came great *despair* upon the Council of Night, which would provoke another regrettable, cosmic clash in which the true heart of the Vheilyel would be exposed.

These were surreal times—the dawn of a once phantasmal era the Urth had ridiculed and scoffed for ages beyond recollection. Truly, these were the days of the fabled Seven Lightnings, invoked in a time far beyond the prevailing hierarchy of the Urth.

For many an Urth did perish in Iddan Revolvings past, but not without relating the treasury of dark secrets they had heaped in their woeful learnings. And amongst these perilous revelations, there came the knowledge of bridging the chasms and thereby enjoining Ru'alameth to the forbidden Dark Xoloth. Keepers of dark wisdom, the Urth were, and now they would use these dark learnings to call upon those shunned, adversaries from beyond, like the desperate cries unto foreign gods to come forth on their behalf. And this, most desperate, proclamation of war against the Daylight, was that very cry unto these supposed gods, the Gods of the Naloz'oth.

And so, it seemed, the creatures from beyond had heeded the desperate cry of the Sons of Darkness. One of their fearsome kind had answered the blasphemous pleas of the Urth . . . once again. Even after bewildering spans of Iddan Revolvings, the things from the void possessed keen knowledge of the other seven T'ohuvohu confined within the vaults of the Daylight. And thus, these had long conspired within that nightmare dwelling of the Dark Xoloth, to exact uncanny revenge upon the Holy Vheilyel. *Nay, they had intensely coveted the destruction of all Ru'alameth!*

Now was that dark advent for those hateful things to emerge from the forbidden void and for the time of their wrath. Now was the dark hour where they would seek to devour and extinguish all light; to devour the very Vheilyel, who were keepers of Ru'alameth.

The Urth thus worshiped these and boldly professed their boastful creed, *There will be Perpetual Night.* For these were the words of the obscene hope that was in them, which they professed, that all Daylight kingdoms must be extinguished in a time to come.

The foul hordes of the serpentine Urth hissed, and they screeched as the revolving, mechanical device before them sinned against the natural order. At long last, the infernal apparatus had been animated by surging bolts of amethyst and pulsating convulsions of unclean luminance. The hordes eagerly crowded the ancient, subterranean shrine and fixated their gaze upon the unholy rift beginning to manifest above the dismal clouds of their revered, Castle Burning Skull. The restless skies became warped, emanating foul, black fumes from the abhorrent realm on the inverted side.

And then, at last, the thing came forth—an eyeless, ghastly face with a pair of arched, vertical fixtures upon its elongated head. Its mouth bore what appeared to be gruesome, jagged teeth and at the height of its abhorrent head, it appeared malformed and contorted. There were dark inscriptions upon its head arches, like some menacing set of etched hieroglyphs, ready to rebuke with unknown curses all who would dare defy. It had now traversed upon Ru'alameth, and its towering, lanky being emanated the same foul vapors intruding from the transgressing rift itself.

There were four, hauntingly elongated arms, twain on each side. And there accompanied the fiend, sevenfold tablets of unknown stone, also inscribed with cryptic runes like the writing upon its head. These hovered and revolved around the archfiend like living shields or hellish servants heralding their dark master.

Alas, let the heavens mourn! For these were the loathsome tablets inflicting terror upon the hearts of the Vheilyel from impossible spans, and now they had come to reveal themselves in the flesh and to lay claim to the apostates of the Daylight!

There was a heavy, shifting haze throughout the T'ohuvohu's body, encompassing its bloodless flesh like dismal vestures woven from the void it had traversed. And when the ghastly vapor shifted, there came the worst horror of its form, those horrid mouths upon the fiend! *So many of them, all throughout its pale, lanky body!*

This was the fabled and dreaded Flesh of Losnou'trum, the flesh of the T'ohuvohu, which was said could not be killed with the weapons of the

Daylight. For their bodies devoured light with these loathsome mouths, and the creatures themselves were said to mercilessly devour Vheilyel of all skill and rank.

The evil Urth Lord was much pleased and uncoiled from his throne. He then raised his deep, ghoulish voice and made proclamation before all.

"O great Gha'shuulmog, Grand T'ohuvohu and Dissolver of Realms, Revenger of the Void, thou art worthy to take possession of this, Ru'alameth, and make it thine own. Thou art worthy to consume all light. We offer unto thee all light that herein dwells. We offer all upon this, thine sacred altar. Go forth now, in all thine power, and take all that is thine!"

The hordes then inclined themselves to the eighth T'ohuvohu, and they chanted obscenities in banished tongues. The hideous Gha'shuulmog looked on with its pale, eyeless face and received their worship.

The Urth Lord then announced to the horde, "We shall now deliver the other T'ohuvohu imprisoned within the Daylight dungeons, and we shall have our revenge. There will be Perpetual Night!"

***

"Papa, that's too scary!" the golden haired Enos interrupted. "That thing really existed?!"

"Yes, son. It still does, actually," the elder Saxfen responded.

"What? Why can't we just kill it or something? It's a Light Eater . . . it eats light. Why would anyone keep it around?"

The youthful, yet aged Shaifetnu and his son rode atop their majestic gethwis as they made their way out of the frozen Oclyd Tower. He calmly explained the nature of the terrible T'ohuvohu.

"Well, it's not so simple, Enos. You see, that creature cannot die. It is consciousness from another realm altogether, from outside Ru'alameth.

As such, it is not affected by the same rules that apply to people on this side. Make sense?"

"I don't know. A little, I guess."

"It's okay if something does not make sense at first, but it will in due time. All things in their time, my son. This is the established order in our realm, all things in their own appointed time."

Saxfen continued to explain and comfort his son, relating how the trespassing creatures from the Dark Xoloth had waged war against the Daylight kingdoms a second time.

***

In the lamentable matter of the Apostasy of Despair, it can be said it originated with the unleashing of the eighth T'ohuvohu upon the realm of the many winged gods. But the first casualties in that awful revolt came with the siege upon Castle Burning Skull of Ga'nost, when there arose twain legions of Sabbayoth, commissioned to retrieve the fugitives, Howarmog and Azbele. It can well be contended that other events could be traced as catalysts to the new rebellion, but the siege upon Ga'nost no doubt gave way to the frightful revelation that an eighth T'ohuvohu now prowled upon the chasms of Ru'alameth.

The Sabbayoth battalions had arrived on the nightmare wastelands of Ga'nost. They had been warned the Urth would deploy new weapons, but they knew not they would come face to face with an unkillable entity from the Dark Xoloth.

Twain legions had traversed the final passageway when there came the sudden, alarming cries of their Sabbayoth Lord, seated upon Highest Ofandynth. Feverish orders came pouring in across the heavens through their Face Sharveth, relating to the warriors the shocking truth.

"Prime Saiorseth!" the Sabbayoth chief shouted across the spectral window.

"Yes, General Dalyorvym. What is my lord's bidding?"

"You must listen to me!"

Saiorseth heeded and noted the disturbed appearance upon Dalyorvym's face. In all the passings of the suns without ceasing, the faithful warrior had never beheld a Sabbayoth Master so alarmed.

"We have terrible news. The Urth, they have committed an unspeakable blasphemy and called forth another thing from the forbidden realms, from the Shunned Beyonds!"

The onlooking, astonished battalions began to murmur amongst themselves when they received the appalling revelation. For no dealings with any of the Shunned Beyonds had ever crossed their paths.

"What? Are they mad? Are you sure, General? Their records were utterly destroyed long ago. This must be deception intended to turn us from our resolve," responded the incredulous Sabbayoth Prime.

"Regrettably, the report is true. You must retreat with your legions at once. You are all in grave peril."

"But the Sacred Utterances were transgressed. Sir, the Covenants . . . they must be avenged!"

"Heed my words! We understand this is well before your time, but the T'ohuvohu are real. They truly exist! They are from a shunned plane known to us as, the Dark Xoloth. You must retreat immediately!"

"The Dark Xoloth?"

The fierce battalions of tried warriors were skillful in the ways of war, but they also were from a younger generation of Vheilyel. They had merely heard the stories of how the elder Vheilyel had perished at the hands of these supposed Light Eaters. But this was said to have transpired in dead epochs past. Only the most aged amongst the many winged gods recalled and survived the siege upon Ru'alameth by those frightful nether things that devoured the constellations.

There were many amongst the warriors of Saiorseth who had not so much as heard mere whispers of this, Dark Xoloth. Knowledge of the obscure, Shunned Beyonds was discretely concealed by the Daylight, as the knowledge of their being tempted many of the elder ones of the Morning Age—for it had become the ruin of them.

The olden legends recounted how seven accursed beings from the forbidden void were imprisoned within seven vaults throughout Ru'alameth. They were cast into formidable prisons along with their servants in what became known as, the Naloz'oth Vaults. And now, the young Sabbayoth were confronted with the supposed reality of a new menace from the rumored, concealed realm.

Legion Prime Saiorseth glanced at his hosts. They were mighty and battle tried. They were celebrated heroes, venerated amongst the luminous rivers of stars and upon luscious, opulent worlds. The thought of vanquishing the fabled monster that had ascended from the Dark Xoloth was inebriating and seductive. Oh, the glory and triumph to be attained!

But the abrupt response that followed was the calamity of them all. The great Sabbayoth Prime amongst them proceeded to utter the words that would condemn them to their doom.

"Master Dalyorvym, respectfully, no foul, trespassing fiend from the obscure crevices of Ru'alameth or any sphere known or unknown, will intimidate us! Sir, we have received our charge, the *D'ath Pithgam* must be avenged!"

The fearless warriors roared at the words of their captain. Naive and filled with self-righteous will, the resolute legions defied the Sabbayoth Lord and they would not be retreating from the face of this evil.

But the commanding master pleaded and insisted, "Return at once! This is no common fiend. There is no honor to be gained if you perish!"

Deaths? Could immortals die? Could the gods be slain? These strange concepts were foreign to the young mind of Saiorseth and his legions of deadly Sabbayoth. All they had ever known was glory and triumph and praise. Mighty terrors not to be scoffed at lightly had perished at the hands of these valiant, white knights. The exotic and bizarre thought of dying was a thing mortal flesh and blood succumbed to. This 'death,' this supposed death, surely did not pertain to them. And so, before Dalyorvym could finish his plea, Saiorseth dismissed the Face Sharveth and ordered his legions to proceed.

"Sabbayoth!" Saiorseth shouted. "We are bound by oath! We are bound to avenge our broken treaties! We will retrieve the transgressors, and we will execute justice!"

The hearts of his warriors were with him. They shouted back and roared with divine bloodlust. Their resolute path was before them as they marched upon the wretched lands of Ga'nost. They treaded alongside the deadly streams of molten ore and beheld the ravished remains of bygone citadels. There were scattered structures formed of unwholesome origin and some appeared for malicious use. There was no sign of life, only abandoned ruins throughout the somber terrain.

But then the monstrous vistas commenced. The valiant Sabbayoth observed as one colossal, bipedal being preoccupied its gaze on some unknown thing underneath the weathered earth. The loathsome giant awaited in what seemed to be a battle stance of sorts. It was a Nofsiun giant, and its fourfold, muscular arms appeared to be readied for the smiting of some unseen foe.

And then the ground slightly trembled, but not from the rumbling, blazing spews of the black mountains that condemned the maddening world. Nay, the shaking thereof arose from some unseen peril underneath the giant's feet. The stealthy menace then finally revealed itself. It was the restless, underground prowling of a massive Griurluch worm.

The hideous worm hungered, and its lust was fixated upon the four-armed giant. It pounced from underneath the immense giant and wrapped its bulging flesh around its prey. The giant then raged and cursed the ghastly worm in some desolate, unknown tongue.

"Let us kill them both, sir. They are an obstruction to our vengeance," said an irate Sabbayoth.

"No, let them slay one another," Saiorseth calmly responded. "We will not meddle our honor in this petty feud between fiends."

The Sabbayoth warriors held their peace as they looked on for an outcome. The savage brutes battled until, suddenly, the Nofsiun frenziedly seized the hellish worm with its beastly set of arms. It pulled its body apart in a burst of rage, compelling the forsaken wasteland to drink a splattered stream of putrid, black ooze. The Nofsiun then erupted into an odious, haunting groan as the Griurluch worm laid motionless on the desecrated ground.

The giant reveled in its slaying of the horrendous worm, but it suddenly held its peace as it sensed the peering eyes of the many winged gods. The monstrous thing perceived the onlooking Vheilyel and approached them to investigate. Saiorseth motioned his warriors to restrain themselves. The giant observed and realized they were indeed Vheilyel. It uttered shameful things again in that awful, shunned tongue.

"That's it, we kill it right now," one demanded.

"Wait, hold steady, I said," their Prime insisted. "Look . . ."

The brute proceeded to prostrate itself after it had culminated its vehement denunciations in that cryptic utterance. But twain legions had no regard for the foul thing's obeisance and returned upon their dutiful march for that coveted conquest at hand.

The nightmare terrain ahead was, likewise, inhabited with similar, towering brutes, and all prostrated themselves before the Sabbayoth as they passed by. But none addressed the gruesome giants and the brutes also held their peace.

These celestial knights had finally reached the malignant citadel that was Castle Burning Skull. The place was quiet. The customary ruckus of riotous creatures, and vanishing and remerging Urth busied with devout pilgrimage, this was all suspiciously absent.

"How rude of the fiends to leave us unattended," said one.

"Let us make sure someone comes to the door," Saiorseth responded.

With that, one Sabbayoth stepped forward and raised his arm to the restless, threatening heavens.

"Ancient voice of Njoorynath, show your might!" he exclaimed.

The swirling, evil skies then responded instantly with a blinding flash of light and the punishing tumult of crashing thunder rumbled the damnable walls of the Urth palace. There was a brief silence, and then came the numberless hordes of jeering Urth, and those foul obscenities of their own craftings. There came with the Urth, beasts fused with beasts, beasts fused with machinery and beasts fused with elements. All these they rendezvoused and swarmed from every crevice of the unholy edifice.

"Well, what's this? This is some welcoming committee," one ridiculed.

And then, there approached one serpentine fiend bearing a discomforting, elongated neck. It proceeded to address the holy legions.

"Noble Sabbayoth, we are most informed of your urgent matters in these, our venerated lands, and we are appreciative of your patience."

The Daylight warriors listened doubtfully as the winged orator continued its taunting hiss.

"As you are well aware, we are bound to honor and observe our holy *D'ath Pithgam,* and we therefore must surrender the offenders as agreed."

The fiend paused momentarily to savor a wicked smirk and savor the carnage it knew would follow.

"However . . ." the orator began. "These are no longer our esteemed, customary times observed of long ago. These are no longer our esteemed times of ancient accords or of feigned formalities the Seven Thrones have succumbed to for revolvings long forgotten . . ."

"What . . . is this fool babbling about. I am weary of his voice," one whispered.

"It appears they are comforted that the rumored adversary from the Shunned Beyonds will save them from us . . ." Saiorseth responded.

He then turned to the Urth's elaborate pontification and put forth his demands.

"Enough! You treacherous fiend! We are not here to be lectured by the filth of Ga'nost. You will surrender the fugitives, Howarmog and Azbele, and you will do this now. Be it known we are prepared to demolish your precious palace and all of Ga'nost, if necessary, for this most heinous breach of the sacred Utterances."

The ghoulish orator glared a murderous gaze at the captain's ambitious threats. It paused as it gathered its forthcoming words carefully. This was it: the Light Eater had been summoned, and a brutal war was now inevitable. The war had come to their very doorstep. After establishing peace for a myriad of millennia from those revered accords within the *Book of Principal Covenants*, a new cosmic clash had now arrived. There was no return from this trespass. The Urth orator retorted and scornfully defied.

"I'm afraid we will not be doing that. There's been a change . . . of plans," it announced.

Saiorseth realized the Urth would not be yielding as expected.

"Alright, brace yourselves. This is going to be messy," he warned his legions.

The monstrous spectators howled and gnashed as their chief orator extended its scaly arm at the invading host. It raised its foul voice, and it contorted into deep, foreboding blasts.

". . . for you see, the time of the Daylight has come to an end!" it jeered. "Now is the time of the Oracle of the Night . . . the Sign of the Eighth is come . . . *there will be Perpetual Night!*"

The invading Sabbayoth drew their burning weapons and light-drifted into battle formation, but the unwavering fiends appeared unfazed at the impending destruction; they merely held their peace.

And then the lurking trespasser from the forbidden plane manifested. That eerie, towering thing manifested upon the restless clouds in those phantasmal vestures of ebon fumes. The seven obscene tablets that revolved around it pulsated cryptically, as if alluding to some impending ruin. And, without warning, the Daylight battalions were deflected by an unseen blast, forcefully scattering them like a vigorous gust scatters fallen leaves.

The sinister silence of the spectating ghouls erupted into howls and jeers, taunts and curses. The Daylight combatants marveled at the great power of the T'ohuvohu as they wrestled to recover themselves from the unknown blast.

The Urth orator extended one final gesture of goodwill with that abhorrent, monstrous voice,

"Join us, O faithful Day Zarrar! Escape the wrath of the Seven Thrones of Ebelsaddon! Save yourselves from the T'ohuvohu! Save yourselves from Gha'shuulmog, Dissolver of Realms!"

Saiorseth rose to his feet. His eyes burned with violent flashes of white light.

"Vile serpents! Perish in the name of the Daylight!!" he exclaimed as his legions surged behind him.

They light-drifted and smote with all fury, but they found their might could not harm the fabled flesh of the T'ohuvohu before them.

Saiorseth anguished to comprehend what grave calamity had befallen them. *What are you?* He pondered in incredulity. And to his own bewilderment, there came trespassing into his fleeting mind, one maddening retort.

"I am . . . the Worthy Priest," said the chilling voice of the arch fiend.

Dismayed and utterly strained, they sought to retreat in disgrace. But the Tablets of Gha'shuulmog had accomplished their deed. For the grip of that lurid *Shadow Terror*, so named, had laid claim to their wavering hearts. It consumed away at the last of their valor. Some amongst them being given over to that maddening delirium that turns the hearts of the Vheilyel away from the wholesome light.

And yet, others sought the oblivion of the holy gods in place, preferring to be slain and therefore severed from all that they loved. And also they would be severed from all who returned their love for Iddan Revolvings without a known end.

The damning report would come to the ears of the Sabbayoth General, Dalyorvym, who had ordered Saiorseth to forfeit their righteous campaign.

The high servant of the Daylight anxiously strolled along a lavish garden overlooking the hallowed lands of Highest Ofandynth. He awaited tidings on the fate of twain legions commissioned to the nightmare world. He dwelt amongst serene, ambient fountains and ethereal songs encompassing a bounty of sweet, floral air. But these had failed to console the war general of his gnawing suspense. Accompanying Dalyorvym, there walked some lovely damsels of the distinguished court, and they too had failed to console his anguish.

The evil tidings finally arrived.

"Sir, the Urth have prevailed against them. None are said to have escaped or survived," said the messenger within the Face Sharveth.

"Understood. It appears the Urth have sealed their fate with the advent of the foul thing they have enjoined themselves to," Dalyorvym responded. "You are dismissed."

"My lord, the brave warriors were warned. There is nothing that could be done to deter them from their duty," one attendant offered.

"We could have forcefully stopped them," he responded.

"They had already arrived to the wastelands," the attendant continued. "We received the news far too late to intervene. You must release yourself of this burden."

"Yes, but the matter is tragic beyond words. The legions of Saiorseth were worthy and honorable. They were faithful and valiant, and now they will no longer join us until unknown revolvings have passed."

"What's this? Are you doubtful of the Lightnings, my lord?" the attendant retorted. "Do you suppose their appearance is in vain?"

"I admit, I have my doubts."

"Doubts? This is silliness and void of reason. You have doubts on the eve of the great Festival?"

The general refrained from elaborating. But deep within his heart, the burning knowledge of the Dark Xoloth had etched terrors upon his soul. Foul visions and oracles which cannot be uttered had returned to his memory. It appeared the things he had learned long ago were coming to life before his very eyes! They haunted the faithful servant of the Daylight and instilled an unwholesome dread upon him, like a pervasive shadow that lived within his noble heart.

"But what exactly, then, are you afraid of, General?" the Vheilyel dame pried.

"I'm afraid of what becomes of the Lightnings . . . after the Festival," he reluctantly admitted.

"You're nervous about this eve's celebration? You should be thrilled and jubilant like the rest of us."

Indeed, Dalyorvym ought to have been filled with joy and with hope that the eve's festivities were nearing their commencement after much patience. But the grim knowledge of the Dark Xoloth did not permit him, its haunting lore filled his heart with dread.

Great, lengthy spans had transpired since he last ventured into the depths of those loathed tomes pertaining to the Shunned Beyonds, those obscure records he had confiscated during early campaigns of his service. Yet, the things he had uncovered so long ago persisted anew like the re-living of a long-forgotten night terror. The matter disturbed him deeply.

For that very eve's festivities were that grand Festival that the concealed volumes alluded to in maddening boasts.

The ancient, dark lore the general had learned would not permit his heart to rest, for it spoke of haughty, daring oracles and dark omens that inverted the hope that the Lightnings promised. The names of the shunned works shall not be recited herein, but they spoke of an eighth Light Eater and of the Festival of the Lightnings; of the mayhem that was to engulf all heavens in perpetual darkness at the time of this same festivity.

"Perhaps, it is the loss of Saiorseth and his legions, and nothing more," Dalyorvym explained.

"My lord," another approached. "It is time to prepare ourselves for the Festival."

"Thank you. We are on our way."

The holy Vheilyel hailed the appearance of the Seven Lightnings with a solemn celebration so named, the Festival of the Lightnings.

The beloved war general and his court made their way through the princely halls of the glorious palace, Haldrulvel of Ofandynth. This was that elevated sanctuary to the south of S'hyeru Kadash.

Dalyorvym had reached the elegant quarters of a costly chamber where there awaited, one worthy pedestal. The column was garnished with a splendid crown, the lovely Atarah Ioz'ev. Dalyorvym and his court approached, and he knelt with his gaze to the polished flooring. There, he would be presented with this crown of honor as was customary to wear when elected to attend these finest of festivities within S'hyeru Kadash.

One presenter solemnly took the beautiful crown from the column and raised it above Dalyorvym's head.

"Take now upon you," the presenter said. "O honorable servant of the Sabbayoth, this holy Atarah Ioz'ev, and with it announce the bliss and favor that it with thee unto all that behold thee."

"There is none equal. There is none rival to that Blessed One," said another. "This unending truth, guard ye evermore and cherish more than thine own self."

They placed the royal crown upon his inclined head, and his kneeling body was suddenly engulfed in gentle, white flames. He was then asked to rise to his feet, as the wondrous notes of serene harpings and soothing flutes graced the air.

He parted from the sanctuary with his company unto the crisp rays of Ofandynth's threefold suns where there awaited the elongated frame of one feathered Soggseraf. Fastened upon the spine of the massive spirit-beast, there sat fourfold velvet seatings, securely adjoined betwixt a dual set of ivory wings. The Soggseraf itself was adorned with golden plates upon the rims of its massive wings. And upon its elegant horns, there appeared an elaborate ornament resembling a royal crown.

"General Dalyorvym, Peace of the Daylight. It is good to see you are well. Let us be on our way," the bleached Soggseraf greeted.

"Ulzrodrem, it is also good to see you, my dear friend. Peace of the Daylight. A great festival is upon us. Let us make haste now."

The imperial Soggseraf proceeded to plunge its elongated frame from the dizzying heights of the tower's podium. They soared above a dazzling sea of drifting, plush clouds, sailing across the swirling, turquoise skies of Ofandynth.

And then, the High Tribunal City of S'hyeru Kadash came into view. Sparse clusters of areal hosts voyaged across the heavens and joyous crowds graced the avenues below. Noble peoples from distant worlds and local citizens alike eagerly gathered for this, most special of festivities of the many winged gods. There could be seen ceremonial, living flames whirling in midair, welcoming guests as jovial cheer and wonderful mirth were found in every place.

Every place, of course, with the exception of those spiteful Urth who dwelt amongst the hierarchies of the Just. The wretched Bogedoth ambassadors in their midst, those resident adversaries, who feigned their smiles and forced their courtesies. These were not permitted to leave their posts, even during the ongoing festivities.

The Bogedoth had always despised the forced diplomacy they were bound to observe. Also, they abhorred the strain upon their minds to maintain a visage of Daylight semblance, that cloak of fairness they were compelled to endure for the entirety of their sojourning upon all Tribunal Halls throughout the stars. This was that ordinance imposed so as to conceal their shame, the ghastly Curse of the Morning, whose serpentine scales resembled the Naloz'oth Soggseraf they had worshiped in dead epochs past.

The emissaries were confined to their posts but the commotion upon the imperial avenues of S'hyeru Kadash provoked much consultation of them.

"Hey, you there. Why so somber?" one stranger inquired of a brooding Bogedoth.

"I am of the Ministry of Scales. I must endure the joy of the Daylight and of their guests," it responded.

"Ah, yes, the Ministry of Scales. This feast must ache you beyond words, seeing how there lives the rumors concerning the Lightnings coming to avenge all the heavens—or some such thing."

"Those are mere stories passed down from the ancient ones. They are tales from a bygone era. Parables and wisdom for our amusement and for our learning. Nothing more," the Bogedoth said.

"Well, seeing you do not believe in the old tales, you probably would not be interested in the recent happenings upon those distant lands of Ga'nost."

"Happenings? Yes, I have heard of Ga'nost. But I have never been to the place. What are these 'happenings' you speak of?"

"Oh, have you not heard? It is said the Great Kel'torh of Ga'nost has conjured up an ineffable beast from the mythic . . . *Dark Xoloth*."

The Bogedoth's eyes grew wide with intrigue.

"You are mad, and you speak falsely. The Throne of Lezuth would not risk their own destruction in summoning the feared dwellers of the shunned void."

"You are correct in one thing. They would not dare commit the unspeakable blasphemy and thereby endanger the entirety of their power and of their kind."

The stranger smiled and continued, "However, what is done cannot be undone, and I lie not. The Urth Oracle is upon us, or so it seems."

The bewildered emissary could not believe what the stranger implied.

"What is this? You speak of the Urth lore in this place? You bare the crest of the Daylight. Do my eyes deceive me? Why does your heart rejoice in this matter?"

"Because a new era is upon us . . . there will be Perpetual Night," said the stranger.

Incredulous at the words uttered before him, the fiendish Bogedoth could not believe he was hearing the Creed of the Night from one such as this. But the matter of the eight Light Eater was spread throughout, and the wavering hearts chose sides. For the dark lore haunted all who gave the slightest credence to the mad visions and the dark omens.

With the unthinkable advent of the eighth T'ohuvohu, the creed of the Urth received great strength. This uttermost trespass was a great omen unto them, the *Sign of the Eighth*. And the timing of the transgression in the eve of the Festival, this greatly inflamed their conviction. Thus, the obscure and concealed lore within the volumes pertaining to the Shunned Beyonds rapidly spread like venom upon the flesh from the spiteful fangs of a viper.

Blissful cheer and mirth enveloped the High Tribunal City and its exalted, neighboring citadels. But mingled throughout, there walked wavering Vheilyel, conspiring with Urth emissaries as the appearance of the eighth Light Eater was covertly discussed. And so, as with the highly esteemed Sabbayoth General, Dalyorvym, those who harbored doubts and treachery were slowly consumed with the haunting visions of the omens they had learned. The things veiled within the dark inscriptions of those cryptic tomes, it appeared, were coming to pass.

Dalyorvym strained himself to abandon from memory the frightful mysteries etched within his soul. He assured himself the dark volumes were poorly understood, misinterpreted, and even mistranslated from vanished tongues. And yet the lengthy lore spoke of these very times, when the Seven Lightnings would appear, and the unthinkable was said to occur, *the monstrous T'ohuvohu were said to be freed from their chains at the time of the Festival of the Lightnings!*

But after much toil and discipline, the good General joined in on the festivities with a merry heart in spite of the troublesome omens he had learned so long ago. And fortunately, for most guests celebrating the festivities of the Lightnings, there reigned within them, a blissful ignorance of the troublesome lore. This, for the time being at the least.

The crowning apex of the Festival was now underway, and it took place within the most revered, ceremonial chamber in all S'hyeru Kadash; that mightiest of chambers, so named, the Courts of the Sapphire Throne.

Dalyorvym and his company had arrived unto their seatings within the vast, colossal courts, where a solemn ceremony was taking place. The grand sanctuary was crowded with faithful Vheilyel from all four corners of Ru'alameth. There were no Urth present of any sort in this place. They were not permitted to gaze upon such hallowed matters of the Daylight from within these courts.

The many winged gods conversed with one another as the elegant, glimmering flames, suspended in midair, graced the atmosphere with a serene ambiance. There were lovely songs and melodies without equal in all Ru'alameth, and these were special works composed for these very occasions. Selected, talented Vheilyel had reserved their most astute compositions for the wondrous observance taking place, and their fervent toilings were manifest to all.

"Do you suppose the Urth will truly be vanquished after all these innumerable ages?" Dalyorvym inquired of his company.

"The Urth have grown quite accustomed to their reign," one responded. "But their thrones may not endure without end."

"Yes, their thrones must cease indeed. But do you suppose their demise is imminent? Until now, the Legend of the Lightnings was merely a whisper amongst us."

"I believe it is imminent. And if the Urth value themselves, they will go peacefully."

"But that is the matter most pressing, you see." Dalyorvym contended. "I do not suspect they will go peacefully. They would not have committed this proclamation of war if they intended to go peacefully."

"Oh, you speak of the matter at Ga'nost. It is merely one place, General, one senseless group determined to destroy themselves."

"You understate the tales of the T'ohuvohu, it seems. The Urth are emboldened," Dalyorvym insisted.

Dalyorvym's companion laughed and challenged, "It is almost as if you know something we do not. What is this you are saying? Is there something you are holding back?"

"I think . . ." Dalyorvym began, but was suddenly halted by the resonating voice of the royal orator.

"Noble Hierarchies of the Daylight, friends near and from far. This is a day triumphant and most memorable—one to be celebrated in ages to come. For this day we are graced with a wonder that shall shake every corner of Ru'alameth."

The crowds erupted in shouts and cheers and lauds of praise. They hailed and applauded as the celestial orator continued.

"And now, your humble servant presents to you, in this our solemn feast, the Festival of the Lightnings. I present to you . . . *the Seventh Lightning*!"

At this, the vast crowds held their peace and they ceased their jubilant praise. Twain, marvel doors opened, and there approached in the serene quietness, the Seventh Lightning, vested in the fine robes of S'hyeru Kadash. He was accompanied by four mighty Sabbayoth, the same warriors Wolsage of the Learners had seen earlier during his sudden flight to meet with his friend, Orilheart.

The fierce, celestial warriors escorted the Seventh Lightning unto the center of the mountainous, domed arena. None dared to make a sound, none dared to offer sweet songs of resonate delight. All held their peace as the Seventh Lightning approached a seated figure at the center of the sanctuary.

The enthroned figure at the center of the Courts was fully engulfed in faint, white flames, and his features could not be seen from the luminance of the flames. No features could be seen, except the curious white locks upon his head that mirrored those of the Seventh Lightning. This was that Worthy One whom the Daylight served. This was He whom they called, the Living One, enthroned upon the Sapphire Throne of S'hyeru Kadash! And he awaited to receive the Seventh Lightning on this, most joyous of occasions.

Upon approaching the Sapphire Throne, the four Sabbayoth escorts were not permitted to proceed further. Instead, they prostrated themselves, with their six wings extended, and the Seventh Lightning proceeded unattended. His silver hair was neatly adorned with costly braces. His head bore a crown of excellent beauty, and his face was shaven, revealing his clean, gallant visage. He extended his right arm unto the white flames encompassing the Living One and he graciously took what appeared to be a golden tablet from his hands.

This tablet was that long-concealed decree purposely omitted from the hallowed inscriptions of the *D'ath Pithgam*. And its name was called, the *Mystery of the Seven O'rahs*. This was that ancient decree long guarded from all peering eyes of Ru'alameth for Iddan Revolvings past and present.

This hidden ordinance was the purpose the Seventh Lightning had appeared upon S'hyeru Kadash. For the sacred Utterances had established that none but this lone Shaifetnu would ever be permitted to read its inscriptions, and thereby fulfil the Decree of the Lightnings,

And none there was, able to unbind from the words of this Decree,
The Lightnings proceed, and they judge the Great Vexation of thee.
A song of sorrows neverending is with them from the faraway lands.
Tremble and fear at the voice of the Seven O'rahs in their hands!
And the time of their voice shall be hidden and veiled,
Until the face of the Seventh amongst them comes near and prevails.

Thus, the thing inscribed upon this, most hallowed relic, was the appointed time when the Ministry of Scales should cease. And now, this silver-haired Shaifetnu had come to receive the hidden Decree. He had come to announce before all, that the time of the Seven Thrones of Ebelsaddon would now end.

He raised the *Mystery of the Seven O'rahs* above his head, as if to signal some grand conquest. And truly, this was a great conquest. After ages of silence, the olden decree was being fulfilled, *the promise to relieve the heavens of the treaties with the Urth had at long last arrived!*

And at that gesture, the myriad of guests throughout the sanctuary erupted anew in shouts and triumphant roarings. Thunderous applause and jubilant music resumed. The many winged gods shouted and greatly extoled the wonder unfolding before their eyes.

The Seventh Lightning himself was most exuberant in the midst of the thunderous crowds. The joy within him compelled him to break forth into a vigorous dance while firmly gripping the sacred relic in his hand. Great happiness therefore increased in all of Highest Ofandynth as all peoples throughout the hallowed lands looked on from every corner of their quarters. For there were generous Face Sharveths furnished everywhere, permitting all attentive onlookers to take part in the occurrence.

And so, day one of the Festival of the Lightnings was triumphant, and all guests throughout Highest Ofandynth shared in the festivities, even from afar.

Chapter 13

The Rogue Emissary

Now, it is needful to recount the matter of the High Bogedoth of Ga'nost, as this pertains to the reckoning of the Urth, which reckoning entails the retrieving of the stolen harp.

Not long prior to the forgoing festivities upon S'hyeru Kadash, there harkened that High Bogedoth of Ga'nost unto an unwavering verdict delivered against his appeal for Denunciation. It appeared he had petitioned for Full Denunciation against the friends of the Fifth Lightning in vain. The Urth emissary, Sandathus, carefully brooded as his own fate was being determined by the woeful denial against this most weighty appeal.

The noble court of the Lesser Nelcailith, those righteous adjudicators of the Daylight Tribunals, they considered the matter before the Aedyr Judge and thus declared, "O Excellent Aedyr, this Lesser Nelcailith shall deny the Bogedoth's petition for Denunciation. Zaamkut for Full Denunciation against the fellows of the Fifth Lightning shall not be lawful."

The High Aedyr judge turned to the Bogedoth and decisively announced, "In accordance with the precepts recognized by the ordinance of Shul-kahn, this appeal shall be Denied."

Sandathus was quite perplexed by the unwavering verdict. In his mind, the Fifth Lightning had clearly indulged that detestable vice of Cowardice. The naive Shaifetnu boy was clearly endangering his friends by bringing them along to this, his pitiful quest for the fabled harp. But the Aedyr had decreed, and there was no dissuading him, for the Lesser Nelcailith were with him. He was now left barren and would be compelled to return as such to the Great Kel'torh of Ga'nost, who would not take his failure lightly. The matter was most burdensome to be left unpunished.

He recalled the fate of the Chief Emissary previous to him and considered it his own fate, as the toilsome predicament of the Lightnings had consumed the Lord of Ga'nost with sore wrath. *There must be a way,* he desperately searched. He had now been ordered to return to the lurid citadel of Castle Burning Skull, where he would relate the demands for the immediate surrender of the fugitives, Howarmog and Azbele. The mere thought of offending the Urth Lord sent cold shivers down his back.

Nonetheless, the Bogedoth, Sandathus, duteously parted the High Tribunal City so as to satisfy the pressing verdict of the Aedyr. But the emissary of evil plotted mischief in his heart against the Night, as he had conceived not to return to the shunned towers of the eon-ridden fortress.

He shuttered in his flight in all its entirety at the thought of reporting to the terrible Urth Lord without securing the much coveted Zaamkut, which thing was necessary if they planned to forego quarrel with the legions of the Sabbayoth and of the Miyshmaoth. Thus, the foul serpent, Sandathus, instead elected to veer course and deviate unto the secretive corners of Ru'alameth, where he would liberally roam the obscure world, so named, Vijuul Kynth. He had determined to assume this cloak of treachery, a rogue and defector against the Kingdom of Darkness—being fully mindful of the grave penalties this treachery would impose. But these were no ordinary times. The dreadful Legend of the Lightnings appeared to be unfolding in the sight of all!

He merged himself into the hidden lands of Vijuul Kynth, and there he dwelt in secret for many years underneath its thirteen lucid moons. This was a land rich in the knowledge of clever devices and of structural wonders. Within this hidden world, there could be seen formidable steel chariots soaring upon the clouds and upon the stars alike. This was that secluded abode of those concealed, gifted peoples, so named, the Kizuul.

And all was well for a time, for this exile of darkness. He feasted and mingled with the refined Kizuul of Vijuul Kynth, and he savored delicacies of much delight. He learned of the mechanical wizardry that did flourish in this hidden gem, positioned deep within the obscure quarters of Ru'alameth. The thirteen moons above varied in size and evoked the feel of one gazing into generous, natural treasuries furnished by the very zenith itself.

The greenery that gracefully dressed Vijuul Kynth was lush and verdant, and the striking heavens mirrored them in hue, like the regal vestments of elegant jade. Also, this was a world rich in sparkling oceans resembling the vaulted, emerald jewels of some celestial monarch, carefully concealed within the hidden regions of the black void.

Dainty, sweet harmonies filled the air as Sandathus calmy sipped some fragrant liquor within his cup. He laughed and ridiculed as he recounted his past life without care. The onlooking Kizuul listened in delight and did not conceal their taunting disbelief.

". . . and they were like, 'Nope. Denied. Cannot help you, pal,'" he narrated his final dealings with the holy tribunals.

"So, these . . . Daylights, as you called them, they trouble you much, you say?" one chimed.

"Yeah, you could say that. That was kind of the point of my story."

"So why don't you look like these 'Urth' people you speak of?"

"Well, that's because I'm special. Your people use that gadget wizardry to accomplish much. But we use our bodies in the same manner to accomplish much. Understand?"

"So, you're saying you have special powers in that frail, skinny body of yours?"

"Well, yeah. You could put it that way."

The encompassing Kizuul audience burst out in laughter, and they scoffed at the excessive claims of the hellish rogue. After all, he resembled their gifted race himself. Surely, this was merely an ordinary commoner at their lounge, one with a bizarre imagination, freely reveling in local feastings, nothing more. They were much amused by his ridiculous stories and enjoyed listening to them, but they did not take to heart what was said.

"He has magical powers, he says!" some laughed and scoffed as they returned to converse amongst themselves.

"Well, do show us your magical powers, Mr. Tared'dom," one pried.

"I can't. You see, it's a little complicated."

"What's the big deal? Are you afraid the big bad lizards are going to come for you?"

"Well, yes, actually. Weren't you paying attention? You see, if I use my magic, this will leave a distinct signature, a mark if you will, which is tracible back to this very place. To me. And then the scary lizards will be able to find me."

The maiden which quarreled with the Bogedoth listened with intrigue, half musing and half reluctant to believe. Sandathus was delighted to ramble on as he delved deeper into one inebriated stupor.

"Well, how convenient is that? You tell us all about your grand, magical powers, only to tell us you can't use them because the lizards will come for you. Tared'dom is probably not even your real name."

Sandathus laughed to himself, struggling to conceal his mirth.

"Did I say something funny?"

"Well, that's another thing. You see, I can't tell you my real name. If I say my name out loud, the vocal vibrations will fuse with the air we breathe, and this will also create a signature, like the one I was telling you about."

"Oh, that's enough for me."

The irate maiden abruptly arose to her feet and went her way.

"Wait, where are you going, my dear? Was it something I said?!" Sandathus laughed.

The now inebriated Urth briefly lamented the parting maiden. He gazed about the vast, open chamber as musicians strummed upon their charming harpsichord and varied lutes. It was a delightful, ironic blend of melodic antiquity and advanced gadget wizardry. The Kizuul danced with some comely strokes of youthful eras as there descended soft, ambient light upon them, complementing their delicate prance.

There attended unto them servants of brass, studiously awaiting to be entreated for their service. These walked upon wheels while others drifted in midair by powers unseen as they devoutly waited on their stellar masters.

"I believe you, Mr. Tared'dom," another maiden interrupted. "I have heard of your ventures, and I find you exhilarating."

"Oh? Well, thank you, my dear. I admit, it gets rather lonely not having anyone to relate to around here."

"Yes," the lovely dame continued. "I especially enjoyed your story about the Urth King, how he humiliates those who fail him. What a total maniac, that guy, right?"

"That's exactly what I'm saying. He's obviously on some sort of power trip."

The two shared some laughs and became acquainted as the night ebbed into the dawn. They strolled along the cool, gentle breeze of moonlit gardens as there drifted above them, neatly arranged tiers of soaring chariots, busily coursing upon orderly orbits.

"What a perfect night," Sandathus said.

"Yes, this was so much fun."

"I think I can see my house from here."

"Hey, Tared'dom. There's something I have to tell you."

"Sure, you can tell me anything."

"Well, not sure how you will take this, but . . . I have to bring you back to Castle Burning Skull."

Sandathus laughed, "Oh, you have to bring me back? Nah, I like it here."

"Unfortunately, I'm serious. You must return to Castle Burning Skull and report to the Great Kel'torh."

"Alright, now it's my turn. There's something heavy on my heart that I have to tell you as well."

"Go on."

"Not sure how you'll take this, but . . . I actually made it all up. Castle Burning Skull . . . the reptile people . . . the Urth King. It's all just a fantasy I dreamt up."

"What? I'm being serious here. You are going back to Castle Burning Skull."

"You can't make me return to a place that does not exist, my dear."

"Well, you tell me if this exists . . ."

The beautiful, young maiden stepped aside, and to the rogue's baffling surprise, her lovely contours deformed into those of the foul, serpentine Urth of the Council of Night! It was the heartless Order of Zayd, skilled assassins and hunters of darkness sent forth to forcefully retrieve the traitor emissary.

Sandathus scrubbed his eyes in disbelief, "What? This isn't happening. I'm in a drunken stupor right now."

The maiden, now fully altered into the form of those serpentine reprobates, instantly drew her dark essence blade and aimed its searing edge at the Bogedoth's neck.

"But this is impossible. How . . . how did you find me? The Yiugmus Tonic, was that it?"

"You got careless, Sandathus. Now, come peacefully or suffer now, the wrath of the Zayd!"

She hissed her hellish utterance, and then there trespassed upon the beautiful, moonlit garden, that oppressive, eerie presence of five additional hunters. Sandathus came to his senses and accepted the gravity of the matter before him. He violently dashed his own blazing weapon against his foe's and flung his sixfold, leathery wings in defiance.

"You didn't think it would be that easy to escape us, did you?" one Zayd hunter challenged.

The Bogedoth then lanced himself into the moonlit zenith, and the six hunters of the Night followed behind. They soared past the unseen orbits of the steel chariots and betwixt legions of enormous towers that graced the Vijuul Kynth city of Nyrathfol. The soaring gargoyles raged against the fleeing rogue, but he skillfully deflected their burning blades with his own foul essence blade and essence shield. They furiously discharged vile orbs of dark ether, but their diligent raids failed to dispose of their fellow Urth.

"Flee the Council of Night as I have!" Sandathus pleaded. "The time of the Urth is come to an end!"

"The Daylight deceives you, Sandathus!" responded the maiden as she flung one deathly blow after another. "Ga'nost has conjured the Gods of the Naloz'oth upon Ru'alameth once again!"

"You lie!" Sandathus exclaimed. "No one would dare such a reckless deed. It is suicide for us all!"

"Fool! The eighth T'ohuvohu is amongst us as we speak! The Dark Xoloth will consume all things. There will be Perpetual Night!"

Outnumbered and exhausted, the Bogedoth refused to yeild as strike after furious strike failed to subdue him. He light-drifted to evade and save his life from the deadly blows. But having done so, there now resurfaced upon the starry gulfs of Ru'alameth, his own unique etching upon the black chasms; his energy signature had been found! This he had long feared because soon, the vile legions of the evil Vheilyel would come for his soul with great vengeance. That hidden gem that was Vijuul Kynth and its pristine, emerald oceans was no longer safe. And so, the serpentine exile proceeded to liberally use his dark powers without regard.

"Sokkunbalah, I command you, come forth!" he shouted.

The quaint, scattered moons then became obstructed from view by one sudden siege of trespassing storm clouds. And from within these unnatural vapors, there emerged the terrible howls of the thing that answered the Bogedoth's call.

And the scaly form of the haughty Naloz'oth intruded upon the Path of the Waking from the depths of the Sithrah with wrathful growls and monstrous blasts of violent flames. The hunters evaded and countered the huge, concealed creature's assaults, but this allowed Sandathus opportunity to smite at his foes. He light-drifted, and one he severed its arms, another its torso, and yet another its wings. He pursued the pained stalkers until they were slain beyond doubt. *We can't leave anything to chance*, he reasoned as he delivered the final blows.

One after the other, the High Ambassador slew his adversaries, but he sought to leave their maiden leader for last. She laid injured atop one exalted pinnacle of the towering structures piercing the night sky. Her wings were severed, and her life within her slowly fled. The rogue concealed his ghastly, scaled form as he approached the dying maiden.

"Tell me, how did you find me," he asked.

"It does not matter. There is nothing you can do. We will always find you. And every time you flee, we will be avenged seven times the greater when you are finally seized."

"I really liked you. We could've been friends. But you couldn't help yourself, could you?" he taunted.

The dying fiend likewise concealed her degenerate state in the hopes of obtaining sympathy from the prevailing emissary.

"I can't live like you," the Urth maiden explained. "Always hiding, never being free to roam the stars again, confined to a single world like the pathetic mortals we scoff and detest."

The rogue leaned in and kissed the anguished huntress.

"Oh . . . it's not so bad," he said.

And with that, Sandathus drove his essence blade through her heart as he held her in his arms. He remained with her lifeless, broken body momentarily until the arrival of the dreadful Kozeroth, those gigantic gatherers of dead Vheilyel that freely traverse the entirety of Ru'alameth in search of new souls to collect. The immense Servant of the Daylight finally manifested and occupied two-thirds of the open night sky from behind the veil of the Sithrah. Those four dreadful faces never ceased to terrorize the exiled rogue.

***

The long-awaited advent, the appearance of the fabled Seven Lightnings, also brought with it an aura of some grand, epic peril the likes of which had not been known by the Vheilyel for epochs immemorable. To some holy Vheilyel, the appearing of the Lightnings seemed like some haunting omen that heralded a great calamity, though the hierarchies of the Daylight were mostly joyous. And this heavenly mirth was in part derived from the peaceful, consoling arms of blissful ignorance that prevailed amongst the Holy Orders.

All of these reluctant, or otherwise oblivious, of the shunned lore pertaining to the Dark Xoloth and the *other* Beyonds were the natural heirs of this bliss. Only as the day approached when the Festival of the Lightnings would be celebrated, did the rumors and gnawing strain begin to spread rapidly. For the reality of the things foretold began to incarnate. Dark, terrible omens against the Daylight, it was whispered, were to culminate at the time of the Festival of the Lightnings.

The Urth perplexed themselves with the perceived injustice of their imminent extinction, while some amongst the faithful to the Daylight were given to doubtful philosophies. These were cast into labyrinthine agonies over the woeful nature of the things lurking within the forbidden spheres. Twain, astral families suppressed the gnawing doubts hungrily prowling within them. Nonetheless, great rifts in thought began to sprout amongst the Vheilyel like the venomous shoots of poisoned weeds that silently diminished their resolve.

And the weeds of doubt flourished throughout the vast, starry field that is Ru'alameth. Unwholesome seeds they were alongside the much-celebrated harvest that was the revealing of the Seven Lightnings. And with these regrettable doubts sown, there came much chaos and unlawful destruction upon the path of the many winged gods.

***

Amongst the violence, grave peril had come to the home world of the orange-haired Learner, Wolsage. Upon the distant lands of Hyirius-nu, there pondered the Sabbayoth, so named, the Omen Breaker, over the curious matters unfolding within the Courts of the Sapphire Throne.

"This is a day most triumphant! What's the matter, Ruvaen?" pried one joyous Vheilyel, expressing concern over her troubled friend.

"Oh, I'm merely considering the appearance of our beloved Seventh Lightning," the Sabbayoth replied. "This is like the dawn of some new era, long thought to have been but a mere parable, not an actual event like the things we are witnessing today. It's truly marvelous to watch unfold."

"Yes, of course it is. But it's a little odd that your Face Sharveth is not open for you to watch along."

"Well, I am in deep thought at the moment, Adelais, and it helps my concentration."

Ruvaen was most concerned over his longtime friend, the young apprentice, Wolsage of the Learners. The mere Learner had been sent to escort and protect the Fifth Lightning, and the wrath of the Night was sure to persecute his dear friend.

And those awful rumors he had heard!

The celestial hall of their gathering was furnished with banqueting guests and lavished with lovely sculptures and a serene ambiance. Its elevated chamber walls were adorned with ancient, proud emblems and curious hieroglyphs. The guests cheered and expressed joy over the lively festivities taking place in S'hyeru Kadash from the comfort of their own distant world.

Adelais continued, "I know what's bothering you."

"Oh, you think so?"

"Yes, I think it's the rumors."

Ruvaen glanced at the warm, comforting eyes of his friend. He was briefly surprised that Adelais had heard of the rumors surrounding far-placed Ga'nost.

"What rumors?"

"The rumors surrounding the Seven Lightnings."

"Oh, that. Well, what's there to worry about?"

"I think you're worried about the Light Eater that is said to have emerged from the dark kingdom of Lezuth."

"Well, I'm not quite convinced the Urth would be so self-destructive as to commit such a heinous act from which there is no return."

"But . . . what if it's true?"

"Then we just seal it up like the others, right?" Ruvaen promptly replied.

"Well, that's the problem. The *others* are said to be released now that the Seventh Lightning is revealed. That's truly troublesome information if you ask me."

"Very well, is it so obvious, then? Yes, that would be a total of eight T'ohuvohu said to bring perpetual darkness upon all of Ru'alameth when the forbidden Dark Xoloth merges and devours all things. You have discerned my mind correctly. This has been troubling me for some time now."

"Yes, more and more of us are hearing these mad rumors of evil, dead gods returning from long-forgotten tombs, but that's all they are . . . rumors, right?" Adelais assured.

"And what about the Veiled Tablet? The *Mystery of the Seven O'rahs*?"

"What about it?"

"Well," Ruvaen began. "It is supposed to contain the time of their release, the release of those monstrous things that are said to be unkillable by Vheilyel. Clearly, they cannot be vanished if they are not first released. And what if one of those things comes here, savoring the opportunity to avenge itself after being confined in the Vaults for so long? Perhaps you are not acquainted with the legends of how the Light Eaters devoured entire constellations, and so they were sealed away in the worlds they coveted."

"Well, if one of those things dared come here to our beloved Hyir-ius-nu, there isn't much we can do, is there? In the end, this could all very well be mere parables and myth."

The words had but left Adelais' mouth when there came a startling, sudden crash upon the merry hall.

"What was that?!" Ruvaen exclaimed.

And then there came a loud voice alerting everyone to the peril that had come upon them without warning.

"Everyone! You must exit this place at once. Neuvundiel is under attack, and this place is going to collapse!"

The banqueting Vheilyel swiftly escaped the crumbling structure and gathered outside, where there appeared those villainous legions of the Kaabaldur Urth. This was that infernal order of destroyers, the Order of Kaabaldur, established to bring lawful destruction upon the worlds in the name of the Seven Thrones of Ebelsaddon.

The skies were plagued with swarming, woeful armies of darkness as they mercilessly trampled the lovely city of Neuvundiel. It was a most astonishing devastation. It was as though the Aedyr Lords upon the Judgment Halls had issued some tragic Zaamkut of Denunciation against them all!

But furthermore bothersome, if this was no lawful scourge, where was the Order of Miyshmaoth? Those fearsome, sentinel giants charged with guarding the fair havens of the Daylight? Something was amiss, it seemed. The Kaabaldur would not be so careless and self-opposing so as to condemn this great city to their own peril. But this violence was nonetheless accomplished, and the invading hosts of the ravaging Kaabaldur desolated the sacred lands of Hyirius-nu and captured its mighty captains.

"This is impossible! How can this be happening?" the baffled Adelais exclaimed at the sight of the unspeakable carnage.

"It's the Miyshmaoth!" Ruvaen frantically exclaimed. "They've let them in, and they have betrayed us all! That's the only explanation, right? Because how could the Aedyr Judges do this to us? This is absolutely reckless. The Urth are emboldened like never before!"

"This is blasphemy!" Adelais shouted. "They'll never get away with this!"

But the murderous Urth Lords prevailed in Hyirius-nu. They marched throughout the peaceful, verdant lands, capturing all peoples and creatures in sight. They drove as many living things unto the edges of the ringed ocean so named, Ittedyn, and they slew them upon the waters. Neither was any sea life in sight spared. All wholesome life was abominable to the serpentine, fallen Vheilyel, for the natural order had been formed by the Living One, and they desired to form an order of their own. And so, a new cosmic revolt had waged war. The Apostasy of Despair had come to the hallowed lands of Hyirius-nu.

The deadly siege upon the cherished world was sudden and without mercy. The grand ocean encompassing the entirety of the world in the form of an emerald ring was defiled and speckled with vermillion from the spilled blood of the peaceful creatures and peoples.

Outnumbered and unprepared for the destruction, the surviving Vheilyel heroically fought nonetheless, refusing to yield. They saved and evacuated as many as they could. But perhaps the greatest tragedy of all was that, amongst their honorable ranks, there were found betrayers who had renounced their oaths. These had succumbed to the seduction and allure of a power presumed superior to that of the Council of Daylight.

The Urth had truly revolted, and there was no returning from this evil. Indeed, the fiends accepted their fate in all these transgressions, and they had placed their hope of deliverance in those things that were said to have returned from the forbidden Dark Xoloth.

***

Although the High Tribunal City feasted and hailed the Festival of the Lightnings, the toilsome matters of judging fates never went unattended. The Aedyr Judges were as perpetual candles that never ceased their flame, and this flame was the judging of matters pertaining to Ru'alameth. For so it was decreed that the Ministry of Fates may never cease their work.

But the shinning flame of the Order of Aedyr had been quietly diminishing from the time of its founding, and their light had slowly veered from its early glory like the passing of a celestial era. This, as the true heart of the celestial judges came forth, and their defects inscribed upon the archives of the Order of Dathmahjen.

And thus, the corrupting influence of the Seven Light Eaters, who were incarcerated throughout Ru'alameth, served to expose the hearts of the may winged gods. Quietly, the Ministry of Fates declined through the ages. Quietly, that is, until the loathsome *Tablets of Gha'shuulmog* intruded upon their plane and thereby greatly augmenting the degeneration of the wavering hearts.

There, upon the hallowed courts of S'hyeru Kadash, there paced the Aedyr, Lurnthalas, unto his designated judgment hall. The grave destruction upon Hyirius-nu would be addressed, and a resolution would be determined. He paced along the elaborate halls of the grand palace, fully clad in the dreadful lightning vestures of his office and accompanied by other Vheilyel of varying orders. They had been previously advised of the tragic occurrences, that they were as the pouncing of a ravenous beast greedily devouring its prey. They were informed of the failure of the Miyshmaoth, who were responsible for the securing and alerting of all menaces. They were informed of the apprehended captains and Aedyr lords.

"Yes, regrettably, the report is true," Lurnthalas announced. "The Urth are become possessed with a maddening scheme. They speak of grand visions of doom against the Daylight and against the Living One himself. Vanities and profanities! They are sieging all places of their choosing now that tidings have spread that Castle Burning Skull has summoned an eighth T'ohuvohu from the Shunned Beyonds."

"Truly, this is madness!" one exclaimed. "How dare they revolt against the Daylight. Do they not cherish their remaining liberty? Do they not appreciate the forbearance that has been with them all these ages?"

"Yes, what exactly is their objective? Do they suppose their fantasies of conquest shall yield any fruit this time?" mused another.

"I shall declare unto thee the reason for their impulse," Lurnthalas interjected as lightning currents surged about his face. "It is the concealed legends. It is the tales and forgotten lore surrounding the Light Eaters.

The matter is obscure, this thou knoweth, for only a few of the living Vheilyel truly witnessed what transpired. And it is for our own wellness that this is so. It is so with the intent that none of us should be seduced by the knowledge of the Shunned Beyonds.

"It is said amongst the Urth that the Living One was not able to return the T'ohuvohu unto that nether void that spewed them. And so, he was compelled to contain and imprison the seven of them in Ru'alameth, within the Vaults of the Naloz'oth. The knowledge of them also being entombed in the sands of eons past."

"What ridiculous claims! Most assuredly, the Living One is able to vanquish them at will," one replied.

The Aedyr Judge continued, "The matter is further laborious, in light of the supposed release of the seven Fiends with the appearance of the fabled Lightnings. It is certainly discomforting that the Living One would elect to contain them here for epochs beyond recollection. Furthermore, to release these destructive creatures after all the fine warriors that have fallen before them; after all the worlds that are said to have perished because of them. And in spite of our formidable weapons, which professedly had no effect on them, these are said to be released upon us again. A most disturbing prophecy, no doubt.

"And hitherto it is said that an eighth one has been admitted from the Shunned Beyonds, which has emboldened the Urth with this most heinous revolt."

Plain reasons and much-desired understandings had been hidden and concealed from the families of the Daylight, as well as the ones of Darkness. Nonetheless, the purpose of this concealment, in truth, was to expose their deepest thoughts because the matter pertained to the uncovering of their true heart.

The celestial judge entered his judgement hall and swiftly discerned the chronicle awaiting him.

"Harken now, O Honorable Tribunal," he announced. "We shall now examine the lamentable matter of Hyirius-nu.

"It is this chamber's record that the Zaamkut of Denunciation was decreed solely against one, Ruvaen, of the Sabbayoth, and none else; and nothing else. Instead, the cherished, ocean-ringed world has been sieged in its entirety by the deadly legions of the Kaabaldur. The Daylight has incurred great losses, including the capturing of high-ranking Aedyrs. The Bogedoth of Zasdeiph may now present their disputation for this excessive use of force."

"Honorable Aedyr, Zasdeiph of the Throne of Yaraath, has cataloged numerous violations against the Principal Covenants by the esteemed city of Neuvundiel and also by the cities surrounding it. These transgressions are enumerated as follows . . ."

The contending Bogedoth recited in detail the damning list of supposed violations against the sacred code, but the heart of the judge drifted to the dialogue he had indulged only moments prior. The chilling thought that the Living One could not return those Outer Things from whence they came perturbed him deeply, and the Bogedoth's case was blurred from his senses.

The honorable Aedyr was long fatigued with this frightful thesis, amongst others. It had secretly eaten away at him for some time. Truly, the damnable Tablets of Gha'shuulmog had accomplished their deed from afar. And now, they had breached the chasms to lay claim and devour the tormented Aedyr's reason and wavering devotion!

The emissary of the shunned, hellish world, Zasdeiph, concluded his indictment.

"And what saith the advocates in these matters?" Lurnthalas queried.

The Dathmahjen Advocates made a spirited defense, detailing the faults within the Bogedoth's outrageous claims against the beautifully adorned world of Hyirius-nu, home of the orange-haired Learner. The right-hand side of the celestial tribunal applauded their eloquence and finesse. But the High Aedyr was disengaged and unimpressed. He looked through his records yet again as he assessed the conflicting testimonies.

"After much consideration, I have reached my ruling," he announced. "In the matter of the brutal siege upon Hyirius-nu, this noble tribunal decrees in favor of the Throne of Zasdeiph. Truly, the *D'ath Pithgam* has been imprudently infringed. There shall be no reinforcements to aid the captured world and the contention of the Bogedoth shall stand."

The Council of Advocates was appalled and gasped in astonishment! They murmured as the Urth discreetly celebrated. But the Prime Advocate pressed the judge and interceded still.

"Honorable Aedyr, we have furnished flawless records that the Bogedoth of Zasdeiph are in grave error. We appeal the Aedyr's decree."

"The advocate's appeal shall not be heard. The Utterances cited by the High Bogedoth shall be observed," he responded.

Hyirius-nu would not be succored by the Daylight.

And with this stern, final decree, an entire world was abandoned to fend for itself against the prevailing hordes of the Order of Kaabaldur.

Alas, the treachery of the Apostasy of Despair! And most wretchedly, the tainted Aedyr had indeed elected to dismiss the evidence presented in exchange for a taste of the Seven Throne's approbation. Indeed, the Bogedoth had previously secured the Zaamkut of Denunciation against Ruvaen, the Omen Breaker, at his own hand. But he could not foresee the ruinous transgression that would follow for reason of his evil deed. The snare had been placed and the Aedyr's reason and integrity had been captured by the Ministry of Scales.

The venomous thoughts within him had dominated at last, and his wisdom and judgment had been deformed. The foul Tablets of Gha'shuulmog had accomplished their work upon him.

And the incident was no isolated happening. This new Apostasy had spread throughout the courts of the holy Tribunals *in all places!*

The elevated Order of Aedyr had been greatly impaired by the mischievous whispers of the events now unfolding before their eyes. Many of them succumbed to the mad visions professed by the Night, and they secretly hoped to gain their favor when the reign of the monstrous T'ohuvohu commenced.

And thus, the sacred judgement halls throughout the Daylight kingdoms became unsound, so the Council of Night prevailed in many a world upon the advent of the eighth Light Eater. For this latest fiend came not on his own, but there also came with him those monstrous tablets from the Shunned Beyonds.

***

"So, Papa . . . why didn't the Living One just stop them all?" the young Enos interrupted. "He could've stepped in and put an end to all their dumb ideas, couldn't he?"

"Yes," said the bearded Shaifetnu father. "Of course, he could have. But you know, the Living One, he is very discerning and prudent. He hides himself, and he does this so people show him what they're truly like. You see, there have always been enemies of the Living One amongst the good Vheilyel. But they hide their contempt against him. They hide their true heart. And so, he in turn hides so they can show everyone what they're truly like. Makes sense?"

"Yeah. I guess that makes sense."

"That's my boy! Understand all this may not have made much sense at the time, but these tragedies were necessary. The Living One is wise because, in so doing, he drew out all of his enemies who loved to hide in the shadows."

Twain, venturing Shaifetnu, continued their sojournings unto the cozy neuf village, Oakendunty Village. They rode atop their regal, striped gethwis underneath the striking, spectral arcs gracing Eofendurk.

It seemed as though only a day had passed since the Shaifetnu prince last beheld those beautiful, roseate skies. But it had been an exhausting sum of lengthy years since he had parted from this, the world of his home and of his heart, with the O'rah Harp in hand.

***

Elsewhere, upon Highest Ofandynth, there came that skillful champion of the Just, the star advocate who had prevailed against Orilheart's adversaries in her time of need. Casdynbiel of the Dathmahjen had been summoned for her skill so she may assist in the matter of the perished legions of Saiorseth, who had fallen in battle upon the nightmare lands of Ga'nost.

The keen assembly of Dathmahjen Advocates railed and denounced within the judgment halls of S'hyeru Kadash. These demanded stern retribution for the slaying of the valiant Sabbayoth, and now the time had come to receive the verdict.

"Therefore, in the discomforting matter of the perished Sabbayoth upon Ga'nost," the Aedyr declared. "The Ministry of Fates hath decreed as follows."

He briefly paused to invoke the sacred pronouncement.

"No intervention shall be afforded."

Murmurs of astonishment and clamors of confoundment erupted in the judgement hall. The Dathmahjen Advocates could not believe their ears. Their loyal warriors would not be avenged? But they perished in dutiful service, seeking to retrieve the transgressors, Howarmog and Azbele, who committed the grave offense of making an attempt on the Fifth Lightning's life! Could this be an error? Or, worse, could this be . . . *treachery*?

"The Council of Advocates shall immediately present their appeal!" Casdynbiel exclaimed.

"The advocate's appeal shall not be heard," the Aedyr responded.

"This is an unjust verdict! There must be justice!" she continued.

"You dare challenge the integrity of the honorable Aedyr?" one Bogedoth denouncer confronted. "Our covenants must be upheld!"

The Dathmahjen defense sensed the brazen taunt. Oh, the insult! The hubris, the gall! Something was amiss.

"The kingdom of Ga'nost has committed multiple, gross breaches against the High Utterances in this matter!" Casdynbiel vehemently insisted. "There must be relief for the Sabbayoth! This is an outrage!"

"The advocate is ordered to refrain from these outbursts. The decree shall stand. The appeal shall not be accepted. The contention in the mouths of the Bogedoth will be observed," the Aedyr calmly declared.

"Nay, excellent, Aedyr! There must be justice!" she shouted, defiantly aiming her finger at the judge.

And with that, the perplexed advocate was apprehended and sent away for reprimands. After the session had concluded, the remaining defense discussed the occurrence in utter confoundment.

"What was that all about?!" Casdynbiel marveled.

"Casdynbiel, perhaps it is best to leave it alone," a fellow Dathmahjen responded.

"Yes, it is not given us to refute the wisdom of the Order of Aedyr," another said.

"Perhaps not, but this is most troublesome and unbecoming," Casdynbiel replied.

"You know, I received word that other Aedyr are also questionably siding with the Bogedoth, some in obvious, blatant defiance, it seems," a third chimed.

"Oh, is that so?" said Casdynbiel.

"Yes, they're letting entire worlds fall, and they're letting hardened renegades go free. All within very short spans of the Prime Iddan."

"Hey, do you suppose this has something to do with the T'ohuvohu sighting?"

"What? What does that have to do with anything? That thing will be dealt with in due time," Casdynbiel assured.

"Oh, I suppose you have not yet heard the tales surrounding the Light Eaters, then?"

"What tales?"

"Well, it is rumored the T'ohuvohu are indestructible, and the Living One cannot vanish them back to the forbidden void, one Shunned Beyond that is called, the Dark Xoloth. Hence, they have been imprisoned here since the Age of the Morning. So, you truly have not heard these tales and the reasons they were contained?"

"Utter nonsense. What is your point?"

And so, another continued the chilling lore surrounding the dreaded creatures. These whispers were the wild seeds of the latest schism that had taken root upon the hosts of the Daylight; venomous rumors that had prevailed throughout the kingdoms of the Vheilyel.

"Well, do not be afraid of the things I will speak of, agreed? But this is what they are saying. They say the Living One . . . *is actually one of them*," one replied.

"What? One of what?"

"They are saying He's also a T'ohuvohu."

"Watch it! How profane is that! How can anyone think that?"

"Yes, I am aware it is a vulgar thought, and I am not saying I believe it, I am merely speaking of the whispers that have taken hold. And I shall come to my point."

"Very well, go on," Casdynbiel reluctantly replied.

"They are saying the Living One is one of them, a Light Eater as they are, and that they have come to return him with them. When this deed is accomplished, the Dark Xoloth will merge with Ru'alameth, and this will extinguish all light from this realm as they have extinguished other realms. All of Ru'alameth will, therefore, become a perpetual void of nether darkness.

"And so, there are many fellow Vheilyel who have secretly embraced this obscene doctrine, creating in them doubts. And now there is a supposed *eighth* Light Eater prowling about. The unspeakable has occurred after the calamity of them so long ago. Therefore, their hearts secretly fear the omen and the doctrine of the Urth."

"This is utter lunacy! I've heard enough," Casdynbiel interrupted.

The group ambled down the refined, opulent avenues of S'hyeru Kadash. There, they would find that their fruitless labors to secure justice for the perished Sabbayoth was indeed but the start of a brewing, falling away most regrettable. For there came turmoil and tumult engaging ahead, vengeful outcries and indignant railings in this, most holy, of Daylight capitols. It was an incensed multitude, a coarse commotion of the mighty. A furious company of armored Sabbayoth feuding against one another ahead. And it appeared to be but a glimpse into the amassing storm clouds of a looming clash within the proud, celestial hierarchies of the Vheilyel.

"What is this commotion about?" Casdynbiel pried into the blusterous crowd.

"There is quarrel concerning the verdict earlier this day regarding the slain Sabbayoth at Ga'nost," one informed.

"Oh . . . what is it that they want?"

"They want to completely demolish the Urth stronghold, Castle Burning Skull, at this very moment. But truly, they would annihilate their entire world."

Thus, there came intense schism amongst the honorable Vheilyel of S'hyeru Kadash that day. Vengeful, Sabbayoth legions demanded retribution, and the Bogedoth emissaries dared gloat in their faces. Only the terrifying Order of Miyshmaoth prevented the infuriated Sabbayoth from castigating the scoffing serpents. They also prevented them from leaving the celestial city in search of retribution, and they issued ominous threats against them if they so defied the Ministry of Wardens.

"This is all our fault! We should have done better today," one advocate lamented.

"No! We did our best, as always. All the evidence needed was presented. Do not burden yourself with what happened. It is beyond our control now," Casdynbiel comforted.

This, she offered to console, but secretly, Casdynbiel wished they could have conducted the matter differently. If only they had presented other examples or presented more compelling exhibits, perhaps this feud could have been averted.

The contending sects could not be restrained, and their quarrel finally seethed. The Sabbayoth unleashed their fury against their giant brethren, the Order of Miyshmaoth, who failed to contain them. Or, rather, the Miyshmaoth elected to yield their might and would not prevent the Sabbayoth from relieving their vengeful hearts, for they also perceived that great injustice was upon them for purposes unknown.

After binding the reluctant Miyshmaoth with potent chains of smoke, the Sabbayoth then unleashed upon the lingering Urth in violent rebukes. But the Bogedoth reveled in the schism, even when their bodies were pierced through with the burning blades of the Daylight. They persisted in their scoffings and in their insults unto death.

"Let it be known!" one dying Urth shouted. "That the time of the Daylight is coming to an end! There will be Perpetual Night!"

This, their vexing creed, did all the emissaries present confess, and the enraged Sabbayoth would not permit such profanities to be uttered in their blessed city. They gathered all servants of the Night at hand that same hour and slew them. The Ministry of Wardens quietly stood down and witnessed the slaying of the emissaries, these also being much grieved with the blasphemies dared uttered upon most sacred, S'hyeru Kadash.

The Miyshmaoth Wardens, therefore, reluctantly yielded. For they, too, had burning contempt for the Urth and compassion for the Sabbayoth slain upon the nightmare lands of Ga'nost.

And all this, in turn, brought further revoltings from the Night, as they would now demand justice for their perished emissaries. Furious Aedyr Lords, upon hearing of the violent clash, they too demanded swift severity against the Sabbayoth involved and against their accomplices.

"Ye fools!" one Aedyr exclaimed with blazing eyes. "That was not prudent. The hordes of the Night shall now siege Highest Ofandynth for this, your careless breach of the olden accords!"

Chapter 14

Oakendunty Anew

Grave destruction loomed underneath the threefold suns of High-est Ofandynth as the Apostasy of Despair had come. And perils also there loomed underneath the spectral arcs of Eofendurk. The Urth had been emboldened to transgress that Supreme Codex governing all starry gulfs throughout Ru'alameth. And now, they would seek to wage war against the Lightnings without securing the proper Denunciations at the hand of the Daylight Tribunals. Or, worse yet, to obtain a corrupt Zaamkut at the hands of betrayers! It had become a matter of discovering the whereabouts of the fabled Lightnings to exact severe violence upon them.

***

And so, two full days had transpired, and then came the third day since the Vheilyel had warned the snow gethwis of the impending ruination that would come upon their cherished mountain. This, Mount Tanlish, was depleting its time, and it was not apparent to Sword of Oakendunty that their friends would heed their passionate pleas and abandon their dwellings.

"Look, over there, hims! What is that?" Qugam shouted as he pointed at some curious object in the sky.

The thing that the startled neuf beheld was but a tiny, glimmering speckle of jade, faintly twinkling in the distance and slowly growing in size.

"That, my dear Qugam, is Pekkudah H'ar," Orilheart proudly announced.

"Him is Pekkudah H'ar?"

"Yup."

"It's the emerald star you said would appear," said Saxfen.

"Yes, I caused it to appear after precisely three days since we warned the gethwis," Orilheart explained. "That should have been enough time for them to consider our prophecy."

The dazzling, glimmering sign was now in full view in all its splendor. There followed the emerald sign, one elongated, luminous trail, and its lucid beauty could be seen upon all the lands of Eofendurk. All creatures and kingdoms underneath the spectral bows of the Sky'erligg gazed upon it and marveled at the astonishing, emerald wonder. It was striking to the senses and gorgeous to the sight. All creatures and peoples underneath the roseate skies beheld it—including the monstrous beast of the watery abyss. The ancient, beastly god curiously gazed upon the soaring marvel.

"And what is this that treads upon my pallid, roseate skies? Why are you here?" the Drukijaken queried. "Do you dare challenge Ruminthumgath, god of Eofendurk?"

The terror lurking underneath the rubied seas mused over the meaning of this strange visitor. *That stunning luminance, that emerald splendor, what is this foreign sight!* Its dazzling blaze mysteriously remained suspended above the gethwi mountain for no apparent reason. The monstrous dweller of the Sea of Nith would now demand answers.

Breathtaking and alluring, the star remained suspended in the same position throughout the day and into the night alike, resembling some enormous, piercing arrow darted from the spectral arcs themselves. The sky wonder steadfastly hung above the gethwi summit like the watchful, fatherly eye of some ethereal guardian from a foreign realm.

"It's beautiful, Orilheart," Saxfen marveled.

"Thank you. I hope it works, though. I sure love all those cuddly gethwis we met. They were so nice to all of us."

"So, is it just gonna stay there and hang around for a while?" said Jix.

"Yes, actually. I want the gethwis to see it for several days and in the same place so they can know this is no ordinary star that is visiting them."

"It is now up to them," Starrelos chimed.

"I still think we should have scared them out of their mountain, which probably would have been more effective," Eluryn insisted.

"Yeah, probably not. You heard them back there, how proud they are of their home," Orilheart retorted as she proceeded to whisper to herself. "Come on, everyone. You can do it. Take a hint . . . please."

The first night of the heavenly marvel soon waned, and the warm morning rays were now upon the formidable Sword of Oakendunty. The four Vheilyel carefully treaded their path while escorting the Fifth Lightning, denying themselves the leisure of light-drifting or Sky Seffinahs to reach that desolate, chastised city that was Ujorg Stone. They were now free to pursue this ambition, where there awaited the O'rah Harp in the bowels of the Drukijaken.

Nonetheless, their cunning and covert labors came to a halt when there arose against them two hundred deadly Kaabaldur Urth. These plated hordes had patiently awaited to secure the much-coveted Denunciation against the Fifth Lightning, and now, the opportune time had come to enforce the lawful decree.

The Sons of Light, it seemed, had failed to shelter Sword of Oakendunty within their judgment halls, as there secretly arose some amongst them proving themselves to be counterfeits. And so, the ongoing Apostasy presented great woe to the four Vheilyel and their young, Shaifetnu Panni.

The spectral, faint image of the Urth legions could be seen advancing towards them within the Path of the Sithra.

"Oh no, Starrelos, are you seeing what I'm seeing?" Orilheart whispered.

"It's them. It appears we have been found. But they are not engaging us," Starrelos noted.

"Wolsage, you stay here with the boys. Starrelos, Eluryn and I will see what this is about," Orilheart instructed.

The three Vheilyel then suddenly vanished out of sight and emerged upon the Path of the Sithrah, where the menacing horde could be fully seen in their dark plates and piercing, sulfur eyes. Wolsage and the three boys now resembled pulsating orbs of light suspended in midair upon the Path of the Waking.

"Whoa, where did they go?" the boys gasped.

"Steady everyone, we have company. They'll be right back."

One boastful Urth orator came forth from amongst the hellish legions, and it hissed Orilheart's name.

"Orilheart of the Eth," it announced. "For the grievous offenses against the hallowed *D'ath Pithgam*, the Throne of Lezuth has obtained lawful Denunciation against the one who is named, the Fifth Lightning. Surrender the Shaifetnu boy at once! Surrender now or face the wrath of the great Ulkazak Knight that stands amongst us and of the Order of Kaabaldur."

The fiendish orator announced the damning sentence as the horde venerated their Black Knight of the Order of Ulkazak. This was that aged destroyer of infamy so great, commissioned by the Great Kel'torh of Ga'nost. This was Dolaam the Perjurer, slayer of Hielandar the Endbringer.

Orilheart was doubtful of the decree against Saxfen. Why would the High Tribunals consult them not in this gravest of matters?

"Something is wrong," Eluryn said. "There is no need to conceal the decree from us. Why would the judgement halls not announce this directly to us?"

"Indeed, and yet they somehow managed to get past the Miyshmaoth," Starrelos noted.

"We need to find answers. There is definitely something wrong," Orilheart agreed.

She then proceeded to defy the order presented to them.

"No, we will not be handing him over at this time," she bravely announced. "We will consult with the High Tribunals, and we will learn of this supposed Denunciation for ourselves."

But the Urth were determined to impose their lawful Zaamkut.

"I am afraid we shall not permit you to do that," the orator scoffed in his deep, sinister voice.

Orilheart then ordered a Face Sharveth to appear, but it would not heed her thoughts.

"What?" she marveled.

"What's the matter?" Starrelos asked.

"I . . . I can't open the Face Sharveth."

"What? Let me try," Starrelos offered, but he was also unable to command the opening.

Eluryn was likewise prevented from reaching the High Tribunals for answers. This, it appeared, was but a clever, treacherous scheme devised against them with the service of the tainted Vheilyel governing the stellar passageways.

"Treachery and malice. There's only one explanation for this," Starrelos said. "It's the Ministry of Wardens. This could only happen with their involvement."

"What? Are you saying they're working with the Urth?" Orilheart marveled.

"Yes, they are interfering with the Sharveths in our sphere. We will now have to rely on our wits to escape these fiends."

"I have to warn Wolsage," Orilheart said, transforming into a hovering orb of light, resembling the boys upon the Path of the Waking. "Keep them busy while I return."

"What? Keep who busy, him?" Qugam asked.

"Wolsage, they're saying they have obtained the Zaamkut to take Saxfen."

"Impossible. Do they not realize who this is?" Wolsage doubted. "Let's find out for ourselves. This matter is far too important and something doesn't seem right."

He ordered the Face Sharveth, but it failed to come forth.

"What?" he bewildered.

"Exactly, there's an interference with the Sharveths so we can't consult with the Ministry of Fates, or anyone else for that matter."

"Well, what did they expect, for us to just hand him over? The Fifth Lightning?" Wolsage scoffed.

"Hold on a minute, what's going on here?" Jix interrupted.

"The Urth are upon us, but there is no time to explain," Orilheart replied.

"Whoa, him evil gods are here?!" Qugam gasped.

"Guys, I can explain later. But for now, you have to listen to me. We are in grave danger. We need to disappear for a moment, and although you won't be able to see us, we can see you at all times. You have to trust us, even if you can't see us. All you have to do is sit still right here and don't go anywhere, okay?"

The boys nodded.

"Wolsage, I charge you; do not lose any of them!" Orilheart continued. "We will make sure this is not the hour of the Urth, and we will ensure they regret this evil deed for all ages to come."

"Be careful, Orilheart," Saxfen pleaded.

"Don't let them get cocky, O," Jix said.

"Don't let the hims escape!" Qugam exclaimed.

"But how did they find us?" Wolsage mused. "Could they really have obtained Zaamkut against us from the judgement halls? This is really troubling."

"Yes, troubling indeed," Orilheart agreed. "It appears the Urth may have breached our ranks."

Twain Vheilyel then vanished out of sight and entered the Restless Lands of the Sithrah, where Starrelos and Eluryn awaited, fully clad in battle plates. The Kaabaldur stood underneath the black suns of Hoviel'iggalot in plates forged of malignant ore, and the foul crescent of their order was upon their chests. Orilheart and Wolsage likewise readied themselves, calling upon their bodies that formidable Eth armor forged from spectral threads of light.

The two hundred Kaabaldur surrounded the company, and their customary diplomacy had reached its threshold. It was now time to take their bounty by violence.

"No more delay!" Dolaam announced. "We shall suffer no further hindrance against our lawful decree."

Dolaam the Perjurer then stretched forth his arm against the outnumbered Vheilyel, and the howls of his legions rivaled the howling tumult of the Sithrah.

But Queen Eluryn raised her voice as her beautiful, emerald eyes changed into luminous orbs of white light.

"Nogzum'thar, I command you," she shouted to the contorted heavens. "Come forth at once from thine dwelling within the depths of the Sithrah!"

The heavens rumbled with the punishing bellow of the fierce Soggseraf, heeding the voice of the Aedyr, Eluryn. The ancient spirit-beast revealed itself underneath the black suns in all its might and fury.

The Kaabaldur light-drifted and dashed their hellish essence blades, but they were skillfully countered by the strength of the war-tried general, Starrelos, and by the dreadful Soggseraf that was with them. And this, Nogzum'thar, shielded with its fourfold, ivory wing and also ruthlessly devoured with massive teeth many an unfortunate Urth who dared confront his Vheilyel Queen.

The feathered Soggseraf towered over the host with its bleached wings outstretched, and it accomplished much chaos against the hordes. But the Kaabaldur were fierce and would not relent.

There were also amongst the Urth battalions, those possessing the scant ability to command wicked beasts scattered throughout the hidden realm. The Kaabaldur called upon these unwholesome dwellers, and they clashed with the fierce Soggseraf who served Eluryn.

Starrelos, with his battle-tested might, was able to harness the aid of spectral weapons that accompanied his every move, and they guarded him like some deadly host of unseen phantoms. The deadly, fiery swords at his command battled and grievously smote on his behalf without prejudice. These were the living, spectral Blades of Nuldric'edul that surrounded the Sabbayoth general like the sworn defenders of some revered monarch.

Orilheart commanded the multitude of ascending shadows within the Sithrah, and they became a dark whirlwind that guarded the three boys with the fierce destruction of punishing bolts.

Wolsage, though the weakest of the group, was also able to shield the quarters of the three boys. He deflected the relentless hordes with furious blows of his own. He light-drifted and smote, all the while commanding the ascending shadows of the Sithrah with the palm of his hand. The howling, mystic air within the Sithrah also heeded his thoughts and became sharpened blades in the same manner as the wind he was able to command upon the Path of the Waking. So mighty were these blades, they pierced the armors forged in abysmal ore. But there were too many adversaries to counter all on his own. They sieged him, and he fell wounded to the ground.

"Orilheart! I can't hold them off much longer!" he shouted.

Starrelos rushed to his aid, but the sheer numbers of the Kaabaldur were quickly draining his strength.

"Starrelos, why aren't they here already?!" Orilheart exclaimed.

"There's a disturbance with my legions as well! I cannot tell if they heard me or if they're on their way!"

"It's the Wardens! It has to be the Miyshmaoth!" Eluryn shouted. "They're shutting us in and drowning us out!"

"The Miyshmaoth are betraying the Daylight," said Wolsage. "We will not spare them for this treachery."

Dolaam became irate.

"Enough of these Day Zarrar!" he shouted.

And with that, the Urth Captain raised his arm above his ghoulish helm and began speaking in some obscure tongue. The contorted zenith of the Sithrah then thundered as if heeding the sinister voice of the Ulka-zak Knight. And at this motion, at the frightful clamor of the menacing thunder, Eluryn's servant mysteriously vanished!

"What?" exclaimed one perplexed Orilheart. "Eluryn, call him back!"

"I'm trying, but it's like he can't hear me anymore," she shouted as she toiled to retrieve Nogzum'thar from its dwelling within the Restless Lands.

Wolsage finally regained his strength and rose to his feet.

"There's too many of them; we need to retreat . . . somehow," Eluryn said.

"Yes, I'm struggling to come up with a distraction . . ." Orilheart replied.

She desperately searched for an escape, but Eluryn suddenly intervened.

"Wait, what's that?" she pointed at some curious commotion in the contorted, blackened sky.

"This is not good. We have to go right now!" Starrelos shouted.

The puzzling aberration underneath the black suns finally came into full view.

"Oh, Great Mebbukah! It's Urth reinforcements!" Orilheart exclaimed in utter disbelief.

And so, there had come newly furnished Urth battalions upon the fiery contention. But to the baffling surprise of the wearied Vheilyel, the newly arrived legions began to smite their own!

The clash became that of brother against brother, serpent against serpent.

Dolaam raged and cursed as he beheld his legions depleted by their own abysmal hordes of darkness. *What cursed scheme is this?* He wondered. He would not be captured this day, nay, not by the Day Zarrar this day.

The infamous Ulkazak Knight fled until a more opportune time would come when he would seek his revenge for this humiliation. This was that grievous humiliation where Dolaam the Perjurer almost prevailed against the Fifth Lightning.

"Hang on, everyone. I can sense our battalions again," Starrelos said. "They will be here very soon now."

"Wait, and my Soggseraf. He can hear me again!" Eluryn exclaimed.

She wasted no time in calling forth Nogzum'thar from his hidden dwelling, and the immense beast quickly responded. He reemerged revitalized and fully healed from his wounds.

The remaining hordes of the Night forfeited their ambition as the intruding army of darkness gained the mastery of the battle. They dispersed all of them in disgrace. All that remained was the succored, Sword of Oakendunty, alongside their mysterious allies—or so they appeared to be.

"What's going on here?" Orilheart said as she gazed at the Urth rogues.

And from their midst, there came their chief to the forefront. He approached the company, and his scaly, serpentine flesh was cloaked in the fair skin of the Vheilyel.

"Servants of the Daylight, we mean you no harm. I am Sandathus of the Order of Bogedoth, High Ambassador of Ga'nost of the Throne of Lezuth."

The four Vheilyel were bewildered and greatly astonished. And although the passing of multiple years had transpired underneath the thirteen moons of Vijuul Kynth, there had merely transpired upon Eofendurk, a mare dozen of days since the neuf village was trampled to the ground. For thus did the aged decree of Unequal Seasons ordain, and therefore, the passing of time was but mare days underneath the Sky'erligg.

The rogue emissary continued, "I have gathered these penitent warriors against their solemn oath in service of the Night. I have done this betrayal at my own peril. Please hear my words."

"Very well, go on," one hesitant Orilheart said.

"My brethren, the Urth, have committed the unforgivable deed of summoning another Light Eater from the Shunned Beyonds, from one that is called, the Dark Xoloth. We want no part in the vengeance against them that follows this irreversible deed."

He glanced at his host and nodded. They then proceeded to transform into pulsating orbs of diminished light. They had breached the Path of the Waking and could now be seen by Saxfen and twain neufs.

The boys screamed in horror at the terrifying sight of the Urth battalions. Eukeris menacingly growled, yet he felt a dread more terrible than he had ever felt in all his years.

"It's alright, boys, calm down," Orilheart comforted. "They mean no harm. They helped us defeat the Kabaaldur that opposed us."

Sandathus beheld Saxfen and proceeded to prostrate himself. His legions also joined in.

"Master, Shaifetnu. I am Sandathus of the Urth. We have come to plead mercy at your hand. We ask but that you remember us. Remember this, our deed we have accomplished this day. Remember us at the hour of our need, at the hour of our condemnation, we plead."

Saxfen was confused. He looked at Orilheart, unsure of what was happening or how to respond.

"Orilheart, what is he talking about?"

Orilheart smiled, herself puzzled, but supposed that they feared the Decree of the Lightnings.

"Remember all that talk about the harp and about the Lightnings? I think they fear . . . the Decree of the Lightnings, my dear Saxfen. The time of the Urth is coming to an end, and these are pleading that you spare them when the time comes."

"Oh, just like the Fire Seer said! Amazing," said the Shaifetnu.

"Yes, but be careful what you promise. Be careful with your words because your words have consequences."

"Well, what do I say?"

"I cannot tell you what to say. This is why you are the Fifth Lightning, because these decisions have to come from you in the sight of the Council of Daylight."

"Oh, I see . . ."

Saxfen pondered for a moment and then exhaled. He cleared his throat and carefully gathered his thoughts.

"Well, they did help you win against the bad Vheilyel, right?"

Orilheart smiled and nodded. He then finally answered the prostrated warriors.

"Sandathus of the Urth, receive our gratitude for your act of kindness this day. I will remember your deed as you have requested, along with these soldiers that are with you."

"Thank you, Master Shaifetnu, Fifth Lightning Bolt of God. We now go in peace to conceal ourselves from our vengeful brethren and from the retribution of the Daylight as well."

And then, there suddenly appeared in the phantasmal silhouette of a light-drift, the blazing essence blade of one unknown combatant of the Sons of Light.

"Away from him, you foul serpent!" commanded a feminine voice.

But the deadly blow was swiftly intercepted by the searing blade of General Starrelos. The prostrated Urth legions then found themselves surrounded by the deadly forces of the Sabbayoth, fully clad in onyx war plates and essence blades drawn.

"General Starrelos, what are you doing? Do not interfere!" shouted the assaulting Sabbayoth.

"Legion Prime, Nemiendyen, these Urth warriors pose no harm. They aided us in defeating the horde of the Night," Starrelos replied.

"What? Is this true?" she glanced at the rest of the group. They nodded in assent.

"Very well then," she said as she withdrew her weapon and ordered her legions to stand down. "Sabbayoth, at ease!"

The rest of the warriors likewise withdrew their weapons.

"We were afraid we would arrive too late. There was a strange disruptance with the Sharveths and . . ."

"Thank you, Legion Prime. All is well now."

"But these Urth . . . they shall be hunted by the Night for this treachery. They must be retained in our custody."

"No, they shall go their way in peace. They have risked their lives to save us from the Kabaaldur this day."

"Yes, please let them go," Saxfen interrupted.

Legion Prime, Nemiendyen, gazed at the infernal battalions and was quietly relieved that the company was well. She then proceeded to trust in the words of General Starrelos.

"Very well, as you wish, my Shaifetnu prince," she concurred.

The onlooking Urth rose to their feet and said their farewells. They parted ways in peace and set out to conceal themselves from the Seven Thrones of Ebelsaddon.

It had been one lengthy, exhausting day, and the nightfall had set in. Sword of Oakendunty would lodge and rest alongside the comforting warmth of their customary, campfire embers.

***

And the rogue Sandathus, along with his devoted combatants, they together traversed the worlds in the hopes of evading the fury of their kin. Thus, they had elected their fate and had assumed the retribution set against them. They had become traitors to the Seven Thrones, and no mercy would be shown for this, their treachery. The horrors that awaited them in the nightmare worlds provoked a dread most profound.

But these, of course, were no ordinary times. This was indeed the advent of the Seven Lightnings. And there now arose a faint hope within this band of rebel Urth. For the Fifth Lightning had given them his word, and he would remember their kindness at the time of their need. A time whispered to be even more terrifying than the tortures of the Night, or even worse, than the dreaded Naloz'oth Vaults of the Daylight.

This terror that some amongst the Urth feared most was indeed the Decree of the Lightnings, which foretold of a time when the exiled Shaifetnu would be restored to their original place in Ru'alameth. And upon their return, there would come with them, those most dreadful servants of the Living One, his mightiest of servants, which also are named, the Devouring Calamities.

And none had ever beheld these servants in the flesh, only there lived whispers of them. For thus did the olden oracle speak of them,

Because they have presumptuously trespassed and devoured the light,
Therefore shall Others come forth and devour at them with light,
Nevermore to escape these servants unbeknownst, the Devouring Lights.

That is, if the Daylight oracles were to be believed. For the Urth had oracles of their own and awful visions most enticing, rivaling those of the Daylight.

Nonetheless, there were those amongst the Urth who feared the inscriptions upon the Veiled Tablet, which also is named, the *Mystery of the Seven O'rahs*. For the appointed time of the Shaifetnu was found therein. And not only so, but also the time when the Urth would be vanquished because the appointed burden of the Ministry of Scales would no longer be necessary. And at last, the ancient treaties and accords with the Urth would finally expire and be satisfied sufficiently.

Fully mindful of these matters and with faint hope in his heart, Sandathus addressed his legions of rogues and commended them for their stand.

"Sons of the Night," he announced. "We have come together this far in our defiance. But in truth, we all know they shall come for me first, as I am the High Ambassador of Ga'nost. So, I plead with you, spare yourselves. Flee each one of you from me and flee the Council of Night with all the zeal that is within you. The Seven Thrones shall not hold back in their brutality. They will show you no mercy for the damage you have done to the Dark Kingdom. But may the mercy of the Shaifetnu princes be with you when they shall arise to recompense the justice that is due for all our deeds of darkness."

The band of rogues sorrowfully looked on, and one by one, they departed each. There remained few that insisted on following, but Sandathus sent them away.

"Master, I will fight by your side until the end!" one exclaimed.

"No, I will not permit you to share in my fate," Sandathus responded.

"Master, let me slay some of them on your behalf!" another demanded.

"No, this is my burden. Hide yourself until the judgement."

Sandathus finally overcame and sent away the sum of his warriors in peace. He sat in the brisk twilight of the ancient, desolate world and brooded over the startling cluster of wandering mountains in the sky, slightly drifting above some jagged monoliths in the distant haze. And then, as he mused alone, there came that chilling voice he had been expecting.

"Sandathus, are they all shunned from thy sight?"

"Yes, Master Uzgerrion, it is done as agreed. You are gracious to spare my warriors."

The Zayd captain then revealed himself, accompanied by twelve additional slayers.

It seemed the High Ambassador had secured a covenant with Ga'nost as the decree of Unequal Seasons afforded them time from the depths of the desolate world they had sought refuge in. He was to freely surrender himself in exchange for the lives of his fighters. The Zayd would not pursue the rogues, as agreed, and neither would they seek them out in the future. It was agreed their capturing and the severe penalties for their treachery would be imposed at the hands of *other* kingdoms, but not at the hands of Ga'nost.

They strapped the Bogedoth's arms with dismal chains of smoke, and they approached the sky chariot before them. The prisoner boarded the cryptic sphere of shifting shadows and dreaded the nightmare torments ahead.

***

Several days had passed since the clash between the High Bogedoth of Ga'nost and Dolaam the Perjurer. The company of the Fifth Lightning had at last entered the royal lands of Nith, where the desolate city of Ujorg Stone beckoned.

But, one morning, something was amiss upon waking from their peaceful slumber. Indeed, something was terribly wrong! Saxfen peacefully laid asleep when there came the taunting scoffs of a familiar voice.

"And what do we have here? Who are you? Why are the winged serpents fighting against you?" the frightful voice said. "You are called what? The Fifth Lightning?"

The haunting voice laughed as it queried the Shaifetnu boy. Saxfen then rose from his slumber, alarmed and perplexed.

"Orilheart, it's back! The voice from my nightmare!"

Orilheart gazed in amazement. She was startled to discover what appeared to be a faint, spectral string above Saxfen's head upon his waking.

"Guys, do you see that?" she said, waving her arm in hopes of dispelling the phantom string.

"I don't see anything, him," Qugam said.

"Yeah, what are we supposed to be looking at?" Jix puzzled.

The other Vheilyel looked on in bewilderment.

"What is that?" Wolsage asked.

"Don't you guys hear that?" Saxfen continued. "How can you not hear that? Make it stop, Orilheart!"

The menacing voice from his dream . . . *it had secretively followed him into the Path of the Waking!* There, it would torment the Fifth Lightning even after waking from his peaceful slumber.

"Tell me, what do you hear, Saxfen?"

"It's the Drukijaken! It's the voice I told you about from my dream the other night. It's talking to me . . . *right now!*"

"Well, what's it saying, Snowball?" Jix laughed.

"It's not funny, this is really scary! How is it you can't hear it? It's asking me questions. It wants to know who I am and why we're going to Nith."

"Okay, calm down, we believe you," Orilheart assured. "The neufs may not be able to see it, but we can see an invisible string above your head."

"This is not good at all," Starrelos urged. "It appears the Drukijaken is a Mind Intruder. A Mind Binding has come upon Saxfen."

"A binding, him?" Qugam pried.

"This 'binding,' is it going to hurt Snowhead?" Jix wondered.

"Not initially," Eluryn replied. "Only torment him day and night. But eventually, it could consume and corrupt his mind. We cannot let that fiend continue doing this to him."

Orilheart was furious. She couldn't believe the Drukijaken would do this to such an innocent, harmless boy.

"You listen to me, foul Drukijaken!" she shouted at Saxfen. "This is Orilheart of the Council of Daylight, and we will show you no mercy when we come for you. You leave Saxfen alone at once!"

But the Drukijaken laughed and taunted more boldly, provoking great strain upon Saxfen's mind.

"Ahhhhh! This is unbearable. The strain on my thoughts, Orilheart. What do we do?"

"We can't face the Drukijaken with Saxfen like this. What do you guys think?" she pondered.

"Well, we need to take him far away so the binding is severed," Starrelos said.

"Yes, we need to take him . . . outside of Eofendurk," Eluryn agreed.

"What? For that, we need a kobanuk. Otherwise, our dear Saxfen could die," said Orilheart.

"Correct. We need a plan." Starrelos said.

"Well, we can't leave him while we go get one. We are sworn to guard the Fifth Lightning and the sacred relics," Wolsage chimed.

"Give me a minute," Orilheart pondered.

"So, what are the odds that the Miyshmaoth will interfere a second time in such a short time span?" Eluryn offered.

"You're right," Orilheart mused. "Not very high. In fact, the traitors who blocked us out recently are probably already incarcerated. We'll have to take our chances. Saxfen can't stay like this. He can't face the monstrous Drukijaken like this. He can barely hold it together."

The four Vheilyel together gazed at Saxfen as he appeared to be lost within himself, within his own thoughts, unable to even listen to their talk.

"Saxfen! Snap out of it. You have to fight it," Orilheart pleaded.

"Huh? What?" Saxfen replied.

It was useless. Saxfen's attention was fully engrossed by an unseen menace, the only trace of which was that loathsome, invisible string atop his silver locks.

The group then prepared for what followed.

"Alright," Orilheart announced. "So, here's what we're going do. We're going to open a Face Sharveth and have the Eth bring us a kobanuk for Saxfen. This, of course, will give us away to the Urth, who are likely salivating on the other side because they insist on having a proper Za-amkut against us. But we will hold them back, as there shouldn't be any interference from the Ministry of Wardens because, well, it would just be so unfortunate if they were permitted to enclose us a second time. We have to take the chance. I see no other way. And while we are at it, we can also consult with the Ministry of Fates to see if the decree against us is legitimate.

"Once we have the kobanuk in our hands, we will take Saxfen to Eylundis, where we will be safe, and it should be far enough for this 'binding' that's on his head to be severed, and he will be free."

"Hey, what about us?" Jix motioned.

"Right, you guys will ride with Eukeris far enough from here so you're not in danger while we fight off the Urth, who will most likely come. Then, we'll find you when Saxfen's mind has been healed, and together, we will confront the Drukijaken as planned."

"Great!" Jix agreed.

"For Sword of Oakendunty!" Qugam cheered, raising his paw above his curled horns.

"For Sword of Oakendunty!" the company exclaimed.

The group wasted no time initiating the plan.

"Okay, Eukeris," Orilheart charged the gethwi. "Go now and keep these little ones safe. Go as we talked about, and we will meet you again when Saxfen is whole again. Don't worry, we will find you."

The gethwi duteously parted with twain neufs mounted upon his back. The four Vheilyel prepared themselves in those regal battle plates they summoned upon their frames.

"Wolsage, you will need to stay with Saxfen at all times and keep him company. If everything goes according to plan, we should have plenty of reinforcements to fight by our side."

"Understood," the Learner replied.

They opened the Face Sharveth and required one celestial kobanuk be sent to them immediately.

"It's on its way, Orilheart," the voice across the opening said.

They then summoned the Ministry of Fates for much-needed answers.

"I am afraid it is true," the Vheilyel on the opposing side lamented. "I'm sorry Orilheart. The Aedyr issued the decree, and your company is in danger of being apprehended by the Sabbayoth if you should continue to resist the Urth."

"What? This is a betrayal of the *D'ath Pithgam*!" she exclaimed. "There must be an inquiry into this."

"Between us, one is underway. Stand fast, Orilheart," the messenger concluded.

The group then patiently awaited in silence.

"So quiet. You think we could get by without trouble?" asked Wolsage.

"Hard to tell. The surprises continue to mount, one after the other," Starrelos replied.

"Look, over there," Eluryn pointed.

"Here we go," Orilheart prepared.

The four peered past the Path of the Waking and beheld the contorted, restless sky of the Sithrah rippling in the manner of their stellar passageways. And traversing through, there came the hordes of the Order of Kaabaldur, clad in their infernal plates and weapons forged of apostate soul essence. They charged, and they raged, but this time, Sword of Oakendunty was prepared.

Orilheart, Eluryn, and Starrelos breached the restless void, emerging anew underneath the black suns of the Sithrah. But the young Learner stayed behind to accompany the Fifth Lightning in the flesh.

"Now, Eluryn!" Orilheart shouted.

Eluryn commanded Nogzum'thar from the hidden depths, and the immense ekeru came forth, unleashing violent rebukes upon the intruders. The elongated spirit-beast spewed damning surges of amethyst bolts, and he brutally scourged with his hulking tail. He crushed with a snout full of spears, and he tore without remorse at the trespassing fiends.

The Urth warriors that escaped the Soggseraf's wrath were met by the raging legions at the command of Starrelos, the Liar's Bane. Though a lawful decree against Saxfen had been declared upon the Daylight Tribunals, the legions of Starrelos had not been advised to contend with the company, at least for the time being. The Sabbayoth therefore breached one opposing, rippling passageway; they soared with vehemence in their breath and they liberally smote at the host of the Kaabaldur.

The plan, it appeared, proceeded in favor of Sword of Oakendunty until there emerged from amongst the Urth, one loathsome fiend of the Order of Yith'doni. These made use of dark knowledge to summon powerful, malignant entities from the depths of the Restless Lands, and they also wielded deadly machinery. The Yith'doni Urth could be seen invoking obscenities so as to allure from the nether depths, one hideous minion sent forth to desecrate the pleasant land underneath the Sky'erligg.

"Come forth!" the Urth magician eerily commanded.

At once, there came the chilling echoes of the creature summoned to battle. It was the haunting cries of one hideous Mevu'yash, as the abominations of their kind were so named. The creature towered over the trees of the field. Its twain heads were covered with horns, and it treaded upon the Path of the Waking on bipedal, hoofed legs. Severed wings could be seen proceeding from its back, and its muscular, lanky arms reached the ground far beneath its deformed set of heads. The thing mindlessly crept toward Sword of Oakendunty in a sort of desperate manner, as if compelled against its will, like some helpless prisoner compelled to its very doom.

"Wolsage!" one alarmed Saxfen shouted. "Look over there, what is that thing? Is it . . . coming this way?!"

"Look away, Saxfen. Remember, we must not fear the form our enemies present themselves in," Wolsage replied, covering the lad's eyes.

Onward, the Mevu'yash trampled the vibrant greenery, all the while leaving a toxic trail of death in the likeness of venomous ooze that devoured with dark hunger from the void. Nogzum'thar battled against the creeping rival from within the Sithrah like some enraged phanthom, but he was unable to hinder its fouling of the pleasant land.

"Starrelos, it's not slowing down!" Eluryn exclaimed. "You have to apprehend that Yith'doni before that thing comes near us; before it destroys all of Nith!"

And so, the fierce general gathered his most potent warriors at hand and charged at the Urth enchanter, light-drifting and fearlessly fending off every fiend obstructing his path.

The Kaabaldur, however, had found venue and surrounded the three other Vheilyel guarding Saxfen. The Sabbayoth legions violently clashed against the hordes, also in defense of the Shaifetnu boy, but the carnage was too much for Saxfen. For there went within him those malicious utterances from the depths of the rubied sea, *and they did persuade the young Shaifetnu to flee against his own senses!*

He could not resist, and he finally gazed at the abhorrence approaching the company. He gasped in utter terror, and while Wolsage was fending off some invisible foe, he escaped the sight of his four celestial guardians. And the matter occurred with great haste. He dashed for safety. He fled for his life at the sight of the monstrous, creeping nightmare. He found himself alone in an open field. Then came anew that hoary, taunting voice of his tormentor.

"But who shall save you from me?" the Drukijaken scoffed. "This is my world. I rule the land and the air. I rule it all from the depths of this watery, red abyss!"

Exhausted and desperate for refuge, Saxfen gazed in search of something to comfort his affliction. He beheld the snowy summit of Mount Tanlish in the far distance. The care of the gentle gethwis comforted him, and their memory brought tears to his eyes.

"And what is this?" the Drukijaken scolded. "You miss . . . your friends? Are they going to help you? Will they dare rise against me? Have they not heard of my wrath in all Eofendurk?!"

Saxfen's heart was filled with love for the snow gethwis, and this did not go unnoticed by the eightfold, prying eyes of the Drukijaken.

"I know. How about we ensure your friends do not intervene in this . . . our little dispute? How about we teach them not to meddle in the matters . . . of the god of Eofendurk!"

And with that, Saxfen suddenly remembered his night terror, where he had foreseen the destruction of the gethwi abode that would follow.

"NOOOO!!" Saxfen screamed and pleaded.

The crisp, roseate skies then became polluted with the haunting clouds of his nightmare. And without mercy, the Drukijaken compelled the dismal vapors to crash down destruction upon Mount Tanlish. Furious discharges of violent bolts came spewing down, and the proud mountain was thus demolished. Saxfen fell to the ground, heartbroken, sobbing for his dear friends, hoping and praying they had heeded their sign and fled for their lives.

And without warning, one terrible, plated Kaabaldur breached the Path of the Waking and seized the weeping Shaifetnu with its scaled claws. It suddenly soared into the blackened heavens with prey in hand. Saxfen quickly grabbed that sacred relic, the Scepter of the Shiggionoth, and he desperately thrust it into the winged villain's throat, tearing into its scaled flesh with those jagged fixtures at its golden apex. The injured fiend cried out in pain and released Saxfen, and both the Shaifetnu and the scepter plunged to the mayhem of the Mevu'yash below. Wolsage was able to catch the falling Saxfen, but the scepter was nonetheless captured by the hellish horde.

"Hey, they took the scepter!" he shouted into the empty, open wind.

The Sabbayoth had, in turn, entrapped the Yith'doni menace. And upon hearing Wolsage's report, Starrelos turned to the captive enchanter and, with burning eyes, slew him asunder. The death provoked the horrid Mevu'yash to forcefully succumb to the dark abyss from whence it had been summoned, and only the foul trail of devouring ooze remained in its stead.

"Eluryn, follow me after them!" Starrelos ordered. "Orilheart and Wolsage, we shall return with the scepter in hand!"

The horde turned fearful when they beheld that their enchanter knight had perished at the hand of the Liar's Bane. The remaining Kaabaldur slowly fled so they could return at a more opportune time.

"Are you okay?" Orilheart asked the Shaifetnu boy as she held him in her arms.

"Yes, now I am," Saxfen sobbed. "But the gethwis . . . Orilheart, my nightmare . . . it came true!"

There would be no mirth and no laughter that night as the company grieved the loss of the gethwi abode and lamented the loss of the Scepter of the Shiggionoth. The Fifth Lightning had escaped yet another peril, but the air was tense and full of heaviness.

***

The crisp, morning rays soon arrived the following day, and Orilheart duteously looked over Saxfen as he rose from his slumber.

"Good morning, Saxfen. How are you feeling?" she asked.

"Honestly, I can't sleep with this thing talking to me in my head. This is torture!" Saxfen replied.

"Right, about that. Hey, look what I have!" Orilheart smiled as she presented Saxfen with a curious ivory object.

"What is it?"

"This, my dear Shaifetnu prince, is a celestial kobanuk."

"Oh, this is what we've been waiting for, right?"

"Yes, my fellow Eth brought it last night while you struggled to get some sleep. Now we should be able to go far away from here, far from the reach of the Drukijaken, and this should make the voice in your head stop. This is all happening so fast, and I wasn't planning for this part for a while, but this is an emergency. You will need to learn how to handle your fears."

"Yeah, sorry about that. I completely panicked back there, didn't I?" Saxfen said, frowning.

"Yes, but there is so much more to it than just trying to be braver. You will need to learn to become a good steward of your heart. Being brave is part of it, but as you will see, always being in control of your own heart is the key to winning against the forces of evil. And so, we will go to Eylundis, where you will learn the Way of the Soulshift."

"Great, whatever that is. So, what do I do with this thing?"

"You put it on, silly," Orilheart laughed.

Saxfen gazed at the lovely craftsmanship of the ivory object, which in appearance resembled a mask with the face of a War Ekeru. He placed the kobanuk on his face and looked at Orilheart.

"Well, how do I look?"

"You look like a mighty War Ekeru," she smiled.

"Wow, like the ones the Fire Seer told us about?"

"Yup, this kobanuk was formed to resemble the War Ekeru in the Fire Seer's stories. It will help you breathe along the way where we're going."

The Shaifetnu boy proudly wore the celestial kobanuk, and though small in stature, the face ornament evoked in him some divine semblance commanding the awe of mere mortals.

"So, are we ready?" said Wolsage.

"Yes, let's get going."

The three then approached the rippling mouth of the nearby Star Sharveth, but not without the maddening voice of the Drukijaken clamoring inside Saxfen in ridicule and boastful threats.

"You think you can escape me?" the Drukijaken scoffed. "I know who you are. I know what you are. You need the harp that resides within my bowels. You shall return . . . and you shall die. You shall know the wrath of the god of Eofendurk!"

The monstrous Drukijaken fumed and howled, and its eightfold eyes burned in the black depths of his lair. It violently surged to the surface as there came that sinister host of unnatural clouds spewing that deathly, red lightning. Its gargantuan, elongated body sat atop the restless waters, and the waters were to him as some lofty, crimson throne. Its broadened maw full of ancient growths cursed the frightened Shaifetnu from afar, and the growths atop its head radiated in a hateful manner, mirroring the creature's wrath.

"Yes, you shall return! This is my world, and you shall die in it!" the terrifying beast vowed.

But as Saxfen stepped betwixt the dazzling Star Sharveth leading unto worlds beyond, leading to the hallowed lands of Eylundis, the Drukijaken's voice inside of him slowly dissolved into a faint ringing until finally, the tormenting voice ceased from his mind. And with it, the faint string above his silver locks dissolved out of sight from the eyes of twain Eth alongside him.

"It worked Orilheart! That awful voice, it's gone from my head now!"

"Yes, we severed that thing's access to your mind so you can rest well again and think clearly."

The comforted Saxfen embraced his longtime friend and exhaled in relief.

"O?" he pried as they ventured upon strange lands.

"Yes?"

"Why do I need a kobanuk to pass through the Star Sharveth? I don't remember hearing my family having to use one of these when they arrived in Eofendurk."

"Oh, of course, they wouldn't need one. They weren't traveling across the worlds like we are. They were sent far, far away, where it would be impossible for the Urth and for the Light Eaters to find them. They were not sent across worlds. They were sent across time. They were sent far into the future."

***

And so, the elder Saxfen and his son Enos journeyed that great pilgrimage from Ujorg Stone City to the rustic lands of Tunjunsora atop their ferocious, striped gethwis.

"So, Papa," Enos mused. "You said the Light Eaters cannot die, and they're still around. They're still out there somewhere. Doesn't that make you afraid? Doesn't that worry you that they'll return?"

"Well, I suppose there could come other evil beings from the Shunned Beyonds and not necessarily from the Dark Xoloth. But rest assured, the eight T'ohuvohu that entered our realm, we stopped them for good.

"Truly, I should have died. But the Decree of the Daylight was with me, and its words were fulfilled through me. We stopped all of them that dared to intrude upon Ru'alameth. If we hadn't, you probably wouldn't have been born, and you would probably still be living with the children of Luwenkith, I think. If we hadn't, I would've failed as the Fifth Lightning."

"You stopped them . . . for good? Are you sure? You mean they can't come back, right?"

"Yes, we stopped them for good, and no, the eight Light Eaters cannot come back. However, as I said, nothing really prevents anyone from opening the forbidden gates again and letting more things in."

"What? Are you serious?"

"No joke."

Enos intently looked upon his father, expecting to learn more about the strange evil creatures, "Well?"

"Well, what?"

"What did you do to them?"

"We . . . expelled them from all Ru'alameth."

"Oh, I see. You sent them back to the Dark Xoloth?"

"No, not quite. That would be too easy on them after all the heartache they caused. As the legend foretold, *They* came for them, those whom the Vheilyel called, the Devouring Calamities. And they took them to a place from which they could never return. This is why I say that the eight Light Eaters will not be bothering anyone ever again."

"Oh, I see, kind of like a prison, then, but outside of Ru'alameth. Can't we just seal up the Dark Xoloth so none of those things get in later? Wouldn't that be easier?"

"Yes, that would be easy, but I'm afraid the Dark Xoloth is not some door anyone can just seal up so nothing goes in or out. It's a realm, a reality, one outside our very own, with its own rules. It's a huge realm like the one we live in, like Ru'alameth. I suppose it's filled with worlds and creatures and things hard to describe. Or, at least, they think there could have been at some point, but the Light Eaters extinguish all light, this we know.

"And so it is said there is no light in the Dark Xoloth. And there isn't only a single entrance. Only the most misguided or evil desire to learn of its ways and of the things that lurk within its endless gulfs of shadow."

Enos pondered over the strange things his father described.

"Okay, but if the eighth Light Eater knew seven of them had already failed and were trapped here, why did it think it could win this time?"

"Yes, I can't really speak as to the reasons for the things it did. But we later found it was those evil tablets, the Tablets of Gha'shuulmog, that caused the Vheilyel to question their loyalty to the Daylight. Those evil tablets were somehow joined to the seven prisoners. And this, in turn, increased the corrupting influence of the Shadow Terror throughout Ru'alameth, especially with the arrival of the eighth Light Eater. It's quite amazing how the power of those evil tablets could be felt from the depths of the Dark Xoloth.

"So that would be why the dark lore about the T'ohuvohu consumed the Vheilyel in such a powerful way when the eighth one came. I'm sure the Urth were very confident that their scheme to bring the tablets into our realm would bring about the end of the Daylight kingdoms. But in the end, their prophecy failed, and it deceived them."

The sojourners had reached the bounds of a certain forest. It was the outskirts of Treewinth Woodlands, and the living trees therein cleared a path upon seeing the snow gethwis of Oclyd Tower. For their gethwi escorts were well acquainted with the living trees and also with the new abode of the neufs.

The guardian trees gave way to that hidden village, and there, they were met by the formidable, hostile keepers of the gate. These wielded sharp spears upon the sight of the Shaifetnu strangers and their striped beasts.

"Halt!" one ordered the travelers. "Identify yourselves, you who intrude upon the house of Oakendunty!"

Saxfen uncovered his head and revealed his silver locks.

"A Shaifetnu . . ." said the lead keeper. "Proceed, Shaifetnu."

Saxfen approached the village, and he was questioned regarding what matters he had regarding Oakendunty.

"It is said all Shaifetnu are departed from Tunjunsora. What business have you amongst us?"

"I am Saxfen of the Sevrinjiv," he replied. "I am here to see the neufs Jix and Qugam."

"Saxfen?" the guard wondered. "My, how you've grown! Come on in, my dear boy."

Saxfen was then happily welcomed amongst the neuf families. He was informed that Jix and Qugam had rebuilt dwellings of their own, and that would be where they could be found. So they made their way through the village until they had finally come upon the abode of Jix, the neuf. Saxfen knocked, his heart pounding with excitement, and there finally came one to the door.

"A Shaifetnu?" said the neuf at the door. "How can I help you?"

Saxfen recognized the voice.

"Jix! It's me, Saxfen!"

Jix's eyes flung open with surprise. Saxfen was now taller than him!

"Wow, Snowhead? Is that really you? You're so much taller now. And that beard! Oh, and is that Eukeris? Come on in!"

The friends embraced again after so many years had passed.

"We thought you had forgotten all about us after you killed the Drukijaken and left with that weird harp in hand. I'm so happy to see you again, Snowball! Come, Qugam is also visiting. He's right over here."

The friends made their way to the cozy rear quarters, where Qugam sat across a soothing fireplace.

"Look, Qugam!" Jix announced. "Saxfen has returned!"

"Saxfen, him? Whoa, you're big now. And that white him!"

Qugam embraced his old friend and was also glad to see the gethwis.

"And who is this little him?"

"This is my son, Enos."

"Wow, so good to meet you, Enos, him! I, too, have little hims of my own now. Let me introduce you to them. Kids, come say hi to Saxfen, him!"

And with that, there came rushing into the cozy chamber, twelve fluttery baby neufs, every one of them curiously gazing at their guests.

"Kids, Saxfen is an old him of ours. This is that him you have heard so much about . . . the him who killed the Drukijaken of Nith!"

The baby neufs gasped and stared in awe. Qugam then proceeded to give the order for a spirited assault. "Attack!" he shouted.

The baby neufs could not believe their ears and proceeded to charge at Saxfen and his guests. They playfully seized him and his son, and they all fell to the floor. They also proceeded to mount twain gethwis without fear, laughing and screaming with excitement that a gethwi had come to visit them. Saxfen laughed as he struggled to rise to his feet.

"Wow, so many baby neufs!" he exclaimed.

"Yeah, they're mostly Qugam's," Jix replied.

The friends shared those familiar laughs they had enjoyed so long ago, and Saxfen had long missed from across the starry gulfs.

"Come, Saxfen, him," Qugam playfully urged. "We have much to talk about!"

And so, the silver-haired hero of the may winged gods began to recount his sojournings after he had parted ways all those years ago with the O'rah Harp in hand. And the night swiftly closed in upon the marry abode as the grand tale upon Saxfen's lips would be heard for the first time by his friends. Their hearts were filled with joy to see one another again, and the radiant bows of the Sky'erligg gently illuminated the born-anew village of the whiskered neufs.

Dream Machine
Books